Again

Again

Sharon Cullars

BRAVA

KENSINGTON PUBLISHING CORP.

http://www.kensingtonbooks.com

BRAVA BOOKS are published by

Kensington Publishing Corp.
850 Third Avenue
New York, NY 10022

All Kensington titles, imprints and distributed lines are available at special quantity discounts for bulk purchases for sales promotion, premiums, fund-raising, educational or institutional use.

Special book excerpts or customized printings can also be created to fit specific needs. For details, write or phone the office of the Kensington Special Sales Manager: Kensington Publishing Corp., 850 Third Avenue, New York, NY 10022. Attn. Special Sales Department. Phone: 1-800-221-2647.

Brava and the B logo Reg. U.S. Pat. & TM Off.

ISBN 0-7582-1370-0

First Kensington Trade Paperback Printing: May 2006
10 9 8 7 6 5 4 3 2 1

Printed in the United States of America

Acknowledgments

Special thanks go to the following who provided encouragement and sometimes sanity throughout the completion of this book: Sabrina Collins, who told me to write another book when I was discouraged from a first attempt; Desiree Dawson, Alexandra Tschaler and Beverly Johns who were enthusiastic readers and gave me much needed critiques. To my agent, Janell Agyeman, who read the first draft and believed in it enough to take me on. And to the Kensington staff who made this final book possible: Kate Duffy, Hilary Sares and Sulay Hernandez.

Prologue

New York—January 1880

The nearly arctic wind bit through his wool coat, chilling flesh and blood. But even the cold could not quell the fetid smell of the open sewer a few feet away. The heat of human waste sent up a vapor visible in the chilled air. Reeking garbage marred the frozen snow drifts piled along the alley floor. Intent on his purpose, Joseph barely noticed the odors. He squeezed his fingers together, trying to get the blood to flow. His leather gloves provided little protection against the unusually cold day.

It wouldn't be long now. He had been waiting nearly forty minutes, yet he knew this alley was where he would find the one he sought. Joseph had studied his quarry for nearly a month now, ever since the coward skulked back into town thinking it was safe to do so. Joseph had passed money around to keep ears and eyes open around the wharfs, piers, and the streets. Three weeks ago, his investment paid off. Charlie Rhodes was back in town. Word on the street was that the man had crossed into Jersey, hiding out until everything had blown over.

For a time, the grisly murder of three men at the warehouse played on the front pages of most of the New York papers, the details glorified for the rabid readers. But with each passing week, and given the low pedigree of the victims, eventually the curious and the sensation hounds found other news to sniff after. Work at the warehouse had resumed and blood was washed away, leaving no reminders of the deaths that had taken place there. It was as though nothing had ever happened.

As though his world had not been torn away, leaving him no foothold.

He knew Charlie took this way home from the job he had gotten as a stevedore. The route was a lone shortcut through the alley a few feet from the hovel Charlie shared with a decrepit prostitute named Sally. Hardly anyone ever came this way, wisely afraid of robbers or mischief makers. Which made Charlie a fool. And which worked into Joseph's plan. A plan he had decided on after Rachel was found.

Nearly a month ago, a dock worker discovered Rachel's body frozen in the East River. By chance, Joseph came across the article in one of the daily periodicals. The other papers hadn't bothered to report the discovery. Even in the one paper, Rachel's death had been summed up in very few words, a toss-away among news about the invention of something called a light bulb and the ever-growing media parade surrounding the Kiehl murder. The poisoning death of the eighty-one-year-old dowager had horrified the city. A Miss Catherine Zell was set to stand trial for the murder. But no one would stand trial for Rachel's death. And with the discovery of her body, Joseph's decision had crystallized within him. No, there would be no hue or cry for the death of a Negro woman, no matter how wonderful or beautiful. And most of those who cared about her either had no power to bring her justice or were too cowardly to come forward. So in the end, he realized what he had to do.

There was something else driving him, also. A half-remembered dream . . . or rather dreams . . . that had been recurring lately. Dreams ensconced in a past that he couldn't decipher but that piqued his suspicions about the workings of this world as well as the one beyond. That gave him hope.

As for these past two months, he had played his part well. Son to his father, friend to his cronies . . . masks that at one time he had worn comfortably. Lately though, the masks had begun to chafe like a hair shirt against the skin—prickly, burning, painful . . . or more like the bars of a prison which he had come to realize enclosed him as much as they once had his mother.

A sudden movement made him turn. A ball of gray scurried out of sight around the corner of a shack a few doors down. He breathed again, not realizing that he had stopped altogether. His pulse was racing. It was just some vermin scrounging for food. He heard its pathetic foraging in the snow, searching for discards from its human counterparts. In that second, his mind wandered as he thought of the rat. It was a second that almost cost him. He turned at another sound and saw the lone body rounding the northern corner of the alley. The newcomer's feet crunched against the snow and the man wheezed into the lapel he held against his face, half hiding his features. Still, Joseph recognized him and knew that his wait had finally come to an end.

It was an early evening and the sun hovered among slate clouds, the sky dimmed by a pall that had settled over the city this winter. A pall that reflected the lifelessness within himself. Today was Friday. Appropriate. Rachel had died on a Friday.

Joseph stepped away from the building where he had been half hiding in wait. Charlie Rhodes stopped abruptly, his body stiffening at the sudden appearance of a stranger before him.

"Yeah? Whatcha want?" Charlie barked, his voice phlegmy. Then his mouth gaped and his eyes bulged with sudden recognition. He put a hand up as though to ward off the devil himself.

"Oh, oh, noww, noww, wait, you . . . you got it all wrong!"

Joseph smirked. "Do I?"

The man began backing away, shaking more from fear than the cold. "Noww, noww, it wasn't me what planned the thing, Joseph. I didn't want no part of it. I tole 'em . . . I tole 'em all it was a bad deal. But that lousy dago, Roberto, he was the one that wanted you dead. And the others, too. It was all them. Not me, Joseph. I just . . . I just went along 'cause they made me. You gotta believe me."

Joseph's hatred made his voice clipped. "All I believe, Charlie, is that you are a liar, a coward, and that you are about to die."

"No!" Charlie yelled out. Joseph advanced as Charlie continued backing away in panic. The predator steadily rounded on his prey, assured that there would be no escape.

Joseph saw Charlie reach inside his coat pocket. He had been expecting it. But he was quicker. He had his knife out before Charlie could clear the ragged tears of his pocket. In two steps, Joseph closed the space that separated them and shoved the blade deep into the other man's stomach until only the Victorian bone of the hilt was visible.

Charlie's eyes widened in pain and horror. Joseph, his soul as cold as his body, felt nothing as he pushed the blade in deeper, as blood spurted out on his gloved hand. Then he pulled the blade free and Charlie's body fell slowly to the ground, his eyes vacant in death. Joseph dropped the knife next to the dead man, blood splattering the snow.

For a few seconds, Joseph stared down at the man who had become his obsession since Rachel's death. Since it seemed his own life had ended.

He bent, reached inside Charlie's pocket. He pulled out the cheap, dulled-blade knife that Charlie hadn't been able to retrieve.

Joseph knew how the accounts of his own death would read. That he had died in a common knife fight. There would be speculation why someone of his station had died so casually. Those who knew him well would guess that it was his debauchery that finally caught up with him. And for once, his father would not be able to sweep away the scandal. Joseph felt a slight satisfaction at the thought.

At least suicide would not be linked with his name. As it hadn't been linked with his mother's.

Joseph cursed the dullness of the blade. It was going to

hurt like the dickens. But it had to appear that there had been a fight. There could be no suspicion of any self-inflicted harm so he could not use his own knife. He opened the coat, tore off a few buttons to make the struggle seem authentic.

He placed the blade at the silk of his waistcoat. Hesitated for a second. The sky had darkened in a matter of minutes. It would be night soon. More than likely he wouldn't be discovered until the next morning, if then. The alley rat would have a meal at least for the night. But these things did not bother him. He was beyond all that. Beyond this life.

He shoved the knife through the material, through the taut skin of his belly. The pain seared, paralyzing him. Immediately, his breath became fire in his lungs. He fell to his knees, his remaining thoughts of her. Remembering. Praying. Hoping.

As he lay taking his last breaths, he smiled a little. Because if his dreams meant what he had begun to realize, that he had lived before, that he had known Rachel before in another incarnation, then he was destined to meet her . . . again.

Chapter 1

Chicago, 2006

In the darkness, Tyne thought she heard him whispering to her. It came like that at times, both memory and fear, followed by a tears-and-sweat struggle to maintain her reality, to know he was not actually there in her room ready to claim her.

She raised her head from her pillow and listened. But the only sound was the distant throb of a motor that grew steadily louder as it approached then ebbed away, leaving her alone again.

Her eyes searched the shadows and found nothing. Still shaky, she let her head fall to the pillow, her forehead sprouting beads of sweat in a room that was sixty degrees on a cool Chicago night. She willed her heart to slow to its normal pace. Emptying her mind of threatening thoughts, she lay quietly until her eyelids grew heavy and consciousness began to die away. Finally she succumbed to the somnolent pull of a tired body and mind.

The dream world quickly sealed her into a vacuum of shapes and faces, a reality recognizable only on a visceral level. Images flitted one after another until her journey reached the last scene, the non-variable in her nightly excursions. Again, she found herself sitting at a long table laden with food she could see but not smell. People, some known, others not, sat talking and eating. The women wore evening gowns, the men, tuxedos. April and Donell sat toward the other end, their heads together in conversation. Everything played as it had before, except this time Eve chattered incessantly in Tyne's ear, some nonsense she couldn't understand. Tyne looked down and saw she was wearing the same green strapless evening gown, a color that shimmered against the latte of her skin. She reached to pick up her fork to taste the leathery meat on her plate, but at that moment, as always, a man's hand fell hard on her bare shoulder. She looked up from her seat.

The table and guests faded away, leaving Tyne and the stranger alone. She stared up where his face should be but saw nothing but a dark void, an abyss into which her soul threatened to fall. She sat trembling, waiting. He reached out to her, the glint of the knife flickering under the light. It touched her throat lightly.

She woke with a start. Sweat trickled down her temples. The digital clock on the nightstand read a little after two, only minutes since she last drifted off. She had a few more hours to get through. Yet she didn't know if she would make it out of the nocturnal web this time. Or the next. One night her heart would simply stop and she would be trapped in her dream world forever.

"You yawning again? Musta been some night. How was he?" Gail smirked. Tyne winced. Gail defined herself by her blatant carnality and referred to herself as an "open sista . . . Big O, that is." Words often tumbled carelessly from her lips. Tyne turned around to the cubicle that faced hers and held up her middle finger. The older woman threw back her head and laughed, causing her medium-length, auburn-by-the-box hair to swing stiffly around her shoulders. Tyne sighed and turned back to her computer.

"Girl, you wouldn't tell a soul if you *was* getting some. Ms. Born-Again-Virgin."

"Mind your business, Gail," Tyne warned over her shoulder. "Besides, the way I hear it, you're getting enough for me and half the female population as it is. Might do you good to abstain for a while."

A few cubicles down, she heard Rhoni cackle, obviously listening. Tyne wondered at her lie. She hadn't heard any gossip about Gail. It just felt good getting a dig in.

Gail harrumphed, mumbling beneath her breath. Tyne smiled to herself, at the same time wishing she had an office instead of a cubicle that sat in a maze of disjointed walls, which didn't provide even the illusion of privacy. She often had to modulate her voice whenever she made a personal call, knowing that Gail, Lem, Rhoni or any of her other nearby co-workers might be listening in.

Not that her life was fascinating. A researcher and copy editor at the *Chicago Clarion*, a small black community newspaper on its last legs, she hardly lived life on the edge. As for her social life, her last relationship had been a couple of years ago and had ended rather badly. Hardly something to divulge to her nosy coworkers. She believed in keeping her personal business to herself. Which made her business that much more intriguing to the busybodies who peppered their lives with the goings-on of other people. Yet they knew more about her than she liked. She shook the flurries out of her head and got back to work.

A few minutes later, in the middle of typing her report for Stan, she hit the Enter key. Nothing. She hit it again. Still nothing. The computer sat frozen. "Damn!" she muttered. She hadn't saved the document for some time and would probably lose several paragraphs if she rebooted.

"Lem," she shouted over her cubicle, "could you come here, please?"

Lem shouted back, "Be right there."

Alem, or Lem as he was known around the office, was the official copy editor as well as the unofficial tech guru. Everyone knew to call him whenever anything broke down, which kept him pretty busy. Being a two-fer on one salary made him indispensable to the paper since it kept down some of the staggering overhead. In the end, this would prove a boon for Lem. Rumors going around now predicted that heads were going to roll, as the paper's circulation had dropped 40 percent from a couple of years ago. Making matters worse, the *Clarion* had just lost a major advertiser this January and stood to lose three more. But if there were going to be any survivors among the carnage, Lem would definitely be one of them. Everyone else, including herself, was dispensable.

Within a minute, he loomed—there was no other word for it—at the entrance to her cubicle. Six feet five, Alem Gebre always had a smile, his teeth luminescent in a walnut-complected face, his Eritrean heritage evident in the broad forehead and slightly flared nose.

"What's going on?" he asked with an accent that always made Gail and a few of the other women suck air through teeth, lick their lips, and, Tyne suspected, clinch their crotches. Yet to Tyne, Lem's cocksure confidence was a turn-off.

"Help," Tyne mock-pleaded. "My computer's locked up again. I don't want to lose this report."

Lem shook his head. "And I bet you didn't save, either."

"Yes, I did . . . well, sort of. But it's been some time, and I'm going to lose a lot of input."

Lem came in and Tyne moved out of her chair to let him sit down. He pressed a series of key combinations and then shook his head.

"Nope. The only thing I can tell you is that we may be able to retrieve something from the auto save files. I have to reboot. Sorry. After that, I'll search through your temp files, see if I can find the last save."

Tyne closed her eyes in frustration, mentally castigating herself for her stupidity. This had happened before; she should have remembered to save every five minutes. Especially on this ancient equipment. The *Clarion* hadn't updated anything since 1998.

The screen flickered as Lem did an Alt-Ctrl-Del and the Microsoft 98 logo appeared. The dialog box asking for username and password followed.

"Your call here." He moved aside, and Tyne sat and plugged

in her personal info. After the computer entered Windows, Lem again took the seat, went into Windows Explorer and did his thing. His nimble fingers tapped a rhythmic litany on the keys that had her temporarily hypnotized. She watched him and an unbidden thought of long, tapering fingers moving along her flesh, caressing slowly, softly, each finger pursuing its own rhythm, coming together in a tingling chord. . . .

"OK, I'm done," he said. "This is the latest auto save, which was a few minutes ago. So whatever you typed after that is lost. Sorry. Wish I could have done better."

"That's OK. No need to apologize. It's my fault. You told me what to do last time, and, of course, I didn't."

"Not that any of you ever listen to me. After all, I'm just the token guy around here."

He smiled, taking the bite out of the criticism, but she knew he really felt this way. He was one of only two men in the seven-person office, including the editor-in-chief, Stan Johnson. Cultural differences between Lem and "the Americans" as well as gender differences between Lem and "the women" sometimes created tension. For all his cockiness, Tyne got the feeling he didn't really like the female adoration. He was probably one of those brothers who liked a good chase and didn't want an easy thing. Probably held fast to his African—and patriarchal—belief that men should do the pursuing. Which put Gail out of the running. But for some reason, she continued to chase. Like now.

"Lem, I think something's wrong with my computer, too." The woman had the nerve to be standing at Tyne's cubicle entrance, looking all helpless and "female." Never mind that she had the heft of a good 190-pound construction worker. Tyne blinked as the woman actually batted her eyelashes.

Lem sighed and nodded to Tyne, then left, following Gail like a reluctant child. Tyne sat at her computer, looked at the temp file, then exhaled in relief to see she was missing only a couple of paragraphs from her report. She began typing, forcing herself to ignore the almost purring sounds of pussy-cat Gail trying to make a kill. The woman was too obvious.

Tyne found Gail antagonizing at times, but in all honesty, she envied her, too. Gail might be shallow, but at least she knew what she wanted. Gail aimed low and achieved what she aimed for. Tyne had aimed high all her life and been miserably disappointed when she fell short. So, she couldn't even really look down on Gail.

Besides, most likely Gail slept well at nights. Didn't have someone chasing her in her dreams, touching her, making her do things—and, for the last few nights, caressing the blade of a knife against her throat.

As Tyne continued typing, her tired mind threatened to shut down. Sleep, elusive at night, threatened to take over in this safe sun-filled place. She battled the lethargy pulling at her lids, slowing her fingers on the keys. Despite her efforts, her breathing deepened, her vision blurred. The sounds of the office—the disparate syncopation of keyboards, ringing phones, Gail's coos—began to fade.

A breath—soft and whispery—grazed her cheek as the hand moved slowly down, its fingers pushing aside the satiny material of her dress, seeking, finding one nipple ready, pliant, massaging it between two fingers, stroking the orb as lips moved to her ear, touching, licking, whispering . . .

"You know what you want. So do I."

Another hand navigated a silky thigh, found the crevice that separated it from its mate, found her bare beneath, wet and waiting . . .

She shook herself awake. Her hands lay motionless on the keyboard. She sat dazed for a moment, trying to grasp what had happened. Just that quickly, she lapsed into a dream state and found him waiting for her. She felt disoriented, unreal—and frightened. The dream had continued where it'd left off. It had followed her here to this innocuous place where sunlight streamed in through large but dirty windows and kept shadows from merging into other shapes. The dream had never invaded her days before, never left her trembling as it did now.

She lifted her fingers, her mind pushing them to finish her

report, but they wouldn't obey. They hovered over the keys, tremulous. Her mouth was dry and she found it hard to swallow. She had to get control over her flayed nerves. If she didn't, she'd have a full panic attack right here in front of everybody.

Tyne stood on wobbly legs, left her cubicle, and headed toward the water fountain. As she passed Rhoni's cubicle, she caught a glimpse of her coworker idly talking on her phone, probably to her boyfriend. Tyne envied the carefree laughter of the young woman. As for herself, she felt like bursting into tears. She reached the fountain and bent to take a few sips. But the water ran dry over her tongue, barely lubricating it. Still, just getting up and walking a few steps had slowed her racing pulse. She took a few lung-cleansing breaths, drank some more water. Feeling better, reality edged back in with the thought that she had several pages to finish on the report before she headed to lunch. She started back, passing Lem on his return, or more likely escape, to his workspace. Obviously relieved to be away from Gail, Lem smiled at Tyne, then disappeared into his haven.

Back in her cubicle, Tyne sat down at her computer, her nerves steadier now. She still had to input the percentages from last quarter; most of the numbers were in red. She positioned her fingers to type and looked at the screen.

Her breath caught in her throat as her eyes read over her last line. It stared back at her, blatant in all caps. Bold. Underlined.

<u>WE'RE GOING TO BE TOGETHER FOREVER</u>

But how? She had fallen asleep. That much she was sure. But somehow, in her sleep, her fingers had typed out a message for her . . . to her. The same message *he* whispered in her ear nearly every night for the past few months, the last thing he said to her before she woke up and escaped.

Chapter 2

We're going to be together forever. The words seared into Tyne's brain as she sat during the train ride home. They were the words she heard in her dreams and lately in the still of her room, between reality and dream. But until this morning, they had stayed safely within the privacy of her room and her head. They had never appeared anywhere else.

As always when she heard them, they brought fear and a need to escape.

This—thing—whatever was happening to her—was getting worse. Most of all, it made no sense. It was ruining her nights and possibly her sanity because she didn't know how long she could go on like this.

Even now, her eyes were heavy, her body craving the sleep that was robbed from her nightly, but fear wouldn't let her drift off. The thought of the train denizens, mostly old, street-wizened men with their own demons, watching her toss and grapple with her nocturnal pursuer, a pursuer who had now chased her into her waking hours, into the safety of her office. . . .

Somehow she had managed to keep it together at work, fighting off an impulse to run and scream and hide. She had sat and stared blindly at the message for a few minutes. Then instinct took over as a finger touched the backspace key and deleted the spectral words. Her fingers finished the report without her, or at least without her conscious self. Her eyes fed her fingers words and numbers from the remaining hand-written pages without thought and meaning, bypassing her brain altogether. She continued in automode for the rest of the morning until she completed the report.

Afterward, she walked the report into Stan's office where she distractedly watched him write in his ledger, waiting for him to acknowledge her. She guessed he was going over the budget. Stan's bald pate gleamed smooth, making him appear younger than his fifty-eight years. Tyne figured he had shaved his head for just that reason, all signs of gray effectively eliminated. His face, when he finally looked up, displayed a series of small moles off his left eye, and a hefty salt-and-pepper mustache that only partially covered his full upper lip. At that moment, the lines that furrowed his forehead were more from worry than age. He looked up, seemingly pissed at the interruption even though he had been bugging her for the report since late yesterday.

"What's up?" he asked, his tone dismissive.

She handed him the report and he nearly snatched it out of her hand.

"Finally. Took you long enough." In the same breath, he laid it on his desk and picked up his pen again. "Can't look at it right now. Gotta go over this budget."

So her surmise had been correct. Normally, she would have started thinking of what provisions she would have to make just in case her salary had been struck through on the ledger. But there was nothing normal about her day, which she was going to bring to an abrupt close, not caring how it might look. She wasn't all that eager to be the good little employee to an employer who was about to kick her ass out on the street.

"Stan, I gotta go home. I'm not feeling well."

He sat up and slammed his pen down with a flourish that was meant to intimidate. It didn't.

"Ah damn it, that's just great! What the hell am I supposed to do if I need changes done to the report? There's no one else here who can do it."

"Just leave any suggestions on my voicemail, and I'll be in early tomorrow and make whatever revisions you need. But right now, I really can't stay."

He studied her face, probably trying to determine just how sick she was. "What's wrong? It's not some woman thing, is it?"

Inwardly, Tyne cringed. She disliked Stan thinking of her in any intimate terms whatsoever, and his mention of her menses was too disturbing.

"No, I'm fighting some sort of bug, Stan, and I know you wouldn't want me spreading germs, considering the staff is already small, and if I stay I could have you down to two people."

She felt no guilt lying to Stan. He lied often enough, calling in sick when everyone knew he was out on the golf course or sitting up in a bar somewhere shooting the shit with some of his journalist buddies. He felt no qualms transgressing the laws he laid down for the underlings. Which was why the employees' loyalty was solely to their paychecks and not to Stan.

"And you'll be in early tomorrow?" He repeated her words, his tone relenting because outside of firing her right then and there, there was nothing he could do.

She nodded. "Going home to dope myself up, and I'll be in bright and early," she assured him, knowing even then she couldn't assure herself. Only the night would tell.

Sitting on the train now, she tried to remember when the dreams had started. Every thought pinpointed the night of the *Clarion* party nearly two months ago. It had been held at the Fairmont in recognition of retired founder Willard Stingley's eighty-fifth birthday, and the staff had been required to attend. Black-tie gala, full-dress, tuxes and gowns. Which made some sense of her dream. Or at least the setting.

She had attended alone, not bothering to go through her book of friends to beg them to share her tedium. She planned to stay only until after the meal, mingle for a half hour, then slip out, but it hadn't worked out that way.

Stan had cornered her and kept her by his side as he made the rounds among the journalist luminaries. Even as he used her, she couldn't bring herself to get angry that he was deliberately giving folks the wrong impression. She found his charade kind of pathetic. Stan, excellent at deadlines and keeping down costs to maintain a crippled paper, had yet to get and keep a woman for more than two dates. Tyne had sidestepped his earlier attempts to expand their professional relationship to something else when she first started working at the *Clarion*. But that didn't keep him from using her. She was thirty to his fifty-eight and he liked people believing that he could "bag a young 'un."

Nothing out of the ordinary had happened that evening. Nothing to warrant the dreams that recreated that night with minor changes. She hadn't worn green that night. April, Donell, and Eve hadn't been there, either.

As for the stranger . . .

She turned from the window to find a grizzled man, probably homeless, staring her down from another seat, his eyes seeking hers. She turned her attention back to the passing buildings outside the train, went back to her thoughts.

The stranger in her dream had no face. She never got a visual sense of what he looked like, not the color of his hair, his eyes or his skin.

She closed her eyes, trying to stave off the memory of the feel of his hands on her skin, the way his fingers traveled down her shoulders and sides, pulling at the soft, green fabric. How his hands cupped her breasts, teased her nipples until her body tensed and her crotch began to cream. How he knew just where to touch her, knew places that caused her body to cry out, places no other lover, either through ignorance or selfishness, had ever explored. . . .

She felt the warmth of his breath as his lips touched her mouth lightly, then forced it open. She tasted the subtle trace of champagne and something unfamiliar on his tongue as it explored her mouth. She felt his hand move down, down. . . .

She woke with a jerk of her head just in time to see the

hand stretching toward her breast. But instead of a tuxedoed, faceless stranger, the old man who had been staring at her a moment—or moments?—before was now leering down at her.

"You weerre moannning," he slurred. "Thought sompin' was wrong wit' you."

"Get away from me," she said between clenched teeth, keeping her voice low, wondering what the man had heard her muttering, worried that he was about to cause a scene. But the other riders weren't even looking at them. They probably assumed the man was begging for money, a normal scenario on Chicago trains.

"Noww, why you acting like I'm doin' sompin' wrong. Just tryin' to helllpp." He turned and staggered away, but paused to look over his shoulder and spew under his breath. "Haughty aasss bitchh . . . nobody want your aasss any damn way." He muttered his way down the aisle, then opened and walked through the door leading to a connecting car.

Tyne raised her hand to push a stray hair out of her eye. Her hand was trembling.

Chapter 3

In the offices of Gaines, Carvelli and Debbs, a small architectural firm located on the fourteenth floor of a North
Michigan high-rise, a stray thought caused David Carvelli's
hand to pause midair as he reached for the plans on his desk.
An impression of skin, cinnamon-touched silk, ran through
his mind for an instant. He shook the image away. Tried hard
to concentrate on the schematics before him.

Still, he had to fight to keep his mind from wandering back
to the dreams, much as it had been doing these last couple of
months. They were threatening to subsume everything in his
life, including his work, and he couldn't afford to let that
happen. Especially not now with the Kershner deal at stake.
He and his partners needed this account to keep the firm
afloat.

After a few minutes of checking the digital designs, he
placed them back on the desk with a sigh. Another flash, this
time just a breath of a remembered scent, took him out of the
moment. The dreams again. It always came back to them.

Dreams he had trouble remembering upon waking. Images
that left his mouth dry, his pulse racing. But in the midst of
the fear, he kept reaching out to someone, trying to touch her.
Sometimes he did touch her. But the dreams only left him
with vague impressions. Nothing ever substantial.

At times, he had awakened to find his hand stroking his
penis, the member fully engorged. He'd been aware of a lin-
gering memory of perfume hanging in the dark. Several

nights in a row, he'd had to masturbate just to relieve the tension, to slow the blood pounding in his head.

Nothing had plagued him this much, not since when he was a child, just after . . .

He tried to cut off the thought he had carelessly summoned. But the memory came flooding back, as though he were eleven years old again standing alongside Terry, his best friend, as both waited in hushed excitement for David to set fire to the spider. David hadn't wanted to but Terry had egged him on, dared him . . .

"C'mon, chicken! Go on, do it!" Terry's red hair seemed to mark his fascination with anything incendiary.

David stiffened at the taunt. He wasn't chicken! What was the big deal anyway? Just set the damn thing on fire, watch it burn. That's all he had to do.

He struck the red ball of the match to the sandpaper strip along the side of the carton. A flame shot up accompanied by the familiar acrid smell. Flickering red and gold light reflected and refracted in two pairs of eager eyes as the boys stood enthralled by the tiny bit of devastation they held. They were ready to watch it take hold of the black widow that had set up residence in the storage room off the kitchen. Liquid black with a spot of orange on its underside, the creature was beautiful in a horrific way. At least to a pair of mischievous boys. David would have liked just to observe the spider in its kingdom, observe it in its predatory glory.

But Terry wanted to see skin, muscle, legs, eyes engulfed in a red blaze, to see the last instinct of his prey chase itself in an attempt to run away from the sizzling pain, to see the body draw up and eventually shrivel in a smoldering mass.

David watched the flame ride down the match. He waited to feel the heat of the advancing flame on his finger.

"C'mon," Terry urged, probably worried that Mrs. Carvelli would come into the anteroom any moment and catch them in flagrante, so to speak. He shook David's arm. The sudden motion made David drop the small torch onto a pile of rags just beneath the ledge where the spider hovered. The pieces of cloth had cleaning solution embedded in their fibers and the small flame licked hungrily at the pile, began consuming it.

Terry, always the self-preservationist, ran from the room without a thought of the trouble he had instigated. David stayed for a heroic few seconds and tried to stamp out the fire, but couldn't. The flames raced along the lower wooden paneling of the room, then latched on to some old cartons in the corner. The crackling grew louder, and smoke began filling the small room, making it hard to breathe. David gave up and ran, fear knocking all thought from his head. For years, he would wonder what would have happened if he'd kept his wits—if he'd remembered the pail in the cabinet beneath the sink, filled it with water and thrown it on the growing flames. He might have extinguished the fire and saved his mother's house. Instead he had followed Terry out the back door, hoping with a child's irrational hope that the problem would right itself on its own, that the fire tearing at the walls of the small room would go no farther . . .

But it had.

As far as his mother was concerned, a candle fell over and burned down the Victorian house in which her mother had been born and later left to her. The house that once stood proudly on the edge of Old Town was long gone. All because of a stupid accident. Worse still, the guilt of a child who couldn't trust his mother to forgive him had stilled his tongue even into his adult years. He accepted the fact that he would never tell his mother, and that, at least on this one thing, he was a coward.

The phone rang, breaking through his reminiscing, momentarily pushing back the guilt. He picked up.

"David Carvelli here."

"Hey Dave," Rick's excited voice came over the line. "Great news. I just talked to Kershner, and he's willing to sit down with us tomorrow at four. So make sure the specs are ready. Dave . . . Dave? You there?"

Dave heard the voice from a distance, as though it was being filtered through a tunnel.

"I'm here. I was just checking something," he said. "Four o'clock is fine. The specs will be done by then. Will Clarence be there?"

"No. It's just us for right now. Just make sure you have the designs ready for Kershner to look at." Rick's voice still sounded far away.

"We'll be ready. We got this." He managed to sound confident, but his stomach fluttered, and not with anticipation.

After he hung up the phone, he contemplated the evening ahead.

He needed to get a good night's sleep to be on his game.

If only those damned dreams would just stop.

Thing was, part of him really didn't want them to go away. He didn't want her to go away.

Tyne started the evening with a scented bath. Vanilla Bean by Yardley. She placed lit candles along the edge of the tub. Their flickering lights set a tranquil mood. Gerald Albright's "I Need You" flowed from the CD player, the seductive strains of his smooth sax filling the small bathroom.

Soaking in the hot water, Tyne turned her mind to family matters, putting aside for the moment the need and fear of sleep. April's wedding was coming up in less than a month, and she had to go to yet another fitting, which was always a pain. Being the maid of honor—as well as the oldest—hardly inured her to the tittering and mania of the younger bridesmaids, most of whom hadn't even hit the quarter mark yet. All the primping, posturing and posing got on her nerves. She noticed their eyes reflected in the mirrors when they looked at themselves and knew with a time-earned intuition that they saw princess lace instead of the shimmering lime satin of the bridesmaid dresses they actually wore. In their minds, they walked down an imaginary aisle to meet a dark, handsome stranger named Rashad, Keith, or maybe Jamal waiting in dreadlocked splendor at the end.

Perhaps she'd had that look a long time ago, but not now. Maybe never again. It vanished along with her once indefatigable hope that she would be settled down by thirty, already into a routine of divvied house responsibilities, with him making romantic meals—her own cooking was ptomaine lousy—and her doing the laundry and cleaning of their large, airy loft. Maybe there would be one or two kids, maybe one of each, a girl and a boy.

That had been her wholehearted plan by twenty-five, twenty-six. By twenty-nine, those plans had become half-hearted, and she decided to concentrate on pushing her career forward. But even that failed to go the way she planned. She had graduated from Northwestern's Medill School of Journalism with grandiose plans of working on a large Chicago paper, hopefully the *Tribune*. But several community papers later, she'd only managed to move down a notch. The market was tight right now, and though she might have gotten better opportunities in a smaller market in a smaller town, she didn't want to leave Chicago, where her family lived—her mother, her sisters April and Tanya, and brother, Tyrone. She just thanked providence for the paycheck—however long that lasted. Next month might see her in the unemployment line.

Another thing to be glad for was April. The family had come close to losing her last spring. Trying to get out of an abusive relationship, April had barely survived the bullet her boyfriend Kendrick fired into her chest after taking her hostage in her downtown office. After shooting her, the fool turned his gun on himself, thankfully.

April had once been single-minded in her pursuit of low-lifes. When anyone asked, she used to say that she liked a little thug in her men, real or not. She'd been contemptuous and casual—and maybe a little guilt-ridden—about her middle-class upbringing, often acting out. It had taken a .38-magnum bullet blowing her chest open to finally blow some sense into her head. When she recovered—after five hours of surgery and nearly a month in the hospital—Donell was waiting for her as he had been waiting for nearly eight years. Donell and April had gone to high school together. Bespeckled and soft-spoken, Tyne knew he was hardly April's initial idea of the man she wanted to wake up to every morning. Too sturdy, too dull, April used to say. Thank God, she'd changed her mind, realizing in time that love might hurt you on occasion, but it wasn't supposed to kill you.

Tyne stood up in the tub, water dripping, suds clinging, and caught her image in the full-length mirror hanging on the door. She studied herself to see what a stranger would see. All the self-love books she had ever read stated that love begins with acceptance of all of one's self, including the physical faults. So she guessed she should accept the slight saddlebags of her hips and the scar that ran along her arm—a souvenir of a bad motorcycle fall; her mother had made sure her father locked up his Harley after that. She looked at her breasts, the way they curved upward, and appreciated that gravity hadn't gotten to them yet. As for her behind, it was nicely rounded like some men seemed to appreciate. Her waist, although not small, was in proportion to her hips and chest. All in all, she had a more than passable body.

But she was a sister who didn't take booty calls, so her nights were solitary. There had been a few boyfriends in the past, but those relationships had been merely fillers; she had known at the onset she wouldn't marry any of them. Put off by the strain of her last thing with Raymond, she'd been celibate for a couple of years and was used to waking up alone. That seemed to be her fate; so be it. She cared, but she wasn't going to languish waiting for someone to come and fill her life, her bed. There were other ways to satisfy herself.

Still, the loneliness seemed to be manifesting itself in these strange dreams. Maybe Gail was right; she needed to get laid. Maybe the dreams would go away if she worked off some of her tension.

Tyne stepped out of the bath and toweled herself off, trying not to think of the many times she had orgasmed these last nights. It wasn't normal, having dreams so vivid, so sensual, they made you come and come hard. Dreams so vivid, they frightened you. How could she desire something, or someone, that frightened her, that made her tremble with yearning and fear? More frightening was the knife that had begun appearing in the dreams lately.

She put on her nightgown and walked to the bedroom. She opened the curtains to let in the illumination from the street-lights below and a bright quarter moon above. Total darkness was no longer a comfort. She popped open the tranquility sound machine she'd purchased on the way home and flipped in the tape labeled "Rain Forest." The soothing rhythm of a light rainfall filled the room. As her head settled into the pillow and her eyes closed, she envisioned herself standing alone under the dripping fronds of lush, tropical trees, felt the warm rain spray on her body, enter her pores, open her up. She was falling, falling . . .

The dinner table was gone. It was just him now. She felt herself opening up to him, her resistance giving way. First one, then two, three fingers eased inside her, then moved up her wet canal while a fourth lightly stroked her clitoris, sending spasms through her body. Her vibrating walls sucked the fingers deeper into her eager crotch, and she began bucking against them, working her body to their rhythm. Lips touched her nipple, then a tongue began tracing the sensitive orb, circling it slowly, keeping time with the fingers moving in, out, in, out. A scent of male musk hovered in the air, mixed with the scent of her excitement . . .

He smelled her scent, bent down to taste her wetness, felt her hips rise, pushing her moist, sex-scented lips against his eager tongue, felt her moving in time with his rhythm.

His tongue moved inside her, teasing her walls, tasting her cream, his lips pumping against her vulva. He heard her moan and it filled him. But just beneath the current of her longing, he felt her resistance, her dishonor. She didn't want to love him, yet she yielded to him with her softness, her wetness. When she moaned again, it signaled submission, not desire. But he refused to hear her tears . . .

David stirred awake at the sound, found his left hand stroking his balls. He felt embarrassed and disgusted. His writhing had caused the sheets to half fall off the bed.

He sat up dazed. Tried to remember. He had more than a slight impression of a woman beneath him, accepting him with desire—and shame.

A scent lingered in the air, a mixture of perfume and sex. He remembered the fleeting image of shimmering green. He had heard a soft, throaty sound, but couldn't remember if it had been hers or his own.

Somewhere in the distance, he had heard someone say, "We're going to be together forever," the voice strangled with desire and anger—and realized that it was his own voice he heard.

He got up, left the room to go downstairs to the kitchen. Along the wall over the stairs hung photos of Ruth (the Big Bambino), Mantle, DiMaggio. These were relics from his father who'd walked out on him and his mother when David was just ten, almost a full year before the fire. They were saved because they had been in the garage instead of the attic.

This was the house he had built for his mother almost three years ago. But just before the move, she'd decided she wanted to stay in her old home instead. The same home they had moved into after the Victorian was destroyed. This one was a Queen Anne built on a lot he purchased in the historic Oak Park district. He had tried to recreate what he had taken from her those many years ago. Walnut woodwork in the front hall, parquet floors, stained glass windows. In the living room, a marble fireplace. Outside a wraparound porch and Palladian windows mimicked the destroyed home. He hadn't even blinked at the expense of building in a historic district; it nearly broke him, but he had thought it worthwhile if it could recompense his past sins.

But his mother had looked at him and said, "This is your house. There's something about you in this place. I can't take it away from you."

No amount of pleading would make her see reason. She was dead wrong. This wasn't *his* place. He couldn't care less about turn-of-the-century homes big enough for a whole family. He would've much preferred a large apartment on North Michigan, sparsely decorated, airy with good lighting. Here, the mixture of rustic and Victorian furniture he had chosen for her matched the architecture of the home.

Still, he couldn't bring himself to put it on the market. Slowly, steadily it'd become the place he looked forward to coming home to every evening after a grueling day. He had even started a garden out back.

Rick had teased him about his "bachelor pad," telling him it was a great setting for a coke party. Or a good fucking Roman orgy with babes straddled over the French-style love seat. He told Dave that maybe he could grow some weed out back, sell it out of the garage. Dave usually laughed with him, sheepishly embarrassed that the house was actually domesticating him.

In the kitchen floor plan, he had deliberately left out a storeroom. Instead, a large pantry stood just off the hallway.

David walked to the faucet, ran the water cold, got a glass, downed it in a few gulps. He felt hot, sweaty, as though he had just been through a strenuous workout—or a prolonged lovemaking session.

He needed a woman. Karen had been gone only two months and already he was falling to pieces. Women might be able to go without for weeks on end, but men were different. He was, anyway.

He ran the water again, downed a second glass, but his thirst wouldn't go away.

Water wasn't what he needed.

What he needed was a good fuck. Then maybe things would get back to normal.

Chapter 4

Jennifer DiMello sat at the breakfast table in Mrs. Carvelli's kitchen. Small, country-styled with maple cabinets and granite counters, it was a cozy, homey place to sit and talk. Just outside the window, she spied a robin wandering along the branches of a sickly looking elm. She figured Dutch elm disease and wondered why Mrs. Carvelli hadn't had it cut down.

"Here you go." Mrs. Carvelli placed a mug of coffee on the table in front of Jennifer. Jennifer studied the older woman as she sat down across from her with her own cup. Early fifties, dark brown hair, lightly graying, with a youthful face that had strong features, but not overwhelming. From the picture in the living room, her son had the masculine version of his mother's Roman nose, broad forehead, and full lips; however, his eyes were green to Mrs. Carvelli's brown. Mrs. Carvelli had a beauty that had settled nicely with age, as well as sophistication by the look of the tailored light blue blouse and darker blue slacks. Diamond studs glinted in her earlobes.

"Thanks for coming over." Mrs. Carvelli's voice was soft, throaty, probably from cigarettes. Jennifer spotted an ashtray on the counter near the coffee machine.

Jennifer lifted her mug to take a sip, pondering what Mrs. Carvelli had just told her about her visions. And her dilemma. "So you never told him you're a seer?"

Mrs. Carvelli shook her head. "No. Though he probably

has some inkling but knowing David, he's scrunched it all down into that little box in his subconscious where he keeps things he doesn't want to deal with." Mrs. Carvelli cocked her head as she looked at the young woman, and Jennifer had the unsettling feeling she was being "read." "I ever tell you about the fire that destroyed my home years ago?"

Jennifer paused her upraised cup. "No, you never told me. What happened?"

"David. I picked up a few impressions from him after it happened. One of the few times I was able to get something after the fact. It was an accident. His friend Terry's shenanigans. David was always letting that boy pull him by the nose. Of course, I didn't tell him I knew because he was already feeling lousy, and there's only so much guilt a kid can handle. Besides, he learned a lesson that day, something I couldn't teach him. Still, I've been waiting all these years for him to say *something* about it. He never has."

Mrs. Carvelli paused contemplatively, took a sip of coffee. "I saw his friend, Terry, drowning in a forest preserve. Soon as I realized it was a premonition, I tried to call his mother, but I couldn't reach them. After it happened, I broke the news to David but I never let on that I knew beforehand. Over the years, there were other things, things I tried to prevent. I kept them to myself because at the time it didn't seem important to upset David's life. Not that he would've listened. He's so much like his father in many ways. Being a stone cold skeptic is one of them. That's why I've pulled you into this little drama. I've been picking up some disturbing things from him lately. I can't talk to him about them because I don't know exactly what's going on. I was hoping you might sense something."

"I'll try, but you know I only see past events, not the future."

Mrs. Carvelli stared bemusedly into her coffee cup as though reading tea dregs. "I think that your visions will be of more help than mine. Jennifer, I've never seen him like this before. And when I say 'seen', I mean his aura. It's been red lately.

Violent red, like blood. David's usually a green. Sometimes orange. Hardly ever red. I've only seen him this color twice in his life, and never this deep a shade. The first time was the night his father walked out on us and told David he wasn't coming back. That nearly destroyed my son. The other time was the day I told him about Terry. But it's not just his aura that's bothering me. There are other things too. I've been picking up some strange visions from him, images I can't quite pin down, but there's almost a violence to them. It's frightening me."

Jennifer sat quiet for a moment, took another sip of coffee. She didn't know about the color of auras or what they meant. She was a psychometrist, a "feeler," sensing impressions and emotions through things people touched. Past impressions, past emotions, never the future. As long as she could remember, she'd had this gift. When she was just seven years old, Jennifer found her friend Emily's necklace lying on the ground near the girl's house a couple of doors away. Emily had been missing for a week. As soon as Jennifer picked up the tiny heart chain, images invaded her mind—Mr. Jakins, his eyes strange, unfocused, his head sweaty; Emily frightened, crying and bleeding. She'd told her mother that Mr. Jakins had hurt Emily, but her mother scolded her for making up lies about their neighbor. No one ever found Emily. When Mr. Jakins finally moved away a year later, Jennifer had been relieved. She was never comfortable around him after the necklace, never comfortable with the way he looked at her and the other children, even though a lot of the kids liked him because he let them use his backyard pool.

Growing up, Jennifer realized that many of the smiling neighbors waving to her hid a lot of sordid sins behind those smiles. By the time Jennifer became a teenager, she knew whom to avoid, whom never to be alone with.

She never told anyone about her gift, not even her parents. But the kids at school must have sensed something about her because they taunted her with "witch bitch" and other cruel names. Jennifer suffered in silence until the day she met Mrs.

Carvelli. An old friend of her mother's, Mrs. Carvelli visited their home one day when Jennifer was just fifteen. And that day changed everything. Jennifer said hello to the woman and hadn't said much else. She hadn't needed to. Mrs. Carvelli looked at the young girl and recognized something in her. Jennifer never knew how. Maybe the woman had read her aura that day. Or maybe she saw something from Jennifer's future. Whatever it was, Mrs. Carvelli had taken the teenage girl aside and told her they had to talk.

That was nearly fifteen years ago. Mrs. Carvelli had kept in touch with the young psychic. But this was the first time the woman ever asked for help. Although she had never met David, Jennifer was glad to help because Mrs. Carvelli had done an extraordinary thing for a young girl not sure of herself or her gift. She had made her feel OK about herself.

"I don't pick up auras," Jennifer said, "but I felt something when I touched the tie clip you gave me. It was strange."

"What?" Mrs. Carvelli leaned forward, a mother's worry and a psychic's curiosity playing on her face. She hadn't asked before, maybe not ready to know then. Now she was.

Jennifer stared into her cup, not wanting to meet the fervor in those brown eyes. The coffee was black the way she liked. Dark enough to reflect her face up at her. The reflection looked fifteen all over again, but she hadn't been that age for a long time.

"Jen, stop stalling. Tell me." Jennifer was used to the commands. Mrs. Carvelli—Jen could never seem to call the woman by her given name, Carmen—didn't like people who dawdled.

The young woman looked up. "I see your son, but it's not his face I'm envisioning. Not like he looks in the picture in the living room. Or rather, when I look at the picture, it's another face superimposed over his. Yet it's him. I'm sure of it."

Mrs. Carvelli leaned back, her expression unreadable, and Jennifer wondered if she had said too much.

"I know that sounds strange . . ." she started.

The older woman quickly shook her head, her eyes fixed in

concentration as though trying to catch something fleeting through her mind. She got up from the chair, scraping it along the linoleum, opened a drawer at the counter and pulled out a pack of cigarettes. She reached for the matches, lit the cigarette, and drew in a long pull before she finally spoke.

"No, Jen, it doesn't sound strange. As a matter of fact, it sounds just about right . . . just about right."

Feeler and seer both looked out the window at the same time, peering at the sickly elm, their thoughts running along the same disturbing line.

New York—June 1879

Standing in the parlor, Joseph Luce stared at the painting of his mother that hung to the right of his own above the fireplace. His father's portrait took space on the left. Below, lining the gilded mantel, sat various curios his father had collected on his many excursions around the world. Three silver monkeys, posed to see, speak, and hear no evil, sat next to an African mask made of rich ebony. This abutted a bronze statue of Buddha that hailed from the Orient. On the other end was a Navajo peace pipe. Center place among the assortment was the cherished miniature replica of Windsor Castle made entirely of gold, presented last year to his father by Queen Victoria during his tenure as honorary emissary for President Hayes. William Luce prided himself on acquiring things, including the woman who later became his wife, the beautiful and winsome debutante, Anne Spaulding, granddaughter of a shipping magnate. She had been displayed, as were his father's other collectibles, as a testament to his extraordinariness.

The triad of gilt-edged paintings hung also as a statement—of power, elegance, and privilege—his father and mother embodying the former, he, the latter. In her portrait, his mother holds her hands solemnly in her lap, her expression one she probably thought at the time was demure and noble. But the painter had caught a steel in her eyes, a hardness that Joseph had similarly observed occasionally in the eyes of felons just released back into the populace, a determination never to be confined again. Gone was the young girl whose vivacity had been dulled and whittled away by the time Joseph was born into this world.

That his mother had enjoyed her life of splendor and luxury Joseph had ignorantly assumed. Yet, given the comforts that even her peers silently begrudged her, being tethered to a man who did not love her must have felt like a prison she could only escape through death. Ten years had passed this very day, ten years since he and his father had found her lying in her bed, the evidence of her departure an empty bottle of laudanum sitting on the bedstand beside her.

The years of his mother's barely expressed disappointments and frustrations sometimes came back to him in snatches, reminiscences that he quickly forced away. He and his father had entered their conspiracy of silence long ago, mentioning her only with reservation, and only when necessary. As for the rest of the world, thanks to his father's station in society (as well as a few tactically greased palms), his mother's death had been ruled a bad heart simply giving out. The word "suicide" would never be paired with her name.

As horrible as finding her body had been, Joseph could not forget the look of peace on her face nor that small smile that had played at her lips. An escapee finally fleeing her prison— and its warden.

William Luce stared down from his portrait, much like Zeus in an eternal frieze of displeasure. The cruelty in his face was unequivocal, the glint in his eyes reproof against a world that fell short of his measure—a world that included his own wife and son. Especially a son whom he considered a profligate unworthy of the family name.

Joseph walked over to the liquor cabinet, reached for the decanter of brandy. He poured a full snifter, emptied it in three long swigs, refilled it to the brim. It was all of ten o'clock in the morning, too early for drink. Had his father been home, he would have lambasted his son for his self-indulgence. But his father was on a trip to New Jersey to settle some matter with one of his steel refineries. Always business.

Joseph was free to enjoy his father's supply of liquor and cigars, the only pleasures the man allowed himself. As far as he knew, his father had never even taken a mistress, an arrangement that was more common than not in their circle. Maybe life would have been better for his mother had he done so, had his father indulged himself even just a bit, allowing imperfection to nick his self-defined veneer. Joseph knew his father's fidelity was due more to his tight thriftiness and self-image as a man of temperance than any real regard for his wife or vows. Women, mistresses, cost money, money that could be better spent being reinvested in his numerous financial enterprises.

Joseph sat on the divan in front of the fireplace, concentrating on the woman who had not only escaped a husband but who had abandoned her son, as well. He knew one day that he would take a wife. It was his duty as heir. Also, his father wanted to make sure there would be a generation born who would be worthier of his money and name than the present successor. But as Joseph stared at Anne Luce's set gaze, he knew that he could never marry a woman he held in such disregard as his father had held his mother. Theirs had been a marriage with rarely an exchange of kind words. Anne's attempts at intimate conversations and loving embraces had been met only with dark silences that delivered more pain than any physical blow ever could. Even as a young boy, he had picked up this tacit hostility and had wondered about it, thinking then that this was what marriage was about.

Looking up at his mother, Joseph vowed that he would only marry for love and not merely for duty—or to acquire a possession to display on his arm. He would love his wife, dearly, madly, completely. He would adore her, worship her so that she would never leave him. The one who finally won his heart would be his forever. Even death would not part them.

Chapter 5

Sitting in the Newberry Library, Rhea Simmons paused at one of the records listed on page 134 of the *African-American Freedmen's Sourcebook*. She'd been leafing through the book all afternoon and the names and text were beginning to blur. She took off her glasses, rubbed her eyes, put the glasses back on. Yes. There it was, the name she had been searching for, for nearly an hour. The listing leapt from a page of the Register of Signatures of Depositors of the Freedmen's Saving and Trust Company, New York 1865–1876.

Record No. 1013 **Record for** Rachel Chase
Date: Feb. 20, 1876
Where born: New York
Where brought up: New York
Residence: 358 W. 15th St.
Age: 24 **Complexion:** Brown
Occupation: Teacher
Works for: Colored School #1
Wife or Husband: George (Attorney)
Children: None
Father: Lawrence Simmons, died on Thompson St., 1873
Mother: Gertrude Olmsted of NY.
Brothers and sisters: Lawrence, Jr. of NY.
Remarks:

This was a start. She would have to research the collections some other day for more information. The research would take a lot of time and effort, but ever since her grandmother had handed her the bundle of letters, her curiosity had been piqued about the woman who'd written them.

Rhea copied the information into her lined notebook, then double-checked to make sure she had written everything correctly. With a sigh, she closed the heavy vellum-bound book, put her pen down and sat back in the chair. In the hour since she'd first arrived, the room had partially filled with people. College students like her, mostly. There were a few older patrons, browsing through large tomes, probably researching their family genealogies. The librarian had told her that the second floor of the Newberry Library held an extensive collection of urban histories, census reports as well as 17,000 genealogies. Here was the place to come to research the past, to find information about somebody who lived and died over a century ago.

Rhea peered around at the bronze-grilled oak cases holding thousands of volumes, the tapered ceiling, the paintings of old Chicago hanging along the wall. The quiet elegance of the room, accented with large windows, marble-and-steel tables, and teak chairs, pulled her into its deliberate illusion of another time, some bygone era where privileged gentlemen sat down to brandied wine and cigars while poring over the news of the day. The plush carpeting muted footsteps, insulating its patrons in a cocoon of studious quiet. The whole room was meant to close out time. Or shut it in.

Rhea looked down again at the information written in her notebook. It was brief, yet it told much. For instance, her grandmother had long ago enlightened her about the early practice of distinguishing status in the colored community by skin tones. Never mind that all were designated "Negro" and were subject to the same discrimination by the majority society. To be too dark among one's own was sometimes an immutable shortcoming, even if one had scads of money. An old adage her grandmother once told her about came to mind:

"If you're white, just right; brown, stick around; black, get back." Unfortunately, the sentiment still survived to a degree. Rhea, medium-complected, still knew what it felt like to be the only black in a class, a room. To not be light enough in some situations, or not dark enough in others. Here in the log the entrant's complexion was a matter of record. Rhea wondered whether it had been used as an identifier or for some discriminatory purpose. Designation "brown." As opposed to what? "Yellow?" "Pearly white?" "Charcoal black?" Was "brown" here a plus or minus?

Rachel Chase had been twenty-four years old in 1876. The earliest letter Rhea held in her possession was dated September 1879, and was addressed to Rhea's great-great-grandmother Sarah Parkins. According to at least one of the letters, Rachel's husband, George, had died in a fire in early 1878. So who was the unnamed "gentleman" mentioned in the letters? Rhea pulled the folded pages of the first missive from her satchel, stared at the browned pages, the partially decipherable words. Some of the words had faded with time, but parts were still legible. It was this particular letter that had started Rhea's quest, that had stayed on her mind, then began to prey on it.

At first glance, it held nothing out of the ordinary. Most of the content was everyday filler that might be found in letters of that time, a lot of chatter about weather, health, and expected travel plans. It was near the end of the letter, two paragraphs in particular, that caught Rhea's eye after the first reading. At the time, she had barely wondered about the allusion to the mysterious gentleman, someone who was obviously Rachel's lover. That Rachel refused to name him began to nag at Rhea. But searching among the subsequent letters, she found no clue as to the man who had brought the young widow so much pain and anguish. Rhea read the words again; she had lost count of the many times she had reread them:

I wrote to the gentleman (I need not divulge his name here to you where prying eyes might find it) just as you suggested. I impressed upon him my desire to cease this madness that has come over both of us. To never again let prior events occur. It is much too dangerous for both of us, given our place in society. Sarah, I implore you not to think less of me for my lapse in judgment and integrity, and hope you do not judge me too harshly. Loneliness for George and a need I cannot understand temporarily did away with my propriety and good sense.

I know there is no future for us. Especially not here, for it was only a few years ago that the whites burned down the colored orphanage on 51st Street, almost killing those precious children. I remember Father had to move us out of the city after the riot because for a long time it was not safe for colored folks to live in New York. Then there were the draft riots years later. And even though the years have passed, the hatred has not. I tremble to think what would happen to us if anyone were to discover our prior assignations. Worse yet, divulge them. Yes, I must find the strength to end that which should never have begun in the first place.

Rhea carefully folded the pages together and returned them to her satchel. What was she chasing? A piece of history? Or a satisfaction to her fervid curiosity? What was the soap-opera fascination that made her read and reread the letters, and now go through stacks of books looking for anything that might bring Rachel forth in her mind as more than a phantom long dead?

She wished she understood what was driving her, but she didn't. What she did know was that she would continue searching until she found out who the "gentleman" was and what had happened to him and Rachel, something not found in any of the letters. The last letter was written in November 1879. Had Sarah moved away? Or had Rachel and her great-great-grandmother ceased communication for other reasons?

Chapter 6

David took a sip from his Manhattan and watched over the rim as Rick tried to engage their waitress with some stupid comment and an even stupider grin. The woman didn't look in the mood to be bothered. She barely broke a smile as she set down the teeming plates of buffalo wings, fries and sour cream in front of them, then rushed away.

After she had gone, Rick looked at David, winked. "I'm wearing her down. I'll give it another two, three weeks before she finally comes around and agrees to have at least one drink with me." He took a gulp from his glass of beer.

David shook his head in mock pity. "Man, you need to give it up. Not gonna happen. At least, not with Ms. Chill over there." He nodded in her direction where the waitress was taking the order at a nearby table. "Look, back to business. I have to tell you I think we really fucked up going in to see Kershner without Clarence. The man barely heard us out and hardly glanced at the plans. After all, this was supposed to be Clarence's deal, and Kershner obviously was expecting him to be there."

Clarence Debbs was their third partner in Gaines, Carvelli and Debbs, the architectural firm they formed three years ago. Lately though, Clarence had been showing signs of wanting to pull out. David suspected their partner was secretly taking on outside projects, a violation of their agreement. That he hadn't shown up for this meeting was a not-so-subtle indication of his lack of interest in the business.

"We have to talk about Clarence, where he stands with the firm, because if he pulls out now—"

"OK, I'll talk with him," Rick said too quickly.

David realized Rick was holding on to a blind loyalty established from years of friendship. David had no such illusions. He hadn't gone to private school, then Yale, with Clarence as Rick had. Rick actually was the one to introduce Clarence to David nearly five years earlier, and David had followed both men's careers as a friendly competitor. Then a couple of years later, Rick suggested the two of them partner up. David agreed to the venture and then had said yes later to bringing Clarence on board, solely on Rick's word. But he was starting to worry that Rick's friendship was coloring his judgment. David had too much invested in the business to just sit and watch it flounder because of Clarence's ambivalence.

"You better do more than talk with him. If he wants out, we should just let him walk. We'll buy out his third . . ."

"No, no, man. I promise, he's not going to walk. He's got a vested interest in our success."

"Does he? Because it looks to me like he's out to fill his own pockets at our expense."

Rick's earlier jovial mood seemed markedly dampened. He poured off the rest of his bottled beer into the glass and gulped it down. "I'll talk to him. I promise. He's not going to screw me—us."

"We'll see." David dipped a buffalo wing in the sour cream, trying to get his appetite back. He had said what he had to, and he would just wait to see what Rick would do. Or more importantly, what Clarence would do. If Rick didn't follow through, then he would.

For the rest of dinner, Rick tried to lighten the mood with his usual stories about his girlfriends. Actually there were two, Melinda and Amy, both of whom David had met a couple of times. Rick rotated them in shifts. Rick scheduled Melinda for sports outings, picnics, day activities. The sultrier Amy was for evenings at upscale restaurants and parties. Rick considered himself a player, but David knew that if Melinda ever showed the slightest interest in getting serious, Rick would be down at the jewelers picking out a ring. As for Amy, Rick used her for show and as a backup in case Melinda walked.

"Heard from Karen lately?" Rick's question came between bites of fries.

The question took David off guard. He didn't want to talk about Karen. After two months, he was still sensitive about how it had ended. A picture popped in his mind, crystalline blue eyes brimming with tears. She had been especially beautiful that night, wearing the lavender dress that clung nicely to her sylphlike figure, her auburn hair elegantly swept up in a bun. She'd brought over dishes of *cavatelli venezziana* and tiramisu from Rosalina's, his favorite Italian restaurant. After dessert, she smiled and pulled out a small, black velvet box. Inside was a solid gold ring. An engagement ring for him that had caught him by surprise. It would have been a lovely evening except that he'd had to admit to her—and himself—that he didn't love her.

The admission had taken them both by surprise. In response, she threw a plate against the dining room wall and accused him of wasting two years of her life. He let her walk out, sorry that he couldn't give her what she wanted. But he hadn't given more than a passing thought to settling down, although sooner or later he knew he would have to. He was already thirty-four and the years were going by fast.

He shook his head, then signaled the waitress for the tab. He didn't feel like talking about Karen, and the problem about Clarence was giving him a headache. He had counted on the Kershner deal coming through, particularly since the last two projects had barely covered costs. Things weren't looking good. He had too much shit to deal with, especially on the little sleep he'd been getting.

He looked at the check, pulled out twenty dollars to cover his half. "Gotta get on home. I got an early morning call in to Larry tomorrow about those condos being planned for Dearborn Street. You're checking on that liability insurer tomorrow, right?"

Rick nodded as he put down his cut and the tip on the table. The waitress came and picked up the bills, then brought back the change. They both stood and walked to the door.

"Sorry about bringing up Karen, man. Thought she might have seen reason and called you by now."

"Why would she? I was the one who rejected her. Most women don't come back for seconds of that."

"I guess. Though that'll teach her to let the man do the asking."

David smiled at his friend's simplistic philosophy on romance. "Anybody ever call you a Neanderthal?"

Rick laughed. "About as often as they call you a noncommitting bastard."

David didn't let Rick see the wince. That had cut too close.

Outside, they parted and David walked to his Lexus. *Noncommitting bastard.* She hadn't exactly called him that; she hadn't needed to. Because they both knew that was exactly what he was.

Maybe such a thing as karma did exist. He had pissed on Karen. Now life was shitting on him, robbing him of his business, even his sleep.

He felt uneasy as he got behind the wheel and pulled off. But anticipating an evening of Ellington and Coltrane along with a glass of wine, his mood lightened a little as he turned off onto the Eisenhower Expressway and drove the nine miles to Oak Park.

David felt a peace descend whenever he drove through the quiet streets of his neighborhood. A mix of Victorian mansions, neoclassical buildings, and Frank Lloyd Wright Prairie homes, the historic area contained an old-world charm and stately beauty that drew the elite, the creative best. Writers, artists, and architects like himself called Oak Park home. Hemingway had been born here. It was a place of tree-lined streets, families old and young, wide lawns and lovely homes.

When people discovered David was an architect living in Oak Park, they invariably asked whether Wright was his inspiration for going into the field. Invariably he told them no.

Wright's style was interior light and open, dramatic spaces in low-hugging, long buildings. David's was eclectic, combining the contemporary and traditional, the utilitarian and the decorative. He was married to no one style.

As uncommitted in work as he was in life.

When he got home, his message light was flashing on the machine. He dropped his keys on the foyer table and hit the play button. The first two messages were from his mother asking him to call, but no detailed message. Something was up, but it must not be an emergency, otherwise she would have said so. He didn't feel like dealing with her tonight. He would call her from the office tomorrow. The last message was from Sherry, asking him to call as soon as he got home.

Sherry was a friend of ten years, beautiful as well as gay. She had been there during the first days after Karen, trying to convince him that he wasn't the total ass he thought he was. She had been empathetic instead of accusing since she had gone through a recent breakup herself.

He dialed Sherry's number, wondering what crisis was up since she had sounded just a little bit desperate in her message. She picked up on the second ring.

"Yeah?" he said without any introduction.

"Good, you're home. Need you badly." He heard a lilt in her voice.

"For what? If it's that faucet again, you should get a plumber and stop being so cheap. My expertise doesn't lean to diddling with washers and pipes. I only design the houses they go in, babe."

"Nope. Not that. I need your body."

There wasn't any misinterpretation. She wasn't asking for a warm body to bed. "Need it for what? What's going on?"

"Wedding. I need an escort. Don't want to go by myself and since Gina's gone . . . C'mon, good food . . ."

"You know how I feel about those things."

"Hey. You should enjoy the irony of someone else falling into the pit you barely escaped. C'mon, it's a friend of mine, and I really want to go and I don't want to go alone. If I ask a girl, I don't want her getting any ideas. You're my safe date. As well as being handsome, you won't clash with my dress."

"Look, Sherry, I'd do almost anything for you but I don't relish getting all dressed up to attend some wedding, especially since . . ."

"I know, I know. Since Karen. But this is a good friend of mine, and I want to be there. And I want a good friend by my side. It'll only be a couple of hours at the most."

David sighed. He didn't want to go. But he didn't want to disappoint Sherry, who had served as arm decoration for at least one of his functions since Karen. It was only fair that he do the same. "When is it?"

"A week from Saturday at seven. First Unitarian Church in Hyde Park. Then there's the reception later. Good food and all the wine you can drink. C'mon, I'll owe you one."

"No, actually, I owe you, remember?"

"Great. I really appreciate this. I promise I won't impose on you again."

Dave chuckled. "Yeah, yeah, yeah. Not until next time when you need something fixed or someone to drop off some Chinese pickup."

"Don't forget the sperm donation I might ask you for one day," she laughed.

Dave nearly choked, then laughed. "Don't even joke about that," he said. "OK, I'll pick you up say six-thirty?"

"Yeah, great. See you then."

David hung up the phone, hung up his jacket, then walked to the living room. He found his jazz compilation CD, put it on. Ellington's "Sophisticated Lady" flowed through the living room, floated up to the rafters, bounced off the windows. He poured a glass of white wine, settled down in his lounger facing the fireplace, pushed off his loafers with his feet, sipped, and closed his eyes. A vestige of the earlier headache still drummed behind his eyelids, and he willed it to go away. If that didn't work, he would have to hunt for some ibuprofen. Relax. That's what he needed to do.

As he listened to the music, the tension began drifting from his limbs. It seeped away, leaving a quiet lethargy in its place. Sleep came unexpectedly, quickly, taking him with it to some other place . . .

He walked slowly, afraid that she might sense him follow-ing behind. The bustle of her lilac skirt swayed with her steps, hypnotizing him as he watched her continue up Broadway. She was wearing one of those ridiculous female concoctions on her head. This was lilac also, velvet, trimmed with tiny roses. He imagined the lustrous auburn hair caught up be-neath, could feel the texture of it as he stroked the corkscrew curls. So different than he had supposed, as he had imagined in his dreams. He remembered the silk of her brown skin, and thought it an inimitable sin to have such loveliness en-shrouded where no eyes could see. Where his eyes in particu-lar were now denied. The spectral scent of jasmine tormented him. There had been the slight essence of that perfect flower between the luscious breasts and he had tasted the salt of her skin. Knew that he had to taste, to touch her one last time. He walked faster.

He didn't know how long he could follow before she sensed him. Sensed the longing trailing her with each step. Would she stop and welcome his "good morning" or would she hasten away as she had before? He didn't know and if he were to be truthful to himself he didn't care. She would not get away from him. He would make her see reason. But he knew that reason had left him a long time ago. It had disap-peared with the first setting of warm brown eyes on him, and a smile from soft, full lips. He was a man possessed, and he knew that he was on the verge of madness. That he would not ever let her go. That if he could not have her here. . . .

She struggled against the hand holding her, pulling her. Fetid smells mixed with the smell of brine, making her gag. The lover held her, his grip tight, desperate. She wanted to pull away, but she couldn't. He was too strong. He wouldn't let her go, had said he would never let her go. She turned to

*see his face, but only saw the glint of the knife as it came to-
ward her. It slid along her neck in a cruel, thin, red line. The
shock of the pain seared as she began to choke on her own
blood flooding her throat, her lungs . . .*

Tyne spluttered awake, coughing. The sound machine was
no longer playing, the waves of the ocean silent. She covered
her mouth with her hand as a spasm wracked her body. She
felt as though she were drowning. But it was her imagination. She wasn't dying. She was safe, sitting up in her bed.
She had swallowed wrong. That was all. Still, fear settled on
her like a cold sheet.

Several moments passed, and the coughing died. The fear
remained.

She pulled her hand away from her mouth, saw the dark
circle of moisture in her palm. It seemed darker than saliva.
The taste in her mouth was salty, metallic.

She rushed from her bed to turn on the wall switch. The
sudden wash of white light made her blink. Everything was
as it should be: the bed, dresser, rattan chair, her bookcase
and nightstand, on which lay the mystery novel she had
started several nights ago. The normalcy of the room said
that nothing was wrong.

She opened her palm to see what she already knew was
there.

A spot of blood, thick and warm, lay in the middle.

She told herself that she had loosened something in her lung.

But when she looked up, she caught sight of her mirror
image. It pulled at her, drew her away from the wall. She
walked slowly to the dresser mirror, her eyes focused on a
space on her neck. When she moved in front of the mirror,
she bent forward to stare at the small streak of red that lined
the middle of her neck.

She reached to touch it, and blood came away on her finger.
She wiped it off and nothing remained. Her neck was not cut.

But she didn't know how the blood had gotten there.

By the time she fell asleep again, she had almost convinced
herself that it was nothing. Almost, but not quite.

Chapter 7

"April, hold still." Tyne bent to straighten the train that had been veering to the left as April walked between the tables in the reception hall. The silk panel tended to sway too much and hitch on April's side. Other than that, the bride was perfect. Luckily no one had paid much attention to the errant train during the ceremony. They had been too entranced by April herself, her glow, her smile. Tyne imagined that love was personified in her sister today, every nuance of it. The girl was just beautiful. She dabbed at a tear building in the corner of her eye. She had on waterproof mascara as a precaution, but still she didn't like appearing so emotional. Today was a day for joy; she managed to put other, more disturbing thoughts away.

April gave her a quick peck on her cheek, then said, "Don't worry about that damn thing. Go on and get you something to drink, stop following me around."

"I'm your maid of honor, I'm supposed to follow you around . . ." but before Tyne could finish the sentence, her sister walked away, winking over her shoulder. Tyne felt as though her sister was walking away for good.

Tears had run during the ceremony, and even before as she helped April dress. Amid the excited retinue of bridesmaids, April had been the serene one, calmly reveling in her moment. When she turned from the mirror and smiled at Tyne, Tyne saw the little twelve-year-old pest who used to follow her around, trying to act all grown with her little, skinny knock-kneed self. Then as April stood there, she morphed into a beautiful woman on the verge of a new life, and Tyne realized their sister-friendship was going to change. With that knowledge, the tears flowed until April came and put a comforting arm around her and whispered, "It's all right. I'm still your little sister." Tyne had blinked, wondering at her sister's sudden sixth sense.

Nearly two hundred guests now filled the Preston Bradley Hall in the Cultural Center. Lights from the hanging Tiffany lamps sparkled against the zodiac signs on the Tiffany-domed ceiling while mosaic scrolls and rosettes adorned the supporting arches. In front of one of these arches, a seven-piece band was playing "Misty." Hundreds of white-linen covered tables sat in the center, where guests sat eating, laughing, and talking. The voices echoed up to the dome, throughout the hall. On the dais that had been set up for the wedding party, the bride rejoined her groom, her hand softly caressing his arm as she sat down next to him. Donell had trimmed his dreads, and looked both nervous and handsome in his tuxedo. Then he smiled at April, and no one else existed for him.

Tyne stood beneath one of the arches taking a breather. She peered around the room, taking in the overwhelming elegance. Crystal glasses, gold silverware, white silk napkins folded in the shape of birds of paradise. . . . April and Donell had gone all out for their fairy-tale day. The hall was actually a gift from April's employer, the Chicago Department of Tourism, where April was an assistant director and which was housed on the first floor of the Cultural Center. April hadn't had to pay for the reception hall at all.

Tyne spotted her mother and Tyrone dancing among the throng of bodies on the floor to the right of the dais. Her brother towered over their mother by two feet and moved to accommodate the difference. Her mother was beaming up at him, at one point putting a hand to his cheek. She was proud. Tyne could see that from where she stood. Tyrone had stepped into their father's shoes today, walking April down

the aisle, smiling proudly as though she were his daughter instead of his sister. Their father, Ernest Jensen, had died of a
heart attack nearly eight years ago when April was still a
teenager. Since then, Tyrone had assumed a protective role
over their sister, which sometimes made her rebel. Today,
though, April had welcomed her brother's arm as he led her
to Donell.

Tyne looked around to try to spot Tanya, but she didn't
see her sister anywhere. Tyne, Tyrone, and Tanya, the three
T's, born in that order, all three names chosen by their father.
April had been christened by their mother; she had insisted
since she knew April would be their last. Her parents had
done well by all their kids. Tyrone was holding his own as a
freelance photographer, while Tanya was a metallurgical en-
gineer at Wode Metallurgical Laboratories. All were success-
ful in their own right, even though at times Tyne felt like the
laggard in the sibling race. Sometimes she found herself si-
multaneously proud and envious, then had to remind herself
that she'd made choices that put her where she was today.

Maybe being laid off would be a blessing in disguise. She
would be forced to take that dangerous step and move out on
her own without a safety net. Freelancing like Tyrone, actually going out in the field and finding stories, submitting articles, and not just sitting at a desk all day checking numbers
and facts. Lord knows, Stan wasn't about to give her that
chance. Not without some horizontal prompting on her part.
Even if by some miracle he played fair and gave her a break,
how many people would actually read her articles? Community
newspapers were hardly stepping stones to Pulitzers.

"OK, what're you doing standing here all alone?" Tanya
came up beside her. Tanya's braids were intertwined with
pearls and a rope of emerald-colored gems. The effect was
regal. They were both wearing the green satin that April, to
their dismay, had chosen, though Tyne's shade was darker.

"You wishing you were up there with somebody of your
own?" Tanya said, leaning her head against Tyne's cheek for
a moment. She was holding a half-filled glass of champagne.

"No more than you," Tyne countered, reaching to grab her sister's champagne glass, but Tanya deftly held it out of the way.

"Get your own. Anyway, you're the oldest. More pressure from the mama-that-be. I have a few good years before I take that step. If I take it at all. I'm comfortable with the way Jason and I are now." Tanya sipped her drink. "Besides, you're the one who wants the house and kids. It's funny when you think about it. April was the one who wanted to be out clubbing and dipping and now look at her. An old married woman. Goddess, doesn't she look beautiful, though?"

"Yes, she does," Tyne answered. Both sisters looked wistfully at their youngest sibling, who was gazing at her groom as though he were a jewel unexpectedly cast her way.

"Thank the Lord that's not Kendrick up there with her, otherwise I'd have had to say something in church." A slight bitterness edged Tanya's voice. Tyne understood. They had both received the late night calls after yet another beating, had gone to the emergency room with April to have the doctors fix blackened eyes, a busted lip, and once a broken arm.

"I really didn't think we would see this day," Tyne said softly.

"Neither did I," Tanya matched her sister's tone. "She came through some shit, but I guess she had to in order to know what a shit-free world smells like. Now, she can appreciate a man who doesn't have to kick her ass to make himself feel big."

Later, Tyne toasted her sister and her new husband followed by Donell's friend and best man, Byron, whose voice shook as he congratulated the couple. Even much later, April stepped down from the dais, finally leaving her man for a moment to mingle with some of her guests. Tyne kept by her side, at intervals smoothing out that damnable panel. She had just stooped for what seemed the hundredth time, then straightened up to see a couple approaching them.

The thing that immediately struck her was what an attractive pair they made. The woman was model tall, long-limbed, full lips, shimmering brunette hair that swung about her shoulders. The man stood slightly taller, with dark brown hair, Mediterranean features, and eyes so light they shone in contrast to his olive skin. The woman stared at Tyne the entire time during her approach. The engagement of eyes made Tyne nervous as she quickly realized she was being checked out and not just casually. Without ceremony, the woman came up and gave April a tight hug and April hugged her back just as enthusiastically.

"Sherry, I'm so glad you came," April said, pulling back with a smile.

Sherry laughed slightly. "Like you would have forgiven me if I hadn't. You are absolutely gorgeous in that dress and the wedding, God, was beautiful!"

"Thanks," April beamed. "Sherry, this is my sister and maid of honor, Tyne."

Sherry held out her hand. "Nice to meet you."

Tyne shook the proffered hand, noting uncomfortably that Sherry held on for a fraction too long.

"Hello, nice to meet one of April's friends," Tyne said, pulling back her hand quickly, but smoothly enough not to offend.

The woman's smile widened and she cocked her head. "Tyne. That's an unusual name. Lovely."

"Yeah, my father's choosing," Tyne said, uneasy under the woman's scrutiny.

Tyne noticed that the man was also staring at her, his gaze searching her face. He seemed familiar, but she didn't know where she might have seen him before.

Sherry spoke up. "April, Tyne, this is a good friend of mine, David Carvelli."

David nodded at April. "I have to agree with Sherry, you make a lovely bride." He turned his gaze on Tyne again. "Your sister is an equally lovely maid of honor." Something in his voice made his friend Sherry gave him a sidelong look, a glance Tyne couldn't interpret.

"Thank you," April said glowing.

Tyne felt David's gaze. She glanced at him, met green eyes, looked away.

"I'm going to go find Mom," she said. "Nice to meet both of you." She headed through the crowd, knowing that she was shirking her duties again. But David Carvelli made her uneasy.

Back at the table, Sherry nudged David as he moved the herb chicken around on his plate with a fork. He wasn't hungry. Actually, he had lost his appetite.

"So, it seems we have the same taste," Sherry said teasingly.

Dave knew whom she was referring to. "What's wrong with looking at a beautiful woman?"

"Nothing, except you weren't just looking. You were practically enthralled. I think you chased her away."

"Well, if she was running away from me, I don't know why. Maybe she didn't like your little come on. I saw that hand thing."

"Hey, I wasn't hitting on her," she smiled. "OK, well, maybe a little. Between the two of us, she probably thought we were going to invite her to a threesome."

David ran a finger along the rim of his glass. "I don't know. I'm pretty sure I've seen her somewhere before."

"Hey, most men think they've seen a beautiful woman somewhere before. Probably in your dreams."

"No . . ." he said thoughtfully. He stared among the cluster of bodies until he spotted her several tables away. She was sitting with an older woman and at least three other people. Her profile was to him. She was smiling, talking.

He couldn't explain his reaction. She was beautiful, but not particularly his type. It wasn't her color. He had dated a black woman before, although that experience hadn't gone down well. No. It was something else. A feeling that was nagging him to distraction.

He'd had this response once before. As a matter of fact, Sherry had been with him that night, too, part of the favor he

owed. It had been an awards ceremony for Chicago architects held at the Fairmont a couple of months back. He'd
taken a breather, stepping out into the foyer. After a few seconds, a woman had come out of another reception hall almost at the same time. They had both looked at one another,
and he stopped, the same sense of recognition coming over
him. At first, she just glanced at him, then she stopped and
stared for a few more seconds. And like today, she had
quickly turned and reentered the room, leaving him alone.

It was the same woman.

He turned to Sherry. "She was there, at the Fairmont. That's
where I saw her before. Remember the awards thing I dragged
you to? I saw her outside in the lobby. She was there."

"Are you sure it's the same woman? That'd be quite a coincidence." Sherry turned to look at the subject of their conversation. "You're probably confusing her with someone else."

David shook his head, certain now that he was looking at
the same woman. Just as he was certain that she had evoked
something in him then that hadn't seemed rational at the
time. That he had stood there pondering the same questions
in his head long after she re-entered her banquet room and
left him staring after. Two encounters, the same reaction. The
same woman.

"Probably in your dreams . . ."

He stood up suddenly, pushing back his chair. Sherry
looked up at him curiously.

"What's wrong?"

Dancers were going out on the floor again. He knew that
he was going to ask her to dance. He wasn't sure what she
was going to say. Might even leave him standing there at her
table looking like a fool, but he was going to take that chance.

"I'm going to dance," he said, not bothering to explain.

"Good luck," she called after him. Amusement was in her
voice.

"Probably in your dreams." Shades of green satin and cinnamon skin . . .

His breath quickened as he navigated the tables to reach her.

Chapter 8

When Tyne looked up, he was standing over her. Her mother stopped midsentence and smiled at the interruption. To the mother of the bride, everybody was a friend today. Tyne was irritated at the incursion and inexplicably nervous. A feeling gnawed in her stomach, and the sensation was moving downward.

Before he walked up, April's friend, Eve, had been talking to her, or more aptly, at her and Tyne had long ago tuned her out, going through the motions of listening. As she looked up at David, her breath caught in her throat, knowing that he had searched her out.

"Tyne," he said her name with an intimacy that belonged between friends, not two people who just met. "Would you like to dance?"

She was about to say no, but her mother prompted, "Go on, enjoy yourself." Her brother smirked, having quickly sized up her reluctance and the dilemma their mother had just put her in. It would never occur to her mother that she wouldn't want to go.

"Um, I was actually going back to my sister," she said, looking up at him.

He stood there, his eyes unwavering. He wasn't leaving. "One dance." The voice was quiet, insistent.

They were at an uncomfortable impasse. Eve looked on with interest, probably reading more into the simple exchange than was warranted. Tyne had two choices, both of

them unappealing. She could either remain seated, and have
him hovering over her or get up and dance with him once, get
it over with.

She pushed her chair back, and he quickly offered his
hand. Dry fingers enclosed hers in a tight grip as though he
were afraid she might change her mind and slip away. He
placed his other hand on the small of her back and steered
her to the already full dance floor. The heat from his fingers
seared through the dress, her back, right down to her limbs.
She found it hard to walk.

The band was playing "Suddenly," a slow oldie by Billy
Ocean. Tyne wondered briefly at April's nostalgia. Most of
the songs she had chosen were from the Seventies and
Eighties. Tyne stiffened involuntarily as David drew her near,
but thankfully he kept a comfortable gap between them. As
they began moving, she caught a whiff of cologne, felt the
toned hardness of his shoulder where her hand rested. Felt a
callus in the palm of the hand that held hers still so tightly
she had to wiggle her fingers to keep the blood flowing. He
loosened his grip.

She didn't look at him, keeping her eyes trained on the
dancers around them. But she knew he was looking at her
with the same concentration he had fixed on her earlier.

"Why did you run?" he asked softly.

She looked up and felt a rise in temperature as she met
those green eyes. She couldn't shake the familiarity, nor the
discomfort.

"What makes you think I was running?"

"Because you were," he said with a certainty that irritated
her.

"No, I wasn't," she insisted. "I was simply going back to
my table. Now let me ask you—why were—are you staring?"

He smiled. "Because I thought I knew you from somewhere."

"And?"

"And you were at the Fairmont a couple months ago. I
saw you in the foyer."

Tyne shook her head. "Yes, I attended a function there, but I don't remember seeing you."

"No reason you should. It was just a quick glance. Except even then I thought I knew you."

"So maybe we've seen each other before in passing. It happens. Now that that mystery is solved, you can stop trying to commit my face to memory."

He laughed. "OK . . . sorry about that. I'll stop with the staring. So, since I have probably less than a few minutes before the song ends, tell me what you were doing at the Fairmont."

"I was at a gathering of black journalists."

He perked up. "You're a journalist?"

"No," she said quickly. "Well, yes and no. I studied journalism but right now I'm a researcher and copy editor for the *Chicago Clarion*."

He shook his head. "Never heard of it."

"Not surprising. It's a small paper with a targeted readership." She couldn't help the defensiveness in her voice.

"Targeted readership?" He raised an eyebrow.

"Mainly African-American. So, what were you doing there that night?" she asked. She wasn't going to be the only one answering questions.

"An awards ceremony for Chicago architects."

"So, you're an architect. Did you receive an award?"

He shook his head. "No, just there to recognize those who did. It'll be sometime before we garner accolades like that."

She saw a momentary flicker of something on his face, then it was gone.

"We?"

"My partners and I. We have a small firm here in Chicago . . . look, I would like to have a longer conversation, away from all the gala. What are you doing later?"

She had started to feel less anxious during the conversation, when it seemed that one dance was all he wanted. Now she stiffened again. "I'm relaxing later. It's been a long day."

He nodded. "Yes, I guess you would be tired. . ."

The song ended and dancers began heading back to their tables. She started to move away, but he held tight. "One more dance?"

"No, like I said before, I have to get back to my sister. Thanks for the dance, but I have to go." This time she pushed away with more strength, forcing him to relinquish his hold. Before he could reach for her again, she maneuvered away from him, leaving him on the dance floor alone.

She didn't turn to see whether he was staring after her. She knew that he was. She passed her mother's table and headed straight for the dais, knowing that he wouldn't follow her there. She would stay there all evening if she had to, tending to April. Waiting for him to leave.

He and Sherry left shortly after his dance with Tyne.

"You're quiet tonight," Sherry said midway during the ride.

"Don't feel like talking." He had barely spoken since leaving the reception, and he felt his mood going from bad to worse.

"She shot you down, huh?"

His throat tightened at the told-you-so tone. She had that damned lilt, which irritated him.

"Like I said . . ." an edge in his voice. His fingers tightened around the wheel, as though closing around someone's neck.

Sherry shut up for the rest of the ride. Though, at times, she peeked over, trying to read him. But even if she had asked what was going on, he couldn't have told her because he didn't know himself. Disparate emotions fought for prominence. Dissatisfaction. Frustration. Anger. Not least of all, desire.

He had been denying the desire from the moment he saw her. From the moment when his dream and reality seem to merge. Yet he didn't believe in predestination, kismet.

When he had held her, pieces of the puzzle seem to come together. The only explanation was that after seeing her months ago, he had incorporated her into his dreams, and seeing her tonight had triggered the memory.

At least now he could put a face to his dream lover. The one he touched at night. Who writhed beneath him, whose musk filled his nose, whose skin and sex he tasted. She saturated his senses, haunted his nights. Yet they were strangers.

After he dropped Sherry off at her apartment, he kept going up Lake Shore Drive to the Gold Coast until he reached Oak Street Beach. He parked in the almost empty lot where only a couple of straggler cars remained. The beach closed at 9:30 and it was after 10 o'clock now. But sometimes couples came to stroll along the beach after hours, even though if they were caught they would get a ticket. The police didn't like stragglers, who were either at risk of committing or being victimized by any number of crimes. As he got out of the car, he noticed the moon was full tonight, suspended like a centerpiece jewel above the lights from the highrises silhouetted across the drive. The nocturnal setting of sky diamonds usually dazzled him. But not tonight.

Often he gravitated to the beach when he didn't want to go home, when he just wanted to think. He found walking along the quiet shore restorative to his soul. Tonight though he wasn't dressed for a walk on the beach. Sand was already seeping into his Prada slip-ons as his feet sank into the surface. The May evening was warm, humid, and he took off his double-breasted jacket, swung it over his shoulder as he continued along the crescent-shaped beach. He spotted a few couples, some walking hand in hand. Tonight was a night for lovers, and he was an intruder in this place of love, lust, or at least, affection.

His first date had ended on this same beach. He'd been fourteen with a desire to impress. Delana—he couldn't remember her last name. He just remembered how beautiful her first name was, how it fit an angelic face with dark curls. They had come here after hours, too, after seeing a movie. They had missed their curfews so, of course, her parents had balked. His mother hadn't seemed worried though. Growing up, there were times when she was inordinately calm despite circumstances, as though she knew everything was going to be all right. She was uncanny that way.

Damn! He had forgotten to return her calls from last week. She probably thought he was trying to avoid her. He'd have to stop by for a visit by way of an apology.

He was trying to remember something. A name. He stopped, and it came to him. The *Clarion*. No, the *Chicago Clarion*. He would look up the number when he got home.

Though he didn't know what he would do with the information. She obviously didn't want to hear from him. But he was up for the challenge.

As he walked, a breeze shored up. He thought he heard a whisper on the wind. *Rachel?*

New York—June 1879

Rachel Chase smiled to herself. The children, a collection of barely contained excitement, were champing at their bits, their faces eager as they watched the minute hand making its final rotation to the three o'clock mark. She had dared them not to fidget during the last minute of the last class before summer break. And they were trying hard to keep still. Yet she amusedly noticed some feet tapping, heard fingers thrumming on desks.

To tell the truth, she couldn't wait for the day to be over, either. Even with the windows opened, the small room was a slowly cooking oven. On better days, she had to keep ice water on hand to make sure the children didn't get overheated and faint. On really bad days, she held the classes outside under a makeshift canopy. Summer brought its ills, and winter wasn't any more merciful when pipes froze over and burst, flooding the building of eight rooms that soon held floors of ice.

If it were in her power, she would give her children the best the New York school district had to offer. Ragged books could finally be thrown away, there would be plenty of chalk for each child, shirts and dresses would be brand new, and shoes with cardboard inserts would be a thing of the past. But these were children of laborers, Negro laborers at that. They considered themselves blessed to have a bit of salt pork with their beans at supper.

At times, she brought food to class, even though Principal Williams discouraged it. He didn't want the rest of the school to think that Rachel's class had special privileges. Still, she often snuck in cookies, crackers, and, on occasion, she smuggled in meat and bread for sandwiches.

Rachel loved her students deeply. They were a comfort in a life that had become desolate since she had no children of her own and now never would. She hadn't been fortunate to be blessed with a child while George was alive, and she could not see herself remarrying. It was simply that her heart had no place for any other man. It had been too hard won by the struggling attorney who had been her brother's friend and who had slowly gained her affections with a sweetness and intelligence that had filled her life. There had been laughter, poems and gifts—nothing large, but so dearly given that they were beyond the measure of the fine jewels worn by society matrons. She fingered the heart-shaped necklace against her throat, George's last anniversary gift to her a month before the fire claimed his life. George's office had been swamped in flames. Even so, he might have been saved except the white firefighters refused to go in to rescue him. Their lives weren't worth risking for a Negro.

Whatever bitterness remained was pressed down hard inside, stored away in some quiet reserve. However, the loneliness was acute, at the surface, a wound that would stay with her a lifetime. Yes, she wanted summer to begin, but she wasn't sure how to keep herself occupied for the three months, how to thwart the solitude her life was becoming, even having moved in with her brother, whose company was sporadic and not always pleasant. Of course, there would be books and some social functions to keep her busy for a while.

She wasn't looking forward to the ball at the end of the month. But Lawrence was insistent that she attend, and to avoid yet another confrontation, she had obliged to go to this one gala.

Lawrence was so eager to get her back into society, to end her grief. And maybe to end her dependence on him.

He was hopeful that she would find someone who could ease past the barriers she had erected around her heart.

But that would never happen.

"Mrs. Chase, Mrs. Chase, it's time, it's time," Luther's voice pealed. She looked into the bright eyes of one of her favorites, impish scamp though he was. Always getting into trouble, but brave enough to own up to his misdeeds. Bright, as were they all. Brighter than their futures, unfortunately. But one could hope. One never knew what the future would hold.

"OK, children," she said, standing at last. "Class is officially over. You all be good and I'll see you back here in September. And remember, learning doesn't stop when the school doors are closed. I know it might be hard, but if you can, find something to read, and I'll be ever so pleased to hear what exciting adventures you discover in those pages."

They nodded, nearly tripping toward the door.

And just as soon as the minute had come and gone, she found herself alone again.

It was a state she realized she would have to get used to.

Chapter 9

"Tyne, could you come in here for a minute," Stan said over the phone.

She closed her eyes as she hung up. She was being summoned—never good. She took a deep breath and got up from her seat. As she passed the other cubicles on her way to Stan's office, she noticed the unusual quiet. No gossiping on the phones, no bantering. Rhoni was actually doing work, and Gail hadn't bothered to come in at all. Rumors had already made the circuit. The *Chicago Clarion* was shutting down. There would be no survivors. When she passed Lem's cubicle, he looked over his shoulder, his face grim.

Stan was waiting for her. No distractions today. He pointed to the seat and she sat down dutifully. His face was unreadable.

"I guess I don't really need to tell you what this is all about?" Stan never beat around the bush.

Tyne felt unusually unruffled. All the apprehension leading up to this moment suddenly left her.

"So, should I start packing up my desk?"

"Tyne, if it were up to me, none of us would be packing. This is Stingley's decision."

Stingley was Allen Stingley Jr., grandson of founder Willard Stingley, and the only son of Allen Sr., the previous owner, who had died from a sudden heart attack over a year ago. Allen Sr. would never have shut the paper down, no matter what. He had seen it as his personal mission to keep the landmark up and running, to maintain one of the few last black-owned newspapers in the country. Allen Jr., however, had been treating the paper more like a dying elephant about to stink up his lawn, and something that was eating up his money, black loyalty be damned. Seemed he had already made preparations for a quick burial. There wasn't even time to mourn.

"The *Clarion*'s been losing too much money. It just doesn't make sense to keep it going."

Spoken like a true company man. Obviously, Stan had been completely indoctrinated by Allen Jr. Tyne wondered how much the editor-in-chief would be walking away with. Probably more than enough to retire comfortably to Florida or even the Caribbean. Then she thought better of it. Stan seemed more a Vegas man, perhaps with aspirations of becoming a high-roller.

She on the other hand would be planning budget meals for the next few months. The safety net was gone. She was on her own.

"Why're you smiling?" He asked, his eyebrows up, looking perplexed.

"Nothing, Stan. Just thinking about future opportunities." As she sat there, she really tried to look on it as a window opening where a door had shut. Now would be her chance to prove herself. No more crunching numbers, checking and rechecking facts for someone else's articles. She smiled a little more.

Stan looked at her like she'd finally lost it. She just shook her head and stood up. "So when is all this going down?"

"Well, we officially close shop two weeks from Friday. We'll finish up this last issue and that'll be it. Allen's going to write a formal farewell, as will I. And as a nod to the past, Allen wants us to dig up the very first editorial done by his grandfather. I think it's a good idea. I'll leave that duty up to you."

Tyne wasn't sure if she was dismissed or not. Then Stan went back to poring over papers on his desk. "That's all, Tyne."

When she got back to her desk, she saw that her message

light was blinking. She dialed into her phone mail, hoping it wasn't some family emergency. April and Donell were on a Mexican cruise, and Tyrone had flown out yesterday morning for a Zimbabwe shoot. But when she checked the message, she heard a strange but familiar voice.

"Tyne, hi. This is David Carvelli. We met at your sister's wedding . . . um . . . I know you're probably wondering why I'm calling you, especially at work. I just—well—I was wondering if maybe you would like to go out to lunch sometime. My treat, of course. Anywhere you want. My cell phone number is 312-777-3232. If I don't answer, just leave a message."

She played the message again. How had he gotten her number? She had told him where she worked, hadn't she? If he called the general number, then he would have gotten Sondra, the receptionist, who would have patched him through.

First a firing and now this. She looked absently at the calendar affixed to the steel cabinet above her desk. Featured for the month of May, the painting of an African-garbed woman accompanied the caption, "A true woman boldly faces life's challenges." The message rang true, yet hollow to her situation. She should call him, tell him no once and for all. Tell him to please just leave her alone. She wasn't ready to deal with him. Especially not now.

Especially since she had thought about him a little too much since the reception, more times than she had admitted to herself until now. It seemed longer than last Saturday since she had looked into a pair of penetrating eyes and wondered why she should know him. Worse still, her dream lover had taken on his face, his voice, and the experience was more intense now that she could picture the one who touched her, whispered to her. Made love to her. It was an intimacy that she didn't think she could handle beyond her dreams.

She hadn't dreamt of the knife since she met him, and the horror of that night with the blood was fading with time. Only the desire remained, and that was disturbing enough.

Phones rang. She had another report to finish, although it seemed a futile task considering that her job was basically gone.

She opened the computer document and began typing. She tried not to think about the message or wonder why she didn't just erase it so the temptation would go away. Why was she intimidated by him? Because he was white? She had never dated interracially before, yet her hesitation seemed to stem from something more that that, although she wasn't certain what. The man just gave her vibes that were totally confusing—and she had to admit, seductive.

She again saw images from the dream from the night before, felt the warm salty taste of fingers slipping into her mouth. She shifted in her seat. The elastic of her panties didn't shift with her and now dug into her skin. Damn.

She got up and pulled at her underwear through her slacks.

"Um, Tyne . . ."

She turned to see Lem standing at her doorway. By the sheepish look on his face, he'd seen her touching herself in a very unbusinesslike way. He didn't seem unpleased. She felt the blood rushing to her face.

"I was . . . uh . . . was there something you wanted, Lem?"

He came in a little farther, and both of them stood side by side. He had almost a foot on her, and made her five feet seven seem that much shorter. "I thought maybe we could commiserate over lunch. Guess you got the word from Stan."

"Yeah," she sat down. "But it was expected. Did you talk with him already?"

Lem nodded. "He called me in early this morning before everyone else."

"So, what're you going to do?" She looked up at him. He didn't seem all that put out. But then again, he had very marketable skills. He wouldn't be out of work for long.

"I've already lined up something at the *Times*," he said, folding his arms, not meeting her eyes, maybe out of guilt. "I've been calling around for months now since February.

Have a friend there who kept an ear open. It's still a copy editor position, but this time with a little more money, and maybe a little more respect in the bargain." He perched on the edge of her bookcase, looking quite comfortable. "What about you?"

Tyne shrugged, embarrassed to admit that she'd been caught with her pants down. Then remembered he had walked in on her adjusting her underwear. "I'm thinking of doing some freelance. I've saved up some money. That, plus the unemployment checks, should keep beans in my bowl for a few months while I look around. I should be fine."

"Yeah, I expect so. You're a very talented woman, much too underutilized here. You need to be somewhere where you can be fully appreciated. So, what about that lunch? My treat."

Tyne wondered at the odds of getting two lunch offers within minutes of each other. Two men, two very different men. One black, the other white, both culturally dissimilar from her. Both appealing. One disturbing for reasons she couldn't understand.

"Yeah, why don't we do Wall Street?" she answered. "I'm in the mood for a good tuna sandwich."

"One o'clock. OK?"

She nodded and he smiled as he left. She heard him whistling down the aisle.

She turned back to the phone, stared at it as though it were an invading enemy. After a moment, she picked it up and waited for the prompt that would allow her to erase the message.

Green eyes flashed in her mind, and her hand paused. In the end, she didn't move to the erase button. Instead, she dialed his number.

Chapter 10

"So, what made you finally decide to call?" When David smiled, his eyes brightened and the dimple in his chin deepened.

Tyne shrugged. "What made you so sure I wouldn't? Especially since you offered me a free lunch anywhere I wanted."

She had chosen the Red Light, which served a Pan-Asian menu. Ray had brought her here once during his wooing phase, when he had cared a damn about making a good impression. She hadn't been back since.

Located on West Randolph, the restaurant wasn't very romantic during the day. She'd wanted to keep things light and casual. She had chosen jeans with a blazer and T-shirt. Again, keeping things casual.

David wore a black suede jacket, black T-shirt and jeans, and still managed to look *GQ* fine. He had strong features, sensual lips, an affable smile. He was not someone who'd have to beg for a lunch date.

"So, it was the free lunch? That's all?" he asked.

On cue, the waitress brought their plates of shumai, small dumplings stuffed with pork and shrimp. They had both ordered glasses of red wine.

Tyne took a sip to settle her nerves. She didn't know why she had called him back or why she had said yes. Maybe it was just the intrigue.

"What else would it be?" she countered, daring him by her

tone to say it was him. But he only shrugged, took his own sip of wine, effectively avoiding the challenge. She was a little satisfied to see that he didn't seem so sure of himself now.

"Don't you want to know why I called?" he asked after a pause, locking eyes with her. She broke away, looked around. The restaurant was nearly full. It was a popular place for lunch, which was one of the reasons she had chosen it. No chance for intimacy.

"I assume you wanted to have lunch with me," she said trying to sound glib but failing.

"Yes, I wanted to have lunch," he started. "No, I take that back. Actually I wanted to have dinner with you, but I knew you'd say no because you wouldn't want to meet in a place where it's dark and close, where the conversation might lead to less than safe subjects."

This was a mistake, she knew now, and she fought an overwhelming impulse to get up and leave. But she didn't want to be accused of running again. "So, what now, you're reading my mind? You don't know what I'd have said if you asked me to dinner." But he was too close to the mark.

"OK. Let's say Friday, then, dinner. You pick the place again."

She looked at him incredulously. "We haven't even finished lunch and you're already deciding on another date. Do you always rush people like this?" Her voice rose an octave.

"No, I don't. I apologize." He did look contrite, almost sheepish as he smiled at her. "If you don't want to, of course, there's no obligation. But I'd like to get to know you better. I'm sorry it came out that way. I tend to get a little pushy when I'm overeager."

She couldn't help the smile. "Overeager?"

"Call it a nagging interest."

"Why nagging?"

"Because I haven't stopped thinking about you since the first time I saw you."

"Since the wedding?"

"No, since the Fairmont—that moment in the foyer. I just lucked out finding you again."

Tyne took a longer swig of wine, almost finishing the glass in a couple of gulps. "Um, I don't know how to respond to that," she said, eyes downcast. She swept a stray crumb from the tablecloth. "Sounds a little obsessive."

He leaned forward, forcing her to look at him. His eyes pierced through, trying to impress a message she didn't want to see. "If a man sees a beautiful woman, it isn't obsessive to think about her for months. To remember how beautiful her eyes are, how biteable her lips, to wonder what it would be like to be alone with her. . . ." His voice was silk.

Tyne edged back into her seat, thrown by the unexpected ardor, the twinge in her crotch and the sudden wetness inside her panties.

"Here you go," their waitress stood at the table with their orders. Tyne took a shaky breath during the respite. She had ordered salmon. David had ordered the grilled bulgoki New York strip. The food smelled delicious, but she'd lost her appetite.

As soon as the waitress left, he said, "I'm sorry. Let's change the subject." He sliced through the tender meat, his long fingers deftly maneuvering the knife. She remembered those fingers, from her dreams, how skilled they were. She shook the image from her mind.

"Tell me what it's like working for a newspaper?" he asked.

"Something like being unemployed. My last day is next Friday." She said this indifferently, even though he was the first person outside the office she had told. She hadn't even mentioned it to her mother.

He stopped mid-chew. "Oh, sorry to hear that. What happened?"

She took a bite of salmon before answering. "Low readership, basically. The paper's been around for over fifty years, but with the economy being what it is and readers opting for the larger, mainstream papers, the *Clarion*'s taken a hit lately. It can't afford to keep running, so my job for the next month or so will be finding another job—or at least, getting some freelance work."

He sat back. "Maybe I can help. I have a friend starting a new magazine. It's going to feature items on the local Chicago scene, specifically from a woman's viewpoint. She's looking for writers. I'll give her a call when I get home."

Tyne smiled, regretting the lunch a little less. "That'd be great. I can give you my resume to pass along to . . . um. . . ."

"Her name's Sherry Fielding. You met her at your sister's wedding."

Tyne's fork paused midair as the memory flashed. Leggy, brunette. A handshake that lasted a little too long for comfort. "Uh, yeah, I remember her." She had to choke the bite down with a long sip of wine.

He smiled. "Don't worry. You only have to tell her no once, and she'll leave you alone. She's not like me." He said this last a little too seriously, making her stomach lurch.

During the rest of their meal they talked about his business. She picked up an ambivalence whenever he spoke about his partners, but she didn't press him. She learned of some of his past projects, including a new building that had just gone up on State Street. It was impressive from what she'd seen. Then he started with his own questions. She tried to keep back much of her personal business, but within the hour, he had managed to pull from her a little about her family, the fact that she liked to go parachuting sometimes. That one particularly got his attention.

"Yeah, where at?" he asked.

"I drive out a little past Naperville. It's a small center that deals mostly with first-timers and jumpers with mid-experience."

"What made you take up jumping?"

She had to think about it. Not about why she did it. But how to convey the reason without sounding like a daredevil. It wasn't easy to explain to people who had never done it or even contemplated it. "I challenged myself one day. I dared myself to do something extraordinary, and I always wondered what skydiving would be like. My father was an avid motorcyclist, my sister Tanya's into deep sea diving. I wanted a challenge all my own, so I signed up for lessons. It was just a matter of going for a personal best."

He nodded. "I know what you mean. I don't parachute, but I do fly. I rent a Cessna every once in a while and fly downstate to a small camp. I like to hike, do a bit of fishing."

At that point, the waitress brought the check, and he passed her his credit card. When the woman left, Tyne thanked him for the lunch.

"So, what about dinner?" he asked, swirling the dregs in his glass around before downing it. In all, they had drunk nearly a whole bottle.

Tyne hesitated. "And if I say no, I can just forget about that job, right?"

The change was sudden. His brows knitted together, and the green of his eyes darkened to hazel. "Let's get one thing straight. I'm not like that. I don't have to blackmail a woman to be with me. If you don't want to have dinner with me, feel free to say so. You can still pass on your resume, and I'll still give it to Sherry."

Despite her apprehension, she smiled. "And if I say yes, do I get the job?"

He looked momentarily thrown, before a smile slowly reemerged and the dimple deepened. "Like I said, one thing doesn't have anything to do with the other. It's just a matter of whether you want to be with me or not."

"Be . . . with you?" she stumbled.

"I'm sorry, let me rephrase. Go out with me. No pressure."

"Sure, no pressure," she said faintly. The waitress came back with his card.

He put it back in his wallet, pulled out another card. He handed it to her across the table.

"This is my number and fax. You can fax your resume

over, and I'll give it to Sherry personally. You'll still have to go through the regular process, but if you can prove you can handle the job, well, I don't see why you shouldn't get it."

"And the dinner?" she asked as she put the card in her purse.

"That ball's in your court—for now."

They left the restaurant, and he walked her to her car. She started to get in, then he reached out, touched her arm lightly.

She didn't have time to respond as his lips came down to meet hers. There wasn't the usual hesitation of a first kiss. He took possession as though he was long used to doing so. As though he had a right. His tongue circled hers hungrily as his arm went around her waist, gathered her closer. She smelled woodsmoke, felt firm muscles beneath his T-shirt as her hands settled on his chest, imagined him without the barrier of cloth. He tasted of the mint he had eaten after his meal, and the cool heat invaded her mouth. She was tasting him, breathing his breath, while his hand moved downward from her waist. The sudden pressure of his hand on her ass shocked her into reality. She pushed him away and found herself gasping. Her panties were wet, her crotch throbbing, crying to be invaded.

"What were you doing?" She couldn't help the shaking in her voice.

He smiled, his eyes bright with longing. "Kissing you."

She felt a desire to slap the smile off his face, a desire to pull him to her, shove her hand down his pants, release him. Instead she said, "You were practically fucking me in the street."

"No." he shook his head as his smile widened. He leaned to whisper in her ear. "Believe me, if I were fucki . . . making love . . . to you, you wouldn't mistake it for a kiss. There'd be no mistaking what I was doing to you." He touched his lips to her ear, moved to her cheek, planted a soft kiss on her jaw-bone. She could hardly breathe.

He walked away, leaving her in that state. She felt a growing anger with herself for showing him her desire. But she was also angry because she knew she was going to call him again and that they were going to be lovers—something he had known all along.

> *When he kissed me, I felt as though one world was closing and another opening up to me. I cannot in decency describe all the feelings that flowed through my body, my soul. I only tell you this, Sarah, so that you'll know that I was under some sort of spell. There is no other way to explain it, to explain why I lost myself. I have confessed my sins to only you and God. Hopefully, God will forgive me as you have done.*
> *You are a sweet and true friend.*
> *Sarah*

Rhea set the letter down on her bed. She would have to put aside the research for a time and study for finals. She had to make up the weeks of not studying, weeks in which she had searched through annals and library aisles, surfed the net, indulged her fixation. Despite her efforts, though, she'd hit a wall. She still hadn't found records of the teachers who'd worked for Colored School #1, the school first built in 1847 for the children of black shipyard workers living in Brooklyn. The school where Rachel worked over one hundred years ago. It was now known as Public School 67 and was located in Fort Greene, an upscale section of Brooklyn. Fort Greene. The postmark of the only surviving envelope from Rachel to her great-great-grandmother was from Fort Greene.

Rhea lay back on the bed, closed her eyes. Tried to rest, but instead, without prompting, began piecing together the mystery of Rachel. She tried to put a face to the young widow. A voice, mannerisms. Had she continued to live alone after her husband was killed? Did she live the rest of her life without a male protector? The Freedmen's record indicated her father had passed away before her husband. Although, there'd been a brother, Lawrence Jr.

Whenever she thought about Rachel, she envisioned someone cultured, delicate, well-spoken. Were those the qualities that drew Rachel's lover to her? That made him flout all society's rules to try to be with her?

Rhea imagined that Rachel had been everything she was not. Or maybe she was just projecting qualities on the dead woman that she wished she had herself.

She never elicited the kind of passion she read in the letters, the kind of fervor that made men crazy. The only attention she generated from the guys she dated was more a mild lust that often culminated in embarrasing gropings, sloppy kisses, and stupid utterances like "I really like the way your breasts look in that sweater." All mundane and stupid.

The letters indicated that Rachel's lover had been a gentleman, someone about society, a sophisticate whose charms had led the young widow to "forget herself," forget that he was white and not a part of her world, that she was black and not a part of his. Their worlds collided one night, a night alluded to in one of the letters. There had been a ball, a colored ball that Rachel's brother had talked her into attending. The same ball the mystery gentleman crashed in a quest to find the young woman he'd followed off the street.

She must have been beautiful that night. Rhea tried to imagine what Rachel might have worn. Pictures of the balls and cotillions of that time showed the black elite of that day dressed in elaborate finery. The women in gowns cinched to emphasize small waists, bodices cut just low enough to attract an admirer's attention. The men in their high-collared suits. It must have been a scandal for a white man to wade into a sea of black folks. There would have been no way for him to blend in. What had been the guests' reactions?

Rhea got up from the bed, put the letters back in the drawer. She turned out the light, got into bed. As she drifted off to sleep, she willed herself to dream about a beautiful ballroom with women in beautiful gowns and distinguished men, all glamoured up in their tuxedos. Instead, she dreamed of groping hands, and someone trying to kiss her, someone with a bad case of halitosis.

Chapter 11

Carmen Carvelli sat at the table watching her son take another bite of the *mezze pennette*. Some people she knew held back on the butter. But she always added extra butter and jumbo shrimp prebasted in white wine, not too much garlic, double the olive oil. That was the way she liked it. Watching David attack the plate, it was obviously the way he liked it, too. A cigarette dangled from the corner of her mouth, and she drew in the nicotine much like a crack addict sucking his pipe, eyes half closed as the smoke invaded her lungs.

David peeked at her disapprovingly, but he had long ago given up trying to make her stop smoking. If she was going to die of lung cancer, she wasn't going to fight against luck or providence. She was set in her ways. The only thing she could do was make her monthly confession, do some penance.

"Aren't you going to eat something?" he asked, his plate still half full.

She shrugged. "I ate earlier. I don't want any more. Go ahead and finish."

He had dropped by unexpectantly just as she was about to sit down to her meal. She'd only made enough for one, but she wasn't going to tell him that. It was enough that he had felt guilty enough to come over. She would keep her hurt to herself.

David wasn't a mama's boy. But he did look after her. His not returning her calls was unlike him, and she knew things were wrong. Things he wouldn't tell her. She could see it in his coloring. The red was almost blood, tinged with green, a darker green. What was it? Red could mean any number of emotions, but with David, it usually signaled anger. It could also mean passion. When she moved her head slightly, she thought she saw a hint of purple around the edge. Frustration?

She stood up, walked past him as he ate. Stood over him for a moment to tousle his thick hair. He'd cut it shorter, but it curled nicely around her fingers.

He looked up, smiled. "Don't you think I'm a little old for that?"

She gave him her irritated mama's face. "It's a mother's privilege to touch her child's hair, no matter how old he thinks he is. So what have you been up to these past weeks?"

A woman. The flash had told her that much. But it'd been too quick. Not Karen. That had been over for weeks now, thank goodness. Someone darker . . . black? Hmm.

"Ma, you're going to get smoke in my clothes," he admonished.

"Sorry." She walked over to the china cabinet, pretended to sweep away a speck of dust, but instead studied David's reflection in the glass. His usually genial features were hardened.

"You haven't told me why you called," he looked over at her. She inhaled, turned around.

"I don't know. I can't remember. It's been so long ."

"Ma, I told you I was sorry. I forgot to call. I wasn't avoiding you."

"See, people forget," she said going back to her seat. "If it was important, it'll come back to me."

David put down his fork.

"I know you're worried about something. Otherwise you wouldn't have called twice."

"I didn't know my calling would upset you. I've just been worried about you, is all." Then almost beneath her breath, "Your dreams . . ."

He fixed her with a stare, his eyes questioning. "Dreams? What are you talking about?" His voice lowered an octave; it always did that when he was upset or threatened. Something sparked from him, shifting his aura. The green was totally suffused in crimson. A dark, menacing red.

She should tell him. Now. Finally. Tell him that she could see things, that she could see things about him. That she always had.

If he didn't believe her, she could recount the time she had kept him from going on his high school sophomore trip to the Rockies. She would tell him how she'd known that one of the buses would swerve, hit the railing, and topple over the embankment—the same bus he would have been on. Bus number 7—a fact never reported in the paper or mentioned by the school administrators.

Or she could tell him how she knew he'd secretly given a girl money for an abortion. Although not the father, David had wanted to help. He promised never to tell anyone, and he hadn't. But Carmen knew even before the knock on the door that evening. She opened it to find a young blond girl standing there, her eyes reddened from crying, asking if "Davey" was home. David never liked being called that.

The older she got, the less attuned she was to her son. It wasn't so much her getting old as it was his pulling away from her, closing her off.

Because deep inside somewhere, he knew. He didn't want to know, but he did. As she looked at him, she realized that he would never admit it to himself, no matter how hard she tried to convince him.

"Call it mother's intuition. I just thought you weren't sleeping well. If I was wrong, I'm sorry. I worry too much."

He nodded slightly. She didn't know if he agreed that she was a worrier, or accepted her explanation. He picked up his fork, polished off the *pennette* within bites. As she smoked, she nearly dropped her cigarette as David's features began morphing into someone else's. Someone handsome, brooding—and very angry.

She blinked the image away with a dawning realization. This wasn't his future she was seeing. It was his past.

His past was catching up with him. No, more like it had already caught him, and was refusing to let go now that it had its quarry.

When he looked at her and smiled, he was David again. The green was chasing away the blood.

It was clear what she had to do. She needed to find out who the other man was. The man whose color was violent red, who for a moment looked at her with torment in his eyes. Begging for release.

Tyne lay the inspirational calendar on top of her stapler, the one she bought to replace the stapler that "walked away" one day and that Stan had refused to replace. Cheap as usual. Inside the box were other items accrued during her four-year tenure at the *Clarion*—her coffee stein, several multicolored pens, a framed quote that said "Believe in Yourself." These were all she had to show for four years.

Four years that she'd included in her resume. She hadn't faxed it yet, and David's card was still burning a hole in her purse. It was deep in the nether regions, jumbled in with her schedule book, her cell phone, her compact, lipstick and keys. The resume was on the screen, waiting. She pressed print and the inkjet groaned to life, and began inching out her professional life, line by line.

If she was going to do this at all, it should be today when she had a fax readily available. Everyone was packing up, getting ready for a quick exit tomorrow when the *Clarion* would close its doors for the last time. There would not be much time then for anything more than carting their possessions to their cars. There would be hugs, some tears, final good-byes. Not for Stan, though, who had sequestered himself in his office, barely peeking out. Probably looking through vacation brochures.

She heard sniffling across the way. She picked up the printed resume ready to walk it over to the fax, but then heard another quivering intake of breath. Gail was taking this hard.

Tyne didn't like the woman, never had. Foul-mouthed, nosy, vindictive when she didn't get her way, Gail had been one of the thorns to working at the *Clarion*. Still Tyne felt for her. Gail's only son was in military school, and that cost. As did her apartment in Chatham. How she had managed all that on an administrative assistant's salary, especially at this paper, Tyne had no idea. She put down the resume, walked over and stood in Gail's doorway. The woman had her back to the entrance, but the steady shaking of her shoulders indicated smothered sobs.

"Gail" she said softly. Gail turned around, tears streaming down her face. Then a torrent spilled forth.

"What the fuck am I gonna do? I got bills to pay, too many of 'em, and Chris's daddy barely sends us what he owes as it is! Damn, that fucking Allen Jr.! His father would've never fucked us over like this!"

Tyne winced at the venom, but entered anyway. "Gail, you've got to stay calm. You're a good assistant and you'll find another job, probably even better than this one. You'll survive." That was the same thing she had been telling herself.

"I know." Gail said. She blew her nose into a tissue she held in her hand. "My son and I will get through this somehow. God won't let us down. Not like this shit-ass paper, taking all your time and energy and giving nothing back in return. I'm glad I'm leaving this shit rag."

Tyne smiled at the woman's about-face. Yeah, Gail was a survivor. She went back to her cubicle to get her resume. Then reached deep inside her purse and dug out David's card. It was nicely embossed with gold lettering on cream-covered paper. Not the cheap kind, but the more expensive stock. She studied his name *David Carvelli, Partner, Gaines, Carvelli, and Debbs, LLP, Designers and developers of residential and commercial properties.* The fax machine was in an empty cubicle just outside Stan's office, but she didn't care at this point. Let him come out and see her using office property for personal reasons. She dialed in the fax number and placed the resume along the ledger.

Her stomach fluttered as the machine fed the paper through. It was too late to stop it. Soon it would be in his hands. Soon he would be calling.

"That's bullshit!"

David paced around the two occupied chairs facing his desk. The window of his office looked out on the beige block structure of the Water Tower and its surrounding park. A survivor of the 1871 fire that devastated the city, the octagonal tower stood as a testament to the resiliency of the past. Across the street, farther north, the black-steeled edifice of the Hancock building hovered over the sidewalks streaming with North Michigan shoppers. The sky was pale blue, no clouds. But a storm was coming. He could feel it brewing inside. A headache blazed behind his eyes. His fingers tightened into a fist.

He rounded his desk and sat down again. Both Rick and Clarence stared at him, one chastened, the other defiant.

Clarence, after having sat silent while Rick tried to stammer out an explanation, spoke up. "What can I tell you, man? It's like I said. Kershner called, said he wanted me to design the condominiums. He's comfortable with me since I designed his home a few years back. Dave, I don't see what the problem is. We're partners and any job I get is one for the partnership."

David looked at Clarence and wondered at his balls. Wondered at Rick's lack of same. Did they really think he was going to eat the bullshit they were trying to feed him?

He sat back in his seat, hands behind his head, a stance more casual than what he was feeling. "Then why the secrecy?" he asked, his voice more controlled than a moment ago. "First, you blow off the meeting Kershner scheduled with *all* of us, and Rick and I walk away with egg on our faces. Then you go and meet with Kershner by yourself without telling us." He looked at Rick, noticed the hangdog expression, "Or at least me."

Clarence leaned forward, putting on his let's-see-reason

face. David thought Clarence resembled a ferret. A sneaky, backstabbing ferret. "Look Dave, stop acting like this is some kind of conspiracy against you. Rick and I contribute as much to this business as you do, if not more."

David slammed forward suddenly. "What the—"

"Let me finish, man! I don't see where you get off acting like we're *your* employees! This is an equal partnership."

"That's right, a partnership!" David rose. "Not Debbs, Inc. but *Gaines, Carvelli and Debbs.*"

Clarence stood, too. "Oh, I see now why my name's last, the reason why I'm supposed to just keep quiet and take shit! A black man goes out, gets him some props and all of a sudden his white *partners* can't stomach the fact that they're not heading the game."

David felt the pulse deepen behind his eyes. His breath quickened, missed a beat. "Don't give me that racism shit! You know this isn't about race! It's about respect!"

"Exactly!"

Rick stood. "OK, guys, your voices are carrying outside this office. You both need to cool it."

"Man, I just need to get out of here," Clarence said. "Rick, I'll call you later." He strode to the door and slammed it behind him.

David felt his anger turn on Rick. Friend or betrayer? He didn't know, couldn't decide right now. But the one thing he knew was that Rick no longer had his back.

"You knew about this, didn't you?" David was surprised at the calm in his voice because inside the storm had broken. He wanted nothing more than to shake the man standing in front of him. Or throw him out the window.

Rick's usually elfin face seemed to shrink. Rick was a shrewd businessman, but David had always known the man's spine wasn't as stiff as it could be. That with a good downpour, all the strength would wash away. Rick might be supportive, but without sterner stuff, that support wasn't worth a damn.

"I only found out yesterday about the meeting. Look, I've

sat down and tried talking to Clar, but, well . . . I think you were right the first time. He doesn't want to be in this partnership. I think we ought to buy him out."

David snorted. "Last year's news. The way I see it, his actions forfeit his right to any damn thing! If he wants outta here, let him walk. I don't give a fuck. And if he thinks he's getting any more out of this arrangement, then let him take us to court. The contract's on our side. He's harmed the partnership with his little side dealings, so he loses his third of the business *and* his investment!"

Rick's usual five-feet eight-inch height actually seemed to shrink. His head shake mimicked the movements of a marionette controlled by an unseen manipulator. "Look, you know that's not going to go down well with Clar. He *will* take us to court, and you and I both know we can't afford to get tied up in litigation. It'll hurt us. You got to see reason—"

"I already see reason. Between the three of us, I'm the only one who sees just how things truly stand. Another thing I see is that you need to grow you a pair if you want to stay in business with me. Because man, this wavering back and forth mealy-mouth shit isn't good for business . . . or for our friendship. You decide."

He didn't need to tell Rick to leave. He simply sat down, swiveled the chair to face the window.

He looked at Rick's reflection in the window, saw the chastised man slink out, heard the click of the door. He stared at the closed door, then let his eyes wander to his own reflection.

He didn't like what he saw. His brows knitted, his jaw tightened. It was as though he were staring at some stranger sitting where his body should be. The man looking back seemed an alien to him. Someone dour, ill-tempered.

He had been losing it a lot lately. Over small things as well as the bigger stuff that would turn a saint into a murderer. Like just now. He had a nagging feeling, just beneath the surface, that had he been alone with Clarence, or better yet, in some out-of-the-way place with no witnesses, he would have beaten his partner unconscious and just left him there to bleed.

What was happening to him? He'd always been passionate, but never out of control. The other day, someone cut him off in traffic, forcing him to jam on his brakes. For half a mile or more, he had followed the fool with thoughts of ramming the man's car. Luckily, he cooled down before the deed got done.

Yesterday, he had even snapped at Debbie because he thought she misplaced a file. He later found it sitting on the end of his desk. The file hadn't even been important. Still, his blood had seethed and his emotions had boiled.

It just seemed as though things kept coming at him. Lack of sleep, although the dreams were fewer now, and a general restlessness. Sometimes, an unsettling feeling of anxiety. Just to be safe, he was avoiding caffeine. He didn't want one cup of coffee sending him off to jail.

The intercom buzzed and Debbie's tinkerbell-like voice piped in. "Dave, that fax you were expecting just came in."

Chapter 12

Tyne ordered iced tea while waiting for Tanya, who was already nine minutes late. The outdoor café along the riverwalk was full of noonday patrons smiling and chatting. She easily spotted the tourists sitting among the regular lunch crowd. The tableau of khaki pants and shorts, multicolored polo shirts, and pastel windbreakers always stood out amid the tailored suits and casual business attire. Plus the tourists tended to gape, as they were doing now as two boats moved up the Chicago River. Some pointed, others snapped pictures. The boat rides were popular, and even though today the wind was up, causing small waves to lap hungrily at the rudders, she could see people sitting on the decks listening to the droning docents regale them with architectural anecdotes.

A blast of wind whipped up, and pages from someone's newspaper lofted on the gust, swirled out into the traffic going east on Wacker. A long cumbersome sheet slapped against the windshield of a Volvo. The car screeched to a stop, and the driver reached out to remove the barrier. The impatient drivers behind him honked their frustration.

"What's going on?" Tanya stood at the table, looking out at the melee. Tyne hadn't seen her walk up.

"Just the Chicago wind acting up again. So, why so late?" Tyne asked as her sister took a seat. "You're usually the one bitching when someone shows up two seconds past due."

Tanya smiled. "Don't beat me up too bad. I got caught up

with errands and lost track. Sorry. Besides, this is my treat. Just relax."

"I've already ordered iced tea for both of us. I told the waiter someone else was coming, so he should be back soon. Thanks in advance for the sumptuous lunch."

Tanya's coffee-brown face glowed with good health, good humor. Tyne could always count on her sister to be there when the edges of her life got a little rough. Tanya was the optimist among the set, the second Mama when things got bad. Miss Picker-upper. She looked particularly engaging, dressed in a dark red blazer and skirt with a tangerine blouse. Her glossy braids hung just past her shoulders. A male passerby craned his head to look back at both of them as he strode up the walk. He winked.

"Gonna try to break my bank, huh?" Tanya said as she settled her purse and several Lord & Taylor bags onto the adjacent seat. "Oh, well. Hey, you know April and Donell get back on Wednesday. I was thinking maybe we ought to get together, go out, just the sisters. Whaddya say? Again, my treat."

Tyne felt an unexpected twinge of anger. She knew she was being overly sensitive but couldn't help it. Tanya was being good-hearted as usual whereas Tyne was being her competitive, bitchy self. It was just that she hated being a charity case, and she averted resentful eyes from the Lord & Taylor bags. Lord only knew when she would be able to go splurge shopping again.

"Sounds good," she said, "but let's go Dutch, or, if you want, we can split the tab between the two of us for April."

Tanya didn't say anything, but looked as though she was making an effort to bite her tongue.

Tyne smiled. "I'm going to be all right, Sis. I'll get through this."

The waiter came back and set tall glasses of tea on the canopied table, then took both their orders. Tyne, pride winning out, ordered a Caesar salad and told the waiter to bring separate checks. Even as she told him, she defied her sister with a look to say anything. Tanya shrugged capitulation. Both knew how long they could lock horns and knew better to avoid the unnecessary drama. The waiter left.

"By the way, I may have a lead on a job writing for a magazine," Tyne said, still somewhat dumbfounded by her good luck.

"That's great, Tyne. Where?"

"It's actually a start-up magazine with a focus on Chicago women. That's about as much as I know right now, but even that little sounds a step up from what I left. I'll actually get to write articles, have a byline."

"How did you hear about it? Someone at work?"

Tyne didn't know where the awkwardness came from. Didn't know why she wanted to keep David a secret. Nothing had happened, maybe nothing would. Still, Tanya had a way of reading her.

"Are you hoarding the information for some future use?" Tanya prompted. "C'mon, what's the secret?"

"Nothing. Actually, I got the lead from someone I met at April's wedding."

"Aaahhh . . . I see. Could it be that guy you were dancing with? The one you got all comfy and cozy with? Verrry niiice."

Tyne nearly spluttered the tea she had been sipping. "How did you—? And, I wasn't *cozy* with him. He just asked me to dance and then he sorta called to ask me out. But we only went out once and that was it. Then he offered to pass my resume on to a friend, no strings." She took a breath. "It's nothing."

"Convince yourself yet?" Tanya smirked.

Another breath. "You're making something out of nothing."

"OK, then, let me go over what you just said so that I know I'm not misunderstanding anything. You met a man at our sister's wedding, you had what looked like a very intimate dance with him—at least from what I saw—and you've already had one date."

"It was lunch, not a date."

"Lunch, then. And he's already offering to help you find

another job. Not bad for a couple of weeks' work. Did I leave anything out?"

"Yeah, the bed-shaking, freaky sex we had," Tyne shot out, causing Tanya's right eyebrow to shoot up.

"What?"

Now Tyne smiled. "Got ya. And tell me you don't think I'm that easy. Skeeza I'm not—yet. But if I get down to my last can of tuna, I may be renting it out soon."

"Girl, pleeze, stop your fantasizing. But really, who is this guy? As your sister, I retain the right to bug you about your love life."

The waiter brought their orders, and Tyne waited for him to leave. "Like I told you, there's nothing. I guess . . . well, he sorta kissed me but—"

"Sorta? Uh huh. Does sorta involve just lips or tongue?"

Tyne looked around embarrassed. "Please. Doesn't matter. Nothing's going to happen. I mean, it can't, especially since I don't want to feel obligated."

"Did he say quid pro quo?"

"No, just the opposite. He told me the decision's mine. Like there's a decision to be made. God, I just met the man, and he's already talking like we've known each other for years. I'm just a little put off by him." She took a bite of her sandwich, but it went down dry. Her pulse was racing.

"Put off? Why? He's not weird, is he?" Tyne could see Tanya's hackles rising. Creep alert. They all had it when it came to the men in each other's lives. Tyne hadn't particularly liked Jason, but he and Tanya were now together for six years, living in peaceful sin. Which kept their mother praying. As she had prayed for April during the Kendrick years.

"No. I mean I don't know. It's just there've been some other things happening. It's nothing I can explain." She had told no one about the dreams. As close as she was to Tanya and April, she had never felt comfortable talking to them about sex. Or specifically the sex she had, wasn't having, was dreaming about. Maybe she had inherited her mother's prudishness.

"Um, Tyne, you're making the kind of sense that's not. Plain and simple. If he gives you bad vibes, just stay away from him, job or no."

Tyne took another bite, looked at the sun-drenched street glutted with folks—folks walking, striding, romping. Glowing faces mirrored the brightness of the day, especially the teenagers. A girl, maybe fifteen, sixteen, pink hair, green eyeshadow, doubled over laughing at something her equally punked-out friends just said. Tyne remembered being that carefree—if not exactly that weird—once, or rather that ignorant of the realities of just living on. Uncertainty, unemployment, sadness, loneliness, the proverbial states of being. Offset by hope, which she still had, love from her family, if nowhere else, sometimes a good glass of wine, a good movie, the touch of someone—something she hadn't had in a long time—except in her dreams. The dreams she had begun to crave even as the fear persisted, even as the lover was fleshed out with thick, wavy brown hair, penetrating green eyes, lips that tasted of mint.

"I can take care of myself. I'm not April, Tanya. It's—he's just about business. Besides, I need this job, if I can even get it. I can't afford to go spending my money like Armageddon's coming." She deliberately let her eyes wander over the bags nearly falling off the chair abutting Tanya's.

"OK, I'm backing off," Tanya sighed. "I don't want an argument with you. I know you can take care of yourself. You're grown enough to know better than to let a man dog you out or to let shit start up in the first place. We've been through this mess with April. I guess I'm just paranoid."

"No, you're not paranoid. You're just being a sister. I like the fact that you've got my back. If for some reason, I do lose my mind and start acting stupid, I'm counting on you to slap me upside my head."

Both sisters smiled, their disagreement smoothed over. Tyne sipped her tea, tried to concentrate on the good things coming up: possibly a new job, maybe meeting new people, and best of all, no more Stan. Things could be worse.

Chapter 13

Time stilled, his lungs burned. Buoyancy gave way to heaviness, but he couldn't stop. He only had half a lap to go. His goal was set, yet his muscles were at war with him. They wanted to stop, to float away. Still, he was master of his body and mind; he wouldn't heed them. He turned his head to swallow air, instead pulled water into his nostrils, his lungs. He stopped, tried to break above the water to gasp the life he needed. But the more he tried, the lower he drifted, his lungs bursting.

Reality became liquid blue, a chloroformed world that eagerly welcomed him into its soundless depths. Below in a blur, he saw the outline of the drain, to the sides, the tiles of the pool. He could hold his breath no longer, and began drinking in his death through his nose, his mouth. This was where he would die. Here.

In a last grasp of consciousness, he wondered why his life wasn't reeling through his mind. His triumphs as well as his regrets. But there was nothing. Just nothingness.

He reached the bottom and waited. It was strange. He could hear music. Faraway, yet familiar. It floated toward him, wafting along the deadly water . . .

Crystal tears mirrored the myriad dancers swirling below, colors sparkled, diamonds glittered. On the dais, an orchestra played "On the Beautiful Blue Danube." The strings blended perfectly with the woodwinds, the tempo precise, flawless. He stared at the musicians. They were all Negroes.

He stood near the entrance of the hall, awed by the regalia, by the decorum. He hadn't known what to expect, but certainly not this.

A few years back, he had read an article in the New York Times *about these colored dances. One of his club acquaintances had snipped it out and passed it around. There were titters and guffaws through the cigar smoke at the sheer thought of Negroes dressing up in finery, trying to imitate their betters. The idea was ludicrous, a caricature worthy of ridicule.*

His thoughts had been far from that issue when he came upon the carriages parked in front of the Waldorf-Astoria. He was hurrying along, mindful that he was already five minutes late to his dinner meeting with Barrett at Delmonico's. Head down against the hat-flapping wind, hand pinning his bowler to his head, he missed seeing the body of green organza stepping out of the carriage. His foot landed hard on the laced hem of the dress.

He looked up with a "Pardon me" on his lips that immediately died when he met the pair of startled eyes framed within a caramel crème face. Tendrils escaped an elegant chignon. Beautiful, he thought. "Negro!" shouted in his head. As soon as the thought whisked through his brain, he banished it.

Her companion—a masculine version of her in a tuxedo adorned with epaulets—tightened his grip on her, coughed his displeasure.

"C'mon, Rachel, let's get inside. Too many rude folks out here."

He would have apologized, but the couple swept past him through the doors of the hotel and left him looking after them. He felt like a slow-witted adolescent or worse, an inmate of Bedlam stunned into inertia. He turned to find the coachman looking on him with much the same estimation. He noted with amazement that the man was white. Never had he encountered this scenario. It was too odd by far.

And why he had entered the hotel, then the hall, he won-

dered even now as his eyes sought out the green organza among the motley of red silk, blue velvet, lavender dupioni. He couldn't help noticing a map of Cuba hanging just to the right of the orchestra. Obviously, these Negroes were adherents of Antonio Maceo, the audacious Cuban who had come to New York just last year in hopes of raising funds for Cuba's uprising against Spain.

Eyes turned to him, danced by in expressions of curiosity, indignation, and in some cases, fear. There was not another white face in the whole room. Still, he would not be intimidated. He would not leave until . . . Then he saw them—or rather her. She had parted with her wraps and stood near a table with the gentleman who had escorted her in. She stood there, a Helen amid the common Trojans, her every movement a measure of grace. The gown was cut off her shoulders, and when she turned he could see the lacy décolletage that concealed and yet teased with the slight impression of cleavage. The dress was demure enough, but inspired a craving to see more.

His legs moved before his mind had decided what he would say. He checked his hat and wrap. Then he circumvented the edge of the dancers, moved toward the table just as the couple sat down. She saw him first, and he couldn't discern her expression. The man was now watching his approach, and half stood as though preparing for an assault. By the time he neared the table, he could feel the eyes on him, could see that some of the dancers had stopped altogether.

He addressed the man first with a half nod. The black man looked at him warily, his body taut. The man was a head taller and could probably overcome him.

"I don't mean to interrupt your evening," he said immediately to allay their worries. "I simply came to apologize. I would have done so outside, but I wasn't given the chance." He turned to her, gave her a full nod. "So, madam, please accept my sincere and humble pardon for my bumbling. I hope I did not soil your dress."

He did not expect a smile. It transformed her features and

he saw that he had earlier mistaken her demeanor as that of a shy fawn. Her voice confirmed his new assessment that here sat a lady who would not be put off by any situation.

"I accept your sincere and humble pardon for your bumbling, as you so put it, but I wonder that such a small transgression warrants this production. I mean, it was an accident, was it not?" Her voice was dulcet and tinged with laughter.

He couldn't believe it. She was actually laughing at him! As was the black man standing near her seat. He could see it in the man's smirk. How dare they!

He bit back his words, aware that he was outnumbered and that he was the interloper. Embarrassed, his first instinct was to make a quick exit, put this matter behind him. But then he looked into eyes sparkling with amusement and more than anything he did not want to leave her with the impression of a withering coward.

"To know that my apology is accepted, would you honor me with a dance?"

He felt some satisfaction to see both smiles fade, to see the fawn return. She was trapped by decorum. To outright reject his offer would be the cusp of rudeness. She couldn't even beg tiredness as an excuse for she had only just arrived. To accept his offer would put her in a socially disadvantageous position. No decent Negro woman would be seen dancing with a white man. It just was not done. All this he knew.

Still, she offered him her hand. He noticed that there was no wedding band. There was daring in her eyes now. She rose in one liquid motion.

"Rachel!" her companion warned. "You will not!"

She calmly turned to the man. "Lawrence, would you have me be rude to someone courteous enough to offer amends? Especially when he did not need to."

"What will people say?" her companion countered.

"What can they say? It's only a dance."

The orchestra had finished the "Blue Danube" and was now beginning the first strains of "Viennese Waltz." The dancers stepped back, creating a berth for the couple. A few women gasped at the sight of his hand going around her waist. There were throat gurgles and indignant whisperings.

But because she looked at him with eyes that dared him to falter, he kept pace with the music, swirling her around stationery bodies. Suddenly, the whole thing seemed comic. Here he was, dancing with a Negro, shirking his dinner with Barrett, who would no doubt call him tonight with exclamations of reproach. But tonight was a night to throw away social recriminations. And it was well worth the small smile that played on her lips. Full and enchanting lips, covered with a rosy hue that played with the contrast of cinnamon . . . no, he had initially thought her skin the color of caramel. A curl hinged near a brow, toying with her lashes.

"So, whom do I have the honor of dancing with?" she asked. "After all, I am probably wrecking my reputation, as my brother was so quick to point out."

He couldn't describe the relief he felt at the designation "brother." It was a relief ill-founded since he wouldn't see her past this night. Past these few moments. Past this dance. As it were, he would not be taking the chance if there were a white guest to relay this back to anyone of consequence. Oh, he had no doubt that the Negroes would talk among themselves, but it would not interrupt his world. She would be the one to bear the brunt of tonight. He would simply have the memory of dancing with a beautiful woman.

"My name is Joseph, Joseph Luce."

She looked startled. "Luce? Not of the Manhattan Luces?"

Now it was his turn to smile. "And how would you know the who is who of Manhattan?"

"And why wouldn't I?" She appeared indignant.

"Well, it's not usual that a . . . a . . . well . . . you know . . ."

"If you finish that sentence this night, and without insulting me, then I will congratulate you on a finesse worthy of the most astute diplomat. Mr. Luce, I not only know about Manhattan society, I also have heard of the Vanderbilts, Carnegies, and Astors. I also know that the present mayor is Edward Cooper, that Hayes is in office, that Mr. Henrik Ibsen

has recently written another play. I believe it's entitled A
Doll's House. *I plan to read it as soon as I get time. Negroes
have an ear to the ground, too."* The coda to this sentence
was another smile that competed with the luminescence of
her eyes.

"I'm sorry if I presumed."

"Like you presumed that an escorted woman would say
yes to your offer . . ."

"And why did you?" He felt defensive.

"Only because you looked so penitent and discomfited, I
thought acceptance would be a saving grace. Of course, I expect an equally graceful exit after the dance has ended. We
don't want to extend the scandal."

He smiled now. "And is this a scandal?"

"It is. And you well know it," she said.

"But as you said, this is only a dance. What more can
come from it?" he asked, realizing that he did not want the
dance to end, that he did not want to leave if it did. But even
now, something was pulling at him. Voices strummed inside
his head, joining the strains of the waltz, the murmur of the
dancers. She was speaking to him, but it seemed to be from a
distance now. She was smiling and beautiful and he thought
that maybe his heart might have stopped.

"I think we've got a pulse. C'mon, c'mon, come on back . . .
there you go. . . ."

David felt pressure against his chest and an overwhelming
need to vomit. He rolled his head on the floor. Water gushed
from his nose, spurted from his mouth in small geysers.

"That's it. Come on back," said a familiar voice. He
opened his eyes to find a man bending over him. Ed, the lifeguard. Standing over them was a woman in a blue bathing
suit. He recognized her as a regular swimmer at the club. Her
ash blond hair was plastered to her skull.

"Oh, thank God," she said. Fear and amazement colored
her eyes.

The relieved lifeguard sat back on his haunches. "Mr.
Carvelli, what were you doing out there? You know you

shouldn't be in the pool before or after hours. You coulda died. Almost did."

David tried to sit up, but his body wouldn't cooperate.

"No, lay still," Ed said, pressing a hand to David's shoulder. "An ambulance is on its way."

David still couldn't speak. All he could do was lay there shivering on the cold, wet floor, his only purview the faces of his rescuers and the chipped white ceiling. Incongruously, the thought passed through his haze that for the fees he was paying, they surely could afford to paint the ceiling. He thought about Ed's words then, and felt nothing. Not fear, not even relief that he was still here. He was numb inside. Ed said that he had almost died. But the lifeguard was wrong. Because he had, in fact, died. If only for a few moments, he had left this life behind. How else to explain the strange episode? He didn't know how to explain it himself. He had left his body and had—his brain tried to reject it—traveled back in time. The memory was still vivid in his mind. Even now, he thought he heard music in the distance. He could still see her smile.

All of a sudden, he began to feel again. An emptiness that threatened to overwhelm him. A loneliness that was more palpable than the restraining hand on his shoulder, the cold that enveloped his body.

He wanted to go back to her. He almost cried.

Chapter 14

David knew before he turned who had entered his room. He smelled the perfume right away. Tabu. After fifteen years, it was her signature scent.

"Who called you?" he asked, knowing the question was abrupt and ungrateful. The EMTs had brought him in only a couple of hours ago, and he had not given any information other than his name, address, and insurance data. The fewer people who knew, the less embarrassed he would be. He already felt ridiculous as it was. He didn't need his mother checking in on him.

"Does it matter how I found out? I'm here." He thought he heard a tremor in her voice. Also anger.

Had to have been one of the nurses or someone at the health club who called her. Maybe someone had gone through his wallet and found her number.

She stood near his bed looking down. Then, suddenly, she slapped his head, lightly. "Idiot!"

"Hey!" He sat up. "What kind of mother love is that?"

"The kind that will keep you from doing something this stupid again! Damn it, David, I've warned you too many times about going swimming alone! Why do you take chances like that? I lose you, I've got nobody."

David lay his head down with a sigh. On top of this disastrous morning, he was going to have to deal with mother guilt again. Damn that nosy ass who called her.

"Sorry, sorry, sorry, and again sorry. Jeez, I just wanted to get some laps in before I went into the office."

"What happened? You get a cramp?"

He shook his head. "I don't know. I probably shouldn't have been out there today. Wasn't feeling at my peak."

He saw the tears brimming in her eyes. They pooled there, refusing to travel down. His mother was resistant to emotional shows, and she probably wasn't going to start now.

"David, I've been going about this all wrong. Trying to protect you. You could've ended up drowned like Terry."

He looked at her, confused. She wasn't making any sense. What did his friend Terry have to do with anything?

"Ma, you're getting worked up over nothing. I'm OK." He *was* OK. No point in telling anyone about what he had envisioned. Since being brought in he had gone over the scene again and again, and was slowly convincing himself that it had been a hallucination. He had read about these types of delusions, usually brought on by the delirium of oxygen deprivation.

"OK? You're laying here in a hospital, almost drowned, and I'm supposed to let you lie to me about being OK. David, you're not OK. Far from it." She paused, reached up to wipe the tears from her eyes. She was silent. He could tell she was pondering something; her eyebrows met the wisps of her bangs.

She walked over and pulled the only chair in the room closer to his bed. She looked determined and he girded himself for a sermon or a diatribe, or a combination of the two.

"David, remember when Bess went away?"

"Bess? What are you bringing up Bess for?" He hadn't thought about his old Labrador in years. She ran away shortly after his father left, and he searched for her for weeks, months even. There hadn't been a tree or storefront window that didn't carry the picture of the two-year-old Lab his father had given him for his eighth birthday. He had gone from door to door within a five-mile radius, asking his neighbors if they had seen his dog. He stopped searching only after the fire the next year. After everything seemed destroyed. Only then did he relinquish any hope that things could go back to the way they used to be. That his father would come back. That was also the year Terry drowned. He shut off the memories; they were too painful. He didn't see why his mother was taking this trek down memory lane, bringing up things he hadn't thought about for a long time, didn't want to think about now. He was irritated and tired.

"I'm leading to a point, so just bear with me. I need to make you understand before something worse happens. I know to you I'm just an obligation . . ."

"Ma . . ."

"Stop interrupting!" she leaned forward and he thought she was going to slap his head again, but then she sat back, her face set like that of a narrator about to impart some heretofore unknown folklore. "I know you love me. I know you do. But I also know you've been carrying around a lot of baggage, not the least of which is your blaming yourself for your father and me breaking up. That would be too much for any ten-year-old to handle, and I tried to tell you then that it wasn't your fault, but you wouldn't set down that burden. You still carry it with you after all these years. And if I haven't said this enough, your father left me, not you. He was an asshole David, and I tried very hard to make sure you didn't grow up to be like him. I think I've been doing a good job . . . so far. If it wasn't bad enough that your father left, Bess goes up and runs away—or so we thought."

His initial resistance wavered at this last sentence. More than anything, he wanted to get up, get dressed and leave, but the doctor wanted to keep him here for at least a day "for observation." He was a prisoner of his own making, and now his mother's captive audience. He had thought he was through with the hurt, but his mother's allusion to Bess's disappearance just brought home the loneliness he had felt at the poolside, the questions he'd asked himself again and again: Why did the ones he love or care about eventually leave him? His father, Bess, even Karen, to an extent—although that had been his own fault. Still, there had been others.

"What do you mean, 'so we thought'? You know something?"

She remained quiet for a few seconds, contemplating. He thought he heard his heartbeat rev up. At least he was alive, but he could only take so much.

She finally spoke. "You remember that house about two blocks down from ours? The one with the blue and white door, yellow awning?"

David nodded. He remembered the house vaguely, remembered specifically how hideous it was. He barely ever passed there, but it had been one of the homes he canvassed in his search for Bess.

"Well, remember there was an an old man who lived there with his daughter? They hardly ever came out. I'm pretty sure he was the one who took Bess."

"What?" Dave jolted up, his pique giving way to anger, and suddenly his inertia was gone. "And you knew this?! You knew all this time and you said nothing! Letting me walk around putting up flyers, knocking on people's doors! Why didn't you tell me before?"

He wanted to lash out at someone, her, the old man. He felt as though his head was about to rip open. He tried to remember the old man, to remember features, coloring, something. He needed some other face to focus his fury on. Someone other than his mother, who was just sitting there calmly.

"I didn't know about it until some time after the man died, David. Bess was gone by then. But—"

"But what?"

"I saw her in my dream. I saw her collar, the red one you bought her the Christmas before she was taken. I felt something was going to happen, but didn't know what. I knew how much she meant . . . your last connection to your father."

This was getting confusing again. "In your dream—what are you talking about?"

His mother's shoulders rose up, her back stiffened. "I saw her in the dream—but too late, and I kept this secret because I didn't think you would understand. But the time's come for me to stop keeping secrets—just as you've been doing. Just like you never told me about the fire, the one that destroyed our home."

His first impulse was to deny it, a vestige of the fear of an eleven-year-old who had taken so much from her. Then he remembered.

"Terry, he told you. Or he told someone else—his parents—and they told you . . ." he reasoned, trying to make the pieces fit into neat little compartments again. Trying not to deal with whatever was coming.

"No. Terry never told anybody, just like he promised you. But I know Terry got you into a lot of other things, things you didn't think I knew about. But I did. I saw. I may not dream or see as much as I once did, but I still see some things."

"See things?" It was worse than he had thought.

"Like this morning. I saw you floating facedown." She said this like a pronouncement, like the crescendo everything else had been leading to. "I tried to think maybe it was just a dream and my irrational fears playing with my mind. But then I knew when I saw you lying in a hospital, this hospital. I knew that I'd almost lost you. I didn't see it in time though, and I'm afraid that something else is going to happen, something worse than this." The tremble was back in her voice.

Disbelief crept in as a small smile on his lips. He had always known his mother was a little eccentric. Actually, more than a little eccentric. He remembered the tarot cards alongside the rosary beads on her bureau and never once growing up questioned the contradiction. Because that was just his mother. Her oddities were a part of her, just like the smoking, or those pearls she always wore whenever she went somewhere upscale. But there had been times . . .

"You're kidding me, right?"

"You want to know why your father left? He left because he didn't want to believe. Or rather, because he started to be-

lieve. He never liked my having an edge over him. It inter-
fered with his agenda of getting women and getting drunk. I
mean what's the fun of cheating if your wife knows beforehand?" She paused, took a breath, continued.

"Actually the main reason he left was that I told him to get
out. I didn't want him influencing you about women. Not
that your father was a bad man, he was just a dick. Why we
ever got together is still a question in my mind. Anyway, I
worked so hard to conform to him, to be how he wanted to
see me. But it gets tiring after a while, David. And as much as
I love you, I can't keep playing this little suburban mama sitting at home drinking tea with a little scotch on the side. I am
who I am."

He didn't want to prolong this drama anymore. He didn't
want to hear this ranting arising from what he was beginning
to suspect was some sort of mental breakdown.

"And who are you supposed to be?" he finally asked, already closing his mind to the answer.

"I am a seer, clairvoyant, a psychic if you will. To put it
simply, I see the future, and yours isn't looking too good
right now."

He blinked quickly, three, four times in succession. A rum-
bling started in his guts, quickly surged up, then burst from
his lips in a laugh that nearly rent him apart and shook the
bed. It poured from him like a gusher, taking his breath away.

Finally it ebbed away, and when the laughter finally de-
serted him, she was still sitting there. She wasn't smiling.

Instead she stood up and said, "I got things to tell you,
David, and I'm not leaving here until you've heard everything
I know about you. And I'm not the only one who knows
you're in trouble. My friend Jennifer DiMello has been seeing
things about you, too."

Jennifer? Who was Jennifer? And what the hell was his
mother talking about?

Suddenly, he was afraid.

Chapter 15

Jennifer went through the stack of answers to the questionnaire Simensen had distributed to its employees a month ago. The questionnaire was ostensibly an assessment of skill levels to determine that each employee was suited to his or her job. In fact, it had been peppered with "flags," specific questions innocuous on the surface but that pinpointed those particular employees who might be prone to unethical behavior. "Might be" was a broad categorization, and it was Jennifer's job to critique the answers and follow up with interviews to ascertain the probability that any of these "flagged" employees would be future trouble.

Simensen, a major Midwest pharmaceutical, was particularly sensitive to the reality of unethical employees. Last year, a shipment of a new FDA-approved drug, Biloxin, was stolen; the boxes were later found in the apartment of a delivery driver. Simensen execs had breathed a sigh of relief at escaping certain liability. Biloxin was a stimulant that was highly toxic at inappropriate doses and might have resulted in deaths had it reached the street.

Jennifer had been with Simensen for almost a year. Ironically, her title was psychometrist, even though it was far removed from her ability as a feeler. In her official capacity as pyschometrist, she was simply someone who administered and interpreted assessment tests. That's how the nonbelievers defined the term. In this capacity, she was more than qualified for the position with a BA and Master's in psychology.

No one here knew about her other ability. The dullheads in charge would hardly be amenable to having a clairvoyant of any kind on staff. Not to say she didn't use her ability now and then. Always by accident though. Like now.

Just a slight impression. A bit of lipstick in the corner of one of the pages. But it was enough. The woman, dark hair, over forty, maybe a few years younger, two bluish pills—no, actually capsules—in her hands. Wariness in her eyes as she swallows the capsules. The sweat bead on her brow and the shakiness of her hands give her away. Possible addict. Maybe doing some personal testing of the product. Jennifer looked at the name. Marilyn Puchinski. The questionnaire is not flagged, but she would put it in the follow-up stack for a possible interview. Better to waylay this one right now then let it fester.

The phone rang. Even before she picked up, she had a feeling of urgency. Something about the ring, which seemed more shrill than usual.

"Jennifer DiMello," she answered.

"Jen? I need your help again." It was Carmen Carvelli. She sounded breathless. Jennifer's stomach lurched, and she immediately felt guilty for the reaction. But there wasn't anything she could do for Mrs. Carvelli's son. It was enough they had identified part of the problem. Past life regression was more than a little out of her expertise. Still, she felt that irritating pull of loyalty.

"I would love to help, Mrs. Carvelli, but if your son's resistant to the whole idea of psychic phenomenon, then I don't see how I can help him."

"I talked to him, Jen. I told him about me. He still says he thinks everything I told him is crazy . . . but I think I convinced him on some level. He's not going to admit it, but I told him things that only he would know. I think I can get him to sit down with you."

Jennifer began tapping fingers on the pile of papers sitting in front of her. "I don't know. I'm not sure I'll be able to do anything with so much resistance."

"That's what I'm telling you. I think part of him is willing to listen now. Please. I told him to come to the house this Friday. It would really help me if you could be there. To feel him out, especially those things I can't pick up."

"I . . ." Jennifer started, wanting desperately to find a way to back out.

"Jen, he almost died today." The voice, strident before, was calm, a fatalist's calm. "If we don't get to him now, I don't know what'll happen next. He needs to be fully prepared, and he can't be unless we know what he's dealing with." Pause. "Please Jen. Don't make me beg past this point."

"Ummm . . ." She hesitated using time she didn't have, adding another questionnaire to the pile. A quick flash of a man, thirty, brownish hair, regular features, staring into a mirror, tears running down his face. Jennifer put the paper down with a sigh. So many people in need.

"OK, I'll be there," she finally said.

"Thanks, Jennifer. I appreciate this," Mrs. Carvelli said, then finally hung up.

Jennifer reached into her special drawer, pulled out a bottle of pink liquid. In the privacy of her office, she took another long sip of Pepto-Bismol.

Tyne crossed her legs, attempting to appear casual, then regretted the move as the other woman focused on their length for a couple of seconds, seconds that made Tyne's breaths constrict before the woman looked away again.

"Nice." Sherry said. Tyne didn't know whether she was talking about the resume or her legs. She shook the thought off. Of course, the woman was referring to the resume.

She glanced over the office while Sherry perused the resume. Impressive. Georgia O'Keeffe reproductions on the walls. A combination of light oak and glass opened up the office's space. Then there was the dazzling view of Lake Michigan. She could see several boats in the distance. All of it served to good effect, which, of course, was the intent. Usually small start-up magazines had to forgo the luxury of décor, directing all monies to production.

"So, you basically did copy editing while at the *Clarion*? But no writing?" Sherry looked up and Tyne knew she was already losing her.

She took a cleansing breath. "I know my history is a bit sketchy, but I have written in the past. You can see that I did some contributing at the *Chicago Herald* before I came to the *Clarion*."

The woman didn't look convinced. "So why did you leave the other paper?"

"More money. And I was told that my position at the *Clarion* would be just a starting point, that my responsibilities would grow from there but that never happened. I promise you though that I can handle whatever you give me. If you're not convinced, give me a probationary period. You assign me whatever . . ."

But Sherry was already shaking her head, peering through the articles Tyne had attached from her days at the *Herald*. "I'm not sure about this. We'll be dealing with some tight deadlines, and this is the first issue, so it's going to have to kick ass. I mean you only have a few samples here, which I have to admit are pretty good . . . still . . ."

Tyne needed to clinch this. This was her job. She knew it. She just had to get over this hurdle. "Give me an assignment, no matter how big or small, and I promise you you won't be disappointed. I really want . . . no, I really *need* . . . this. Just give me a chance to prove myself."

There was silence while Sherry once again peered over the resume as though she wasn't sure she hadn't missed anything the first few times around. Tyne felt a ping of guilt at the masked hope that her association with David would help her clear the hurdle. Especially since she had been so adamant at not owing him anything and doing this on her own. She knew coming in that she could do the job, but that other applicants would probably have a better track record. Yet they weren't as desperate as she was, and she knew now that she was desperate enough to exploit whatever ties she had to get this.

"OK." Tyne sat up at the one word. Sherry's eyes were still elsewhere on the resume, and Tyne wondered if she had heard the word at all.

Sherry looked up, settled back in her seat. "I'll give you a chance to show me what you can do. First of all, let me tell you a little about the magazine and what we're going to be about. The magazine will be called *Elan.* The audience I'm aiming for will be diverse in race, orientation, marital status and income level. I don't want the same fluff the other women's magazines offer. So we'll be focusing on relevant issues that affect all women whether they're a young college student just starting out, a married mother of two, a lesbian facing discrimination, a black woman dealing with harassment, or a retiree grandmother wondering how to make her pension stretch past a couple of years. Many editors usually center on one market and that alone. But I think that we can do better without diluting our impact. I'm only going to bring on about eight writers. That'll include you. But again, this is provisional, a test period. If I like what you do, we'll talk about salary and benefits. And if I don't . . ." Sherry shrugged.

"I understand," Tyne quickly filled in. "So where do we go from here?"

Sherry reached over her desk, nearly knocking off a small statuette of two intertwined women as she reached for a folder. "Here's an article I actually had planned to do myself. Let's see what you can do with it."

Tyne tried to hide the smile as she reached for the folder being handed to her. She didn't want to seem satisfied. But inside, she was kicking up heels and doing somersaults. She opened up the folder, read the notes, saw the address. She nodded, and at the same time wondered what she had just let herself in for.

David sat on the edge of the bed, staring at the rays of a new sun barely breaking the horizon. Last night, he hadn't dreamed at all, and when he awakened, his body felt as though he had fought a battle in which he was fairly throttled. He was still recovering from his near-drowning, but had been able to go into the office yesterday for a few hours to do some follow-up calls. When he checked his e-mails, he wasn't surprised to find one from Clarence officially giving notice that he was terminating the partnership. Rick had been out of the office most of the day with meetings, saving both of them an awkward confrontation. He hadn't told anybody about his close call; instead he told Debbie that he had taken a day off to fight a cold.

He didn't want to go in today. It just didn't seem worth it. He loved being an architect, but he didn't like the hassles of keeping a business afloat, especially when others in the boat were tearing holes in it. Sometimes, he thought it might be better if he just walked away and took a position with another firm, a well-established firm where someone else had to deal with the headaches and all he had to do was design buildings.

He hadn't let himself think about the last couple of days. He didn't want to deal with Friday coming up. Why had he let his mother talk him into it?

But he knew the answer. She had told him things about himself. Things she shouldn't possibly know. Yet she did. In the hospital, she had regaled him with events that happened in high school and college—including the near-suspension he had never told her about, fights he'd gotten into, stupid daredevil stunts that had almost cost him a limb or two. Hell, she even knew when he lost his virginity and to whom, which was something considering he barely remembered the girl's name.

He was fighting to keep his world straight. There were rules that were supposed to operate, reactions that by logic should follow certain actions. But those rules were breaking down. As angry as he had been with his father for leaving, he probably understood a little better why the man had walked away from the marriage, from his mother. He had to fight not to take flight himself, just get on a train or plane and not look back. But he was different from his father; he knew his responsibilities. He would never leave her, no matter how crazy things got.

He got up, put on his robe, went downstairs creaking like an old man. He needed to get back to the gym, work out a little. His muscles were atrophying.

He stopped at the answering machine. He had forgotten to pick up his messages yesterday. There was only one. From Sherry. He listened as she filled him in on the new employment status of his "girlfriend." He blinked at the emphasis on the last word.

Surprisingly, he was ambivalent at the news. He should be glad but he wasn't certain how he felt. Just a couple of weeks ago, Tyne had attached to every thought, shadowing his work and his play. He had jerked off continuously to the image of her. But the dreams were fading now, and oddly, when he thought of her, he thought of green organza and tight curls. But that image was not hers.

He remembered the kiss and her subsequent shock. He had seen himself in smoky eyes, seen a man driven by passion. He'd stepped back that time, and he wasn't sure he could do that again.

He strolled to the kitchen, put coffee in the coffeemaker, then sat down and waited for it to brew. He ran fingers over tired eyes, through his hair, yawning. It was as though he hadn't slept at all. By the time the aroma of coffee filled the kitchen, he had already decided he wasn't going into the office. He got out the bowls, eggs, butter, the makings for homemade pancakes. The day was blossoming like a marigold, yellow and white against a clear sky. The clouds were lacy, the kind that adorned rather than obscured a mellow sun. This was a day to go jogging, throw around a football, or go swim . . . The thought cut off. It would be some time before he ventured into the water again. One day he would. But not today. Today, he would enjoy being alive. There was something about nearly dying that put priorities in perspective.

Today, work wasn't a priority. He would let Clarence walk, let him take his damn money without any argument. If Rick wanted to leave, too, then fine. They could both go. He'd deal.

But today, he didn't have to deal. He wanted a time-out. No calls or meetings. No confrontations. Just a chance to enjoy a beautiful day. But he didn't want to enjoy it alone.

He mixed the batter, turned on the radio to the soft jazz station. Boney James's sax weaved around the pop and sizzle of butter, of batter being poured into the skillet. He whistled along. He felt like a picnic. Maybe he'd pack up some cheese and crackers, wine, find some good company. He played with the idea, let it loiter in his mind, at turns rejecting then calling it back. Her number was upstairs, but would she be home? More important, would she come? He didn't know when she was due to start her new job, didn't know much about her at all. He flipped a pancake, caught it in the pan.

He missed her, missed touching her in his dreams. That was just how weird this was. He was missing someone he barely knew. Why Tyne instead of the many other women he'd dated? Why was she so embedded in his psyche that she now seemed an integral part of him? Standing at the stove, he let his mind wander back to the kiss, let himself remember how soft her lips had been, how warm and liquid, how sweet she had tasted. A sexual surge went through him, and he felt himself growing hard. He turned off the stove, left the kitchen. He took the stairs two at a time, wondering at his urgency.

He had placed the original fax copy in a folder and brought it home. Even then, he told himself there was no reason to keep it, to just toss it. He never did. The folder was on his nightstand.

The phone rang four times with no answer and he nearly hung up.

"Hello?" her voice came over the phone. She sounded breathless, and so near, as though she were standing next to him. As though he could just reach out and touch her. His throat constricted, and suddenly he was back in grammar school, hands sweating, calling his first crush, wanting to hear her voice, fearing what he might hear in it.

"I hear congratulations are in order," he said finally.

"Oh . . . thanks." Her hesitation caused his stomach to flinch. Suddenly, the ambivalence was gone. He wanted her. Had wanted her before they ever met. Most of all he wanted her to want him, wanted to know how it felt to touch her, to hear her moan, bury himself inside her so deep that he'd lose himself and never find his way back out. Already his body was crying out for her.

"If you're not busy today, I thought we might celebrate, maybe a picnic in Grant Park. I'll supply the food and wine. It'd be a shame to waste such a beautiful day." He tried to sound casual but he heard the plea beneath the words, was afraid that she would hear it too and that she would bolt again. Much as she had done at the wedding.

But instead she said, "A picnic? Funny. I don't picture you as the picnic type."

"Oh? And how exactly do you picture me?" He didn't want to admit to himself just how important her answer was.

"I don't know. I hadn't really thought about it. I guess I picture you as the active type, you know flying around in your plane, maybe waterskiing, but not exactly lolling around on the grass eating pâté. Anyway, thanks for the invitation, but I have some errands to do today."

He swallowed the disappointment, thought of something else. "Well, don't underestimate the pleasure of grass lolling and pâté eating, especially if it's at—oh let's say, a Ravinia concert, maybe listening to Wynton Marsalis or Tony Bennett?"

"So, are you inviting me to Ravinia?" she asked.

"If you're game. Ravinia's on Friday nights, but I can check the schedule, see who's playing this Friday. What kind of music do you listen to?"

"Usually smooth jazz, some R & B, a little classical, especially Handel."

He wasn't much into classical, but he would leave himself

open to the experience. "Then, let's do Ravinia. I'll pack us a basket. What do you like?"

"Surprise me. I'll take a chance on the food and the music."

He liked the idea of surprising her, of guessing her tastes, her desires.

"Friday, then. They usually start around eight, but traffic to Ravinia is heavy, so I'll pick you up at around six-thirty. That'll give us time to get there and find a spot."

"OK, let me give you my address."

He didn't remind her that he already had it from the resume.

"Or better yet, let's meet outside my office," she said. "I start the job Thursday."

He heard the lilt in her voice as she said "my office," felt good knowing he'd had a part in putting that lilt there.

"It'll be more convenient since I live far south in Hyde Park, and it doesn't make sense for you to drive all that way south when we'll just have to drive north again. Do you know the office address?"

"Yeah, I know it. I've been there before. It's on Erie. I'll pick you up at six-thirty then."

"OK." She said good-bye and was gone.

But with that one word, he felt the hell of the last few weeks ebb away. He was determined to hold on to that feeling. He picked up the phone and dialed another number. Five rings and her machine picked up. He left the message, knowing that she would be disappointed that he wouldn't be able to make it on Friday. But his mother would just have to understand. Besides, there was probably a reasonable explanation for why she knew the things that she did. There had to be.

New York—July 1879

"See here, Luce, what Trenton brought back from London." Barrett smirked as he leafed through a gazette with a nude woman of Raphaelite proportions on its cover. They were sitting in their usual room at Delmonico's, having just finished a three-course lunch that included an appetizer of smoked salmon with fennel followed by a main course of roasted leg of lamb, broiled potatoes, a large garden salad along with a magnum of Veuve Clicquot champagne. They had topped it off with chef Ranhofer's luscious creation, Baked Alaska, served with a bottle of port. The lunch was in celebration of Reese Trenton's return from his four-month European tour. Among the gifts he had brought back was one particular item of prurient interest. Barrett's fixed stare was matched by a wide grin as he turned another page.

"How can I see anything, Barrett, if you refuse to unhand the thing?" Joseph said sourly.

Barrett raised an eyebrow. "Why the foul mood, Luce? Lose at cards again?" alluding to Joseph's infamous predilection for gambling. And not always in the finer places.

"As a matter of fact, no. I won a couple of thousand last night."

"You'd better be careful, Luce," Trenton warned. "There're unsavory characters in the Tenderloin who would be all too willing to unencumber you of your monetary burden."

"I am well aware of the perils, Trent. Which is why I always carry a little something with me." Without flourish, Joseph retrieved a switchblade from his coat pocket and placed it squarely on the table next to his plate. "I don't take needless chances," he said, finishing off his glass of port. "And I've had occasion to use this to its full extent. Needless to say, that 'gentleman' will no longer be bothering myself or anyone else for that matter."

An awkward silence followed. "Still . . ." Trenton started.

Joseph gave Trenton a look that said he didn't want to pursue the subject any further. "Still what, friend?" Then, turning to Barrett, "I *still* haven't seen what all the fuss is about," Joseph said, tearing the gazette from Barrett's unresisting hand. "So, what do we have here?" The cover read simply *THE PEARL, A Journal of Facetive and Voluptuous Reading.*

"It's amazing the things you can find in Old Europe," Barrett said, leaning to peer over Joseph's shoulder as Joseph turned the pages. "It seems our boy made good use of his time on the other side of the Atlantic. No Tower of London for you, hey, Trent?"

Trenton smiled. "Just came out this month. As good as the pictures are, the prose is even better. Quite extraordinary, really. A great resource for lonely nights, if you know what I mean. Nothing like it here on these American shores." His smile broadened. "I can tell you boys approve."

In the pages, Joseph found a collection of limericks and stories, the language blue and uninhibited, accompanied by pictures of couples in stages of undress and copulation. He read several passages from one story of two randy cousins, the words deliberately chosen to elicit a sexual response. He was embarrassed to feel himself stiffening a little.

Trenton nodded as though he was privy to Joseph's bodily reaction. "Puts you in a certain way, doesn't it? Think I might head on over to one of the houses after lunch, get me some good ole American cunny."

"What American?" Barrett sneered. "Since most of the whores are either Irish or Italian, it's more like good ole immigrant cunny."

"Whatever, Barrett. A whore is a whore, as far as I'm concerned," Trenton said, draining another glass of port. "Just as long as I don't pick up any those foreign diseases. Half these girls don't know what a bar of soap looks like."

Joseph listened halfheartedly to the exchange. He hadn't made a visit to a whorehouse in over a month. This past week, his thoughts had been elsewhere. Ever since the evening of the Negro cotillion. But this was not a fact he could divulge to his friends.

They would never understand.

Oh, they might understand patronizing a Negro whore,

which they had done on occasion. But this plethora of feelings for a Negro woman who wasn't in the business of selling her body would not go over well. The thought of a Negro woman being considered of decent society would be amusing to them. They would not understand his growing need beyond a mere call of the flesh. A call pulling him to someone far removed from his world.

Because he couldn't understand it himself.

Couldn't fathom the desire to talk with her again or to see her smiling up at him once more.

As it were, he had already taken measures to find her.

Barrett's voice cut in. "From the look on his face, I think Luce here is planning a similar rendezvous, wouldn't you say, Trent?"

Trenton laughed, then poured another glass of sherry. "I'd definitely say there's something . . . or someone . . . on the boy's mind. So, Luce, do you have a particular wench you're planning to see?"

Joseph smiled, but said nothing. Instead he poured himself a glass, thought about soft caramel skin ensheathed in green. Thought about what it might feel like to touch that skin, kiss those full lips.

Unexpectedly, he stiffened more. Took a swig to waylay the direction his thoughts were taking. To take an edge off the acute anticipation of what he would do once he saw her again.

Chapter 16

Tyne's feet hurt. It was her first day out "in the field" and she should have known better than to wear two-inch slingbacks, but she had opted for style over comfort. A pain stabbed through her little toe as she climbed the stairs to the graystone. This would be the last time she would make this mistake. Even with her car, she still had to pound pavement, pound it good and hard. As hard and sore as the small corn emerging on her toe. But this was where she wanted to be— where all her work and years, and hopes and disappointments had finally brought her.

Tyne rang the doorbell, then warily looked back at a group of three or four teenage boys loudly talking outside a corner liquor store. If ever a nuclear apocalypse were to erupt and wipe out ninety percent of the world's population, one could rest assured that there would be someone who would open up a liquor store amidst the devastation. And there would be those, only breaths away from death, who would reach for a bottle to drown away their last few seconds of sorrow and horror.

The air smelled of sulfur or something as toxic, which was why she was here.

"Yeah?" a voice said from behind the door.

Tyne turned back and smiled. "Regina Stewart?"

A head of curlers appeared and a pair of eyes peeked from around the door.

"Who wants to know?"

"My name's Tyne Jensen. We spoke yesterday on the phone about my interviewing you for a magazine article." Tyne tried to keep her face and tone neutral. Overfriendliness in the situation might come off as patronizing.

The woman edged a little more from behind the door. Tyne's immediate impression was of purple—dark purple shirt and lilac sweat pants. A sparkle of amethyst in a silver teardrop dangled from an ear. The woman was petite and thin, her features molded by the hardness of someone who had to deal with the streets on a daily basis, and who had probably lost more than her share of battles. The eyes relayed an old woman's cynicism, yet Regina Stewart was twenty-eight according to the notes Sherry had given her.

Regina peered at Tyne for a few seconds, then emerged in whole from behind the door. "I dunno. I don't want no trouble with the city."

Tyne heard fear. She understood. Distrust of authority ran deep in some neighborhoods, especially where the struggling, the have-nots, and the never-would-haves lived. Paranoia was passed along like a virus through murmurs and rumors. Tyne had only a few seconds to overcome this distrust or she would get nothing. Already the woman was backing off from her initial interest in getting the truth told and her name immortalized—at least for this issue. Yet Tyne couldn't promise her that there wouldn't be retaliation. All she could promise was that she would be heard.

"Are you still interested in getting rid of the dump site? Because it's not going to go away on its own. It's going to take people speaking up, telling their stories. You can help make things better or you can remain silent and let things stay the way they are. It's up to you."

An eternity of silence ticked away as the woman gazed past Tyne's shoulder, looking toward the group of boys. Tyne felt her body stiffening with the tension. So much depended on this interview, this one chance to prove herself. She also had a chance with this story to make a difference in her own way. She needed to get inside that house, past the invisible barriers Regina Stewart was quickly erecting.

After a few seconds, Regina made her decision. "OK, I'll tell you what I know." She sounded tired and defeated already, but she opened the screen door and stepped aside to let Tyne enter. "Not that it's gonna mean much of a damn. They still gonna dump their shit out back 'cause it ain't their kids what's got to play around here."

Tyne followed the woman through a wide foyer.

"You can have a seat over there," she said, pointing to a chair.

Over there was a pleasant surprise, and Tyne inwardly berated her elitism. She had expected something different, something more pedestrian than the antique oak furniture, buffed to brilliance, and a fireplace that served as the centerpiece of the large airy living room. A few brown dhurrie rugs were thrown around the hardwood floor. A sun room extended the length of the living area, and sheer beige curtains blew with a breeze, catching onto an oak table on which sat a vase of wildflowers. The smell outside was tempered by their scent.

Tyne took the seat offered just opposite the fireplace. Regina sat down in an upholstered wing chair. Regina must have noticed Tyne's surprise because she said, "This was my mama's furniture. My mama and her mama lived here for a long time, long before things got bad. They always had good stuff and took pride in this home. I guess I musta inherited that pride, too. Things are bad out there; I won't let them get that way in here."

"Want something to drink?" Regina offered and Tyne shook her head. Instead she pulled out her tape recorder and placed it on a nearby table. "Like I told you on the phone, I'll be recording this so that I make sure I get the story as accurate as possible." Then she began with her notes. "How long has the dump been behind this block?"

Regina was already shaking her head. "That's just it. It's not supposed to be a dump. It was a vacant lot next to a building the city was supposed to tear down a long time ago. Now, the building's overrun with people selling and buying drugs. As if that wasn't bad enough, last year sometime—I think it was summer—all these trucks started pulling up in the middle of the night and dumping all sorts of garbage on the lot, mainly old tires and batteries and God knows what else. And the kids being the fools they are sometimes get up in there and start setting fire to the tires. That's why I make sure my kids stay away from there, especially Cassandra 'cause she already got an asthma problem."

"And you reported this to the city?" Tyne asked.

Regina looked insulted. "Of course I did, and not just me, either. There's a group of us who've been calling downtown as well as to that good-for-nothing-but-collecting-our-votes alderman for the past year, and still nothing. Even just a couple of nights ago, them trucks were out there. Like we can't hear them! You should see that mess they left behind!"

Tyne knew she would have to in order to relay the devastation fully. She would ask Sherry about getting a photographer to take a few shots of the dump. "Has anyone found out who the dumpers are?"

Regina nodded. "Mrs. Calhoun waited up one night and stood on the corner, which was a pretty foolhardy thing for her to do with these gangs running up and down the street selling their shit, but she waited for the trucks, and she saw the name on one of them. It's that tire plant about twenty blocks down, Webber Tires. It's bad enough we can smell the smoke all this way. Now, they're dumping their old tires over here and anything else they got no more use for. See they know they can't go to just any place and do that, because someone would get after them about not having permits. Besides, it's probably a longer trip to where they should be dumping. So the lazy asses just come here, figuring nobody's gonna say nothin' 'cause who gives a shit about a bunch of poor folks? You know the city doesn't and especially not the cops, otherwise they would be trying to clear out these gangs."

She continued. "We already got folks around here getting

sick from the stink in the air, and now we have to deal with this. My daughter's asthma is much worse than what it used to be, and Jeneva Trainor's daughter was just diagnosed with some sorta blood cancer. This keeps up, it's gonna get as bad as Altgeld Gardens."

Tyne knew Altgeld Gardens. A housing development on the far southeast side of Chicago, the name was synonymous with toxic waste dumping. Unfortunately for the residents, the dumping by local steel mills had contaminated the soil and waters around the community, and coincidentally the rates of cancer and birth deformities had gone up. The residents cried racism because everyone knew that this would not happen on the north side of town. Especially not near neighborhoods like the Gold Coast, Lincoln Park, or Wrigleysville.

"That's why when that other woman called, I thought that maybe now we can take it to the press, maybe put pressure on the city to do something. But I don't want no more trouble than what I already got. None of us can afford that."

Tyne steadily took notes that would supplement the tape. "You said a group of you have been calling downtown. Do you think the others would be willing to tell their stories, especially . . . um . . . what was her name again, Ms. Trainor?"

"Yeah, that's it. It's spelled T-R-A-I-N-O-R. As for them talking, I don't know. You'd have to ask them. Jeneva lives a couple of doors down. As for Mrs. Calhoun, she's a widow who lives across the street. This used to be a nice area, and it might be again if people would care and do something about the crime and the dumping."

Regina gave more names and addresses, related other illnesses that might or might not be associated with the dumping. Or with the toxins in the air from the plant. Tyne would call to try to schedule an appointment with Webber, but she wouldn't hold out hope that they would talk to her. Anyway, it wasn't their story. This story belonged to the victims of what was clearly a case of environmental racism. What was happening here was a travesty.

By the end of the interview, Regina seemed much more relaxed, was even smiling a little. Tyne knew that change wouldn't come quickly, if it came at all. Still, she was giving them a chance to have their voices heard. Just maybe the city would be embarrassed enough to at least call an investigation.

Tyne thanked Regina as they both stood. Tyne caught a glimpse of two framed pictures on the mantle she hadn't noticed before. A girl and a boy, around ten or eleven, both with big grins for the camera. They were beautiful children, and they deserved a better life than what they were getting here.

She promised herself she would write the best story she had ever written. She silently promised those two smiling faces that she would try to make things better, if only through the might of her pen.

Tyne checked the artillery for the night: orange-rind-laced chamomile tea, an extra comforter, and the cozy mystery she'd been trying to finish for nearly a month. She set the sound machine for "gentle rainfall" and a soft patter filled the room as she settled in between cool sheets that gave her a momentary chill. Even without the aids, her tired body and aching limbs promised to pull her into a deep slumber.

When she'd first gotten home from the office, she'd been all too glad to kick off her shoes and disrobe. She'd been too tired to do anything but pop a Lean Cuisine into the microwave and settle in front of the television for a few hours. Yet the exhaustion had felt good because it was from doing work she liked. No more mind-numbing rewrites and fact checks that had inundated her days at the *Clarion*. When she'd gotten back to the offices at *Elan*, she had eagerly typed up a first draft for the Stewart story, planning the direction she wanted to take the piece.

Laying aside thoughts of work, she picked up the novel, but after just a few minutes, the words began to blur as she felt herself giving way.

The music played in her head even here in the quiet of her sitting room. Days had passed and still her heartbeat sped, making her have to catch her breath at times.

She tried not to remember the pressure of his hand on her waist. The feel of his breath on her brow. The firm grip of his hand.

She had been dreaming of his smile. It didn't make sense. She felt as though she were losing herself.

It was bad enough that she had incurred her brother's ire, and that, yes, some people had begun to talk. There were whispers now.

But why? What had she really done but flout some unwritten rule? The man had not disrespected her. If anything, for those few moments they had danced, he had treated her with nothing but courtesy.

But it wasn't the courtesy she was remembering. It was the fire that had been in his eyes when he looked at her. Not a lust, but a burgeoning desire.

And if she was to be truthful with herself, the desire had reached her, had touched her. Was now becoming her own. She had wanted the dance to continue, but had nodded her acquiescence as he took leave of her in the silent room. The music had stopped and no one had said a word as he led her back to the table. Lawrence, still stunned, had not acknowledged the man further, except to turn away.

Unruffled, the stranger had not responded to the slight, but had walked through the berth made by quiet dancers and retrieved his coat and hat at the door.

Only then did the room began to move again. And uncomfortably the eyes had remained focused on her.

Lawrence stood then.

"We have to leave," he had said with a finality that brooked no resistance. And she gave none. He took her hand, escorted her to the door.

Something had changed that night. Somehow life had become life again and not an endless existence of days to get through. She actually woke with a smile this morning.

She wasn't foolish enough not to know that there would be consequences for her defiance. But she could live with that. Because now she knew that she could feel again.

If not love, then something else . . . something she didn't want to put words to because it wouldn't be decent. Yet it was this not-too-decent feeling that made her remember she was a woman and had known a man in her life. In the private moments of her bedroom.

Soon the scandal would die down, and she would have nothing more than a memory. And the ordinariness of her life would resume.

But, she also knew that the pain of losing George would eventually loosen its grip, would begin to ebb into something less intrusive, less acute.

And maybe, one day . . . not in the near future, but one day . . . she might let herself love again.

She picked up the monogrammed handkerchief she was mending for Lawrence. It had been a gift from Mother the first Christmas after Lawrence passed the New York bar. Much used, he was loath to throw it out.

The ringing bell caught her by surprise, made her prick herself. She quickly put the wounded finger in her mouth to suck the blood away, then walked to the foyer to open the door.

When she saw who was standing outside, her heart nearly stopped. It was as though she had summoned him with her thoughts. But how had he found her?

Her eyes scanned the surrounding street to see who might be witness to this unusual scene. But there was no one walking about. Lord knew there would be further scandal if anyone saw him standing on the stoop. And even more if she actually allowed him inside.

Still, she stood aside to let him enter. And Joseph Luce smiled.

Tyne woke up to the dark room, tried to remember the dream. But unlike other nights and other dreams, she found it hard to hold on to the tenuous impressions. The only thing she was sure of was that in the dream David had been smiling at her. And she had waited for him not with dread, but with a quiet anticipation.

Chapter 17

The retiring sunlight skirted along the waves in long beacons of burnt gold. Because of their late start, David was avoiding the Kennedy, which was sure to be bumper to bumper with rush hour commuters trying to get home. Instead they were taking Lake Shore Drive where the traffic was slightly better. To the right, Lake Michigan was points of fire at intervals, a mirror to the sky's blazing orange.

The coming evening promised cooler temperatures, and in anticipation David had brought an extra blanket. In the backseat sat the basket packed with a bottle of chilled Santa Margarita Pinot Grigio, salami, ham, turkey, olives, prosciutto parma, Italian bread, smoked salmon, and cream cheese. For dessert, there were slices of apple pie and small berries known as frutti di bosca. Just in case she didn't want liquor, he had made lemonade, the way his mother made it. Tyne was bound to like something, and he was very interested to know what she would choose—and whether he had chosen well. She sat next to him, her perfume a distraction to his driving. Light, floral, he had smelled it that day at lunch and would now remember the scent as something uniquely hers. He talked inanely of his workday, concentrating on the project he had just bid on, leaving out the friction between him and his partners. All the while he talked, he tried not to think of the alluring contour of her thigh apparent in the dark slacks she was wearing.

She hadn't asked about the headliner, and he hadn't offered the information, hoping to surprise her and hoping that the surprise would be welcome. She was trusting him for a good evening, and he would do everything to provide it.

"How long had you known you wanted to be an architect?" she asked.

The question took him by surprise. He thought about it for a second. He had never pinpointed the beginning of his desire to design buildings, yet he knew he hadn't always wanted to be an architect. He remembered a childhood fantasy about one day becoming a fireman. But that was long before the summer of the fire, the summer when everything went to hell. "I guess after taking a couple of drafting classes back in high school. I seemed to have a knack for it, and the ambition grew from there."

He stopped short as they hit a stall. He bit back a curse, looked at his watch. Almost seven-fifteen. He had hoped to be there about seven-thirty, but at this rate, they weren't going to make it.

She noticed the motion and again apologized for keeping him waiting for almost twenty minutes. He understood. She had already explained about the rewrite that had taken longer than anticipated. Some story about pollution in a depressed neighborhood. Even though he wasn't looking directly at her, he could feel her enthusiasm as she talked, knew her eyes were beaming.

"Next week, I've scheduled a couple more interviews. I really think this is going to be a good story." He liked the excitement in her voice.

"I want to thank you for passing on my resume. I might not have ever gotten anything this good."

"Well, Sherry seems very happy with your eagerness and drive."

"So, you two been talking about me?" The tone was more amused than paranoid, but he answered carefully.

"She just called to thank me for sending you over, that's all. So there's gratitude all around. Here, let's have some music." He reached over and turned on the radio. Al Hirt's "Cotton Candy" was playing.

"Jazz man, are you?"

"I don't think the word aficionado accurately describes my obsession. I probably have every jazz record, tape, and CD there is. I may start my day with Miles or end it with Goodman. Fall asleep to Coltrane, take a run with Jarreau. But jazz isn't my only passion. There's REO Speedwagon, Fleetwood Mac, ELO, EWF."

"Earth, Wind and Fire? God, I love them! After the Love Is Gone, Love's Holiday . . ."

". . . The Way of the World," he added enthusiastically, loving this meshing of the minds.

"I always liked the oldies, even as a teenager. I didn't care too much for many of the groups out of the eighties. Anyway, I remember playing "After the Love" so many times following a breakup that my mother finally burst into my room and confiscated my CD player, told me she wasn't having her daughter going crazy stupid over some slim-hipped jim who didn't know how to treat me right anyway."

"Yeah, I think we all had those types of breakups," he chimed in. "Actually, mine happened in grammar school, and it wasn't music but phone calls. I think I must've called her nearly seventy times, trying to make her take me back. Her mother finally called my mother and pleaded with her to make me stop. My mother disconnected the phone for a whole weekend and told me to get over myself, that if the girl didn't want me, I better stop trying to force a thing that didn't fit."

They were finally on North Ridge Avenue, and the steady stream of cars had thinned a bit. He pressed down on the gas, and the speedometer moved up to sixty-five. Once they were on Green Bay Road, they would almost be there.

"Your mother sounds a little like my mother," she laughed. "They'd probably get along great."

A bit of guilt flitted through his conscience and he mentally swatted it away. His mother hadn't returned his message, and he imagined her sitting, watching her reality show, already hitting her second package of Camels. Inwardly cursing her wayward son. Or probably putting a curse on him. Another thought he quickly shook away. His mother was not a witch. But, hell, she was as close as they came.

Jennifer pulled up to the address Mrs. Carvelli had given her. The woman was already there, waiting on the porch.

Jennifer got out of the car, walked up the path. Rhododendrons grew in profusion on either side of the stairs. The house was a St. Anne Victorian with a wraparound porch and bay windows. Much more old-fashioned and elaborate than she would have attributed to a single man. Maybe he bought it with thoughts of a family in the future.

Carmen Carvelli looked upset as she waited for Jennifer to climb the steps.

"So how are we going to do this?" Jennifer asked. "I mean we can pick out one or two of his things and try to get an impression that way, but, of course, direct personal contact is always best—if he'll let me touch him, that is. The visions will be much stronger and . . ."

"We're doing this without him," Mrs. Carvelli said definitively, her eyebrows fierce straight rods, her eyes thunderous.

Jennifer looked at the locked door, confused. "But . . ."

"Don't worry," Mrs. Carvelli said as she reached into her purse and pulled out a key. "I always keep a spare in case of emergencies. Despite my dense-headed son's knack for avoiding the obvious, this is an emergency."

She put the key in the lock, then after a couple of tugs on the knob, pushed open the heavy oak door. "He still hasn't fixed that," she said under her breath.

Then they were inside the foyer. Jennifer took in the cherry wood staircase, the large oriental throw rug, the antique table with phone and answering machine just past the door. Off to the left was the living room. Again, antique furniture, and an overall impression of dark woods. The whole effect was turn-of-the-century elegance.

Mrs. Carvelli headed for the stairs, then stopped and turned to Jennifer. "He built this, you know. Said it was for me, but he's all through this house. I can't explain it, but this house is him, and he doesn't know it." Then she started up the stairs and Jennifer didn't have any other choice but to follow. She felt like a trespasser as she glimpsed the black-and-white photos lining the stairway wall. She recognized Babe Ruth, but not the others.

This was someone's home, someone who didn't believe in the paranormal, let alone psychics. She could only guess what his reaction would be if he knew that she was now approaching a door that opened on what looked like his bedroom. But his mother was leading like an advance scout of an infantry, marching steadily on with the fierce determination of battle heat. Jennifer began to wonder what she had gotten herself into.

She watched as Mrs. Carvelli beelined to a bureau, pulled out a drawer and searched through its contents before retrieving a navy-and-gold striped tie. The woman turned and held it out to Jennifer, a fire in her eyes. Jennifer fought an urge to step back, to shrink from the mania that had overtaken the woman. Instead she tentatively took the silky material in her left hand, closed her eyes. Let her mind go blank, tried to receive an impression. But seconds passed and there was still nothing.

"Are you getting anything?" Jennifer heard the voice through her haze. "That's the tie he had on that evening at my house—when he turned into someone else. Or at least, that's what I thought I saw." Jennifer detected the uncertainty in the older woman's voice, the first sign of withdrawal. Maybe the woman was only now realizing she had overstepped some invisible boundary, a trust broken between parent and child.

"No," Jennifer answered simply. Mrs. Carvelli's face fell a

little, her determination petering out. But then a second wind came from somewhere and Mrs. Carvelli turned to the dresser. She opened a wooden box that sat on top, pulled out the first thing she touched. A diamond stud earring. Jennifer was confused for a second, until she realized the earring belonged to David. She knew men pierced their ears nowadays, but she hadn't realized that Mrs. Carvelli's son was one of them. Jennifer held out her hand, and Mrs. Carvelli dropped the delicate piece of jewelry into it.

Immediately, Jennifer got a flash of a woman. Auburn hair, blue eyes that glittered as she fastened the earring into the man's ear.

The flash ended. It was something, but not what they needed. It didn't tell them anything that might or might not stave off the impending storm that seemed to be hovering above them. She felt Mrs. Carvelli staring at her. Jennifer shook her head. But the woman only turned and looked over the canvas of the dresser, searching for something else.

Jennifer started toward the dresser to put the earring back in its place. Her nervousness made her legs quaky, and she accidentally brushed against the edge of the bed.

Mrs. Carvelli's son, David—his face contorted in pain, sorrow—thrashed in his dreams. And then his face morphed back and forth into another's. The face she had seen superimposed over his photo. He was murmuring something—a name—Ra . . . Rachel?

Mrs. Carvelli was shaking her. "What is it? What did you see?"

Jennifer shook off the remnant of the vision before telling the woman about the alternating faces.

The older woman nodded. "I bet you it's the same man I saw. Did you see anything else? Hear anything?"

Jennifer hesitated, not sure of what she'd heard. "He seemed to call out a name. Someone named . . . I think, Rachel."

Mrs. Carvelli pondered this before reaching inside the large, black handbag hanging from her shoulder. She pulled out a pack of cigarettes, took one, lit it. Then through a curl of smoke, said, "Must be someone he knows . . . or knew. But at least we have more than we had before."

Rachel. Jennifer wondered if that was the name of the girl Mrs. Carvelli had mentioned in their phone conversation the other evening. A young woman Mrs. Carvelli said she had a vision of a couple of nights ago. She'd said the girl was in her late teens, early twenties, reading through a bunch of letters. Mrs. Carvelli didn't know how the girl figured into all of this, but that she was somehow a key to something missing.

Could she be Rachel?

And if not, then who?

Chapter 18

A slight breeze tickled her hair, sweeping a tendril into her eye. Tyne pushed it away. The smell of crushed grass joined the medley of deli aromas from hundreds of picnic baskets. From a full expanse, she could see hundreds of heads swaying to the rhythm of the saxophone as couples lay in various positions of repose. On the Pavilion stage, Wynton Marsalis fronted the Chicago Jazz Orchestra, and their horns filled the evening with the strains of Duke Ellington's "Take the A Train." She and David sat along the edge of the lawn, and were among the lucky few who could actually see part of the stage. Along the perimeters, a state-of-the-art sound system broadcast the concert to the rest of the listeners.

"How is it?" The sudden rush of words brushed her ear and a tingle vibrated down her spine. She turned and his face was so close, she found herself looking at the indentation in his chin. She scanned the slightly full lips, traveled up to the eyes, their color dark in the night. But they reflected the lights all around them. She had to bend in close to his ear to speak.

"It's great. I really like Wynton Marsalis. How did you know?"

He shrugged to say he didn't. They both turned back to the music, and the night. Even as she listened, her body throbbed with the music, with expectation. No, she wasn't going to sleep with him. Not tonight. Yet, she had to admonish herself for peeking at the hard line of muscle visible through his jeans, the impression of pectorals through his shirt.

She knew that on occasion, throughout the performance, he peeked at her, too. She knew that his eyes searched her profile, sometimes traveled the length of her body, explored her curves. She was wearing slacks, so there wasn't much to see. Yet, she felt as though he saw her bared and open.

After the first set, the orchestra segued into "Get Close." A hand appeared, holding a small berry to her mouth. She was already stuffed from the various meats, cheeses, and breads he had packed. She had drunk glasses of both lemonade and a light wine, tasted a scrumptious slice of apple pie. She barely had room for anything else, but she opened her mouth to let him move the berry in. Her tongue brushed his finger, and she felt his body stiffen inches away.

There was an eclipse as his head blocked the light. He touched her lips lightly with his tongue, left a trail of moisture across them. He smelled of berries and wine. An accompanying moisture crept from the crevice of her other lips, and she resisted a compelling need to pull him to her. Instead, she moved her head back to break the spell of intimacy he was creating.

He moved back then, but his eyes bored into her, as though he needed to find some way to penetrate her. She wanted him to penetrate her—with tongue, fingers, penis. She wanted to feel his mouth discovering those curves he had only so far explored with his eyes.

Not tonight she told herself again, tried to tell him with her eyes. But they both knew she lied. Thank goodness she had packed a box of condoms. She bought them the other week on a whim she hadn't wanted to explain to herself. That same whim had made her pack them into her purse only days before. It'd been so long, she no longer had a prescription for the pill. Strange how the subconscious makes the conscious self submit to its desire. How denial gives way to acquiescence, surrender.

He turned back to the music, and she let her eyes go to the stage. But she no longer saw the musicians, barely heard the music. Only felt his fingers close over hers. They stayed that way for the rest of the concert.

David held her hand as he forced the key to turn in the lock. He always had trouble with the knob and it usually took two hands to maneuver. But he refused to let her go, and had to put some extra single-handed muscle into the tug before the knob finally turned. This was on his to-do list, but with everything going on, he hadn't had time for minor fix-its around the house. At the moment, he had other matters on his mind.

He had been careful not to pressure her. In the car, he simply asked whether she would like to see the house he'd built for his mother that he was temporarily living in. Because that was how he saw it. A temporary arrangement until he could finally convince his mother to take his gift—or sell it.

She hadn't answered right away. He had taken her silence as a flat-out "no." But then she turned to him, and said so softly he wasn't sure he heard her, "Yes." Both of them knew she was answering the tacit question hidden beneath the spoken one. For the rest of the ride, they were quiet, simply listening to the local jazz station, each lost in anticipation.

Now he studied her as she studied the living room. He was pleased at the awe he saw in her eyes.

"You designed and built this? God, I'm impressed. It's beautiful, David, it really is."

He liked the way she said his name. "I actually built it for my mother, but she said that it was more me than her. I don't see what she's talking about." He thought about fixing her a drink, decided against it.

Tyne nodded. "I do. I see exactly what she's talking about," she said as she swiveled around, looking at the wood beams, the bay windows, the hardwood floors. "There's just something, the strength of the lines, maybe even the antiquity."

He shook his head. "That's just it. I'm Mr. Modern. Give me clean lines and surfaces, a bareness and minimalism."

"Which explains the Victorian furniture," she said teasingly. "I can see the minimalism in the detail of the brocade here, the finely detailed carving of the wood"—she traced the material of a wing-backed chair, looked around—"the oriental rugs, the hurricane lamp."

He chuckled. "Well, it's not exactly Eero Saarinen, I have to admit. Actually, I did buy the furniture with my mother in mind . . . but it's kind of grown on me."

He walked up to her, caught and deliberately held her eyes, traced a finger along her cheek.

"Well, I like it," she said softly. Her eyes were warm, liquid desire.

"What else do you like?" he asked, his breath shallow, his throat constricting. He heard the pounding of blood in his ears. The pace quickened as she smiled. He throbbed with need, resisting an urge to rush. He wanted to savor every second, to take it so slow it hurt.

"About what?" she whispered, her voice breathless.

He didn't answer. Instead he lowered his lips to hers, tasted the tart and sweet, the sugar and spice, deepened the kiss to taste more and was rewarded with a soft moan that vibrated through him. He drew her into his arms, pressing his growing tumescence into her stomach. The discomfort only added an edge to the pleasure. His hand wandered down the arch of her spine, settled on the roundness of her behind, squeezed lightly. Heat emanated from her flesh, seared through his own.

It was as though he were drowning again, only this time he eagerly welcomed the death that awaited him. She was pulling him into her depths with her lips, her hands that moved along his back, the feel of her body yielding to his.

He stood there for more moments than in a span, entirely lost in her. When he pulled back, it was to get much needed air. He saw that her state was not much better than his. Her eyes were glazed and hooded, her breaths soft pants, her lips moist from the kiss. She stepped back unsteadily.

"Tell me if I'm going too fast," he offered between his own quickened breaths.

"No. The pace is just fine." She smiled, then became serious. "I have some—I mean in my purse."

He knew where she was going. "I have my own upstairs. Ready to see the other parts of the house?"

She chuckled. "Now why do I have the feeling you're not inviting me to see your kitchen?"

He smiled back. "Your call. I got a real sturdy table . . ." Then he stopped. "Sorry, that was crude."

"Only if you're a prude, which I'm not. Look, I want to do this just as much as you do. So, let me see whatever room you got to show me." He heard an avidity in her voice that matched his own. He hadn't realized until this moment how starved he had been.

"OK, then." He took her hand, led her to the stairs. The trip was the longest he had ever taken, and it seemed they would never reach the top. As he passed the picture of Mantle, it seemed as though the man winked at him. An illusion. Yet the smile appeared brighter than usual.

"Here it is," he said with unneeded fanfare as he pushed the door open and hit the light switch on the wall. He stood at the entry to let her enter first and he followed. He stopped, wondering at the scent of Tabu in the air. He thought of his mother, then shook the thought from his head. Another illusion. Yet the smell seemed strong, and it threw him for a second.

"Hhmm, smells good in here," she said, turning to him. "But it's a little lighter than what I'd expect you to wear."

Then he knew. His mother *had* been here. He only parsed the thought for a second. He would deal with that later. But for right now . . .

"My mother. She has a key. She must have dropped something off," he said quickly, maybe too quickly because her right eyebrow went up a little.

"You don't have to explain. Your business is your own."

"I don't sleep around," he said, feeling defensive now.

"Neither do I," she countered. "As a matter of fact, it's been awhile."

"Oh?"

"About two years," she said cautiously, looking at him to gauge his reaction.

"It's been a few months for me, which, for a man, is saying something. I came out of a long relationship. It was a bad breakup."

She nodded. "Me, too. But I'd rather not talk about it, not now anyway." He understood and closed the space between them. His fingers played with a tendril of hair that fell over her eye. Then a finger trailed down her cheek, her chin, detoured down her throat, to the crevice exposed by the opened top buttons. The finger paused as he waited for a protest that didn't come. Instead, there was a small catch of breath. A breath of anticipation.

He let the finger travel down the warm chasm between the soft mounds of her cleavage. His other hand began to maneuver the buttons, to free her flesh. With each opened button, the blood rushing in his ears, his head, became louder until he thought that she must hear it, too. Every motion was new; every motion familiar, resounding with the echoes of his dreams and something else.

He released her from the constraints of a lacy, low-cut bra, caught his breath as he stood enthralled by the sight of cinnamon tipped with cocoa. A temptation for the lips. His mouth closed eagerly over a nipple, eliciting a soft gasp, a small wave in the ocean pounding in his head. He suckled like a newborn babe tasting his first milk. The taste was exquisite. Hands raked his curls, pulled his head in closer. He had to steady himself with his hands straddling both her hips. She pushed into him, nearly knocking them both over. He released the nipple, only to begin a slow baptism of the other one.

After several excruciating moments in which he didn't

know that time still moved, he reluctantly released the nipple, but eagerly found her lips again. Unlike the first kisses that had been firm, but controlled, his exploration now was almost brutal. His tongue grappled with hers, advancing like an invader instead of a guest. Melded together, he deliberately backed her to the edge of the bed, then moved his weight to force them down onto the mattress, which gave way with a slight groan.

He buried his head in the crook of her neck, his lips leaving a trail of moisture as he moved to the luxuriant softness between her breasts, his hand busying with the button on her slacks. He found the zipper and eased it down, then sat up as he pulled the pants over her hips, tugged them until they came off. Then he eased fingers beneath the wet crotch of her panties, found a pool of viscous moisture, a well of hot silky cream. He softly touched the soaking lips, moved up to the clitoris, began moving in a purposeful rhythm.

"Ohhh, God." He heard the tortured sound from far away, from a distant shore. He pulled down her panties, then navigated southward, his lips moving along the island of her taut stomach, to the curly thatch that teased his nose, his tongue. Her scent was sweet, sweaty. He touched her clit lightly with his tongue, felt her hips jerk. He held them steady, holding her prisoner to his ministrations. He grazed her with his teeth, alternating nibbles with licks around the tiny orb until he felt tremors moving through her. Her gasps sounded like the sobs of the tortured, but he would not stop. Her cream was oozing into his mouth and he drank liberally, slaking a thirst he had let go unquenched too long. He pushed his tongue inside her.

He felt it when she came, felt her walls spasming, heard the unintelligible gurglings, as though she were ululating in some unknown language. He reluctantly released her to stand up and quickly shed his own clothes. As he took off his layers, he watched her, taking in her beauty as she lay prone trying to recover from her first orgasm. But he wasn't about to let her.

She could barely move. The pleasure was too paralyzing. She heard him taking off his clothes, felt the air vibrate at his approach. She lifted her head, saw him hovering over the bed naked. He wasn't the specter of her dreams anymore. He was here, flesh and blood. Blood moved through his flesh now, suffusing his penis until it stood erect from his body, turning the head a reddish purple.

"I've waited for you," she thought she heard him whisper, but quickly dismissed it as something she'd misheard. There was too much going on in her head, not the least of which was that she was about to make love with someone she barely knew—and yet she did know him, knew him just like this, as he stood now reaching inside the drawer of his nightstand. He pulled out a square package, tore it open with deft fingers, and she watched in studied fascination as he pulled and stretched the latex over his elongated member. She throbbed with a renewed need.

He sank his knees into the mattress on either side of her, positioned himself until there was no view but his face. He filled her visual world as he would soon fill her. The nerves in her body called out to him, and she knew he heard. Knew he smelled her anticipation. She saw moisture on his face and didn't know whether it was his sweat or her juice. Slowly, he lowered his body and shifted until the head of his penis pressed against her opening.

"Are you ready?" His breath tickled her lips. She didn't have a chance to answer as his tongue pushed into her mouth, as his penis pushed into her body. A double invasion. He lay still for a second, his body embedded in hers. Then slowly, slowly he began to move inside her. The bed springs echoed his tempo, trilling a chorus as he began moving a little faster, thrusting a little deeper. She had known the feel of men inside her before, but what she felt now defied the history of every lover she had ever had. The sensations were too varied, contradictory. Inside, the ribbed sheath of his penis raked against her walls, causing a friction so good it bordered on pain, while his thrusting punished her clitoris with nerve-screaming pleasure. He sucked her tongue, swirling the taste of her sex in her mouth, while his fingers clutched her ass, his fingernails imprinting themselves in her bountiful flesh. There was no relief, no chance to catch a breath, to escape the rapture.

His thrusts demanded her capitulation, her temporary relinquishment of her humanity. Trembling beneath him, she was no longer Tyne, an educated, self-possessed, independent woman. Instead, she was an extension of his body, a capillary through which his need, desire, even his life, flowed. He was the same for her. His hunger scared and exhilarated her. Her hunger frightened and enthralled her. She clutched the firm mounds of his ass, unceremoniously pushing him even farther up her canal. The moan that escaped this time was from him.

They drank each other, grinding their hips together, demanding a denouement that was swiftly rising, threatening to sweep both of them out on its tide. Saliva, sweat, heat, tears mixed and fused the air with the smell of sex, an amalgam of their essence, a child born of their desire and need.

A sensation started moving from her crotch, moving upward to her stomach, outward to her limbs. It was more than she could hold in her body. She released it through the scream against his lips, through the nails that ran streams of red down his back. Soon, the smell of blood joined the other smells. She didn't care to see sunlight again if she could keep this moment. No food or water would ever sate her. Just him inside her.

A violent convulsion shook his frame against hers, and he buried his face in her nape, his rapid breaths burning through her skin. His weight went dead and settled fully on top of her, making it hard for her to draw in breath. But if she had to die like this, so be it.

An eternity of seconds passed before she realized she would have to move or suffocate for real. She began to sidle from beneath him, and he responded by shifting his weight off her to lay beside her. His breathing sounded like an asthmatic foraging in a field of poppies. Or the screeching blurt of bellows. For a moment, she wondered if he was going to hyperventilate.

After a few seconds, his breathing became less agitated.

"You're all right?" she asked between her own shaky breaths.

He said nothing but she felt him nod. A sliver of sexual pride ran through her at the damage she had done. He was a quivering mess beside her. But then again, she wasn't in any better shape.

She raised up to get off the bed, but he reached out a hand to still her. It slowly moved up to cover a breast, began a slight caress. The twinge in her crotch took her by surprise.

"What?" she asked incredulously. He couldn't possibly. . . . But then she noticed he was no longer limp, the crown of his head growing darker.

He winked, smiled, then reached over and licked her lower lip—and began where he left off.

New York—July 1879

It was just a rose. A beautiful yellow rose waiting for her on the doorstep. Thankfully it was early yet, too early for Lawrence to have come home and discovered it there on the porch to their brownstone. She would not want to raise his suspicions when she could not name her suitor, nor allow for a time for the two men to meet. She picked up the flower and looked around, knowing that he was no longer there, but wishing that he were. She smelled the flower. The scent was heady in the heat of the early afternoon. It would die soon.

The gesture was sweet and unassuming, somewhat contrary to what she had come to know of him in the three weeks since he had found her again. He did not seem one for simple gifts. He had been very disappointed when she refused the emerald necklace he tried to give her on their last meeting. There had been other attempts at gifts, none accepted.

He did not seem to understand that this could not be, this

association he was so desperately pursuing. Anything between them, any more than what had already gone before, would be the unraveling of them both. They had their places in this world . . . and it wasn't together.

And yet . . . She stroked the petals. So soft, one slightly bruised, but this did not detract from its beauty.

She must put a stop to this courting.

Because it could not be. This hope for more.

Still, she couldn't help the smile that touched her lips, nor the warmth that ran through her as she remembered how first his hand, then his lips had covered hers, and how his brown eyes had nearly swallowed her whole.

The ringing phone pulled her reluctantly from her dream. Half asleep, Tyne wrestled with the sheets, blindly reaching for the nightstand lamp. The clock said two-forty. She picked up the receiver, hoping bad news wasn't on the other end.

"Tyne?"

The sound of David's voice woke her fully. She sat up, pulled the sheet around her, feeling self-conscious, wondering why. Then remembered the very intimate dream she'd been having about him, in a place that seemed from another time.

"David, hi . . . what . . . what's going on?"

"I know, I know . . . it's late . . . too late to be calling, right?" He laughed softly, warmly.

"Well, no . . . is everything all right?"

"Yeah, it is. I just . . . I was just dreaming about you and I woke up needing to hear your voice."

Tyne felt a warm surge. "Funny, I was just dreaming about you, too."

"Was it a nice dream?" The purr in his voice made her take an unsteady breath.

"Very nice. So what were you dreaming about me?"

"It was strange, really. I couldn't see your face clearly, but I knew it was you. We were talking about books, some of the classics, and you were laughing at something I'd said. It was such a wonderful sound, your laughter. And I woke up wanting to hear that sound again. Only thing is, even though I knew it was your voice, it was different somehow. I know this must sound weird."

Tyne heard the uncertainty in his voice. She wondered about her own dream, the man who was David and somehow wasn't.

"So, what did you dream about me?" he asked.

Suddenly embarrassed, she didn't want to tell him the intimate details, even after last night, or especially after last night. And there was something about her dreams that still brought a chill to her. Even though she hadn't dreamed about the knife in a while, yet whenever she was with her dream lover, the dream David, there was a sense of danger, a sense that she wasn't safe. Sometimes there was an overwhelming need to get away. Although that hadn't been the case with tonight's dream.

"It was nothing really . . ."

"That bad, huh?" he teased.

"No, nothing like that. I'd just rather not talk about it. But, it's nice that you called though."

A silence then, "Sometimes I just want to talk to someone. Reaching out isn't always easy. And when you do, you hope you don't get burned. That's why I want you to know, it wasn't just about the sex . . . I mean last night."

She smiled. "That's good to know. Like I said, I don't do that usually, hardly ever. And never after just one date. Last night was different, though . . . special." Even as she said this, she wondered whether she had revealed too much.

"For me, too." Another silence. "I would never admit this to my mother, I mean she's into all this predestination and kismet stuff, but sometimes you wonder if fate has something to do with the people we meet . . ."

"So, you think we were meant to find each other?" She tried to put a lilt in her voice, didn't quite succeed. Because she didn't think the idea was as farfetched as she wanted to make it sound. And the alternative was inexplicably disturbing.

"I know, I know . . . it sounds like a line. Just forget it. Tell me about you, Tyne."

"Tell you about what?"

"I don't know . . . your likes, dislikes . . . I want to know everything."

"It's late, David."

"I know. But I have these feelings, and I can't explain why the connection with you was so immediate, but it was. I just need to know why."

"Sounds like you don't want to have these feelings . . ."

"No, I like what's happening. Which is why I want to know more about you."

She sighed. "David, I could tell you the colors I like, the music I listen to, the foods I crave, but I don't think it could really tell you about me. The thing you need to know is that I'm just a woman who wants what other women want . . . someone I can be comfortable with, can talk to, laugh with. I've had good relationships, as well as bad, and I know I don't want to be hurt again. Have you ever hurt anyone, David?"

She heard him hesitate. "There was someone I hurt, hurt really bad . . ." And he told her about his last girlfriend, Karen, how he had walked away—or rather, let her walk away, how his heart hadn't been open. "I wasn't ready—then." There was a pause that she knew she was supposed to fill, an inference she was meant to make but she held off, not wanting to assume too soon.

As though talking about Karen had opened a valve to his memories, he told her about other girlfriends, his first crush. A girl named Delana.

"I hate to admit this, but I've never been in love before," he said with a hint of sadness.

"Before when?"

He didn't answer, and she didn't want him to. It was too soon. And she wasn't yet sure of her own feelings. They only had one night between them.

She told him about her own failed romances and only

when she had concluded her list did she realize that she had never really loved any of them. No one had ever come close enough to make her want to open her heart. She had spent more time guarding it instead.

He related other things to her. A best friend drowned, a father who had walked away.

"I've done many things that I'm ashamed of," he said quietly. Another silence, and then, "I burned down my mother's house a long time ago. It's something I haven't ever been able to fully tell her . . . and right now, I don't know why I'm telling you. I guess I finally needed to tell somebody." He told her how the fire got started, about how he had run instead of trying to put it out.

She heard the guilt in his voice, wanted to appease it somehow. "Maybe, one day you'll be able to tell her everything. After all, it was an accident, and you were just a child, if a little mischievous. There's only so long you should have to hold on to guilt, David. Sometimes, you just have to let things go and go on living."

"Thanks for that, Tyne. I'm glad I told you."

After that, they talked for hours. And when she finally hung up, dawn was breaking and it was time to get up.

Chapter 19

Rhea sat quietly at the kitchen table studying the old photo. Her grandmother stood at the old chrome stove she'd had for nearly thirty years frying bacon in a skillet. She was humming like she always did while cooking.

The picture was creased at the corners, the sepia tones faded, making the colors indistinguishable. Rhea had to peer closely to discern the details of the faces captured in grain for over a century. The two women stood side by side, their heads adorned with hats sporting large, curving feathers. The taller of the two was her great-great-grandmother, Sarah. The other, according to her grandmother, was Rachel Chase. Both women were attractive, their smiles radiating even through the damage that age had done to the photo.

Her grandmother had unearthed the picture the other day from one of the many stashes she had sequestered away in the old attic.

"I shouldn't even give this to you," she admonished. "It's not normal for a young girl to be so obsessed with the past. You should be going out, celebrating the end of finals, not laying around here reading letters from the dead." But then her grandmother pointed to each of the women captured within the picture.

"This here is my grandmother, Sarah. A beautiful woman." Rhea heard the pride in her grandmother's voice as the older woman stared at her own grandmother.

"She was a stylish woman in her day. And did she ever

love her hats! Custom made. Never went to church without a one-of-a-kind on top of her head. I always walked a little taller whenever I was with her. She and my grandfather sat on several boards, including a Negro savings and loan. You better believe that was a double feat for a colored woman back then. Now I'm not certain here, but I seem to recall my mother showing me this same picture one time and calling the other woman Aunt Rachel. Not that she was really my mother's aunt, just someone my mother had an affection for. Has to be the same Rachel my grandmother corresponded with."

Rhea looked at the second woman in the picture, trying to impress the image on her brain.

"Guess now you can put a face to the ghost," her grandmother echoed her thoughts before going back to the business of making breakfast.

As is often the case, reality conflicted with fantasy. For some reason, she had imagined Rachel Chase as a demure, delicate flower. But the woman in the photo was taller than she'd imagined, and even with her small waist (no doubt courtesy of a corset), she was no shrinking violet. She would have been considered "statuesque" in her day, "stacked" by today's lingo. The smile on her face was hardly demure.

"It was a shame what happened," her grandmother said almost as an afterthought as she put the several sausage patties in an iron skillet.

"What do you mean? What happened?" Rhea stopped midtrack on her trek out of the kitchen. She detected the pity in her grandmother's voice, and at that moment realized she had overlooked a very important source of information right under her nose. But she had assumed that because her grandmother never offered much about the woman who wrote the letters, she didn't know anything.

"It's strange how things start coming back to you. But I remember now how my mother once told me about her Aunt Rachel being killed. My first thought back then was that neither grandmama nor granddaddy had a sister. Then Mama showed me the picture and told me about her mother's best friend who she had loved like an auntie. Anyway, the way my mother told it, Rachel disappeared one day. At first, everyone assumed she had upped and left New York, especially since she'd lost her husband. But sometime later that winter, they found her body frozen in the East River."

Her grandmother flipped over the sausage, her recollection seemingly at an end.

"Well?" Rhea prodded, stepping closer to her grandmother. Near enough that the popping grease caught her on the wrist. She stepped back.

"Well what?" her grandmother said irritably. One of the sausage patties was smoking.

"Well, what happened to her? Did she fall in?"

"Uh, uh. Not likely, unless a corpse can drop itself into the water. Let's just say someone left her with an extra smile—on her neck."

This time Rhea stepped back in shock. Not that her grandmother ever had any subtlety. Her philosophy on death was simple: Death was death no matter how it came to you. A slit throat would be no more or less shocking than a heart attack in bed. "No one leaves this world healthy" she'd often heard her grandmother say. Still, Rhea couldn't or didn't want to fathom the beautiful woman in the picture stilled so brutally, her life robbed at the edge of a knife.

"Did they ever catch who did it?" The question came out a slight whine.

But her grandmother just shrugged. "If they did, no one told me. Could be they did. Maybe not. Who's to know? It was such a long time ago. Still, it was a pity. Such a pretty woman."

The one other thing Rhea knew about photographs: they kept the dead alive. Smiles couldn't be forgotten so readily. She knew she would see Rachel's smile in her dreams for a long time to come.

"Don't take that tone with me! I'm your mother, not your girlfriend!"

"Then act like a mother and stop snooping through my bedroom!"

"I am acting like a mother! That's what mothers do, snoop! Especially when their kids don't do like they promised!" Carmen Carvelli stood with her arms akimbo, defiance making her smooth skin look aged. But she stood behind an aegis of righteous anger that protected her from her own doubts.

"If you hadn't noticed, Ma, I'm no longer a kid!"

David paced up and down her living room like a trapped animal. Like he wanted to pounce at her. Maybe claw out her throat. But then again, she had to admit to herself that she'd gone too far this time, actually breaking into his house. If you can call using an emergency key "breaking in."

"I'm sorry, but you promised me you'd come by Friday," her tone capitulated, even if her stance didn't. "It was important, and I wasn't about to beg you."

"No, you just decided to rummage through my house, my room. For what? What were you looking for?"

Her first instinct was to lie, immediately followed by the realization that she had lied way too much already, a choice she now regretted. No, there would be no more lies. But her resolve was fading in the face of David's anger. His aura was blood red. Her hands trembled. She wanted—no, needed—a cigarette bad, real bad. She started for the kitchen, then remembered in her first half step that she had smoked her last one that morning with her coffee. She glanced longingly at the butts lying in the ashtray on her living room table before turning her eyes back to her son.

"David, do you ever have memories or strange dreams where you seem to be someone else?"

He stopped midpace and looked at her. She caught the startled look before he was able to quickly tuck it away, his angry mask back in place.

"What kind of craziness is that?" His voice was strained, the pitch off. It didn't sound like him.

"No crazier than everything I've told you in the last week. Besides, reincarnation is . . ."

". . . a whole bunch of shit that con men—or women—try to pawn off on hapless fools so they'll believe in hope past this life," he said angrily before falling hard into one of her wing-back chairs. It shook with the impact of his weight.

She sat down in an adjacent chair and said in her tone of reason, "Much like people believe in a heaven once they leave this plane. Are they hapless fools for believing there's a higher power, a better place than this?"

David said nothing, just sat there brooding like a petulant boy, looking down at the area rug. He looked almost like the ten-year-old who had always butted heads with her. Only now, he was a man, a very angry man. She didn't understand the anger. It was disproportionate to her small infraction. It couldn't be just the snooping. He'd definitely been surprised that she knew his dreams, or part of them anyway.

When he was growing up, she'd been careful not to force her theology on him. She had only made him go to church up until his thirteenth birthday when he decided definitely that he would no longer go to church. She knew that if he didn't want to believe in things beyond this world, she wasn't going to change his mind at that point. But she did believe in a higher power, just as she believed there were malevolent powers at work also. Powers that were at work now. She didn't know much about reincarnation. She'd only encountered a few souls that had returned to this earth, and they had hardly been aware of their past life, or in some cases, lives. But David's case was different. He was having memories, and they were starting to manifest in dreams. What worried her was that they weren't going to stay confined to the safety of those dreams.

Because sitting in her chair right now, she saw a soul going through a metamorphosis. What was scarier, David was becoming someone she didn't know, someone volatile, someone in emotional pain.

She wanted to touch him, to comfort him, to read him, to

pick up something so she could stave off the calamity she was sure would happen.

Instead she asked, "David, don't you believe in anything?"

Just as quickly, the red began to waver, the anger to seep from the planes of his face. As he thought about the question, he seemed almost lost as he shook his head. "I believe in you, Ma. That you have a gift. I believe that there's good in the world. But I know there's a whole lot of evil to go up against that good. And there's always love."

A slight green softened the red, began pushing it away.

A small smile played at her lips. "Are you in love, David?"

Finally, he looked up at her, and said hesitatingly, "I don't know. I don't know what this is. It's so much that I think it's going to drive me crazy."

Carmen Carvelli realized at that moment that there was another piece of the conundrum that had just settled into place.

"Tell me about her, David."

New York—August 1879

Until he saw the hansom pull up outside the boarding room he'd let for the afternoon, Joseph wasn't sure she would come. Both of them had much to lose by this rendezvous. Yet neither of them seemed able to overcome what had taken possession of them both. If love could split open a heart, his had already been rived in two. He looked around the room, regretted its despair. The only thing to temper the ugliness was a yellow rose he had placed in a glass vase on top of an old bureau.

As he watched Rachel from the upper window, a doubt blazed, telling him that she would not take the stairs leading to the building. That she would not knock on the door to this room. That she would reenter the cab and leave this place and his life forever.

His heart leapt as she ascended to the building's entrance

and was let in by the proprietor. Finally, the knock on his own door came and he hastened to answer in case she should change her mind and decide to turn away.

All reservations fled as he saw her standing there, lovely and vulnerable. Her eyes were hesitant, but there was desire there also. He pulled her into the room, pulled her to him, found her lips. They opened softly, eagerly.

He stopped, catching his breath. "Are you sure?" he asked, hoping not to hear anything other than yes.

"I would not be here if I had any doubts." But then she smiled guiltily. "To be honest, I might have some. I just don't hear them as well as I used to." She was breathless, and he didn't know whether it was due to nervousness or desire. Or maybe fear. There could be unwanted consequences.

"I have a rubber shield for . . ." he started, then noticing the lowering of her eyes, realized she didn't want to hear the rude aspects of what they were about to do.

"Thank you," she said, and this barely above a whisper. He held her again.

"I love you, Rachel," he breathed into her hair, his fingers tangling in the coils. Only when the words had left his lips did he realize that he had never said this to anyone. Not to his mother, never to his father. At least he had loved his mother, in a fashion, although she had not returned the affection. Not really. He had only been a link in the chain binding her to her prison.

"I don't think I've ever felt anything like this before. It's wonderful."

She was silent for a moment, as though she had to think of a response. For that interminable second, his heart froze, as he wondered if he were truly alone, even with her standing here in front of him. That he had grown up without affection, he had long come to terms with. That this might be so for the rest of his life, he could not fathom. To love and to have it returned was something that he had only hoped for. He had waited for the woman whose soul would reach out to his, through touch or word. And she was standing here with him now.

Please love me, he pleaded silently.

Her eyes gave him his answer and he allowed himself to breathe again.

She began unbuttoning her dress jacket. He barely registered an impression of lilac trimmed with a darker hue, his senses too heady to care about sartorial details. A white shift fell to the floor. He helped her out of the full skirt, her bustle and bindings until she stood wonderfully naked before him. There was no bashfulness, no feminine coyness, just a trust that was openly given.

As he touched her, he wondered how skin could be dark yet so soft. Until this moment, he had only thought that a virtue of white flesh. But as he buried his face in her bared breasts, he knew this was not so. Her moan was the sound of angels.

He shed the rest of their clothes and carried her to the bed, a pallet really. But it would do.

He laid her down gently. Emboldened by the desire in her eyes, he began exploring all of her contours with hands, mouth, tongue, his touch causing her to sigh, moan or, at times, softly laugh. The savor and smell of her drove him on, making him desperate to consume all of her. Slowly he moved his lips down the taut, soft stomach, farther down still until he found her creamy moisture. He tasted her and she gasped. He realized then that despite years of marriage, she was still innocent to much of lovemaking. He welcomed the opportunity to teach her.

He moved his tongue inside her, around the walls of her sex, inhaling the pungency, loving its flavor. She clutched his head, pushed him farther into her wet mound until he would have blissfully drowned. Not wanting her to come just then, he pushed against the force of her hand, released himself, his face wet with her moisture, loving her obvious desire for him.

He shifted, and with his fingers began stroking the orb of pleasure he'd learned about in the arms of an older and experienced lover, a friend of his mother's who had eagerly schooled him in the craft of lovemaking when he was fifteen. Since his introduction, only on rare occasions had he truly cared about his partner's total pleasure; if his lover happened to find satisfaction, it was usually secondary to his own. With Rachel, though, he wanted her to know every facet of delight that he could bring her.

His mouth followed a trail upward until they touched on the delicate curves of her breasts. He took a nipple into his mouth, tenderly bit it while his fingers sinuously moved into the folds of her other lips that were moist and hot to his touch. Rachel moaned as his fingers entered her, as her wellspring sucked him in eagerly. He moved his mouth up, gathered her mouth into his, stifling her moans as he trailed his tongue along her own, as his thumb circled the swollen nub of flesh between her thighs, as his other fingers increased their pace, in and out, in and out, until she began to tremble as though in a fit of ague. Her hips swayed upward, unencumbered by shame, abandoned to the ecstasy he was bringing.

His fingers rapidly moved in and out, driving her onward until he felt a shudder go through her. She gasped with her orgasm, mouth opened, eyes half lidded. He had never seen anything so sensuous.

Ready, he shifted his body over her, heard an intake of breath as he entered, a possession so sweet he froze a second to weigh the look of pleasure on her face, a look he hoped to see for the rest of his life. He began a motion, found a rhythm, moving her hips and thighs along with his to a measure, a pace that mimicked their initial dance, first slow, slow, then moving faster, quicker, a heady race seeking a final denouement. His thrusts became desperate as he sought to go even deeper. She groaned and wrapped her thighs tightly around his back, letting him possess her totally. The pallet shook with their pulse, banged the wall, the floor.

A violent shudder snaked through her body, vibrated through his own. She grasped his shoulders, her fingernails biting through his flesh until the explosive quake ebbed to just a tremor. She gasped for air.

He buried his face in the nape of her throat, closed out the world as he inhaled her scent. Still buried deep within her, he slowed his motion, waiting for her to recover so that he could bring her again.

He heard her breaths slow, knew she was ready.

He pushed deeper into her, heard her gasp again. Driven like a madman, he could not stop as he pounded, plunged, and plundered, his lips devouring her mouth, her face, every inch of flesh his mouth could reach.

The blood rushed to his head, and his heartbeats drowned out every other sound. Eyes half closed, he watched her mouth form a perfect "O," knew she was coming again. Between the whirring of sound in his ears and the gales of his own breath, he heard her scream his name, heard her declare her love in a strangled cry.

Her ecstasy brought forth his own. His body trembled as his seed threatened to overflow the protection shielding her. And for that moment, he regretted the piece of rubber, wishing he could fill her with a child that would be all their own. Heady with his orgasm, he yelled her name and the sound of it reverberated to the cracked ceiling of the room, bounced off the unpainted wood walls. The shaking floor caused the vase with the yellow rose to topple off the bureau. It shattered against the wood floorboards.

"Shut it up, up thar!" They heard a thump beneath them. The landlady was hitting the ceiling with something, probably a broomstick. The anger in her voice shook them from their haze. Looking at each other, they suddenly broke into laughter. He held her body tightly against his, both sweaty and exhausted, until their mirth was spent.

For a long while, they lay together, no words exchanged, none needed for those moments. But all too soon, it was time for her to go. He found that he could barely stand the thought of her leaving.

He held her hand as she moved to rise from the bed. "Promise you'll see me again."

She hesitated too long. Her eyes glittered as though she were near tears.

"Joseph, this was wonderful, but . . . it can't go on. This . . . today . . . cannot happen again. There are too many eyes and ears on me. If we were discovered, I wouldn't be able to hold my head up ever again, nor show my face to my friends . . . or my brother. I am so grateful for today, you cannot know how much. You've shown me that life is still in me, something I thought was gone for good. And most of all, you've made me remember love."

He stood, held her. "We can find a way to be together . . . to make love again."

She pushed him away, her expression wounded. "Is this all you want then?"

He shook his head. "No, you know I want more than this."

"But what then, Joseph? What can we possibly have here together? There aren't many places we can live as man and wife."

"There are places . . ." he pondered quickly, feeling her slipping away. "In Europe, Paris maybe. We . . . we could go there."

"And would you leave all of your wealth and family behind?"

"Trust me Rachel, I have no reason to stay on these shores. If I can have you with me somewhere else, then that is the place where I want to be. But can you leave your brother, your world, and be with me forever?"

When she lowered her head and said nothing, his heart contracted. She dressed, refusing to answer his persistent requests.

She finally stood at the door, and he thought that he had lost her for good.

Before she opened the door, though, she turned to him. "I'll . . . see you again."

Her voice sounded so mournful, he wasn't sure that she was glad of it.

Then she opened the door and was gone.

Chapter 20

Tyne parked her car in a lot filled with trucks, Volvos, and sedans. As she got out, an overwhelming stench of rubber flayed her lungs, causing her to cough. She noticed two Beamers and a Benz in the reserved area. Management, no doubt. Webber's main office, factory, and ancillary buildings occupied an entire expanse for miles. To the east were a few industrial plants, including a petroleum refinery and a smelting plant, most of which were closed down due to a series of economic slumps. But Webber Tires was still trudging on, if not exactly flourishing.

Tyne didn't expect much of an interview. She had only made the call as a matter of journalistic courtesy, more than half expecting to be refused, and was surprised when she was not. Alexander Webber had even sounded downright jovial when she called. "Sure, sure thing. I welcome the opportunity to clear things up. How's Tuesday for you?" They scheduled to meet at nine the next day.

She was wearing Hush Puppies low-heeled pumps this time. She needed the extra comfort to offset what would likely be a very tense interview, despite the owner's seeming acquiescence. She fully expected to be bullshitted, to have to wade deep in defensive rhetoric, but that was OK, she was ready. She would let them have their paragraph; the real story was the community and its residents.

She followed the shrubby path leading to the front of the red brick building. A glass door didn't ameliorate the dingy

ugliness of the facade, which was exacerbated by the surrounding gray adjuncts whose large smokestacks belched out
gloomy, grayish black plumes. The whole picture was de-
pressing. As was the sunless sky peering darkly upon the con-
crete landscaping. Not exactly Dickensian, but definitely not
corporate modern chic.

Through the glass doors, a few feet ahead, she found the
bare bones reception area that fronted a cubicle network.
The blonde sitting at the desk was bleached, starched, and
rouged, but nothing could mask the wear of time. Crows' feet
defied the pink pearl lipstick, and brown-gray roots stood
starkly against the strawberry blond frizz. Tyne imagined that
the woman had sat in that same chair for decades with no expectation or desire other than bringing home a biweekly check
and relaxing each night at her local bar. Tyne noticed the
ringless finger. Either dearth, death or divorce. Or alternative
lifestyle.

"Yes, whom do you wish to see?" The diction was overly
precise.

"I have a nine o'clock appointment with Mr. Webber. The
name's Tyne Jensen from *Elan* magazine."

The woman brightened. "Oh, yes, he's expecting you."
The woman buzzed the intercom, picked up the phone, and
announced Tyne, her head bobbing. She hung up.

"Right this way." The receptionist rose from her seat, the
action hitching an already short, hot pink leather skirt up
fleshy, varicosed thighs. Tyne heard the swish of nylon rub-
bing together as the woman led her through a maze of inter-
connecting cubicles where mostly women sat entering data
on prehistoric looking computers. Tyne was briefly reminded
of her years at the *Clarion*. The same office ghetto peopled by
underappreciated females. In this case, all white. The receptionist stopped at an office along the southwest wall. Inside,
a fiftyish-looking man sat at an oversized cherry wood desk
adorned with two gold pens upright in an embossed stand.
Standard office gear that usually only impressed the owner.
The gold nameplate with black lettering read ALEXANDER

WEBBER. He had been scribbling something with an ordinary Bic pen on a pad, but looked up on cue as the receptionist entered. Tyne had the feeling that the "busy owner" scenario had been staged for her benefit. The receptionist left them alone.

Webber rose and came around the desk, his right hand extended. "Ms. Jensen." He shook her hand with two hearty shakes. "Glad to meet you. Please, have a seat. Would you care for a cup of coffee, or tea perhaps? I believe we have herbal."

Tyne shook her head. "No, no thank you. And again, thank you for your time. This shouldn't take too long. I just need to ask a few questions to clear up some points on the story I'm doing. I'm going to record for accuracy," she said as she took out a small recorder from her bag and turned it on.

"Yes, yes," he said smiling. "I understand that there've been a few unfortunate incidents with a couple of our drivers. And before you get to your questions, let me just say that those drivers have been severely reprimanded. We here at Webber are dedicated to environmental safety and would never knowingly jeopardize the comfort or safety of our neighbors."

Tyne shifted in her seat. "That's good to know, Mr. Webber. But, correct me if I'm wrong, this isn't the first time your company has been cited for illegal dumping. I checked the EPA's records on Webber Tires, and found at least five earlier infractions."

Webber shook his head, the smile gone. "Those were trumped-up allegations," he said sternly. "There was never any connection to us."

"But the old tires found dumped had your brand on them."

Webber sat forward, his blue eyes lucent spheres surrounding small dots hardly amounting to pupils. "Let me tell you something about how vicious this business can get. Yes, those tires had our name on them. But anyone could have bought those tires at any auto body shop. We distribute to

many places, Ms. Jensen. Now, I'll admit that these latest incidents were our doing, and I've taken care of the matter. But
there's no way I'm going to admit to any wrongdoing that
someone else has been throwing off on us. After all, it's my
family's name on this business."

Tyne heard the shake in his voice, and knew that she had a
potential powder keg here. She'd run into his kind before,
pleasant so long as you stuck with "soft" questions that didn't
ruffle or threaten to make them look less than saintly. She
wasn't about to buy into some convoluted conspiracy theory
that defied reason.

"Why would anyone want to frame you for illegal dumping? What's to be gained?"

He shook his head at her like she was woefully naïve.
"Competition in a niche industry gets ugly in a shaky economy. If Webber accrued enough violations, we might be
forced to shut down, which would make our competitors
very happy, considering Webber is the forerunner manufac-
turer of tires in the Midwest."

"But, Mr. Webber, someone outside the industry would
still say that it was more likely that it was one or more of
your employees who was responsible. What makes you so
certain that it wasn't one of your employees?"

He leaned forward, his fingers templed. "Because on those
dates we supposedly 'dumped,' I had no drivers out."

"How convenient," Tyne said, keeping her voice neutral.

He leaned back, the smile reappearing. "Yes, convenient.
But true. And make sure you put that in the article."

Tyne was already editing the information in her head. At
least, he'd admitted to the current dumping. She would put
his theory in the story and let the readers decide if that on five
occasions someone set Webber up.

"So, I'm assuming there'll be no more dumping in the
Roseland community."

"You can rest assured that there'll be no more problems
from us." He smiled the benevolent smile of an angel.

Tyne figured that smile hid a whole lot of sins, but she didn't have the time or resources to do much digging. She got little else from him, not even the names of the offending drivers.

Twenty minutes later, she barely responded to the cheerful good-bye from Ms. Bleached and Rouged as she exited the building.

"I hate when I'm being lied to," Tyne said between bites of spiced coleslaw. She had already torn through a serving of rib tips that left her fingers stained with Ruby's special ginger BBQ sauce. Her sisters sat in the other chair of a corner booth a few feet from the door, their usual place at Ruby's Original Soul Food. It was busy for a Wednesday evening, but that was how good the food was.

"Well, what did you expect him to say?" Tanya asked, licking sauce from her own fingers, then mimicked, "Oh, yes Ms. Reporter, I did the dirt and I'm gonna keep on doing it, too."

April, the newlywed glow still apparent on her face, chuckled. "I'm with Tanya. He was hardly going to admit more than what it took to keep the egg off his face. Sounds like he was playing you from the start. You know, admit only so much to appear cooperative, but then stonewall on the rest."

Tyne nodded. "That's OK. He sounded like an idiot, and I'm expecting my readers to see through that whole smoke-screen. Anyway, at least I'm getting somewhere on the article. I've interviewed most of the neighbors and there are some pretty good stories there."

"OK, on to something juicier," Tanya said, her eyes mischievous. "How's it going with Mr. White and Wonderful?"

Tyne nearly choked on her bite of baked beans. She peered around at the surrounding tables, but folks were busy chowing down. She didn't want ears pricking, listening to her business.

"Oh, please say that a little louder." Tyne threw daggers at her sister. "I don't think the next table heard you."

"Well, if you're ashamed of your doings . . ." Tanya smiled. "Sooo, how much doing have you been doing, anyway? Can we talk baseball parlance with bases, or—no, let's do football. Any touchdowns?"

"Yeah, do tell," a smiling April interjected. "I want to hear about someone else's sex life for a change. Y'all been harping on mine long enough."

Tyne laid down her fork, her hunger taking an unexpected hiatus. The other Friday was—hell, she didn't know what it was. A dalliance? A moment of insanity? And the long phone call they had had the night after where they had revealed so much? She thought they'd really connected that night, more so than when they had connected sexually. Which made the weeklong silence painful. She'd even left a message on his machine, but no word since, not a call or a note. Hell, not a greeting card even just to say "Hi." She didn't want to admit to her sisters that she was starting to feel used, stupid even. That he had left her longing for him, had touched her in a way she hadn't experienced before. But she didn't want to hold on to this feeling anymore. She wanted to throw away the disappointment and get on with her life.

"Yes, there was a touchdown, as you so metaphorically put it. Last Friday. But it seems it's going to be the only score, so I'd rather not talk about it."

Tanya's eyes cut stone. "The mo-fo hasn't called? Sheesh, I hate to say this . . ."

"Then don't. I'm already kicking my own ass for not picking up the signals. Of course, it was going too fast, and it was just too intense."

April shook her head. Another no vote. "Don't ever let someone use you. I know you know this already, but you're worth better than that. At least, that's what I remember a couple of sisters telling me. 'Hold out for the best' they said, and I finally heard them. And I thank both of you. So now it's my turn to give out some advice. Don't walk down my road. I don't care if he is a friend of a friend. I have a good mind to call Sherry and tell her . . ."

"Don't you dare!" Tyne warned. "We're talking about my job here, OK? And it's not her business anyway."

"Look, we're not going to beat you up about this," Tanya said. "We just don't want you getting hurt. If he's already acting like a dick, just leave him alone, I don't care how cute he is."

"Yeah, he is cute," Tyne said underneath her breath. "Man of my dreams."

"What was that?" Tanya asked.

"Nothing. I guess I'm meant to be alone."

"Bullshit," April said. Both sisters looked at their younger sibling with raised eyebrows. She wasn't usually given to cuss words.

"Whaat?" she looked back at them. "It is bullshit. Because Tyne, you know you're a beautiful, intelligent woman, so stop acting like you're the wallflower no one wants. Now, question—was the sex good, at least?"

The smile bloomed before she could stop it. She had re-lived that night every night since. He wasn't in her dreams anymore. He was in her skin, her blood. She remembered his smell, their smell. She remembered how their merging nearly ripped her soul, and tore her body with pleasure.

"Oh yeah, it was good, if that smile's any indication," Tanya said. "Well, at least you got you some. Finally an end to the drought. That's what you got to do, put it in perspective. It was sex, nothing else."

Tyne nodded. "Yeah, it was just sex. Nothing more," she mimicked her sister's words, a smile plastered on her face. But there was that ache inside, because even in the short time she'd known him, it had seemed much more than that. Damn, how had she let herself get hurt again?

Chapter 21

David sat at his desk looking at the signatures on the Declaration of Dissolution of Partnership. The black ink glared, each stroke a mark against him. Yeah, he'd expected Clarence to walk. That wasn't a big surprise, as he had given his notice a couple of weeks ago. This just made it official. What threw him was Rick's signature on the line beneath Clarence's. Not that he hadn't anticipated that Rick might make that move sooner or later, but anticipation is one thing, reality another. Rick hadn't even bothered to notify him beforehand. He felt as though someone had lobbed into his guts at full speed. Rick had weighed friendships, both his and Clarence's, and had decided that Clarence's was worth more.

David started to crumple the paper, then stopped. It was a formal document that would have to be filed away for record. Just as he would file away his severed partnerships, and, in Rick's case, a friendship. He laid the document on the desk and as his hands smoothed over the crinkled paper, his mind tried to fathom how everything had unraveled so quickly. Especially with Rick.

He and Rick went back nearly seven years. They had met as competitors bidding on a municipal water project for their respective firms, and in the end, Rick's firm got the project. Still, David admired Rick's savvy, a combination of salesman glitz and statesman tact which he used to good stead when dealing with the city politicos. Rick once said, "It's not who you know, but who you don't. When you figure that out, that's where you focus." And Rick had gone through otherwise closed doors, garnering favors and later, contracts.

Rick once told David that it was David's obvious talent and innate ability to assess a client's unspoken—and sometimes unknown—need that made him think they should combine forces. They had started out as two, and then had brought Clarence on board shortly after. Even then, David had been wary. In too many circles, Clarence Debbs was labeled a recalcitrant self-aggrandizer, but Rick had assured David that those were sour grapes. David knew that racism pegged a lot of black architects as hard to work with or incompetent. And Clarence had proved his competency and superiority fast enough.

But like the saying, "where's there's smoke . . ." within a year or two, certain things began to confirm that the wagging tongues knew what they were talking about. Clarence slowly began to show another side to his professionalism. Like his bulldogging for projects that he was always too reticent about, jealously guarding important details from him and Rick. Then there was his making unilateral decisions that contradicted prior agreements between the partners. David had put up with it because of Rick's incessant excuses. But the main reason was always that Clarence could take away their clients.

"Clarence knows a lot of people. We need that network, man, because if Clar decides to walk, you can bet we lose half our client base and goodwill," Rick had said on more than one occasion.

The thought made his fingers form a half fist. Well, Clar was walking, and Rick was walking right along with him. Fine. Damn it, it was going to have to be fine, because he was on his fucking own right now.

He would have to make calls to their clients, let them know where things stood and gauge which ones might stay with him. He sighed. Most of these clients had been brought in by either Rick or Clar. In the end, most likely they would

go with them, no matter how much damage control David
tried to do.

He felt the nerve drumming in his temple above his right
eye. It did that whenever he was stressed. He needed to get
out of here. The office, big as it was, was too confining right
now.

Even as he grabbed his suit jacket from the coat stand, he
knew where he was heading. Debbie told him earlier that
Rick had called to say he wouldn't be in. David had a good
idea where his turncoat partner was sitting right now, even
this early.

He left instructions with Debbie to tell anyone calling that
he would be out for most of the morning, then headed for the
elevator that led down to the underground garage. Within
minutes, he was in his car headed up Michigan Avenue. Even
at just past ten, the shoppers were out in full force. July was
a heavy tourist month with lots of pedestrian traffic on
North Michigan because of the upscale stores. He continued
north on Lake Shore Drive, until he got to Fullerton and then
turned right onto north Lincoln. Soon, he was at his destination. It took less than ten minutes. He lucked out as a car
pulled out of a parking space just as he pulled up.

He got out, spotted Rick's red Jaguar parked a couple of
cars down. The meter flag was down, signaling he would be
in there for a while.

Over the doors hung the familiar white sign emblazoned
with a red lion crest. The Red Lion was a gambling hall in
the 1930s, but its main claim to fame was that it sat across
from the Biograph Theater where John Dillinger was gunned
down. Just inside the worn wooden doors was a diligent re-
creation of an English pub, right down to the cozy fireplace
and wooden tables along the wall. On the television the
black-and-white image of Peter Sellers played on the screen.
David recognized the movie—one of his least favorites, *Dr.
Strangelove.*

This was Rick's main haunt, the place he came to unwind.

David had never figured out why. The crowd here was more into discussions of literature and politics; Rick was more into sports and women. Still, the place had a little something for everybody. David sometimes came for their Red Light nights where aspiring writers read erotic prose.

The sun filtered starkly through the windows, illuminating everything in a whitish-yellow tinge. He spotted Rick sitting by himself at one of the tables farthest from the bar. He was nursing a mug of beer, his face half turned to the wall. He was wearing his Yale University T-shirt and jeans. He must have sensed something, because he looked up just as David walked up to the table. The man flinched.

David stood looking down at his friend—soon to be former—with whom he had shared many intimate conversations. To whom he had told a lot of secrets. But right now he was looking at a stranger. Maybe he had never known the man at all. He saw the fear in Rick's eyes.

"What's the matter, Rick? Not glad to see me?" David slid into the opposite chair.

"Should've known you'd come looking for me." Rick took a sip of beer. "And you don't need to tell me what I did was fucked up. I know it, man, I know it." He sounded defeated by his conscience.

"Then why?" David asked as a waitress started to walk up to him. He shook his head, and she stopped midstride and turned to go back to the bar. "This has to be the lowest stunt you've ever pulled, and believe me, I've been around to see a lot of the shit you've done. So, no honor among partners anymore? The least you could've done was let me know before the final papers came. I deserved that much respect. Even Clarence gave me that bit of nothing."

Rick shut his eyes, opened them. "It's not about you, man. It's simply business. When I realized Clarence was going to take nearly everybody, including the clients I brought in . . . man, he's been working us from day one. So what was I supposed to do? Especially when Clarence offered me a copartnership in the firm he's starting up. If it wasn't for the bills . . . Man, I just bought Melinda an engagement ring the other week. Three carats. It put me back almost five thou. I'm sorry, Dave, but I have a future to plan for, and I've got to go where my money's going."

David's pulse was racing, and he fought to control his voice. When he spoke, he sounded almost neutral. "And you didn't have faith in the two of us to keep it going . . . like we did before Clarence even signed on. Let's face it, I'm the talent behind the business. You and Clarence barely have the vision to put a couple of Lego buildings together."

Rick had been avoiding eye contact, but now he looked at David, his initial remorse no longer visible. "You're full of it, David. You know that? You try to make it seem that the only problem is Clar, but in these past weeks, hell, months even, things have been going on with you, and you haven't even bothered to be straight with me. I don't know if you've got some emotional shit you're dealing with . . . but you've been more than distracted lately. I tried to bring it up, but you never wanted to talk about it. Yeah, you've got the talent, but you've lost the drive, and I don't know when it left you, but, man, from what I'm looking at, it's gone. Ask yourself, do you even want to be in your own business? And be honest with yourself, if not with me."

The veins were popping in David's head. "What the fuck do you think I've been doing for the past three years? Playing? Of course, I want to be in business!" his voice rose a decibel level, causing two men sitting at the bar to look over their shoulders at them. "You talk about your bills. What do you think your little stunt's going to do to me? It's going to pull me under. Did you even think about that?"

Rick slowly shook his head. "Maybe not. Look, I'm sorry, and I know that's not worth much of anything right now. Maybe I can talk to Clar. . ."

"Don't bother." He stood abruptly, causing the chair to scrape against the old, wooden floor. "Just let me know what I've got to do to bring this farce to an end. You know where to reach me. I'll be in *my* office. I expect you and Clarence to clear your shit out of my space by the end of the week. I'm going to be headhunting for some newer heads. Hopefully, these'll be attached to bodies with souls in them."

He left Rick sitting there, his glass mug half full, his eyes mournful. The sun was warm and welcoming. It didn't do him one damn bit of good. It might as well have been raining.

Back in the car, David didn't know where to go. He didn't feel like going back to the office. The same office he would probably have to move out of in a matter of months if he couldn't find someone else to help with the expenses. He definitely didn't feel like going home.

In the past, whenever he was this unfocused, he would get on the phone to Sherry. But now he was thinking of someone else. He reached for his cell phone, stopped. She would wonder why he hadn't called her back. And what could he tell her? *"I had this dream of you dead, with me standing over you, and when I woke up, I had blood on my hand."* Most likely she would think he was nuts.

But he needed to see her. Had to. He started his car, and turned into the traffic heading back south.

Tyne sat looking at the proofs Carole, the production manager, had left on her desk. The article read very well, and the photo of Regina Stewart and her children juxtaposed against the picture of the dumping ground was visually effective. She was about to buzz Carole when a movement in her doorway made her look up. She expected to see Carole or maybe Sherry. But it was neither.

"Hey . . . I mean how . . . ?" she stuttered, taken by surprise at the pleasure of seeing him, then angry at herself for that pleasure. But he stood there looking so good, and she wanted so much to be wrapped in those arms "So, what makes you drop in? Looking for a booty call?"

She saw the wince. He stepped all the way in. It might have been her imagination, but he seemed taller and older. Definitely troubled.

"I deserve that, I do," he said wearily.

"So, why're you here? I haven't forgotten a date we made, have I? Oh, no, that's right. 'cause how could there be a date when there hasn't been any more calls or contact, period. Look, I wasn't looking for a relationship, but I was certainly expecting some respect."

"And you have it," he conceded, then walked over to take one of the seats facing her desk. "My not calling hasn't anything to do with you. I've been going through some shi . . . stuff, and it's been . . . I mean, I've been . . ."

"Busy?" she filled in.

He nodded. "Pretty much."

"Well, I'm busy now, so thanks for dropping by, but I've got to get back to work." She picked up the proofs again, went through the motions of reading, her eyes unseeing, her pulse racing. But he still sat there, refusing to take the cue.

She looked up, found him staring at her, his green eyes unreadable. No, not exactly unreadable. She let herself forget her anger, even her desire. She let herself see him, and saw just the edges of his pain. She saw it in those eyes, in the stiff jawline, as though he had to clench his jaws to hold something back. No, this wasn't about her.

She sighed. "Tell me what's going on."

His eyes flickered, and he sat back, his body wilting slightly.

"There's been some problems with my business."

"Like what?"

And he told her. Quietly. Not a placid calm, or a defeated peace. But a slow simmering stillness before the hurricane. She saw the way he flexed his fingers, how they settled into a fist, relaxed, only to flex again. She understood the anger. Betrayal was soul-cutting, heart-searing, especially from a friend. She already hated the unseen, unknown Rick. With the thought, she analyzed that she felt deeply enough to resent those who hurt him, as though it were her obligation to keep harm away from him. But that was the duty of a lover in love. What was she, exactly? They had slept together only once. When she had awakened next to him following hours of vigorous lovemaking, she had spied on the stranger as he slept and wondered how long it would take to get to know him.

She didn't know what to say, so she asked, "Are you a good architect?"

"You've seen an example of my work. What do you think?"

There was a spark in that question, and she smiled. "I think you are very talented, but then again, you know that. I also think you're going to survive this setback. In another few years, you won't even remember the asses you worked with. And I really think you're underestimating your sales-manship. After all, you sold me on you, and trust me, I'm not an easy sell."

He laughed. She liked the sound of it and the crinkling around his eyes. But then the laughter petered out. The way he stared at her now was too intense.

"I wanted to see you. I let things keep me away. It won't happen again."

"Whoa," she laughed nervously. "You don't need to pledge your troth." She couldn't explain her desire to back away, physically, emotionally. Suddenly, it was like the space around her had contracted, and was slowly closing in around her. The feeling was inexplicable.

"Let's start again," he continued. "Let me cook you dinner tonight . . . that is, if you don't have any plans."

She didn't. But for a second she didn't want him to know that. She knew she was being ridiculous. She'd have dinner with him, with some reservation.

"All right—depending on two things, though."

His left eyebrow shot up. His smile was wicked. A good look on him. Her pulse quickened.

"And what's that?" The smile was in his voice.

"Well, of course, the menu."

He leaned forward, said seductively, "Just tell me what you want."

Things stirred, not the least her crotch. How could the man make her moist just with his voice?

"I just want something light, maybe a salad. . . ."

"Uh uhn," he shook his head. 'No rabbit food, at least not for the main course. You like halibut?"

"Yes," she said, resting her chin in her hand.

"Then I'll pick up a pound. Do you like pasta?"

She wondered if the man always needed to be in control. Still, she felt her smile widening.

"Yes, I like pasta. What about elbow macaroni?"

"Yeah, we could do that. Or we could do better. Ever had pasta ramone?"

She shook her head. "Well," he said, "it's linguini tossed with sauteed garlic, black olives, fresh basil, proscuitto, and tomatoes . . . I can promise you I'll make it as good as possible."

His eyes were hooded as he talked, as though recounting the ingredients was a seductive experience for him. She would never hear the word "linguini" again without thinking of how the sound of it could purr from a man's lips.

"Sounds good," she said weakly. Her temperature shot up a degree or two.

"So, what was the second condition?" he asked.

"Huh?" Then she remembered and reluctantly said, "No sex."

She saw him try to hide his shock, but he said, "Sure, OK. I don't want to rush anything."

Now she felt defensive. "I mean, we went a little fast last time. I think we need to pull back a little."

"Sure, sure," he agreed distractedly, the nod of his head not enthusiastic at all.

"I just want to go slow this time, OK?"

"Ok," he said in capitulation. "OK. That's fine, no sex. Until when?"

She smiled. "We'll play it by ear."

Chapter 22

Inner resolve is a true possibility when temptation isn't within sight. Like that last piece of chocolate cheesecake with chocolate shavings; that last cigarette; that half-filled glass of Chianti . . . or the well-defined abs of a man who's had to take his shirt off because he spilled marinara sauce on it. Not deliberately. Accidents happen. At the sight of hard muscles, resolve flies right out the window and throws a smirk over its wing.

Part of it was her fault. She'd offered him a shoulder rub, because during the meal he had seemed tense, and she'd suspected that his mind was still on the occurrences of the day. After dessert, he sat in one of the winged chairs in the living room while she stood over him. Even though he had put on a clean shirt, she could feel every tendon through the material, the image of his naked torso playing in her mind as her fingers kneaded the taut muscles.

As he started to relax, he leaned back to rest his head on her stomach. The lights were at half-dim. Neither of them was playing fair. Especially when a hand reached up to caress her cheek.

"Stop it," she whispered.

He seemed to realize he was breaking a promise, because the hand went down, and he said, "I'm sorry." But his head remained on her stomach, his eyes shut.

From her vantage, she could see the shadow of hair on his chest. She remembered how soft it felt, feathery, like down.

Instinctively, and against her conscious will, her hand moved to touch the bare flesh below his throat. She heard the intake of breath, felt the pulse at his throat speed up.

She told herself to stop, but there was the throbbing between her legs that was calling attention to itself. It made her realize she had lied. When she told him she wanted to take it slow, she had meant it. Then. But that declaration seemed a million moments ago, before her fingers touched him again, felt the heat of his flesh melding with her own.

He bent to kiss her wrist, and the touch of his lips was the catalyst she needed. The permission to betray herself again.

She pulled her hands away, and he looked up like a child whose treat had been cruelly snatched away. She smiled and circled him. Then slowly she lowered herself to her knees, reached over, unbelted and unbuttoned his pants. Slowly, pulled down the zipper.

"But I thought you wanted . . ." he started.

"That's what I thought I wanted." She released him from his constraints. "But right now, this is what I want." She took him into her mouth.

She heard an intake of breath, then a moan that seemed to reverberate through the rafters of the room. She felt the muscles of his thighs tighten beneath her hands, relax, tighten again. Her tongue circled the furrowed flesh, running rings around the natural grooves. She tasted him, realized that she liked it. Liked the tang of the moisture leaking from him. And the strangled animal groans her ministrations elicited.

There were pauses in his breathing, followed by strained exhalations. Then a sudden weight of a hand on the back of her head, guiding her. She took his cue, began sucking with a pressure that drew him farther inside her mouth. Yet there was more of him than she could hold.

He was moments from coming. She could feel the trembling in his limbs. But suddenly he pushed her away, disgorging his member from her mouth with the motion.

He shook his head. "No, not yet," he said breathlessly. "Why don't you join me?" Before she could answer, he stood up, pulling her up with him, and began unbuttoning her blouse, almost tearing the seed pearls in the process. The silk slid from her skin and fell to the floor in a languid pool of golden-brown. He hooked eager fingers beneath her bra straps, wrenched them down. Within seconds, she was naked from the waist up, and the current in the room, as well as the excitement of the moment, teased her nipples into hard pebbles. His fingers gently grazed them, then he grazed each with his tongue. Her knees buckled.

"How far do you want to go?" he breathed. "Because I don't want you to do this just for me."

Her answer was to reach for the button of his shirt, then stare into those green, almost hazel eyes. "I'm not doing this for you. I'm being totally selfish. I want you . . . your body . . ." She pushed the shirt over his shoulders, yanked it down his arms.

"Hey, what about my mind?" he grinned.

She smiled. "Some other time. Right now, nature calls."

They undressed each other quickly, and as they stood naked, his eyes roamed the landscape of her body with undeniable appreciation. Then without ceremony, he pulled her to the floor on top of him so abruptly that she let out an "oomph." His hands gripped the plump cheeks of her ass, began kneading the soft flesh. She felt his hardened penis against her stomach and began moving against it, causing him to inhale sharply. His hands soon stopped their kneading and replaced the touch with soft, whispery caresses that caused her crotch to contract with spasms. One of his fingers played along her crevice as his lips grabbed hers and began licking them. His finger moved to the delicate wall dividing both entryways, moved past the moist canal, up to her clitoris, started teasing her orb just as his tongue began playing along hers. She ground her pelvis against him, desperately claiming her own pleasure, listening to the symphony of quickly pumping blood and intertwined breaths playing in her ears.

He guided her onto his shaft. Holding her hips, he moved

her up, down, in an achingly slow and steady pace that was thrilling and killing, for right now she thought she could die with the pleasure of it, the way he filled her, sated her. She felt her eyes go back into her head. She had heard about this phenomenon from other bragging women, and had thought they were doing just that—bragging. But now she knew how it could happen.

"Ooooh, fuck," she moaned.

"My thoughts exactly," he whispered back and with a deft motion, changed their positions until he was on top of her. Straddled on his elbows, he quickened his thrusting, causing a friction that drove her to a climax she couldn't stop. Her inner walls throbbed against the invading hardness, and she drew in shallow breaths as her lungs seemed to shatter with the rest of her body.

She put her arms around his waist and wrapped her legs around his firm thighs. His body had the first sheen of perspiration. She stroked along the dampness of his skin, then reciprocated the ass affection with gentle strokes along his cheeks.

"I want . . . I want . . ." he exerted but couldn't seem to finish the sentence. Instead, he placed his mouth over hers until she was able to pull his ragged breaths into her needy lungs. The wave that washed over her once had hardly ebbed away before it began building again. Now his pace was frantic, his hips pounding her body into the carpeting, almost through the floor. Not one for passivity, she pounded back just as hard and eagerly met each thrust. The wave was gathering force, this one threatening a cyclonic power that would rip her apart, render her in pieces. She didn't care. His desperation was born of sex, but also, she knew, of anger and frustration. He was expelling his demons inside her, and she was his willing exorcist.

She reached a point where she wanted to devour him, subsume his body into hers in every possible way. Instinctively, she began nibbling his lips and drawing them into her mouth as though she would swallow them. At the same time, her other lips sucked along the piston that was drilling inside her, and her canal pulled him up even farther.

She was going to come again—now. She felt the beginning of a tremor in him that was steadily growing. They would leave this torrent together, ride the wave at the same time. She clutched his hips frantically, pushing in . . . in . . . in . . . and then he flooded her, and deep in the nether region of sane consciousness, buried beneath the morass of sexual mania, a little voice admonished that they had just done something stupid. They had forgotten protection. But it was too late now, now as her vaginal muscles joyfully squeezed out every bit of moisture it could sap from him and mix with her own.

The "ohh, God" that escaped from her was both a vocalization of the blessing of mind-numbing pleasure and a curse on the reality that she would now have to test herself and deal with the consequences.

He gave one final heave, then collapsed his full weight on her for a few seconds as she breathlessly relived the déjà vu of their first encounter. A few more seconds passed and he finally shifted off her, and she was able to breathe again. His own breathing was distressed. But as she peered over at him, he seemed much more relaxed.

"Can you stay the night?" he asked once he could breathe.

She started to shake her head no. It didn't seem like a good idea. She had no change of clothes for work tomorrow, would have to get up that much earlier to drop by her apartment to dress before heading to the office. But then she detected a desperation in his eyes that he wasn't even trying to hide. She reached over to stroke his chin.

"What's wrong?" she asked, and realized she had almost cooed like a mother to a child.

"I need you," he said so baldly that her first reaction was the caution one got when a seemingly normal person, on further acquaintance, doesn't seem quite as normal as one thought. Because his words were those said to someone you loved, someone you had invested time and emotion in. They were too blatant, too fraught with complications. She didn't want any complications in her life, not now, not for a long time.

But she turned to those eyes and couldn't find the word "no." Instead she nodded. He rose from the floor then and held out his hand. She took it, and he helped her up. Then, still holding hands, they walked to the stairs and ascended to the bedroom.

Blood was everywhere. On the walls, which were already stained with vile human secretions; on the wooden floor, where the viscous fluid slowly seeped into the fibers of the wood and pooled between the crevices of the boards. Soon, the hue would be an indelible tale-tell witness of what had happened, long after every other evidence had been disposed of. Long after her voice stopped haunting his dreams. Long after he was laid cold in his grave.

He bent to run a finger through one of the cork screw curls. Its end was soaked with blood. The knife felt warm in his hands still. Actually, it was the warmth of her life staining it.

He turned her over and peered into dulled brown eyes that accused him in their lifelessness. Gone was the sparkle, sometimes mischievous, sometimes amorous, sometimes fearful—that used to meet him. Now, the deadness of her eyes convicted him where he stood, even if a jury would never do so. The guilt of this night, this black, merciless night, would hound his waking hours, haunt his dreams, submerge his peace, indict his soul. There would now always be blood on his hands. For that reason alone, he would never allow himself another moment of happiness. Not that he would ever find it again. What joy he would have had, might have had, lay now at his feet in her perfect form. Strangely, in death, she had managed to escape its pall. Her skin was still luminescent, still smooth. If it weren't for the vacuous eyes, the blood soaking her throat, the collar of her green dress, the dark auburn of her hair . . . he might hold to the illusion that somewhere inside, she still lived.

He reached a shaky hand to touch her cheek. It was warm, soft, defying death even as it stiffened her body.

He bent further, let his lips graze hers one last time. Their warmth was a mockery. Her lips were never this still beneath his. They always answered his touch, willingly or not.

He saw a tear fall on her face, and for a second was confused. It rolled down her cheek and mixed with the puddle of blood. He realized then that he was crying. It scared him. He hadn't cried since he was a child. But now, another tear fell, and another.

Through his grief, he knew what he would have to do. She was gone. There was no way to bring her back. Her brother would be searching for her soon. She wasn't an ordinary Negress. She was the daughter of a prominent Negro publisher, now deceased, and the widow of a prominent Negro lawyer. She had a place in their society. So, yes, she would be missed. There would be a hue and cry for vengeance if it were ever discovered that she had been murdered.

Which was why he could not let her be found.

He knew what he had to do. It wasn't her anymore. It was just a body now. Yet, he couldn't resist calling her name one last time.

"Rachel."

Then he began to cry in earnest.

Tyne pushed through the sleep-cloud that fogged her mind. The dream-world still tugged at her, reached out cold fingers to pull her back. But her feet ran as fast as they could, ran toward the name hailing her, pleading with her to hurry. The name reverberated around her . . . "*Rachel . . . Rachel . . . Rachel. . . .*

"Rachel . . . Rachel. . . ."

The sound woke her. She slowly opened her eyes, lay there for a moment, not remembering. Gradually, disorientation gave way to familiarity. Shaking off sleep, she became aware of her surroundings. Recognized the curtains that hung at the moon-bathed window, saw the winged-back chair that was a silhouette in front of it. Sometime during the night or early morning, he had retrieved her clothes and laid them neatly on the chair's back.

He was shifting in his sleep, murmuring. Then she heard the name again, just as she had heard it in her dream. "Rachel." He strangled on the syllables, his voice choked with emotion—with . . . grief, she realized. She sat up, turned. His back was to her, shuddering. He was crying in his sleep. Was calling to a woman—a woman named Rachel. Someone he'd never mentioned before. And obviously a woman who meant a lot to him, and whose loss he freely felt in his unconscious state. So he'd lied about never having been in love. But why?

A pang of jealousy moved through her, pushed away affection, gratification. She didn't want to be solace for some lost love he was still pining for. Didn't want to be a secondhand replacement to someone else's warmth in his bed. She looked over at the clock. It was almost four anyway. She might as well get home to get ready for work.

She shifted off the mattress delicately, grabbed her clothes from the chair, and started for the door. She would dress downstairs to make sure she didn't wake him. She turned at the door to look at him. The shuddering had stopped. There was only the peaceful up and down motion of deep breathing. She opened the door, shut it lightly and made her escape.

Chapter 23

Rhea looked again, covertly darting her eyes from the woman to a row of books sitting on a nearby table. But the glance confirmed what she had suspected for moments now—the woman *was* staring at her. Had been staring for some time.

Rhea looked around the room. There was a black girl, about her age, a few tables over reading a book. In a chair beneath one of the windows, an older black man sat leafing through a paper.

So why was the white woman staring at her? Yet there wasn't that look of disdain, the curling up of the nose to say: "What are *you* doing here?"

It wasn't a sexual thing, either. She wasn't getting that type of vibe. Besides, the woman had to be in her fifties, with graying hair and not-so-supple skin. Still, she was nice-looking for someone that age. No, it wasn't that. It was more like . . . like the woman was trying to figure out whether she knew Rhea or where she knew her from.

Rhea realized she had let her glance last too long. Because now the woman was rising from her chair—and was walking toward her. Rhea quickly tried to feign interest in one of the reference books she had just opened. But the woman stopped at her table and stood over her. Rhea recognized the scent of Tabu that her mother used to wear.

"Excuse me," the woman said, her voice a soft rasp. "I don't mean to disturb you, but may I speak with you for a moment?" Before Rhea could come up with some reasonable excuse why she wanted to be left alone, the woman sat down in the opposite chair, setting her large purse on the chair beside her.

"I really got to get back to my studying, so if you wouldn't mind . . ." Rhea started.

"Yes, I know," the woman interrupted. "Your 'studying' is why I'm here . . . at least, I think it is. I can't be quite sure. My premonition wasn't too specific. But I knew I'd find you here. I need to talk with you." The woman stopped, looked around the library with interest. "I always liked the Newberry, but I admit I haven't been here in quite a while. I see they've changed it some."

Rhea's exasperation was rising. Usually, she was over-accommodating to the point that friends used to take it for granted that she would do whatever requested, no matter how extreme the favor. Her grandmother got after her about that. "You let people walk over you enough, you won't be able to wipe off the shit they leave on you." Only recently had she taken the words to heart. Some people didn't like it, so she was down by a couple of "friends." Still there was something about her, maybe her youngish face, that made her too approachable by beggars, fools, and crazy people. She was pegging the woman as the last of the three.

"Look, I really don't have time."

The woman was reaching into her purse and pulled out a pack of Camels, looked up as she seemed to remember where she was. Shaking her head, she put them back. "What was that? Oh, yes, I won't bother you for long. And no, I'm not some crazy woman. I'm something loopier than that. I'm a psychic."

Rhea had had enough. She slammed her book closed, rose to leave. Then the woman said something extraordinary.

"I need to know who Rachel is."

Rhea froze in the middle of pushing back her chair. "What?" But, of course, it was a coincidence, or something like that because . . .

"Rachel is the name; I've been hearing it quite a bit lately. Yesterday I had a premonition of you sitting here at the Newberry, and I knew I had to find you. I'm not certain what your connection is to this woman. I have to admit, sometimes my signals can be off a little," the woman said, staring at Rhea's face curiously. "But I have a feeling that I'm right on target. You see, I think Rachel is the key to something that I need to find out. So I need you to tell me about her."

Rhea didn't know whether to sit down or leave. Her instincts were divided, pulling at each other.

"I hope I don't have to do some parlor tricks to keep you here. By the way, my name's Carmen, Carmen Carvelli. And I think your name is hhhmm . . . Thea? No, not Thea, but something close to it."

Rhea's legs felt shaky and she finally sat down. The woman leaned forward. "I didn't come here to shock you, or to bother you. But I do need information from you. It's very important. So please tell me, who is Rachel?"

Rhea only knew one Rachel. It was impossible that this woman would know that. Maybe her grandmother had told her. . . .

"How do you know about Rachel?"

The woman's smile was docile, but Rhea could see the exasperation in her eyes. "Like I told you, I'm psychic. Guess I'll have to prove it, won't I? Um, let's see . . ." She stared at Rhea, a look that went on a little too long, and now Rhea was starting to worry about her safety. She peeked over at the overweight librarian, but even if she called out for help, his girth would impede an immediate response. Which wouldn't help her if this woman had a knife or a gun.

"You're going to get a B on your history final, and let's see . . . yes, I believe you're going to get an A in music. So, you're a violinist? I know, you don't believe me now, but wait a week. That's when your grades are due. Then if I leave my number with you, you'll call and tell me what I need to know?"

Rhea didn't know what to think. Of course, there were

ways this woman could have found out about her courses. Maybe, she was even stalking her. Still those grades would be nice—if it were true. Rhea admonished herself for the thought. There was no way.

"If you're a psychic, why can't you find out about Rachel yourself?"

The woman shook her head. "Doesn't work that way. Wish it did. Could save me a lot of aggravation. But you see, sweetie, you're my link. I don't know why or how. I just go where the signs lead me. I've done this before, and I'm hardly ever wrong. Now we can meet up after you get your grades, or you can call. Or better yet, you can just tell me what I want to know now, and I'll be out of your hair in a matter of minutes. The choice is yours."

Rhea couldn't explain the sudden defensiveness she felt over Rachel. Rachel had been hers for weeks now, the puzzle, the enigma that she had been slowly uncovering. Suddenly, here was this woman, who had to be some sort of kook. Yet if telling her the truth would make her go away . . . and she didn't have to tell all she knew. . . .

"Why do you want to know about Rachel? I mean, what do you already know about her?" Rhea asked.

The woman named Carmen Carvelli—or at least who claimed the name—seem to ponder the question, as though she were trying to decide how much to tell Rhea. Rhea decided if there was going to be an exchange, it was going to be quid pro quo. She wasn't saying anything until she'd figured out the woman's angle and what game she was playing at.

The woman came to a decision. "Rachel figures into the life of someone very dear to me," she said.

Rhea smiled inwardly. She knew it. This woman didn't even know Rachel wasn't alive. She thought Rachel was a living blood-and-guts person.

"I also know she's been dead for some time," the woman continued. "I've picked up that much, at least. But I don't know when she died—or for that matter, when she lived. I don't know the circumstances of her life or death. I just know that she did exist. And because she did, someone's suffering now."

This woman wasn't making any sense! How could Rachel's life—or for that matter, her death—over a hundred years ago have anything to do with the present. Unless . . . unless this was about money. Maybe there was some property some-where, a house, old jewelry that was unclaimed, that this woman was trying to get ahold of. Somehow she'd found out about Rhea's research. Probably through her grandmother, who might have told the woman in innocence, not knowing she was a con artist.

"Did my grandmother tell you about me?" she asked, not trying to keep the suspicion out of her voice.

"I don't know your grandmother, dear. Really, I don't. By the way, the man getting up from the chair. The dark-haired one in the blue blazer and brown pants . . . Lord, what was he thinking? . . . he's about to stumble."

As both Rhea and Carmen Carvelli watched, the man began walking toward the double glass doors of the room. He made it halfway across and then—he stumbled. Just a lit-tle bit. But enough.

Rhea's nerve endings were near to snapping. "He's work-ing with you," she accused. "You must think I'm stupid." Why did everyone think she was so gullible?

Mrs. Carvelli smiled again, but the smile didn't reach her brown and unnerving eyes. "How unfortunate to be so cyni-cal so young. Here, one more parlor trick for you. My last one for today. That piece of paper you were looking for this morning—the one with what's-his-name's phone number—Ronald . . . aahh, yeah. It's in the front compartment, not the inside like you thought. By the way, I don't see a future with him . . . which I think might be good for you because I think he's gay."

Rhea sat unblinking. It seemed she had forgotten how. These were tricks. But she had to see for herself. She had looked everywhere for that piece of paper this morning. No one knew that she even had it as she had copied his number from a friend's phone book—on the sly, of course. But she rummaged through the front pocket of her purse, touched on her mascara, her lip gloss, a nail file, a paper clip, her grandmother's receipt from the cleaners (she still needed to pick up her grandmother's lavender dress), and deep, deep down she felt the edge of a torn sheet of paper, pulled it out—and found Ron's number, hastily scribbled in red ink. Ron, the tight end on the school's football team, the one who half-smiled at her that one time, so she'd let herself think that maybe, somehow. . . . But, she guessed it wouldn't be the case. Not now. Because this woman wasn't the phony she had first thought.

Rhea sighed and sat back in her seat. "What exactly do you want to know?"

Carmen Carvelli smiled. This time the smile did reach her eyes. They were beautiful.

"Everything you know, dear. Everything."

Rhea began her tale. In the back of her mind, she anticipated receiving her final grades. A, B and an A. Not bad.

Chapter 24

David's smile was a facile copy, stretching muscles that didn't want to work. The man sitting across the desk from him seemed nervous one moment, cocksure the next. Thirtyish, but already balding, his features were normal but asymmetric. The blue eyes were icy, the mouth a thin bow. David peered at the resume again. Langston Murphy, Developer. Not a long time in the business since his credentials only stretched back five years with a little-known firm called Anders & Sons. David figured a Murphy wasn't exactly a "Son" and probably didn't have much of a chance of achieving partner status, thus his seeking other opportunities. He had called David early this morning, asking for this meeting. Or rather, this impromptu interview. David reluctantly agreed to see him. Obviously, the word was out, even before he had taken steps to find replacements for Rick and Clarence.

Meanwhile, his erstwhile partners had already cleared out their offices, not bothering to fight for the space. David found out that they were renting an office a little farther north in Old Town. Not cheap, since realty there was astronomical, but the area was trendy. Probably Clarence's choice, who figured a little more wasted money would impress.

David sat half-listening to Langston delineate his work history, which wasn't anything extraordinary. A school, some low-income housing on the near South Side. David looked at the photos of the jobs—again, nothing impressive.

Even as he pretended to listen, he sat wondering why Tyne hadn't returned his calls. Seven of them all together, left over a space of five days and nights. The time expanse between today and the wonderful night they had spent together. At least, it had been wonderful for him. Maybe, this was payback for his not calling after their first time together. Or maybe, she was really busy. Or maybe . . . He did a mental shake. There were two many *maybes*, not the least of which might be she had tired of him. Or maybe she regretted sleeping with him.

They had been physically intimate, but without the emotional intimacy that should precede the act of two bodies coming together. To him, the sex hadn't been just sex, no matter what she'd said. It had been a culmination of months of expectation, a waiting for someone coming over the horizon—and he had known she would be there. His dreams had led him to her.

He could believe in prescience, could allow himself to believe that he had a little of his mother's "gift." But what he didn't want to believe is that all of that had led to just physical encounters and that was all he should expect—or want.

"So I think that I have something to contribute." The words interrupted his thoughts.

David looked down at the paltry resume again, thought on the old adage about beggars not being choosers. Looked into the eager, almost desperate, eyes of the man in front of him.

"I'll think about it and give you a call," was all he would promise. There had to be someone better. He didn't ever want to settle.

He stood up, signaling the end of the meeting. When he shook Langston Murphy's hand, his own hand came away with the slight dew of palm sweat.

He told the man to shut the door behind him. Once it was closed, David reached for the phone.

Sherry sipped a can of Diet Pepsi while watching two monkeys caw to each other, their spidery legs dangling from fake branches against a blue-lit backdrop of trees and mountains. One monkey began teasing the other, reaching over to tag his partner on the cheek. The other took the bait and followed suit as the first began swinging through the intertwined branches, leading a merry chase. They were happy despite their captivity. Or more likely because they weren't aware they were captives, having known no other home but this.

Sherry looked over at David, who seemed distracted as he watched the same tag-race game. This early weekday morning, they were the only ones here. She could tell that his mind wasn't with his body, that he was functioning on automode. No wonder with all the crap coming down on him. Damn that Rick! She had only met the guy a few times since he and David became partners, usually at some formal functions, and once at a Cubs game at Wrigley Field. From the first handshake, the way he had held on just a little too long, and his pathetic attempts to impress her with his credentials, she had immediately sized him up as a smarmy weasel, more suited to selling used cars than architectural services. Still, she had held her tongue. She held it now because frankly it wouldn't do any good to tell David he shouldn't have gone into business with the little putz. David was only too conscious that he had made an error in judgment.

"You know, you can start breathing any time now," she said, watching him. "If you stay in that position too long, the attendants will mistake you for one of the props and put you in storage."

She thought she detected a glimmer of a smile. He straightened from his half-stoop over the bar fronting the monkey display. But the glimmer became a shadow, and as quickly disappeared.

"So now you got me here, you need to unload, start unloading. Otherwise, I got to get back to work, because the monkeys aren't doing it for me."

He half turned, his eyes finally connecting with hers. They were a dull reminiscence of their usual carefree glint. "What's been going on? I haven't seen you in a while," he said quietly.

So, he was going for the small talk. Major avoidance—typical Dave move. She sighed as she realized she had to play along, or else he'd stand here for half the day pulling this James Dean nonsense.

"I'm doing fine. Matter of fact, I met somebody at a party a few weeks ago. I would have called, but you've been pretty much out of touch. Guess someone's been keeping you busy."

She saw a flicker, then stone. "Yeah, I've been busy," he said. "How's she working out?"

Sherry knew who he meant. "OK, I didn't know I had to give you a report on your recruit, but I can honestly say she's working out fine. Then you should know that since you two seem to be . . . um, 'friendly.' "

"I'm glad," he said, his attention back on the monkeys, who were swinging back and forth on a couple of limbs. "I haven't talked to her in a few days. I figured she was busy working on an assignment. That she was too busy to call."

Sherry's hackles went up. Trouble in paradise, already? No way did she want to get in the middle of this, which, if things were going southward, would mean an awkward situation for her. "OK, not trying to be callous, but whatever's going on is between the two of you, so please don't try to pull me in. All I can tell you is that I'm not working her to death, so if she's not calling, well . . ." She shrugged.

He was quiet for a moment, his repose thoughful. Then in an upbeat tone he turned and asked, "So who's this someone you met? Give me credentials, so I'll know if she's good enough or not." This was said with a smile that fell flat.

"Candy," she answered.

"Aahh, c'mon, Candy?" he stood up straighter, his smile broader. "Sounds like a *Penthouse* playmate. I thought you were into the mother earth intellectual."

"Hey, you're prejudging. Candy is short for Candace, and she's a graduate of Vassar who's currently pursuing a PhD in Greco-Roman history at Northwestern. So, her intellect is very stimulating."

"Uh huh, yeah, right, her intellect. Give me the numbers."

Sherry shook her head. "Why are men so focused on the visuals? Don't you know there are other attributes to a woman?"

"And again, uh huh," he said, throwing her a look. She was glad to see the twinkle back in the eyes, though.

"OK, OK. Something like 38-26-37."

"Not bad, not bad," he nodded.

Sherry was more at ease with the buddy-buddy exchange that was the norm of their conversations. She didn't like to see him down, of course, but she felt helpless to make him feel better. She didn't want to complicate her life, so she didn't particularly want to know if things weren't working out between him and Tyne, especially since she had decided to keep Tyne on permanently. *Elan*'s first issue was due to hit the stands in a few weeks. They were running Tyne's story on the cover.

"Yeah, well, we've been out a few times now," she said before draining the last of her Pepsi. "And as much as I would like to stand here all day talking about her inimitable charms, I got a column to write and some proofs to go through. So, if you feel like shooting the breeze some more, let's get together later after work. What about The Closet?"

Already he was shaking his head. "You know how I feel being around a bunch of male-hating females."

"David, we're not male-haters, just female appreciators. And you know the place is male-friendly, so don't even start. Besides, you got to pick last time. And I know you want to talk about something, something you obviously don't feel comfortable talking about here."

He shook his head, the action one of sad defeat. "I guess I just wanted to know I still had a friend in the city. I seem to be a pariah lately."

"OK, if you're through attending your solo pity party, I can promise you you have plenty of friends, and as for that double-crossing asshole, you're better off without him. You have enough talent and perseverance to get through this setback. As for your love life, you make your own choices. You walked away from Karen, which I'm not saying was a bad thing, but again your choice. I'm not sure what's going on between you and Tyne, but if it's not meant to be, no use trying to force it. Maybe she needs some breathing space."

Consternation froze his features, as though the object of his frustration were standing before him. "Hey, I'm not crowding her. She's the one who thought I was trying to throw her off, but I wasn't. I don't know if she's trying to get back at me or what. All I know is she's not returning any of my calls. So I guess it's over." He sighed, his shoulders sagging again. "Whatever it was."

"I suggest you ask her then. Although, I am *not* suggesting you bring this to the office. Leave a message asking her to let you know whether you should even bother calling again. And if she ignores that message, well then fuck her. Or rather, stop fucking her. And get on with your love life. Cause you have to know you're a stud. Hell, even I've noticed, woman appreciator that I am. So you definitely won't be lonely for long."

He seemed to ponder her words. "Yeah, you're right. Thanks. I knew you would put things in perspective. Sometimes, I just need a swift kick in the ass to get me going again. I always know you have the shoes to get the job done." He looked down at her red Manolo Blahnik slingbacks that matched her red pantsuit. Pointy-toed with four-inch heels.

They started for the exit, and just in time. Sherry could hear the echos of tiny voices rounding the bend near the entrance on the other side. The exhuberant yelps echoed through the building. Sherry, not much for children, thought sadly that it was too bad that such excited innocence would be muted one day. But that was the way of the world.

New York—September 1879

Joseph stared at the words, rereading them, first in sequence, then skipping to those few killing passages, trying to find meaning in them. Or rather, to find anything but what the words actually said, to read some latent message in the letter that said he was still part of her, that they could still be together. But the pain radiating in his head told him that the words truthfully spoke their only message—she would not see him again. Ever. She stated that she could not continue with this "madness," the word underlined twice. That "the price was too high" for both of them to continue their affair. The knife in his heart turned to see her signature, so beautifully written, as though the missive were nothing more than an invitation to tea.

He tossed the pages and they drifted downward onto the oriental carpeting of his room. Pacing between the bed and the windows, he looked out at points as though he expected to see her walking up the circular driveway.

Price too high? The words rang like a hollow bell in his head. What price was too high for her? To leave a bunch of uppity Negroes who thought their world was the height of society, when in fact it was nothing more than grand pretensions and apery? He was the one who would be throwing everything away! Who would be walking away from the true society with all of its luxuries and privileges. And he would be doing it for her! But obviously that wasn't enough. What more could he do to prove his love?

He had felt tremendous heartache when his mother left him, when he finally understood that she had held him in so little regard that she hadn't even taken pains to disguise her suicide or to make sure he wouldn't have to see her like that. What had hurt most was how easy it had been for her to leave him, as though he and his father were indistinguishable. As though his love wasn't enough to make her overcome her unhappiness.

He had thought the pain of losing her incomparable—until this moment.

Outside, the gardener was setting down the autumn floral to replace the summer blooms now dying. Fall was near; everything was destined for death. Soon, the trees whose leaves were only now starting to turn would be bare, their naked branches making the landscape gloomy and dark. Inside his soul, it was winter already, everything cold and fading.

Except the ember still burning, that refused even with her words to die away. If he had any pride left, he would toss away the letter and with it every memory of her. She wasn't worth it, he tried to tell himself. He had been crazy, yes "mad" as she so cruelly put it, to have even entertained the thought of more than just a dalliance with her.

The sun was setting, causing shadows to play along the walls. Unkindly, as though the devil were mocking him, one of the shadows seem sylphlike, its outline feminine, a specter to momentarily taunt him. He looked around. The English wood furnishings were rich and elegant, a nod to his mother's sedate tastes. The massive canopied bed was too big for just one, but he had never had a desire to share it with another. Until Rachel. Of course, she had never been to his room. One of his many regrets was the dreadful places he had to use for their unions, rooms that could not but further degrade her.

In a fairer world, he would have been able to bring her home as his bride, welcomed by both his father and mother, still alive. And he would have found a purpose and happiness to his existence other than this meaningless pursuit of the next drink or next poker game. At twenty-eight, he was in danger of having wasted his whole youth. Rachel had finally brought clarity to his life with the realization that all the wealth and accumulation in the world was nothing without love. His mother had understood that in the end.

Until this moment, he hadn't thought on the unfairness of Negroes being deemed second-class citizens—not even that, really—in this world. That had never been a concern of his. They had been no more than apparitions in his life. Not for a million years would he have ever thought to actually have a real conversation with one, be able to joke or laugh, or give his heart to one. But he had. And the world would not, could not acknowledge his love.

Love. Yes, he still did love her. And always would.

Anger surged. How could she say their love was over? It couldn't be so easy for her to walk away, to pretend that nothing had happened between them. No, it couldn't be over. He wouldn't let it be.

He would find her, make her see reason.

Convince her that they had to be together somehow.

He *would* convince her, or die trying.

Chapter 25

"Tyne!"

Even before Tyne turned around, she recognized the voice and that accent. It had been nearly four months since she saw Lem that last day at the *Clarion*. He seemed taller, but maybe that was a trick of distance, which he was closing at a rapid rate, his long strides encompassing two or three squares of sidewalk with each step. She stood waiting in front of the cathedral-inspired Tribune Tower. Its clock tower reached toward a sky marred with slate-colored clouds, the kind that hoarded water like a miser before pouring forth like a reborn philanthropist. Despite the overcast day and threat of downpour, people were milling about, even at five-thirty. As he neared, Lem made them all look like Lilliputians.

He reached her and she held out a hand ready to shake. Instead, he pulled her into a tight hug that took her by surprise. He had never been this expressive back at the *Clarion*, but she found herself enthusiastically returning the embrace.

"Lem, it's been months. How're you doing?" She smiled up at the grin beaming down at her. The hug loosened, but his hand remained on one shoulder.

"Can't complain. Well, yeah I can but I won't. You know, I was just thinking of you the other day, wondering what you were up to. Heard you were working at some magazine now."

"Yeah, it's a new one coming out in a few weeks. It's called

Elan and best of all, I get to do actual reporting." She squealed like a schoolgirl. "My story's going to be on the cover."

His smile widened. "Congratulations. I always knew you'd make your mark somewhere. When I think of all the time we wasted at that place . . ."

"Hey, at least no one can say we didn't pay our dues. Where're you headed?"

"To the train, which"—he looked at his watch—"I'm missing right now. But never mind. Where're you on your way to?"

"I was going to do some shopping."

"Got time for a cup of coffee? Starbucks?" The look he gave her was little-boy-hopeful, and she found that she didn't want to say no, even though it would throw her off schedule because most of the Michigan Avenue shops closed by six, not to mention the torrent of rain that would probably greet them after they finished; one of the items she had planned to buy was an umbrella. Even with these valid reasons to turn him down, she nodded. His smile widened as he took her arm, then escorted her across a bridge congested with frazzled pedestrians rushing to trains and buses.

They reached Starbucks and found that despite the impending downpour, or because of it, nearly all the tables were taken. Breaking her daily habit of decaf latte, Tyne ordered a mochaccino, deciding on a splurge since she couldn't shop. Lem ordered a decaf espresso. They located a table along the wall that was half hidden by the counter and shifted onto the gray vinyl chairs.

As Lem began describing his months at the *Sun-Times*, Tyne examined his face. The lines around the eyes were new. So was the monotone that made his words flat, lifeless. The earlier smile was gone, replaced by an uncharacteristic somberness that he had never displayed at the *Clarion*. He finished, took a sip, then said, "So, how's it going with the magazine? Sounds great from what you told me."

"Uhn, uhn. You don't get away with that sad look and expect me to just segue into how good my job is. What's wrong, Lem? Don't you like your job?"

"Damn, Tyne. Got that reporter's instinct already," he laughed, but the sound rang hollow.

"No, I just got eyes and ears. Your mouth is saying one thing, but your tone and face are saying something else."

He stretched his long length of leg and edged a foot alongside hers, black leather nearly touching her taupe suede. Then he took a deep breath and said, "You're right. I don't know what's wrong. I just don't get any joy out of what I do, anymore. At least back at the *Clarion*, I had more responsibilities to keep me distracted. What's that American saying? 'Out of the pan into the hot grease'?"

Tyne smiled. "That's 'out of the frying pan, into the fire.' Lem, I can't believe you're going to just settle for mediocrity when you know you can do better. What about working with computers? You know your way around them more than a lot of people do. You just have to figure out what you want to do and take steps to get there. Then maybe luck will meet you half way. Look at me. I thought I'd be at the *Clarion* or some other small paper for the rest of my career. Then this came along."

Some of the sadness seemed to evaporate around him, letting his features relax back into a semblance of his old self. His shoulders straightened a little. Maybe he felt obligated by the passion in her voice, or maybe she had actually pierced through his despondency.

"How did you find this job anyway?" he asked.

Tyne's mind skirted over things she didn't want to think about. She was suddenly uncomfortable about her luck, how she had come about it. "Actually, a friend of a friend of my sister told me about it, and I grabbed at the chance. I know, sheer luck. But I also knew that I could take the opportunity and make it work for me. It seems to be for now. Who knows what's going to happen in the future? But for right now, I'm happy . . . with my career."

He cocked his head to the side, suddenly more alert. "I heard a pause there. So you're happy with your career? What about everything else?"

She shrugged. "Well, my sister got married a few months ago. I told you about the wedding plans. Anyway, she and her husband are still in newlywed heaven. As for the rest of my family, they're all doing well. And as for me, I'm healthy, paying off my bills on time—thank God—and things seem to be working out. Overall, I can say that I'm content." She nodded distractedly, her eyes on her cup. She realized that her voice had petered out at the end, as though uncertain or unconvinced at her own words.

Lem leaned back, took a sip of coffee. "There's a saying back in my homeland, 'Happiness can grow from a little contentment.' So it's good you're content . . . right?"

She looked at him, biting back a surge of resentment that really wasn't directed at him. More at herself. "Yeah, I'm fine. Why, don't I seem fine?"

"Well, yes and no. I may not have the reporter's nose, but like you said, I can see and hear. Now it's your face that's contradicting your words."

Tyne sat quiet for a moment, pulled back to that night. The initial hurt of David's calling out another name no longer flared inside. It had ebbed away with each succeeding day. This wasn't something unique. It had happened to countless women before her. Besides, he owed her nothing. Still, for those intimate hours, she had felt completely joined with him, and she'd thought he'd felt the same. The same level of desire if not love, because it wasn't love between them. But there was definitely this pull, this need to be close to him. But it was over now.

Tyne didn't want to talk about herself anymore. "Have you heard from Gail or the others? I wonder how they're doing?"

He half smiled. She was on the defensive and they both knew it. But he answered, "Gail called me a few times, then showed up at my door one evening a few weeks back. She brought over this big serving of baby back ribs and collard greens."

"Oh, oh . . ." Tyne said, suddenly remembering that Lem was a Muslim. They paused, then both broke into simultaneous laughter. Tyne knew she shouldn't be laughing at the woman, but couldn't help feeling a somewhat guilty satisfaction that Gail had finally had a sort of comeuppance.

Lem stopped laughing, but a smile hung at his lips. "Of course, I had to explain to her why I couldn't partake of her offering. She looked absolutely devastated. She had totally forgotten the small fact about my being a Muslim. But I thanked her anyway. And then . . ."

Tyne leaned forward. "Nooo! You and she didn't . . ." she started, then caught herself. "No, no I'm sorry, that's none of my business."

His smile widened. "Actually no. But not from her not trying. It became somewhat uncomfortable after a while, so she finally left. Anyway, during our conversation, she told me that she had found work as an assistant in a law firm on the north side. Seems she worked in a law office before. As for the others, I haven't heard anything."

"Well, good for her." Despite her laughter, she was glad that Gail had found something to keep a roof over her head and her son's.

Lem's face became more thoughtful. "Tyne, I think you know that I would never . . . well, at least not with Gail. She's just not my type. Maybe some men like that kind of aggressiveness, but I never did. I like women who are confident in themselves without flaunting it. That's why I always admired you."

Tyne felt her fingers tighten around the cup handle. She had seen this look before—sheepish, uncertain, hopeful, asking her to look behind the words spoken, find the tacit message. Lem was a sweet guy, nice, handsome even. So why was she automatically saying no? She had always thought him overconfident, the same thing he had just accused Gail of being. But the months seemed to have changed him. She heard the humility in his voice, saw it in the way he didn't attempt to hold her eyes, but rather moved them over his cup, the table, then up to the couple who had just entered the shop.

"Why, thank you, Lem. A woman likes to be admired." She prayed he would leave it at that.

But then he settled his eyes on her, and there was no mistaking the look. "Can I be forward and ask if you're seeing someone?"

If she said "yes," would she be lying? But she had to be honest with herself. She *wasn't* seeing anyone. She was free to do whatever she pleased.

"I'm not looking for anything right now, Lem," she stated firmly, although friendly enough not to wound. "There was someone . . . I mean . . . I don't know." She hadn't meant to admit even that much.

"OK." His whole body seem to back away with the one word. "Then I'll leave that alone. But like you said, you have to grab at an opportunity. I let too many pass by when we were working together. I guess it was just the pleasure of seeing you again that made me try. I hope I didn't make a fool of myself."

She reached out to touch his hand on the table. "No, Lem, you didn't. I'm just not at a place where I would be comfortable dating, and I don't want to lead you on."

He shook his head. "I would never think that about you. Thank you for at least being honest."

After that, they maintained a stream of safe subjects, from his photography hobby to her favorite singer, Dianne Reeves. Then their cups were drained, and outside the first sounds of rain drummed against the windows and sidewalks. Tyne looked out.

"Oh, well. Looks like we're in for a wet commute." She turned back to him. "But it's been good seeing you again. Let's keep in touch." She reached in her purse and pulled out a business card that had been delivered to her office just last week. Embossed in gold lettering, it was above the pale of every other card she had ever had. For no other reason, she felt a surge of pride, feeling now that she was heading in the right direction.

Lem seemed impressed as he looked at the card, then placed it carefully in the side pocket of his suit jacket. Almost on signal, they stood in unison. He reached over and lightly kissed her left cheek. He never wore aftershave, but somehow there was always a smell of herbs about him, the kind newly pulled from the earth. No one had marketed this smell yet, but they should.

As they walked out, dark spots appeared on their shirts as droplets hit with rhythmic consistency. She would be soaked way before she could catch a bus to where she'd parked her car. Lem gave one last nod, then merged into the moving body of people in stages of rain gear.

Tyne stood outside the shop a for a few seconds as she tracked his diminishing figure, entirely surrendering to the rain. Finally, she ducked her head and began her headlong trek to the bus stop, knowing that trying to shop for an umbrella right now would be futile. Anyway, she kind of liked the feel of the rain on her skin.

Strange, how someone could make a rainy day seem brighter.

Chapter 26

Tyne peered down, saw a woman's body floating in the murky river miles below. The skirt of her dress temporarily ballooned as water filled its interior, then slowly settled around the contours of her legs. Small waves lapped at the corpse, welcoming it into a foamy embrace. The moonlight barely underscored shapes and shadows, still Tyne could see the man standing near the edge of the pier as he stared down at the body. His head was bare, his hair dark. His hands were stained with something darker. A glint of light caught her eye; something metal lay at his feet.

From the distance, she heard him speaking. There was no one else around . . . no one living, at least, and she wondered whether he was addressing himself or the lady in the water. She could not hear the exact words, but the tenor of his voice spoke sadness, great sadness. He edged closer to the river, until the tips of his shoes peeked over the pier's border. He rocked forward as though trying to gain a momentum to throw himself off the pier, but then leaned back again, his body still.

He bent, picked up the piece of metal. Its tip caught and curved the moonlight, shafted it up at her as the unknown man held it in his hand, held it to the sky. She saw that it was a knife, not a utensil but a weapon. There was the same dark stain along its perimeter, muting its luster. She realized now that the dark stain must be blood. Was it the woman's . . . the one in the river?

As though he could see her, or maybe attempting to address God himself, the man turned his face skyward. His visage was dark, like the rift in the sky just before thunder tears through it. All of the anger mankind had ever known was stamped there in his features, and he looked not so much a man as a demon dressed in human clothing.

Still, she recognized him, the one who had invaded her dreams, the one who had brought pleasure and terror to her. And in the second of recognition, she saw the features morph into those of someone more familiar, someone whose face was etched already in her psyche, her soul even. And the anger was even more lethal as he stared at her with such hatred that it seemed he would pull her from the sky, tear her body in two.

He shook his fist that held the knife and it was as though the knife split through her even with the distance between them. He shouted, and it was not the sound of a human, but that of a wounded animal, the roar of an injured creature seeking to hurt those within its reach.

Then the knife reached through the miles, found her throat, slit it in one motion. The hot blaze of pain caused her to scream . . . yet no sound would come, her voice choked with gushing blood.

Darkness and fear surrounded her. And with her dying breath she wondered: Why had David killed her?

Tyne woke with a start, trembling, trying to push the remnant of the dream from her mind. But it refused to meld into the nothingness where dreams go upon waking. Instead, it crystallized into horrible images that seared her brain, the last scene more soul-shaking: David slitting her throat, his eyes cruelly piercing her soul even as the blade pierced her flesh.

She told herself it was just a dream, but even as she settled her head on her pillow, pulled the comforter around her trying to quell the tremors that shook her body, closed her eyes, David's angry face was there to meet her.

She could not sleep for the rest of the night.

New York—October 1879

The sun was at its peak on an unusually warm Saturday afternoon, casting brilliant rays on the streets below. Whatever snows were predicted had held off, and the warmth gave the illusion of a cheerful summer day. Yet a dark dread had taken hold and wouldn't let go. Rachel's heart pounded frantically, her breath caught in her throat at intervals. Her stomach quivered. He was somewhere near. She could feel him. Walking amid the crowd of bodies along Broadway, she turned left, right, nearly stumbling as she did so. The sea of top hats and parasols made it hard to distinguish one body in the mass, yet she knew he was here, watching her. As he had done before.

Only last week, she had been coming out of a shop that catered to Negro patrons on Sixth, when she felt the insistent tug on her arm. Before she could escape, he had maneuvered her into a nearby entrance, away from the stream of bodies, away from prying eyes. He had stood there, his expression that of a madman's, his voice trembling as he told her that he must—no, *needed*—to see her again. Couldn't go on without her.

Her fear had merged with desire, feeding one another, confusing her. For a second, seeing the pain in his eyes, she had been tempted to say "yes" if only to stop that pain. Instead, pulling on a quickly dwindling resource of strength, she had told him to let go of her arm and stop making a spectacle. She threatened to hail an officer, knowing full well that the police might not intervene on her behalf. Despite her protests, her blood had warmed at his nearness. His breath caressed her cheek, stirring emotions, not all of them unpleasant. She had inhaled sharply as his lips touched skin, then trailed along her jawbone toward her lips, making her remember other sweeter occasions. Making her throb in places she did not want to remember. Then thankfully he pulled back, giving her respite, but even that small touch had left her quivering. She heard the desperation in his voice when he spoke.

"Can't you see what your absence is doing to me? I'll go crazy if you don't come away with me now! Rachel, we can leave the States, go to Italy, France! We can live in Paris just as I said before. I can... I can get work there... somewhere. I'll do anything! I'll load boats, haul boxes! All we'd need is just a small apartment, maybe near the Seine. You'd like that. We wouldn't need much... just each other. We could be happy together. Why can't you see that?"

She silently shook her head, her mind torn. Always, it seemed her heart and flesh were ready to betray her. All she had to do was reach up, place her lips on his, welcome his embrace. Instead, she jerked her arm away and fled into the crowd, praying he wouldn't follow. He hadn't.

Now at the corner of Eighteenth Street, the feeling pursued her like a phantom. Sometimes she wondered if she would ever be free of him—or if she could at least free her heart. She had several errands to run, not the least of which was to purchase a few reams of paper at Macy's. Classes had reconvened in September and, as always, the school had limited supplies to parcel out among the students. Whenever they ran short, she felt it her duty to put forth the money to make up the lack. Once she had the reams in hand, she could take one of the new elevated trains running along Sixth Avenue and make her way home.

With her focus on what she needed to do, other thoughts tried to push their way past her defenses. Part of her even now remembered the route to the apartment where they had met weeks ago, although it seemed a lifetime. It would be so easy to ride the blocks to 26th Street, and navigate all of the perils of the Tenderloin just to be in his arms again. To feel alive again.

But she could not. Somewhere she must find the strength not to go back. Again.

Maybe if she left the city for a bit.... Maybe, she could even visit Sarah and see little Angela, her precious goddaughter. As she walked, the thought became more than a mere prick, and began to grow and take hold as she crossed the street with the throng of afternoon shoppers and businessmen. That's what she would do. She needed to talk with Sarah face to face. Maybe the physical proximity to her friend would give her the strength she needed to get through nights when her body called out to him. Sarah, her friend, her touchstone, who had not judged her when she first confessed her sins in her letters, would know how to overcome this insanity. And with distance, maybe she could finally exorcise him from her soul.

The thought revived her a bit, and she walked toward the eleven buildings that housed Macy's on their ground levels. The red star on the entrance banner beckoned a flurry of shoppers to try wares, including clothes, jewelry, toiletries, plants, toys, dolls, and other miscellany. Just a few years ago, the Strauss brothers had opened their china store, and folks now flocked to admire the extensive display of tableware and glassware. Whenever she had the time, she would stop to look at the offerings, mentally adding to the list of items she could purchase with her next paycheck. Lawrence liked the best, especially when they had friends over for the occasional small dinner. She spotted a handsome plate and bowl set with gold-plated roses lining the edges. Gold-plated cutlery finished the ensemble. Maybe next time she would get the set. But today she had no time for dawdling. She was eager to quit the shopping district as soon as possible and recover to the safety of her home.

She had just neared the stationery area when she felt an overwhelming desire to turn. And there he stood near the entrance of the store, his top hat askew, his coat unbuttoned, desperately looking around . . . searching for her. She quickly turned her back, hastened her steps toward a large display sign, indicating a ten percent sale on writing implements. Behind the large placard, strategically placed next to a Greek revival column, she stood, almost sure she would lose her lunch. She could not take this any longer.

She had to impress upon him that she would never change her mind. She had to make him see reason because neither of them could go on like this. She just needed time to talk with him, to make him understand all they had to lose. A letter was not enough to make him see this. He needed to hear her say it as many times as it would take for the message finally to get through to him. Still, she would have to give Lawrence a plausible reason for her tardiness. He was becoming suspicious of late. And she had told him her shopping outing would be no more than an hour.

She debated facing Lawrence's mounting suspicions, weighing them against Joseph's increasing obsession. And realized she was left with only one choice.

With a nervous breath, she stepped from behind the sign. At that moment, he looked up and saw her.

He did not exactly run, but his pace quickened, probably due to his fear that she would escape him again. But she held to her place, resisting the need to flee. Soon, he was standing in front of her, his face hard with barely contained fury. She felt faint.

"Come with me," he demanded without even the ceremony of a hello. They were past that now. Once lovers, now combatants. He took her arm, turned her around, maneuvering her to the door. Heads swiveled, expressions of disapproval following them in their wake. A white man and Negro woman were a sight under any circumstance. Probably they thought she was being escorted out because of larceny or some other perceived crime.

She had to move quickly to keep step with him. Then finally they were outside.

"My carriage is around the corner."

"Where are we going then?" Although she already knew. And the thought made her knees nearly give way.

"To the apartment."

She tried to pull her arm away, but he only tightened his grip. "Joseph, I will not compromise myself again. I'll only *talk* with you, nothing more. There are things that need to be said. And you will hear me, finally." She was glad that her voice did not shake because inside she was trembling.

His eyes wavered for a second. "All right, Rachel, we will talk. But you will hear me, also."

She detected the smell of whisky about him as well as something else. Her apprehension grew with the thought that liquor might induce other feelings in him. But she swallowed her caution, determining that the risk was worth it. This would end. It had to.

When they reached the brougham, she stepped in and Joseph got in beside her, his hand still clutching her arm.

And with a slight nod from the driver, they took off.

Chapter 27

Carmen Carvelli vigorously rubbed the rosary beads in quick succession, reciting her morning litany with each one. Her eyes looked heavenward as she broke off and whispered, "Please God, give me the strength to do what must be done."

Sunlight filtered through the gauze of the blue bedroom curtains, casting a bluish-green haze on the walls. The scent of last night's rose incense lingered slightly.

She'd looked at the cards last night, and what she'd seen had chilled her. Three successive turns; each time the death card figured prominently. All three times, they seem to point to David.

Since meeting Rhea, she nearly had the full story. Or at least a major part of it. She just didn't know who the entire cast was. And she didn't know how this was going to play out, here and now.

Someone was going to die. Either David. Or someone close to David.

The cards said so.

It had taken some convincing to get Rhea to give over custody of one of the letters. But she had convinced the girl to meet her at the library again, convinced her with a mother's sincerity that she would take care of the cherished item, which would be returned promptly. Still, the girl's eyes had looked at her suspiciously, even as she handed over the letter during their arranged meeting at the library. Carmen practically had to tug the papers from the girl's hand.

Then she called Jennifer over for tea. She hadn't told the psychic what she planned.

Instead, when Jennifer sat down at the kitchen table, the letter was already there to be pushed aside as the cup was placed on the table. Jennifer's hand had slightly touched one of the sheets, and Carmen held her breath.

The look that froze on the woman's face morphed from shock to horror. She had drawn back her hand as though it had been singed by fire. Then she looked at Carmen with wounded dignity.

"Was this a test?" Jennifer accused.

Carmen didn't answer the question, but simply asked, "What did you see?"

At first, the young woman sat there quietly defiant, resentful about being tricked. But the images in her head needed exorcising. To do that, she would have to pick up the pages again, which she did.

"Read it," Carmen encouraged. Jennifer read over the words, words more suited to a time past, but whose sentiments reverberated to anyone who had loved someone she shouldn't. And had tried to get away.

With the prolonged contact, Jennifer's hand visibly shook.

"There's violence here," she started, and couldn't seem to finish her sentence. "And death. A horrible death. It's—it's . . ." she stalled, took a deep breath, her emotions causing her to strain with the effort. "The woman who wrote this . . . this woman died at someone's hand. She was horribly murdered." Her strength petered out. She looked physically exhausted, as though the exertion had crossed from visual to physical empathy. As though she felt the pain the dead woman must have felt.

Carmen felt sad and frightened. Her suspicions were falling into place, settling into jigsawed grooves that were merging into a tableau of pain and violence, two words she never wanted to associate with her son.

"I see the man holding the knife," Jennifer continued. "His face is familiar, but I don't . . ." Recognition morphed into a newer horror. "I've seen his face before. It's the same face that lay over your son's picture that day, the face I described to you."

The face that Carmen had seen when she looked at David and saw someone else sitting there. Someone with a handsome face—and an angry soul.

Later, she'd turned to the cards in a desperate act, hoping they would refute everything that the fates seemed to be declaring. David had killed before. He would either die, maybe in some karmic retribution, or he would repeat the actions of a past life. A life that was pulling forward in time, obscuring the present with its hatred, venom, whatever it was that this man had felt for the woman who wrote the letter.

Rachel.

She needed to find the woman who had died. And who must now have been reborn. The woman whose present soul was a siren's call to the soul of the man she once loved. The man who had killed her. The man who was now her son.

Once she found this woman, she would do whatever was necessary to make sure that past deeds remained unrealized. Even if it meant that she would have to go to the extreme to save her son's soul.

Tears fell onto the beads. She rubbed them harder until the blood infused her fingers.

Chapter 28

Tyne held up the dress, turned it one way, then another, examining the lucent sequins that accentuated the luster of the black silk. Nice, classy, but a little too suggestive for the party. Its length would show more than an appreciative view of thigh. She didn't want him to get any ideas that this was more than just a get-together between two friends, a celebration for the magazine, or specifically, a launch party hyping the success of *Elan's* first issue. She might be opening up a can of worms, but she refused to go stag again. She'd had too many of those evenings back at the dull but mandatory *Clarion* parties where the founder was dutifully lauded and sycophants preened for an opportunity to be noticed. Since her brother was off on another one of his photo shoots, this time in the Ivory Coast, steadily collecting a photologue of the changing African topography, he wasn't available as her fallback date. So in the end, she'd called Lem, which was, in fact, a return call. He'd phoned earlier in the week to say hello and left a message. The timing seemed karmic, so she'd called and invited him to the gala. He had readily said yes, and for a second, she'd hesitated at the fervor of his answer.

Looking through the closet, a green shimmer caught her eye. She reached for it and pulled out the half-hidden dress, one of her former favorites almost forgotten since it started tightening around the midriff a couple of years ago. But in the last weeks, she'd dropped some pounds, not consciously but due more to a consistent neglect to eat. She remembered the excitement she'd felt when she first found the dress in a small boutique near Oak Street, and the immense pleasure she'd also felt when it had slid smoothly over her skin, clinging nicely to her curves.

The pleasure was just as sweet this time around. The silk felt like warm water as it flowed effortlessly down her body, falling against her in just the right places. Its satin caught the diminishing sunrays filtering through the window, contouring the dress in shadows and light, so that some patches of green seemed darker. The asymmetrical bias hemline touched just above her right knee and slanted down her left knee in soft pleats. The V-plunge didn't expose too much, but gave a suggestive view of cleavage. It looked tasteful but not demure.

She was putting on her small gold hoops when the doorbell rang. He had arrived. She took a deep breath then walked out of the bedroom, unconsciously circumventing the pile of boxes she had never unpacked that rested against the wall in the hallway. When she opened the door, she was greeted with a luminous smile that made his smooth dark skin glow. Handsome and fit in an elegant tux, he temporarily made her rue her "friends only" stipulation. She wondered what it might feel like to rest her head against his chest and be bathed in his scent, which this night was a hint of something earthy. She missed being held, and the thought immediately brought on a remembered impression of hands pressing into her flesh. Strong, supple fingers with neatly buffed nails that had softly traced along her pliant skin, pale flesh reddened with desire that meshed against her own. . . . She mentally shook the thought away, determined to pay attention to the man standing in front of her.

"You look gorgeous," Lem said, his eyes moving briefly along her curves before settling on her face again. Tyne suspected that he was fighting to keep his expression neutral, to not let her see how much this evening meant to him. She fought to keep her tone impassive but cheerful as she thanked him. She wanted everything smooth this evening, no snags or entanglements. No expectations. This was part duty, free food and drinks, and hopefully some fun, which she had been miss-ing these last weeks.

There was one snag that she couldn't avoid though. David would be there. She knew it, felt it in her bones. She had mentally scripted the few words she would say to him if he cornered her. But she was hoping that wouldn't happen, that beyond a nod of greeting, she wouldn't have to speak to him at all. She had the strategy mapped out. Dance floor; she would only dance with Lem. Sherry would be another buffer; David wasn't likely to make a scene in front of his friend. Still, she knew she should explain why she had pulled away, why she hadn't returned his calls in almost a month.

Yet, she would never, could never have called out another's name, as he had that night they were in bed.

"Are you ready?" Lem asked.

"Just let me get my coat."

September had come on with strong gusts and tempera-tures dipping into the low 50s and high 40s. She wrapped herself in her beige cashmere coat, preparing to deal with the brunt of the cool evening.

But she wasn't sure she was prepared for the tempest that might await her.

Sherry checked over the salmon mousse baguettes and cold canapé assortment the caterer had just set up on one of the tables. On another table sat hot tureens of sliced turkey and sliced beef immersed in gravies. Another table hosted miniature chicken drumsticks slightly basted with lemon gar-lic butter. Yet another held chilled bottles of Cristal, while a fifth featured cases holding complimentary silver pens with the name *Elan* embossed on them. These she would pass out to the guests at the end of the evening.

Guests were already trickling into the very popular Terrace Room, one of several private event rooms housed in the Ritz Carlton. Sherry had pulled some strings (and tugged at some unwilling arms) to get this place. Insulated from the chillier Chicago clime, the room offered an illusionary tropical setting with an indoor rock garden surrounding a small, trickling pond. Overhead, the skylight broadcast a cloudless evening sky, with the last amber and golden hues merging into a slate gray which would darken into a rich ebony within a half hour. Already a full moon was taking center stage.

She was expecting nearly two hundred guests tonight, friends and acquaintances lured by the promise of good food and music and a lot of conviviality. She was no stranger to gala events, having grown up in a family where her parents celebrated everything they considered pivotal to their success.

Her invitation to the celebrations stopped after she introduced her then-girlfriend, Gina, to her parents. Her mother had choked out an explanation during one of her awkward visits to the apartment. "It's just too much on us right now, what with the downturn in the market. You understand, don't you honey?" Her mother had come as close to perspiring as Sherry had ever seen her. Embarrassed and hurt, Sherry had merely nodded her expected understanding. Later that same year, the hurt was amplified when her parents somehow managed to find funds to purchase a new yacht in which they sailed around the Caribbean.

Her parents would not be here tonight. She had not invited them. Even if she had, she wasn't certain whether they would have come. For her peace of mind, she didn't want to know.

Sherry looked up in time to see David coming through the doors. He wore brooding very well. Too well, as a matter of fact. He had settled into gloom like a well-worn but comfortable coat. Despondency had sunken his cheekbones a little, accentuating the angular planes of his face. He had lost weight, but still managed to fill out his tux quite nicely. At that moment, he spotted her, gave her a slight wave and started over. Sherry noticed a few female heads turn to scope him as he made his way across the room.

"You're the only one I know who can look this good and still look ill at the same time," she said as he reached her. "You shouldn't have come . . ."

"Thanks for the welcome," he said dryly.

She had been joking, but she could see the shadows beneath his eyes. He wasn't getting enough sleep.

"Just kidding. You know I want you here." She grabbed his neck to plant a kiss on his cheek. Then she let him go and looked into those near hazel eyes. At times, the color seemed to shift with his mood. "So how's the new guy working out?" He had hired a new architect, managing to lure him from a prestigious firm with the promise of a full partnership within a couple of years. The guy was talented and more than made up for the loss of David's former partners.

"Fine, fine," he answered distractedly, his eyes wandering the room, looking for something. Or someone.

"She's not here yet," Sherry said.

David's eyes tended to darken whenever he heard Tyne's name, so Sherry had begun to avoid saying it in his presence. Despite her disdain for disagreeable situations, she was barely managing to stay away from the fray. She had even started maneuvering her time to make certain David never ran into Tyne during his visits to her office. She would have liked to have avoided this altogether, and if Tyne wasn't such a good journalist and writer (not to mention April's sister), she might have decided not to keep her on staff. She hated whatever was happening to David, or whatever he was allowing to happen to himself. She couldn't understand his depth of emotion over this one affair, which was just one of many that he'd had since she'd known him. There was nothing substantial about this particular one. After all, it wasn't as though they'd been seriously dating. Still, what she thought had been just a momentary fuckfest was obviously something more to her friend.

She tugged at his lapel. "You're going to be good, right? Don't let me have to whip you," she threatened lightly, putting on her mock Mother Superior face.

He laughed. "Yes, ma'am. I'm just here for the booze. Show me the way to the bar."

"Actually, no bar. But staff is passing out glasses of Cristal over there, so feel free. There's good food all around, even got those drumsticks you like. So, we're going to have fun, right?"

He nodded distractedly, eyeing the table with the liquor. "Right. Lots of fun."

As he walked away, her stomach knotted. Especially when she saw Tyne enter the room on the arm of a stranger. She looked at David's receding back. He reached the table then looked up. Sherry didn't have to see his face to know that he had seen Tyne and her date—and that he was throwing knives in her direction.

Sherry felt she might actually get sick at her own party.

Chapter 29

He felt sick. No, not just sick. More like he was on the edge of death, but couldn't pinpoint what was wrong. That wasn't right, either, because he knew what was wrong. Or the who of it. Everything else was good. So, his life should be better. But she was the constant thorn in his side, the skipped beat of his heart, the longing that couldn't be sated.

Things were good at the office. Dan Hammond, his new hire, had skill and talent, as well as a savvy belying his twenty-eight years. The two of them already had bids in on a couple of city projects, and had survived the weeding out process. There were now only three firms they were up against. It didn't even faze him that one of the firms was the newly formed *Debbs & Gaines*. He was past that betrayal, and the hurt no longer gnawed at his guts.

His nights were better. The dreams didn't plague him anymore. His sleep was almost eventless, just the regular abstract scenes that had been commonplace in his dream world. That is, before the other dreams had taken over and nearly driven him crazy.

Now, the star of those dreams stood in the doorway—on the arm of someone else. Suddenly the climate of the room seemed extremely warm as he watched the couple enter and head for Sherry. Damn, she looked beautiful tonight. He had almost forgotten how beautiful she was. In the weeks of her silence, he had forced his mind to erase her, just as his dreams began edging her out of focus.

Looking at her now, it was hard to breathe, as though someone had turned down the oxygen in the room. Beads of sweat emerged on his brow. They hadn't been there a minute ago.

A waiter handed him a glass of champagne. He downed it in two gulps and realized that his thirst wasn't quenched. He nodded to the waiter and received another glass. Sipping evenly, he positioned himself to casually observe the trio. Sherry's smile was warm and cordial. Watching his friend, he felt an irrational resentment, knowing even as he acknowledged the feeling, that it was childish and silly. Of course, Sherry was going to be friendly to all of her guests. She wasn't the keeper of his personal enmity.

Tyne's smile broadened as the three of them laughed about something. For that second, there was nothing else. In a room of glass and crystal, her smile's brilliance overwhelmed the glitter and sparkle that illuminated the room. A warmth stirred in his stomach and he wasn't sure whether it was Tyne or the alcohol. The earlier sick feeling he'd experienced upon seeing her slowly morphed into something pleasurable, something desirable. Something that moved like tentacles through his bloodstream. He sipped and the tentacles spread out. The tension in his bunched muscles seeped away. He drained the second glass as the couple took leave of Sherry, turning to scope the room. Then her eyes met his.

The pleasant warmth torched, became a painful conflagration as those liquid eyes blankly acknowledged his, then quickly turned away. Tyne turned her back to him, and the tendrils spiked like knives, cutting him. They sliced through his guts as he watched her take her partner's arm in a display of possessiveness that spoke of some intimacy between them.

Something was growing inside him. Something feral, angry. Lethal. At that moment, he would have gladly wrapped his hands around her throat, squeezed until he felt the bones give way. Those lovely eyes would bulge from their sockets, screaming with fear. He wanted to make her feel his pain, the knives tearing through him.

"Hello." A voice broke into his thoughts. He turned to find a tall, thirtyish redhead standing next to him. She held her own glass of champagne, the rim edged with burgundy lipstick. A pricey scent drifted between them, settling in their airspace. Soft hair escaped from a ball at her nape, and blue eyes peered through silver wire rims that added a sultry sophistication and complemented the silver beaded gown clinging to her slight curves. She reminded him of Karen. He took all of this in even as she covertly checked him out.

"You're David Carvelli, aren't you? Well, actually I know you are because Sherry already told me." Her eyes twinkled with amusement and confidence. This was a woman who had already weighed and measured the odds of both rejection and conquest, and had decided that conquest was more probable. David stemmed the volcano inside him, thinking that maybe here was the distraction he needed to get him through the night. To take his mind off of more violent thoughts.

"Why are you so curious about me?" he asked more abruptly than he meant.

Her confidence seemed to waver a second, then refocused with a renewed verve. She was recalculating the challenge, probably wondering if he was worth the risk. Usually Sherry warned him when someone had marked him, but she hadn't this time, making him wonder if she was the instigator.

"I saw you one day at Sherry's office. I was leaving, you were coming in. You looked all intense, brooding. I thought then that here was a man who could stand some cheering up. I've been known to bring in the sunshine on occasion. If you're willing to try me."

"Depends on what kind of cheering up you had in mind." He reached for another glass of champagne, his senses expanding. The colors of the gowns, the flowers, the intermingling scents of attar, perfume, cologne, hot cuisine, the murmurings and laughter—all were amplified, making his pulse race. Everything was too bright, too loud.

". . . up to you." He caught the tail end of the sentence and realized he had momentarily faded her out. His eyes caught his quarry, in a far corner of the room, far away from him.

She wasn't going to get away that easily. The alcohol churned in his stomach, fed out to his nerves, emboldened them.

Tonight, things would get settled.

The warmth of Lem's fingers tingled her bare back where they lay. She ignored the sensation as she and Lem talked with Carole Penzer, *Elan*'s copy editor. Carole was twenty-five, nice, but with a sometimes irritating perkiness that had yet to be tempered by experience. She beamed as she discussed plans to one day become managing editor. Tyne couldn't help but smile at such naïve optimism. Still, one never knew which way the wind would blow—and what it would carry in: good fortune, opportunity, or something else. Something like the persistent dread she had been fighting since she saw David.

It really shouldn't be this hard. She had dealt with former lovers before. That was the problem, though. She *wasn't* dealing. Instead, she was running, as she had the first time she met him and he set her emotions in a flurry. She was being a coward. Instead of going up to him and saying hello, she was avoiding him and hoping to providence that he wouldn't seek her out.

Lem nodded as Carole admitted that her job wasn't always as stimulating as she'd like and was something she hoped not to be doing for too long. He commiserated with his own anecdotes, his voice not betraying the disappointment Tyne had detected that rainy day at Starbucks. She tried to listen fully, but her focus wavered even as her body strained against an irrational fear that refused to be contained. There was expectancy, a lull before a hurricane, the itching of the skin when someone was staring into your back, about to plunge a dagger into it.

"Hello, Tyne."

The conversation stopped as all three turned to acknowledge the newcomer. Tyne's fear deepened, but she stood calmly, her eyes momentarily focusing to the right of him before they settled on those eyes. Lem's fingers still rested possessively on her back. She noted that this fact was not lost on David as she watched him stiffen, his eyes narrow. Then he seemed to recall himself and let his features relax. He was going to play casual. She would play along, despite a sudden shift in temperature that was turning her flesh molten.

"David, how are you?" she asked, pleased that her voice was steady. The glare of chandelier lights behind him seem to cast a halo around his head and the illusion was off-putting. Hundreds of people were in the room, including Lem who stood next to her, but they might as well have been in another galaxy. It was a scene from a movie, where the supporting cast dims out and the light brightens around the lovers. All her senses were attuned to the man standing in front of her. A smile played around his lips, but an angry fire burned from his eyes. She knew she could never be alone with him again.

"How do you *think* I am?" His voice was bitter, the planes and angles in his face hard and unforgiving. Lem's arm enclosed her waist like a shield as he sized up the situation.

The forgotten Carole tittered nervously. "I think I see Sherry over there. I should, um . . . um . . ." She left the sentence hanging as she scampered out of harm's way.

"David, this isn't the place . . ." Tyne started.

"Then what place is good for you, since you've been avoiding me for weeks."

She heard the pain in the words, and felt guilt rising to join her trepidation.

"Look, is there a problem?" Lem piped in, his voice a register lower, his grip around Tyne a bit tighter.

David turned his glare on the taller man. "This is between me and Tyne."

"Well, I think you should let it go for tonight. Like the lady said, this isn't the place."

David's smile was nasty. "And you're the one who's going

to decide what happens here? You might be in for more than you can handle."

"Trust me, I can handle anything you got," Lem said softly, but his fingers bit into Tyne's waist causing her to wince.

"David!" Tyne pleaded.

Her voice was part of a chorus. Sherry stood at David's side, staring up at him, eyes furious. Both of them had spoken at once. People nearby stopped chatting, feeling the threat of something in the air.

"What the hell is going on?" Sherry said to David, her voice low, but audible enough to the four of them.

David lost the smirk, and turned a chastened face to his friend, whose expression was livid.

"You had better not be messing up my party, David!" she warned. "This isn't the place to settle your petty resentments, so don't start anything! If you can't handle your liquor, I suggest you leave now before you make a scene."

David opened his mouth to say something, then quickly shut it. Sherry had forced him to see himself through someone else's eyes, and the image was disturbing. Tyne saw several emotions juxtaposed on his face, all at war with each other.

He turned his eyes to Tyne again, and her breath caught in her throat. The pain was raw, and it shone harshly through prisms of green, gold, and brown. She wanted to say she was sorry for dismissing him so casually, but she figured that time had passed. There was nothing between them now but hurt and animosity, and the best thing was to stay out of each other's way.

"Tyne . . ." he started, then seemed not to know what to say. So he said nothing as he turned abruptly and strode from the room, causing curious heads to turn in his wake. Tyne hadn't realized she had been holding her breath until she began breathing again, slow deep pulls of oxygen that would help calm her racing pulse.

"So, who the hell was that?" Lem asked, his eyes staring at

the doorway where his sudden nemesis had exited. Sherry stood for a second longer, staring in the same direction, then just walked away. She had the presence to stop to acknowledge her guests. Tyne figured she was giving some explanation to those close enough to have heard the exchange.

"He's a friend. Or I guess now, a former friend," she said quietly.

Lem looked at her. "Well, from what I could see, he probably thought he was more than a friend. Bad breakup?"

Tyne was embarrassed. She didn't like airing her business, and David had practically broadcast it to everyone within ear distance. She especially didn't like the impression it might have given Lem, who had always respected her. She didn't want to appear a heartless bitch who used and tossed away men without batting a lid.

"There wasn't a breakup. Just a misunderstanding."

"No, sweetie, that wasn't a misunderstanding, that was a declaration of war," Lem looked at her with concern. "Maybe you should get something to protect yourself."

Tyne was already shaking her head. "It's not like that. David wouldn't hurt me. He's not capable."

"Tyne, one thing you have to learn: *anybody* is capable of *anything*. I know from personal experience. I had an uncle who you would have thought was the most loving man in the world, but that didn't stop him from unloading a gun into his wife. Never knew why. And the way that man was looking at you, well, just promise me you'll take some precautions, all right?"

"Lem, I promise you nothing is going to happen. People get angry without going crazy. He's angry, I'll grant you, but there wasn't that much between us. It was just a thing, a stupid lapse in my better judgment. It won't happen again."

"Well, you're intelligent enough to know the score, so I'll back off." He looked around, spotted the table laden with food. "Let's try to enjoy the rest of the evening as best we can. I came here for a good time."

Tyne forced the smile and nodded. "So did I." She pushed

David's face from her mind, intent on enjoying the celebration. But throughout the rest of the evening, no matter how hard she tried, the image loomed large and angry and violent.

At one point, she shuddered as though the Chicago chill had seeped through the caulked windows into the room and entered her bones. She ignored it as she bit down on a mini-drumstick, her tongue tasting lemon butter, her brain registering nothing but a tiny verve of fear.

Chapter 30

He sat waiting in the starkly cold night. To keep warm, he kept the engine running. A Stan Getz CD was playing, a personal favorite, but not even the alluring strains of the tenor sax could stop the blaze that was steadily building. An ache pounded behind his eyes, and his mouth was dry, the early beginnings of a hangover that shouldn't be because he had drunk no more than two glasses of champagne.

His body didn't feel right. The hands that gripped the wheel felt foreign, his fingers unfamiliarly shorter, thicker. He took his left hand off the wheel, flexed the fingers to throw off the sensation of estrangement from his body, from himself. Thoughts canvassed his brain; some he let in, others he flung away, refusing to listen.

But the logical part of him that had now dwindled to just a speck would not peter out, but instead shouted with a dying voice: *This is crazy! Just drive away!* This voice he refused to hear, shutting it out until it was just a whimper, an echo of a pestering insect. He wasn't crazy or acting irrationally. She was the one who was being irrational. He just wanted to talk to her, find out what he did wrong and try to make things right again. So that she would let him back in. Because he missed her. As much as he tried to deny it to himself, he longed for her heat that kept him warm during the night. He wanted, no he needed, to smell her scent, a pungent mixture of cream and sweat that suffused his room after she'd come, sometimes softly, sometimes violently enough to shift the mattress.

This was her fault! All she had to do was answer one of his calls. Just one. Instead she'd shut him out entirely. She'd tossed him away like garbage, like he didn't matter, like it had been nothing but some sort of sick game between them.

An hour passed, and the combination of cold along with a steadily growing stiffness in his limbs almost decided the matter. He sighed in defeat and set the wheel to maneuver out of the parking space.

Before he got in a full turn, a sedan pulled up and parked a couple of cars in front of him. With only the street lights and a hazy moon, the color was indecipherable, but the car was an older Ford model, something driven by someone with a whole lot of loyalty, or by someone with no taste or money to get something newer. Despite the threadbare look of the vehicle, something made him watch carefully, the hair on his neck moving, causing his skin to itch.

A man got out of the car. David strained to see his features. Same height and lankiness as the guy at the party. The man walked to the passenger side, opened the door, and a woman got out. Even in the darkness, he recognized the silhouette of her profile, the elegant neckline. She was home.

The thudding headache that had receded in the hour came back with a full rush, causing a sharp pain that momentarily caused him to shut his eyes. He didn't want to watch the pair walk through the entrance of the building. He didn't want to visualize them taking the stairs to her apartment, then standing at her door while she made her decision. Maybe it would be nothing more than a kiss on the lips. But then kisses could become more. She could open the door, let him inside—inside her apartment, her body, her soul, even. David would forever be shut out.

That wasn't an option.

They entered her building and he waited. And waited. Ten minutes passed, fifteen. Nearly twenty and he thought about getting out and ringing the bell. Even knowing that when she realized it was him, she would never buzz him up. But he needed to do something tangible, to move his stiff limbs, to walk the pavement, to feel the smooth metal of the bell button beneath his finger. To let her know that he wasn't going anywhere.

Before he reached for the handle, the entrance door opened and a figure stepped out. Tall and lanky. His proportions seemed abnormal, belonging to a nocturnal creature lurking in the dark instead of a human male. What did she see in this guy anyway? Yet David's peeve was tempered by a trickle of relief that nothing had happened, couldn't have happened in so short a time.

The figure got into his car, warmed up the engine then drove off. David sat for a moment longer, then finally opened his door and got out. A chilled wind hit him in the face. The temperature had dropped since he arrived, and the climate was more wintry than autumn. He walked the few steps to the building door, each step seeming like miles. He'd only been here once, a month or so ago. He'd dropped by on a whim only to find her not home and had left without leaving her a note.

But that was when he thought there would be other days to visit. He hadn't gotten the chance to see her apartment, let alone stay there, or to become familiar with her domestic habits, discover her idiosyncrasies. Sometimes he would imagine waking up beside her in her bed, sunlight streaming through her windows. The fantasy had played out with her making strawberry pancakes for breakfast, after which they would sit down to a leisurely meal at the kitchen table. A hundred times he had tried to picture how the rooms of her apartment were set up, how walls merged into each other, making cubby areas where she would have placed a painting, a knick knack, something that was entirely her taste.

This building was a three-flat that had been converted into a condominium. Hyde Park was sated with such edifices, old brownstones that managed to maintain their veneer of state-

liness despite the fading years. The stone lintel along the door
was chipped by weather and the door needed a new coating
of paint. The bell was cold to his touch, but the chill he felt
had nothing to do with the weather.

Again, the tiny voice tried to warn him. He ignored it, and
it drifted away on another cold breeze. As he pressed the bell,
he imagined it resounding through her apartment. Maybe she
was half dressed now, already preparing for bed. It was almost midnight.

The buzzer surprised him. He was sure that she would
have intercomed to find out who was calling. He pushed the
door open immediately before the buzzer stopped, then took
the stairs two at a time, eager to close the distance. He heard
the door open, and she said softly down the stairs, "Lem?"

He paused midflight. She was expecting the other one, the
man from the party. Which explained why she had buzzed
him in so readily. She still hadn't looked down the stairwell
to see who was ascending. Were she and that guy planning a
night together? But why had he driven away then?

"Did you forget something?" she asked down the three
flights. Her voice was light, even maybe a little flirty. The
pain throbbed, and his left hand formed into a fist.

Then she did look down.

And the world stopped.

Chapter 31

New York—October 1879

Rachel watched the words form on the page with each pen stroke, the letters round and cursive, slanting to the right. They pled for forgiveness, for understanding. The plea was in part to Sarah, to whom she was divulging her latest folly. The thought of it made her quake. Why had she believed she could meet with him and make him end his attentions? That it would go no further than words? She could barely write of the events of her last meeting with him nor the violence that had ensued. In those words not written, but understood, the letter was also a plea to God; to George, gone these many months, whose image now vacillated in her memory, if not in her heart; and to Lawrence, to whom she had lied again and again.

A breeze blew the hem of the white gauze curtain toward the writing desk and it caught. She brushed it away, her eye breaking from the page to look out the window. A hansom was passing by, and a woman sat inside. Although Rachel could not make out the woman's features, by the elaborate feathered hat, she guessed it was Twila Dabney, the eldest of Reverend Dabney's three unmarried daughters. An advocate for the rights of coloreds, Reverend Dabney often allowed like-minded groups to use Lafayette Avenue Presbyterian Church as a meeting ground. Earlier in the century, the church had served as a junction of the Underground Railroad and its illustrious history was known by all the city. In keeping with the standing of their esteemed father and his venerated church, the daughters felt duty-bound to serve as their father's unofficial ambassadors to the colored community, to represent Negro womanhood as vessels of staunch Christianity and female purity. Therefore, husbands would only inconvenience their mission. The sisters visited the sick, organized fund-raisers for those suffering in their finances, and held women's meetings wherein they promulgated the rules of virtue by which all decent Negro women were to adhere if they would hold their heads up and march in God's holy army. Twila was the banner waver and the horn blower for this righteous militia. A militia to which Rachel no longer belonged.

Not that anyone exactly knew of her fall. Nor had she been branded a pariah. At least, not yet. But what could only be guessed at caused tongues to whisper, eyes to cast her way then quickly shift in another direction, and her own brother to call her virtue into question. Two nights ago, at dinner, he had berated her over the table that held a platter of roast pheasant, a bowl of steamed baby carrots and broccoli, a tureen of gravy to be poured over creamed potatoes that sat beside it. But her culinary efforts were ignored that night as Lawrence sat for all the world like a god enthroned on Mt. Olympus.

"So you're telling me you spent all that time shopping?" he asked, his eyes skewing her from across the table.

"That's what I said Lawrence. Why are you questioning me?"

"Because I saw no packages, dear sister. I find it hard to believe that you could not find at least one item in nearly three hours of *shopping*."

She put down her fork and met his stare with more aplomb than she felt. But she refused to be intimidated. "Then tell me where you think I was and what you think I was doing. Tell me right now. And be careful what you say because it could change everything between us."

She knew Lawrence. He would never confront her outright. He would never accuse her of impropriety. He would mask it with a sermon on decorum, on what appeared seemly or unseemly.

Lawrence's brow creased. It was a high and stately brow, usually bare of lines. His hair was oiled and looked luminously ebon, except for flecks of premature gray dotting his sideburns. "When you are seen in the presence of a white man, the same man with whom you created a spectacle months ago, you should then be more circumspect in your actions to diminish, not exacerbate, the damage you have already caused. The only thing a woman has is her good name, and you seem not only willing, but determined, to tarnish that. If George were alive . . . but then again, none of this would be happening if George hadn't died in the fire. Or would it?"

At the mention of her dead husband's name, tears pricked. Shame immobilized her. "You don't understand, Lawrence," she said softly. But of course he wouldn't understand; she barely understood herself. How could she forget who she was and demean herself, her family, and most of all, George's memory?

As though he read her mind, Lawrence said, "Remember, it is George's name you are soiling also."

His authoritarian tone raised her hackles. It always had, even when they were children. Lawrence, older by six years, had lorded over her, always echoing their father's dictates, as though she were too naïve to understand without interpretation. Their parents would always tell her to "mind your brother, he knows better." Lawrence the good student, the obedient son had been the example held up to her as a standard to attain.

But looking across the dinner table at her brother, who relied on her to provide meals since he had never found a woman who could meet those high standards he set for himself and everyone else, she momentarily could forgive herself for her lapse. It was human. Besides, it was over. She had ended it for good two days before. The day of her shopping venture.

In mortified retrospect, she thought for the hundredth time how she had let it start in the first place and had a hard time reconciling how she had taken leave of all that mattered to her these last months. As much as Lawrence suspected, he didn't know the true extent, the breadth of what had gone before. How it had diverged from mild flirtation to something more ardent, something desperate, extending beyond propriety, igniting a passion she had never known, not even with George. Most devastating of all, how she had not found the strength to stop herself. Grief, loneliness, the need for consolation that she still hadn't found, had propelled her into Joseph's arms time and time again.

Brown eyes still accused her as she dismissed their passion in the words she now wrote to her dear friend Sarah. She closed her eyes, and the memory of demanding fingers on her arm caused her to rub the offended area. He had tried to keep her from walking out the door of the apartment he rented on 26th and Seventh in the Tenderloin District. But she had broken away finally and had shunned his offer of a cab, even though walking through the streets of tenements, saloons, and whorehouses was a risk no decent woman should take. Especially a Negro woman, who was all too often considered fair game. Still she had walked until she hailed her own cab, warily eyeing the men, mainly Irish, hanging in front of the saloons who had shouted out indecent proposals, causing her alarm. Afterward, at home, she had berated herself for allowing this further descent, for allowing herself to become involved with someone who nominally was of the upper class but whose actions were no better than those of a wastrel. Even his reason for renting the apartment in so horrid a place had given her pause. A regular gambler, he frequented the infamous gambling dens in the area, often playing into the early morning hours. Instead of trying to get a cab back to his family's estate, he would stay overnight, a knife beneath his pillow should any of the local denizens take it upon themselves to try to relieve him of his money. That is, if he had not gambled it all away.

His last words to her, half slurred by the absinthe he had drunk during her visit, had followed her out the door: "We're going to be together forever! You'll never get away from me!" The taste of absinthe clung to her lips where he had torn hers apart. Her thighs were bruised from where he had forced them apart and taken her on the floor.

But never again, she vowed silently to herself as she ended the letter. A vow she had made before.

Chicago, 2006

Tyne watched him climb the stairs, and each step that brought him closer rang a death knell inside her. Fear rooted her there in the half-lit hallway even as her instinct told her to get into the apartment and lock the door. But, she reasoned, that would be overreacting. All he wanted to do was talk. She would let him. She owed him that much, at least.

Still, as he advanced up the last flight, his body rigid in motion, her whole being told her to get away. But it was already too late. He had reached the landing and within a few steps, stood towering over her. Before, his stature had been a point of attraction and, at times, comfort. Now his height threatened, and she realized that as lean as he was (he had lost considerable weight), his whole body exuded strength. Maybe it was the anger, but his face seemed different, transformed, as though a stranger stood before her—a stranger who wanted to hurt her.

"Let's go inside," he said so softly that at first she wasn't sure she had heard him.

"We can talk out here," she countered as softly.

He smirked. "Still not the right time and place? What, are you afraid to be alone with me now?"

"No," she lied wearily, and more bravely than she felt.

"It's just that it's late, and I'm tired. Anything you have to say, you can say to me out here."

"What, with witnesses?" he half joked, but the words were strangely ominous to her. "Do you really want your neighbors to know your business?"

"No, but what I don't want is a prolonged fight, which I know is going to happen if we go inside. I'm sorry if I hurt you, David, but it's over. Just let it go."

She didn't know it was possible for him to look any angrier. "So, you decide that it's over, and I'm just supposed to go away like an obedient dog. You walk away with no explanation, and leave me racking my brain trying to figure out what the hell I did to make you treat me like a leper."

His voice had risen during the tirade, and she realized that she *didn't* want the neighbors to hear. He was too far gone to care about causing a scene.

With a sigh, she headed inside the apartment, knowing he would follow. She locked the door behind them, her back to him for a moment as she gathered strength to turn around to face the storm. When she did turn, she leaned back against the door as though it could give her the emotional support she needed. She *was* tired, tired of hiding, of running. Her fear began to ebb as she thought about the release of resolution.

"Look, I know I should have at least talked to you when you called. But, I thought you'd understand when I didn't call back."

"Understand what?" he challenged.

She hesitated a moment, her eyes settling on the picture on the wall behind him. It was of a mountain stream, quiet and reflective. She wished for that retreat now, to be away from here. She talked to the picture instead as she said, "You *know* what. That I didn't want to see you again. That it was over."

He shifted and at first she thought he was going to close the space between them. She straightened in anticipation of what could turn into something physical. But he just stood there, looking bewildered.

"Well, excuse me for not picking up on your ambiguous signals. But if someone decides to break up with me, I usually want an explanation why."

She moved from her resting place against the door, walked around him to the kitchenette that fronted the living room. She opened the refrigerator and brought out a pitcher of orange juice, retrieved a glass from a cabinet, then poured herself a drink. She sipped, quietly deliberating how much to tell him.

He stood on the other side of the counter, glaring at her nerve to ignore him yet again. She thought he looked a few steps away from losing it entirely. Some of the fear began moving in again. She put the emptied glass down and looked at him finally, keeping the counter between them.

"I didn't want . . . I mean I don't want . . ." she started, not sure what she meant to say. But her hesitancy only made him look at her as though she was a blithering idiot. She decided that bluntness was needed. Or a lie, even.

"Look, what happened between us was a mistake, and I don't want to continue making the same mistake. I just thought it should end before somebody got hurt." Yet she remembered the hurt she'd felt when he called out another woman's name. She realized only at that moment how much she'd let herself become emotionally invested in something that hadn't even had a chance to develop. She had been falling in love and hadn't known it.

"And you don't think you've hurt me? You don't think I have feelings?" Consciously, or unconsciously, his finger thrust at the middle of his chest. "Or was I just some walking dildo that you could use then toss away without a thought? Because that's how you've made me feel."

He *was* hurt. She could see that, had been trying to avoid seeing it. Because the pain in his eyes was harder to bear than his justified anger. She had never wanted to hurt him.

"Didn't you have any feelings for me at all?" he asked, the tone sounding much like the wounded voice of a child who had just realized the extent of the cruelty in the world.

"I do care, David, and that's why I'm putting a stop to this. This—thing—between us isn't going anywhere. You have issues, and so do I. And whoever this Rachel is, you have to come to terms with . . ."

He was shaking his head, confused. "Rachel? Who . . . what, what are you talking about?"

Now she felt the first twinge of anger. He was going to play her like she was some fool. "Look, you don't have to tell me who she is because it doesn't matter anymore. So, please don't lie to me, because I really don't give a damn." Her voice was tight with indignation. "You're not the only player out there, but I thought, at least, you were smarter than the others. But then, that was my mistake. And I don't intend to be on somebody's rotation. I won't let myself be used like that again." Even as she said this, she knew that her anger was out of place. They had never claimed monogamy, or anything other than a mutual infatuation. Still, she felt betrayed.

"Is this what this is about?" he asked incredulously. "You think I've been fooling around? Look, I haven't seen anyone but you these past few months. And I don't know where you got the idea that there's someone else, but there isn't, Tyne, I swear. There's just you. Only you."

The words were so sincere, she nearly accepted them as truth. Nearly.

"But you called out her name, David. No, you cried out her name . . . in your sleep. Rachel. That's the name you called. So, what am I supposed to think? Because my name is definitely not Rachel. It seems to me that I was just filling someone else's place in your bed."

He shook his head for more than a second, denying her accusation with motion, as though he had lost the power of words. But then he spoke. "I—I don't know what you think you heard, but it wasn't—Look, I've only known one Rachel in all my life and that was my father's aunt, and I definitely wouldn't have been calling out her name. It must have been a dream. That's the only explanation. Tyne, you walked out on me because of a dream."

She wanted to believe him. Men had fantasies and dreams. But the emotion in his voice when he called out that name was not something arising from a dream. There had been too much passion and pain in his voice. As well as regret. Whether he refused to admit it, he loved . . . or had loved . . . this woman. So, he was lying to her; she wasn't about to be another man's fool. Raymond had more than ripped away the protection around her heart, and it still hadn't healed yet.

"David, please I don't want to hear anymore. Just go now. It's late." She walked to the door, opened it and stood waiting. But he didn't budge.

"No, I'm not going until this is straightened out," he declared with a finality that bordered on the irrational. He just stood there, daring her, knowing that she couldn't physically remove him. Which left her with little choice.

"David, I will call the police if you don't leave now. I don't know what else to do or say to convince you that it's over, no matter what reasons or excuses you give. It just doesn't matter now."

"Don't say that," he pleaded.

"I'm saying it. It's over. Get out."

Something strange happened then. Something frightening. One moment David was standing a few feet away, pleading with his eyes. Then he was there, in front of her, staring down.

But it wasn't him.

Those features, handsome still, belonged to somebody else. He tore her hands away from the door and shut it firmly.

Tyne opened her mouth to scream, but the sound caught in her throat, causing her to choke. The stranger who was David—who was not David—slowly bent his head and settled his lips on hers, first lightly then with a desperate control. The tongue that invaded her mouth tasted of champagne and some other liquor she couldn't name. A moment stretched out past endurance before he finally pulled back. Tyne gasped for air, realizing she had stopped breathing through the kiss. The eyes that met hers were no longer green or hazel, but some darker color. Brown, maybe, but in the dimmed shadows of her living room, they appeared black. A black that expressed heat and cold, love and hate.

A voice that wasn't David's, full of restrained anger said, "I told you that we would be together forever, Rachel."

As she slipped away, her body sliding to the floor, her last conscious thought was that she had heard that voice before. In her dreams.

Chapter 32

Carmen swerved to get out of the way of the oncoming car. It had pulled out of an alley unexpectantly and would have hit her side on, except for her desperate maneuvering. The driver threw her the finger, the silhouette of which she could barely make out in the glare of a street light.

Carmen continued east along Fifty-fourth, relying on the landmarks of her dream to guide her. There, just at the corner was the street sign she had seen so clearly last night—Ellis Street. The corner building was a brownstone just as it had appeared in her vision. She was getting close. A map of the city lay open and neglected on the passenger seat.

"I've got to get to him," she whispered to herself, but the nervousness of her voice only increased her anxiety. "Please, God, let me get to him in time." She had tried calling him nearly all day, but he never returned any of her calls.

She tried not to think about the gun that she had stashed in the glove compartment. She had bought it in an outlying suburb just this morning with this night in mind.

She desperately hoped she wouldn't need it. But if she had to, she would use it. To save David from himself. If he was still David anymore.

New York—November 14, 1879

"Keep your mind on the game, why don' cha?" the dealer bellowed. Joseph, lost in the golden glow of his whiskey, set the glass on the table next to the spot where his cards lay facedown. He'd played three bad hands already and lost nearly half of the money he'd brought with him. He'd had bad nights before but had never been this deep in the hole so early on. This game started off badly, which meant that it would end that way. His luck never turned around once it settled into a pattern.

Losing money was usually a painful experience. But his mind and senses were dulled tonight, partially by the whiskey, but mostly through one of Dr. Lakehurst's famous (or infamous, depending on what side of the moral road you traveled) egg creams that he had drunk earlier at the bar. The syrup and soda water were a tasty blend, but it was the dash of heroin that made it quite splendid. The good doctor himself sat across from Joseph, having earlier doled out a few packets of the powder to the owner of the establishment as a means of settling an outstanding debt. Smoke from the doctor's perfecto cigar wafted upward, joining the haze created by the numerous cigarettes and cigars in the ill-ventilated bar room. Clatters of glasses, bursts of raucous hilarity from drunken patrons and the women who serviced them, the mixed odors of unwashed bodies and various intoxicants served as a backdrop to the game in progress.

Joseph picked up his cards and cursed. Two deuces, a trey, a nine and a seven. Another damnable hand. He slammed the cards on the table and winced as Charlie Rhodes set down a straight flush, and groaned as the doctor laid down a full house. At least Roberto Salvatori had a worse hand than himself.

The doctor chuckled. "Looks like the devil's got your luck tied up somewhere, Joseph. You might think about stopping before you lose everything."

"And you might think about minding your business," Joseph shot back, pushing his lost currency to the middle of the table where it was eagerly swept up by the doctor.

"But then my business is good tonight," the winner said, his face beaming, unoffended by Joseph's retort. Winning money often made one benevolent. Just as losing often made one vile. Tonight, Joseph felt very uncharitable. An unchecked anger simmered beneath the surface, waiting for a point of explosion. But this moment wasn't it.

Though he knew that tonight there would be a reckoning.

He abruptly slid back his chair, causing it to scrape against the wooden floor. He stood, picked up the glass, drained it, set it on the table again. Then he grabbed his coat from the hook on the adjacent wall and donned it before bending to pick up his hat from the floor.

"On second thought, gentlemen, I think I will take the kind doctor's advice, and save myself from abject penury. At least for tonight. Perhaps, tomorrow, Doctor, good luck will blow my way." He settled the hat on top of his head.

"The way yer been playin' lately, it'll be the stink of the Hudson fartin' in yer face, more like," Charlie piped in, and the table erupted in laughter. The gap between Charlie's teeth was a dark vacuum, and his already ruddy skin was blooming a dark crimson in his mirth. Stan O'Brien, the dealer, an old Irish reprobate with a bald pate and sparse, white whiskers, showed his near toothless gums in a smoke-choked guffaw, his cigarette dangling precariously from the side of his open mouth.

Joseph forced a smile. "Gentlemen, I will see you on the 'morrow, and then we shall see where fortune rests her head. Until then, I'll take my leave of this motley crew for someplace that is less redolent of vermin."

"Aaahh, I think the rich man, he insults us," Roberto muttered beneath ponderous muttonchops. Of the four, Roberto was the one with the stench attesting to long hours loading and unloading ships on the waterfront, with too little money to afford a decent dwelling that included indoor plumbing.

His hope to extend the few measly dollars he earned in a week was obviously dashed tonight. His black eyes glared at Joseph, settling his life's resentment on the object of benevolence that had been blessed with fortunes he himself could never dream of.

Joseph had run into his type before, sometimes at a poker table, sometimes on the docks, other times in the dens and whorehouses in the Tenderloin, or on Mulberry Bend in the Five Points district. They all saw a golden boy who had occasion to enjoy the pleasures of both worlds, a world of large mansions and lazy days waited on by dutiful servants, with time to dabble on the less savory side of existence, an existence of wine, women, and drugs. No one man should have everything was their silent and verbal sentiment. More than a few times, some reckless soul thought to act on that sentiment. More than a few times, they lived—and on one occasion, died—to regret it.

Attuned to these resentments, he was always aware of the eyes that followed him, that sized him up. He knew Roberto's stare cut blades through his back as he walked away. Those eyes were joined by others, predatory and calculating in their scrutiny. But he made it to the door unscathed.

Outside, a chilled November wind scurried the litter along the street. Several Negroes huddled together in front of the opposite building, a dilapidated two-story clapboard that housed one of the few brothels that serviced nonwhites. The irony was that whether a whore was black or not, it was the white brothel owner who determined to whom her wares would be sold. Money was a major factor, money that too often Negro laborers rarely had. Not that there wasn't a healthy market for black skin, even without Negro patronage. For that matter, there was a discernible and measurable taste for every shade of chocolate, including the more popular caramel and café au lait. Whether the hair was kinky or straight, the nose flared or keen, the face bare or with artifice, white men gathered to taste and feed. And drain. And fill. And feel. And add their own currency to the accounting of mulattoes that inhabited the mostly black denizenship of the Tenderloin and elsewhere.

Until Rachel, Joseph's taste had not run that course. He was wont to satisfy his needs in the Irish brothels that inundated parts of the Five Points, so named because of the five intersecting streets, Mulberry, Anthony, Cross, Orange, and Little Water. Within those corners was every vice that man or devil had ever invented, as well as an excruciating poverty, evidenced by overfilled tenements that weren't habitable for the basest barnyard animals. But newly arrived immigrants as well as Negroes, with little choice for accommodations, preferred a leaky, crumbling roof to no roof at all.

Joseph walked briskly down Thirty-ninth Street, then walked north along Seventh Avenue to Forty-second Street, passing dance halls and saloons along the way. The night dwellers were in various stages of inebriation, celebrating another Friday night. In front of La Maison de Plaisir, one of the pretentious French bordellos whose pimps sought out French immigrant women to exploit, two men were engaged in fisticuffs, surrounded by onlookers cheering them on.

He spotted a hansom and flagged it down. The driver slowed the horses, his cabbie hat pulled down over his brow so that his features were indistinguishable, even under the glare of the gaslight. Joseph got into the carriage, and shouted an address to the driver. The cab took off.

Joseph settled back against the leather, wrinkling his nose at a distasteful odor, something with the pungency of rotting onions. His head was throbbing now, and he massaged his brow with his fingers. What he needed was one of his nightly elixirs, wine laced with absinthe, which had a palliative effect against the stresses in his life. One of which he was going to deal with tonight.

He had given her no choice. The letter he'd sent had made it plain that she risked his exposing her secret—to her brother, her minister, and all those good Negro folk—if she did not comply.

He knew that he could not force her back into a relationship. But he needed to see her one last time. Just one more time to taste her softness, smell the scent of her love.

Then he would exorcise his demons once and for all.

Chicago, 2006

Consciousness returned in a haze of lines and angles. Slowly the lines and angles came together to form a face looming over her. The face was familiar, but it took her a few seconds to remember the name attached to it.

"David?" she whispered as he helped her sit up.

The haze moved out of her brain as her eyes focused. She looked around, slowly recalling where she was. She was at home, in her apartment. But for some reason, she was sitting on the floor.

"What happened?" she asked groggily.

David gently helped her to her feet. "You fainted. I don't know, one minute you were standing there with the door open, then you got this strange look, like you were frightened. I didn't know what was happening to you. God, Tyne, were you that scared of me? You have to know I wouldn't hurt you."

She shook her head slowly, more to clear away the fuzz than in answer to his question. Yet, she did remember fear, but of someone else.

"I don't know what happened. . . ." But even as she said this, images began replaying in her head. They had been arguing. She remembered his face, hard and angry. Then she told him to get out. She opened the door . . . and . . . and . . . he came at her. After that, everything was black.

Still, what she remembered hastened the rate of her breathing, the pulse of her heart. She had known this fear before, this terror that had consumed her for so many nights in her forever dream-dance of pursuit and evasion, which always ended with her pursuer finally subduing her. But then gradually the dream phantom had morphed into David, and she had found that she no longer wanted to run.

But those had been dreams. This was real. The fear was real. David was real. Her need to get away from him was real, also.

"David, please can you just go?" she pleaded.

He moved to touch her cheek, his face concerned, but she stepped back. "I don't want to leave you like this," he said quietly.

"David, don't you understand, you're the one making me like this! I can't deal with you right now! So, please, for the last time, just go!"

For the first time since she saw him on the stairs, his reason seemed to return. His eyes said there was more to be said, but after a moment, he turned to walk to the door. He paused, his back to her.

"It may not mean anything anymore, Tyne, but . . . I love . . ." The last word caught in his throat. Her breath caught also. Her tears were unexpected. The tears in his voice were just as painful. She didn't want to love him.

The phone rang, startling the quiet between them. He turned to look at her, his emotions naked and raw. Both of them stood unmoving, as though the ringing phone tethered them to their spots. As the call went to her answering machine, she expected to hear her mother's voice or that of one of her sisters. A male voice came on instead. An accented voice. Lem.

"Tyne, I know I just left. But I had to call to let you know how much I enjoyed myself tonight. I was just . . . well . . . I thought maybe we might get together again. As friends, of course. I know I shouldn't be calling so late. You're probably getting ready for bed now so I'll just call again tomorrow."

Tyne closed her eyes. Why did Lem have to call now?

"That's the man you were with at the party tonight, isn't it?" David's voice was so strained, it didn't sound like his own.

"David, I don't have to explain anything. You don't have that right anymore."

That knocked the anger out of him. "Did I ever have, Tyne?" he asked with sad resignation.

She sighed. "No, David, you never did. I was never yours."

Something seemed to go through him, something that visibly shook him. She couldn't take this any longer. She needed him to go, or she would collapse from her own sadness.

She started to the door, then heard a sound that hovered between a breath and a sob. She turned to tell him he had to leave. And stopped in half-motion.

Standing in profile was a stranger, his shoulders sloped, his head bowed, almost mournfully. The stranger said nothing.

The shock of this stranger standing before her broke through Tyne's memory block. This had happened before, only minutes ago.

Her whole body shook as he turned to her.

He looked at her in confusion, then seemed to remember who she was.

But the name he called out wasn't hers. Yet it was a name she'd heard before.

"Rachel?"

Chapter 33

New York—November 14, 1879

She would not, could not, she told herself, her hand nervously tightening around the green silk reticule that held the letter. The seed pearls adorning the purse seemed to burn through her gloves, searing her fingers. The illusory pain was both a beckon and an accusation. She should have thrown the letter away when it arrived in her mail over a week ago. Most of all, she should not have even opened it once she saw the postmark. Still, the pull had been too great, and she had opened the missive, and with each sentence, her horror had grown. Even now, she could remember nearly every word.

> *Rachel,*
>
> *I know that mine is the last face you would ever want to look upon again, and I have no doubt that you meant the words you last spoke to me, harsh words that ripped through my heart and left it in pieces. I am, therefore, appealing to your compassion, a trait of which I know you have an abundance and of which I hope you will spare a miniscule portion for me, your once lover, your forever love. You claimed that our love is over, but*

if what you felt was even one-tenth a measure of the fire that still burns inside me, I know that you still carry an ember of the passion that was ours. For a man starving for warmth, that ember is enough to carry me through the years in which you will deny me your presence, your touch, your smile.

As a starving man, I will do whatever I need to do to receive the sustenance I crave. And I crave you, you alone. There is no one else in this world but you. In my heart, my soul, my very dreams, there is always your beauty, your charm that is yours alone. I could marry any one of a number of beautiful women, cultured and suitable for a man of my position. But I find that my heart could never let them in because it brims full.

Do not think ill of me for these next words, but understand the desperation behind them. I must see you again, and if you do not oblige me just one more meeting, one last chance to savor your love, then I will not be responsible for what you will force me to do. Your standing, your relations with your brother, your church, your community will be little more than strewn rubble to be tossed away. I shall enlighten any who will hear me of the times we met, the love we made, the love you declared then so cruelly rescinded.

Understand, I do this not out of hatred or bitterness, but from a love that now tortures and consumes me. I shall die from it if I cannot have this one solace, a solace that will have to last me a lifetime, however brief or protracted that may be.

This coming Friday the 14th, at 8:00, I will have a calash waiting for you in front of Castle Belvedere in Central Park, the spot where you often came to meet me. Whatever you need to do to get away, whatever subterfuge, whatever dis-

*sembling you must do, please do so. The calash
will bring you to me. Even if for only an hour, we
will be together.*

Please do not disappoint me.

*Yours,
Joseph*

The room was filled with the Who's Who of the colored
elite. In the corner, chatting with Twila Dabney and her sisters, Flora and Esther, sat Miss Susan Maria Smith, from
Weeksville, Brooklyn, the first colored woman valedictorian
of the New York Medical College for Women and the first
ever to practice medicine in the state of New York. Lawrence
often mentioned Miss Smith with a paradoxical mixture of
racial pride and male resentment for a woman who was audacious enough to pursue and achieve that which was denied
to many colored men. Across the room, Mrs. Sarah Smith
Tompkins Garnett fanned herself against the temperature of
the overheated room. The public school principal was a personal heroine to Rachel, and Rachel often held the woman
up to her sixth grade class as an example of how far they
could go and what they could achieve if they set their minds
to the course. In the large chair next to the blazing fireplace
sat the illustrious abolitionist and journalist, Frederick Douglass, who was wiping away a bead of sweat with his handkerchief. His untamed hair and whiskers were even whiter
than last year when she had seen him at George's funeral. He
had purchased a home just a couple of years ago in Washing-
ton, D.C., but the distance never prevented him from answering a summon of duty. He and her father had been fellow
journalists and great friends. He was almost like a second father to her.

There were only about twenty souls stuffed into the
moderate-sized living room of the parsonage where the
Reverend lived with his daughters. They were gathered to
hear the appeal from Edwin McCabe, who was seeking financing of the migration of thousands of colored families

from the south to Kansas, in a movement referred to as the
"Exoduster." The native New Yorker had left his job on Wall
Street with dreams of establishing an all-black metropolis out
west; he was a major organizer of the movement. He sat now
with the Reverend, both men to the left of Douglass. The
Reverend stood up, the gleam of sweat on his brow visible in
the light of the oil lamps. A large, sturdy man (his daughters
took after him), he introduced the speaker. The gathered
guests welcomed Mr. McCabe with a warm applause. Rachel
clapped her hands mechanically, too aware of Lawrence sitting next to her. Lawrence often served in the capacity of attorney for the church, and was called whenever funds were at
issue. Mr. McCabe's voice boomed in the room, his expression assured as he was a man on a godly mission who did not
question the godliness of those assembled before him.

"Good friends, I thank you for your welcome, and for the
generosity of your time. I ask that you extend that generosity
even further to help those of our race who have not had the
fortunes God has blessed many of you with. As many of you
no doubt know, the colored families living in the south often
live in peril, especially since Congress passed the Civil Rights
Act, giving the Negro man the right to vote. Just a few years
back, in the great state of Mississippi, the white folks who
wanted to deny the Negro his vote used everything from po-
litical assassinations to intimidation to keep the Negro from
exercising his God-given rights as well as those privileges recently afforded to him by law.

"Unlike those of us in the North, our sisters and brethren
in the South have few expectations and even fewer choices.
Those who want to stand up and be counted as men are often
shot down like mongrel dogs. No, the white man will not let
them live in peace and with dignity. So, I say that if whites
and coloreds cannot live peaceably together, then let the two
races abide apart, with equal liberties and opportunities, and
no resentments for one by the other."

At this moment, McCabe paused for effect. Twila, ever dutiful, brought out a heretofore unseen glass of water, and

walked it to the speaker. He nodded gratefully as he took the glass and sipped at the refreshment. Twila waited as McCabe sipped some more. Then he gave her back the now half-filled glass and she took it away, gingerly stepping back to her place in the corner of the room.

Lawrence took this moment to lean over and whisper, "Are you all right? You look ill."

Rachel was aware of the lateness of the hour as well as what day it was. Friday, the 14th. The speaker began again, and Lawrence cast a quizzical glance at her, waiting for her answer.

She looked around at all the illustrious people gathered in the well-furnished room. This was her place in society. These people gathered here were people she admired and respected and whose respect she desperately wanted to keep. She imagined the disdain they would have for her if they were to discover how she had fallen.

In the end, she had no other choice. To maintain her place, to keep her good name, she would have to prostitute herself this one last time. She determined not to think about how she missed him, missed his touch, his voice. If she allowed herself that bit of truth, she would be lost.

She leaned toward her brother. "I think I should leave. It's overly warm in here, and I am feeling somewhat faint."

He moved as though to get up, but she stayed his action with a hand on his arm. "You are needed here, Lawrence. I will hail a cab."

"I will not leave you unescorted so late in the evening. I will come with you." Again the authoritarian voice, tempered with actual brotherly concern.

"Lawrence, I'd rather you didn't. You know I don't like a lot of fuss. Besides, the house is so near, I don't need an escort. Really, I'll be all right if you just don't make a grand production of this."

Lawrence looked undecided for a few moments. McCabe was talking about the thousands of dollars needed to purchase more land in Kansas for those families preparing for the move. Lawrence's ear was turned to this. The issue of money had arisen, the main reason his presence had been requested. Depending on how much financing would be needed, papers would have to be drawn up. It was important that he hear the rest of the speech so that he would be better informed for his talk with McCabe and the Reverend. This, Rachel knew, and she could see in her brother's face the moment he acquiesced to her request. He settled fully into his seat again.

"Well, I should be home no later than ten. I'll have to stay afterward to talk with the Reverend and Mr. McCabe. If you're sure you'll be all right . . ."

"I'm sure, Lawrence," she said calmly, even though she quaked inside. She rose in one move, motioning Twila that she was leaving. Unexpectedly, Twila rose also and followed Rachel out into the foyer where she gathered her coat from one of the coat hooks.

"Rachel, dear, is there anything wrong?" Twila asked, concern in her voice, but avid curiosity in her eyes, light brown eyes the color of topaz that were complemented by a brown and tan suede dress and lustrous light brown hair. The woman's upswept chignon added another inch to her already towering six feet. Not exactly beautiful, but handsome nonetheless, Twila's stature lent an inherent authority that she used to her advantage whenever she wanted to persuade someone to do her bidding, or to gently extract information. Rachel looked the woman in the eye, trying not to feel intimidation in addition to the other emotions coursing through her.

"There's nothing particularly wrong. I'm just not feeling myself tonight and thought it best to quit the evening now. Lawrence will stay, of course, to confer with your father later. He knows how important this evening is."

"I am sorry that you have to leave. I so rarely get to see you these days. It seems you've been . . . distracted . . . for the past few months. I do so miss our teas together. Maybe we can plan for something next week. Just us girls, Flora, Esther, Adele Watkins, and Bertha Mason. You know Bertha just gave birth last month and is slowly working her way back into the social calendar. We would just love to sit down with you and catch up on old business."

Rachel blinked, but smiled. "Of course, tea would be nice. I miss you all also, and apologize for past distractions that have kept me away. I promise you, though, I will not allow that to happen again."

Twila smiled widely. "I'm so glad to hear that. We would not want to lose the pleasure of your intercourse."

Rachel blinked at Twila's choice of wording, but only nodded as she finished buttoning her coat.

Twila opened the door. "Shall we say here, next Wednesday, then? Noon?"

"Yes, that will be fine, Twila. Absolutely lovely."

Rachel then escaped into the cold and only felt safe once Twila had finally closed the door. Providence was being either cruel or kind, as she spotted a hansom cab that had just turned onto the street of stately brownstones. She hailed it, and it obediently stopped.

The air was chilled, and she found herself trembling as she descended the stairs and waited for the driver to descend from his seat to help her into the cab. Even as the door closed against the cold, she found herself still trembling and knew that it was not the climate that had her in such a state.

She closed her eyes and prayed this night would end quickly.

Chapter 34

Chicago, 2006

Rachel? Why was he calling her that damned name?
The man took a step toward her and Tyne stepped back,
nearly knocking over a table situated near the door.

"Rachel, please don't run from me. Not again." He reached
out a hand, his eyes begging her.

Tyne fought through her panic and confusion, trying to
grab hold to some shred of reason. Anything to explain away
what was happening before her eyes. To explain how it could
be happening at all.

Either she was going crazy. And that frightened her.

Or this was truly happening. And that terrified her to the
core.

She was close to the door, but she knew he would be there
even before she could get it open.

Somehow she had to reason with him. Reason with this
stranger, who should be David. Who was David. She had to
convince him to go . . . or to let her go.

"I thought I had lost you, Rachel. Please, love, don't be
frightened. I won't hurt you . . . not like before."

He moved so quickly she didn't have a chance to evade his
grasp. His hand closed firmly around her arm, but not
roughly. A gentle vise. He pulled her close enough for her to
look up into his face, to see his features.

She couldn't believe the change. There was nothing left of David, as though he had been totally subsumed by the stranger. Yet, for some reason, the face was familiar. Or felt like it should be. The smell of liquor was warm on his breath. And his eyes had the dangerous edge of someone not clearly sober. Or sane.

"I'm . . . not . . . I'm not who you think I am. My name's Tyne, not Rachel. David, please let go of me."

His eyes hardened. "Why are you playing these games with me? Of course, you're Rachel! And please do not try to confuse me by calling me by another name. You know I'm Joseph."

"Joseph?" she whispered. No, his name was David. And hers was Tyne. And this wasn't happening. She was asleep, having another dream. A nightmare.

Another dream. A dream lover like David . . . but not David. Someone who could strike desire and fear. All of it so familiar.

He closed his eyes, his face in a grimace as though he were in pain. "For so long I thought you were . . ." He stopped, drew in an audible breath. Then pulled her completely to him.

His lips found hers and in her shock, she let him kiss her. Let him because she was afraid of what he would do if she resisted. He didn't invade her mouth, just let his lips wander along hers. She tasted him, felt the contours of his body. So familiar.

Yes, he had kissed her before. Had held her before this moment.

And not just in her dreams.

He pulled back finally and his eyes were clouded over. He stared at her, confused, as though he wasn't sure who she was. Then he released her and stepped away.

She knew that if she was going to escape, now was the time to do it, when he seemed so lost. Instead, she continued standing there, watching as his shoulders slumped and his face fell. The sadness emanating from him was almost palpable. It almost smothered her. He looked around the apartment as though seeing where he was for the first time.

"This isn't right. It isn't real," he said mournfully. "This place . . . you. It's all just a trick of my mind. A strange delusion somehow. My Rachel is gone, forever gone."

The grief in his voice struck a plaintive note. She'd heard that same note in David's voice that night when she'd run from him. And although the voices were different, they were echoes of one another. As though both were from the same man. As though this stranger named Joseph and the man she knew as David were—

Something inside her tried to hold on to a truth that was evasive, a truth that was so painful she didn't think she could stand to know it. But she reached beyond her fear and disbelief. Began gleaning the logic from the chaos before her.

The dreams. How they had pulled her to David and, at the same time, made her so afraid of him. The otherworldliness, the undeniable attraction. . . . But they were just dreams. They couldn't have been anything else. Could they?

The stranger stood unmoving, looking downward now at something unseen at his feet. Then he said, "My love's dead."

What was he seeing? Whatever it was had increased his sorrow greatly. He seemed paralyzed by the emotion. She stepped closer, keeping a safe distance. He lifted his head for a moment to look at her but his eyes were immediately drawn back to the unseen apparition.

"My beautiful Rachel. I killed her."

Tyne blinked at the confession. Killed her?

She didn't have to see his face to know that he was crying.

She should leave. Right now, just turn and walk out the door. She should find a phone, call the police, get him some help. But how could she explain that this stranger was and wasn't the man she knew as David Carvelli? The police would think she was the crazy one. Maybe, she was. Maybe she was only imagining the change, seeing David as someone totally different.

In the end, though, she knew she wasn't crazy or imagining things. Just as she knew she wouldn't leave. Even as everything inside her resisted, tried to block out the madness of this night. Told her to run. Told her she was in danger.

Instead, she accepted the duality that was David . . . and Joseph. That they were the same. And that they both mourned a woman named Rachel. A woman they both had loved. Still loved. A woman Joseph just admitted killing.

She should have been afraid, but her earlier fear was gone, replaced by an overwhelming sadness. And as she stood watching the man she had made love with, made love to, saw him swallowed into someone else, she could finally admit her deepening feelings, though she had tried so hard to deny them these past weeks. She couldn't bear to see him so tormented. And even though he wasn't David physically, she knew that the anguish the stranger felt was also David's anguish. His pain belonged to David.

Whatever she had to do to stop that pain, she would.

Even if she had to become Rachel to do it.

She just didn't know how.

New York—November 14, 1879

The calash was there, just as he had promised. It was a dark silhouette beneath the gaslight that darkly illuminated the stones of the medieval-looking folly known as Castle Belvedere. There were just a few souls wandering around the serpentine paths, one of the reasons Joseph had decided to make the park, and particularly this out-of-the-way spot, their meeting place. He would often drive her from here, going to his apartment or some other secluded place. During those times, when she had stood before the battlements of the building, anticipation had built, making her feel giddy and sullied at the same time. And, like a whore, she had gone willingly.

Now, she was not willing, even though her blood coursed to those intimate parts of her body in expectation of his touch. As she descended from the cab and approached the calash, the shadow that was the driver became more distinct. He must have been given a description because he stepped down from his seat and approached her.

"Would you be named Rachel, ma'am?" he said with a thick Irish brogue. The "ma'am" would have been at Joseph's insistence; white men did not address a colored woman with such deference. Especially not a man from the street, as surely this man was.

"Yes, I am Rachel. Where are we going?" she asked as he led her to the calash, then helped her up the two-wheeled vehicle into the hooded interior of soft leather seating. The comfort of the carriage made her feel even more like a bought woman. Joseph always provided nice transports to their secret places, places that invariably would be stark and spare, with maybe a table and chair, and always a bed. With clean sheets. He provided that little comfort, at least. He never gave her much time to notice the ugliness of their surroundings, his ardor eclipsing every sense she had.

The driver did not answer her question, but proceeded along the lane leading them out of the park. At the exit, he veered the horses south, taking them down Fifth Avenue. They drove along, but her mind was blind to the sights they passed. Twenty minutes seemed more like an hour, and she drew her coat tightly around her, feeling a chill where there was none. Her mind came out of its fog after a time only when she realized they were passing the rebuilt Madison Square Theatre.

The sight of the building now jarred her. It meant they were on Twenty-fourth Street. Joseph's apartment was on Twenty-sixth. They had passed the turn.

Confused, and a little frightened, she demanded against the wind, "Driver, where are you taking me?"

He half turned his head and his words seemed lost in the clatter of horses' hooves and the rush of air caused by their swift pace. "The Points, ma'am," drifted to her, and for a moment, she thought she had misheard him. But they were still going southward, and a dread took hold, bringing a new level of fear. Five Points. A district so infamous that decent folk only deign to read about it in the newspaper. It was the site of murders, thievery, and debauchery on a level that no city had ever seen before. More important, it was the site of the 1863 Draft Riots sixteen years earlier, where white men and women ran rampant, targeting innocent Negroes to assault. By the end of the riots, more than two thousand souls were lost.

She yelled to the driver to stop, but he kept his speed, ignoring her plea. She did not want to go to that place. If she thought she'd been diminished by her assignations in The Tenderloin, there would be no washing off the filth that would cover her soul just by stepping foot in Five Points. Only the worst or poorest souls dwelled there, and now he was making her an honorary resident of that damnable place, even if for a short period of time.

Her pleas went unheeded for the remainder of the ride. They passed Eleventh Street, Tenth, Ninth before the driver turned east on Eighth. This was some horrible nightmare. Each passing mile brought her closer to something she couldn't imagine. They reached The Bowery, where the driver then turned southward. Thirty-five minutes had already passed. Even if Joseph did not keep her for an hour, there would be no way that she could get home before Lawrence did. She would have to lie, knowing that Lawrence would not believe her. That he had stopped believing her a long time ago.

The smell of overrun sewers hit her abruptly, causing her to gag. Mixed with the sickening odor was the brine of the East River. She had never been this far south in the city. Outside of her honeymoon in Chicago and her years in Tennessee at Fisk, Fort Greene had basically encompassed her entire world. She had always felt safe there, far removed from many of the ills most colored women had to endure. Now she had put herself in harm's way because of her weakness of spirit.

The driver finally pulled over on a long, narrow street that was strewn with debris. Of the gas lamps that stood on either side of the street, only a few seemed to be working, leaving most of the buildings looming ugly in the dim light of a wan moon. In a few of the doorways, men and women loitered, their talk loud and strident. Many of the buildings appeared to be shops of various sorts. In front of a pawnbroker shop, two men stood arguing animatedly. Next to it was a structure barely more than a shanty that passed itself off as a hotel. Another building, this one two-storied, had a sign announcing itself as a boardinghouse. In front of this was parked a hansom cab. The distant strains of a player piano and discordant singing indicated a concert saloon nearby.

The driver stepped down from his seat and rounded to where she sat, then put out his hand. She sat for a moment, resistant to his tacit signal to step down. But then the door to the cab across the street opened, and a man in a dark coat and hat stepped down. He walked toward them, his pace slow and deliberate. As he neared, his features became clear and achingly familiar. Her heart jumped at the hardness of his face, a face that she hadn't seen in the three weeks since she had left his apartment vowing never to see him again.

Even then, both of them had known that she was fooling herself. Because here he was again and here was she. He stood near the calash now. The driver stepped aside. This time it was Joseph's hand that beckoned, and after a hesitant moment, she gingerly took it, her body warming at the first contact.

Desire battled fear and indignation. "Why did you bring me here to this place?" she demanded as soon as she alit.

He smiled, but it did not soften his face.

"So that we are far from any distractions and so that there is no chance of you easily making off into the night. Tonight, we will not be interrupted and you will not leave me . . . until I say."

Her tongue failed her. She had never seen him like this before, and she realized that he had lied. This would not be a matter of an hour, or a night, for that matter. For it was apparent now that he would never leave her alone.

She was silent as he led her across the lane to the boarding-house from where the hansom cab had since departed.

He stopped at the bottom of three stairs that led up to the entrance, indicating that she should precede him. He followed her and she could feel his presence behind her. He pulled a key from inside his coat and opened the plain-looking door.

A stifling darkness obscured the immediate interior. He was waiting at the door, again signaling for her to proceed. With no further protest, she stepped blindly into hell.

Chapter 35

Chicago, 2006

He didn't respond as she stepped a little closer. His eyes still stared downward at a horror only he could see.

"Dav . . . Joseph, talk to me," Tyne encouraged softly. "Tell me what you're seeing." And with a faith she couldn't explain, she asked, "Is it me you see lying there?"

The man named Joseph lifted his head and turned to her. His face was contorted with his confusion and despair. "Rachel? But . . . it isn't you, is it? After all, how could you be here?" He looked down, then at her again, as though trying to decide between reality and illusion. "I killed you," he said in a voice strained with remorse and disbelief.

She edged closer. "No, David. I'm here, standing next to you. Please, try to understand that what you're seeing there on the floor isn't real. But I *am* real, Dav . . . I mean, Joseph. I'm right here, alive."

For a second, it seemed as though he did understand as he stared at her, trying to comprehend. But just as suddenly a blaze of fury swept over his face. "What kind of trickery is this? You are not Rachel! You can't be her because she lies here dead at my feet! And she's lying there because of me! Because of me." This last trailed off in a moan. "I did this to her!"

He looked at Tyne again with such incredible anger, she

had to resist the urge to take a step back. He railed at her. "What did you think to gain by trying to make me believe Rachel is alive, and that you are her? Yes, you may resemble her . . . but you are not her! Because she was my everything. . . ." He looked somberly at the empty floor, all of the anger visibly seeping from him. His voice was dead as he said, "And now I have nothing."

Still uncertain of the rightness of what she was doing, Tyne reached out a tentative hand and laid it gently on his arm. "Tell me what happened to her, Joseph."

She could feel his body trembling. Then he let out a wretched cry and said, "Dear, God, all I wanted to do was see her one last time, just one more time. I would have let her go. But . . . oh, God . . . everything is so blurred, I can't even remember. . . ."

She gripped him tighter, moved until she was a breath away from him. "Try to remember, Joseph. What happened to Rachel?"

New York—November 14, 1879

Joseph wanted to savor this evening, this hour. He had to restrain the craving that had nearly overtaken him the moment he saw her, the second he touched her hand. Her scent was soft jasmine and permeated the space around her. She sat in one of the two chairs, looking up at him with trepidation. He didn't want to see that fear there, had not wanted her to feel threatened in any way. But how could she not? He had summoned her with a threat and then had brought her here to this godforsaken place to force her to do that which she would not willingly do.

A bottle of absinthe rested on a three-legged wooden table next to the only window. The table's surface was scratched and bruised from years of overuse and the wear of time. Everything in the room was worn, tired, a pall to the eyes. By contrast, Rachel's beauty shone like a precious diamond. In his desire to have her alone, he had paid the owner, a Mrs. Doggel, fifty dollars for the whole night with the stipulation that she was not to stay in the downstairs room where she usually slept. Not tonight. The old hag had happily snatched the money from his hand, then winked obscenely. "Rest assured, Mista, that ole bed up der has seen betta days, but she'll do you well, nice and sturdy." This had been followed by an equally obscene cackle that had made his skin crawl.

The bed did look sturdy. The legs were of oak, although quite scarred. He had also paid to have the mattress changed and had checked earlier to make sure his instructions were followed. There were also clean sheets, although somewhat faded to a mottled gray from their original white. He never wanted to soil her with someone else's filth.

Joseph saw her note the direction of his gaze, saw a shade of color flood her caramel skin. Skin so soft, like the gossamer wings of a butterfly. Poetic hyperbole, he knew, but there was no other way to describe his pleasure in touching her. He felt himself stiffening, readying for her. But not yet. To distract himself, he grabbed one of the glass cups on the table. He poured the absinthe into the glass, then asked with his eyes whether he should do the same for her. She shook her head. She never did indulge in this sin, at least.

The liquor went down raw, a fire in his throat. It seared its way to his stomach, settled there, quietly simmering like the waters of Parnassus. No, not Parnassus, that elicitor of poetry, whose waters quench appetites and desires. If anything, his desires were stoked, aided by the liquor as well as the heroin he had earlier imbibed. Time was passing quickly; there was not much left of it. If he was to keep his word to her, he would have to move now.

In two strides, he walked to Rachel and abruptly pulled her up from the chair. The sudden motion caused her to inhale sharply. He closed his arms around her waist, and without a word, brought his lips down on hers.

Her lips were not compliant, and he felt her whole body stiffen against his assault. He could not help but compare this kiss to their first, when again she had stiffened against his sudden act, unexpected because moments before he had been sitting demurely in one of her parlor chairs in the house she shared with her brother. It had been his third visit, that one as furtive as the preceding two. From the moment he had left the ball weeks before, he knew that he would see her again, somehow. After diligently seeking out her address from sources around town, he had staked out her home for nearly a week until he knew her and her brother's comings and goings, the exact times when they both left for work, when they returned. Her brother, the attorney, never returned until evening, leaving many hours between his return and that of his sister's from her teaching duties at the school where classes ended in the early afternoon.

Though surprised when she answered the bell that first time and found him at her door, she had not denied him entry nor courtesy. Her graciousness had given him hope, and had emboldened him then much as the liquor emboldened him now. Their first kiss had been sweet; this one was bittersweet. Now, just like the first time, he felt her resistance give way, felt her body mold into his, her mouth soften, allowing his tongue access to her own.

Several intoxicating moments passed before he pulled away. She was breathing hard, her eyes luminous, her desire apparent. Still, she said breathlessly, "This *is* the last time. And if you dare threaten me again, I will simply leave the city and go someplace where you can never find me."

The defiance, instead of tempering his ardor, set it ablaze. "There is no place you can go, Rachel, where I will not find you. Forever isn't hardly enough time for us."

"You're mad!"

"If loving you is madness, then yes I am mad. I freely admit it. And like a happy lunatic, I welcome the madness and will enjoy its every pleasure."

Unceremoniously, he grabbed the lacing of her bodice, and with a deftness of habit, unlaced the top of her dress. She did not protest, but neither did she aid him. After bodice, skirt, bustle, underwear, and shoes had been nearly ripped from her, she stood nude, her arms around her breasts as though to hide them from him. He pulled her arms away and settled his tongue on a nipple, knowing the pleasure this would elicit. With satisfaction, he heard her barely stifled moan.

His lips traveled along her breasts, nape, shoulders, touching every contour with the renewed vigor of an explorer too long kept from his quest. He could feel the stirrings and shudders, her body's betrayal of her will.

He stopped only to finally lead her to the bed. He gave her a little shove, and she dropped onto the mattress with a small bounce. He then positioned her, hindered by her disobliging limbs. Letting lust take him, he shed his own clothes hastily. He joined her, resuming his trek along her body with tongue, lips, fingers, hands. Despite his varied attentions, she lay there as though dead or dying, her whole body stiff, unresponsive. Not even the earlier shudder. He lifted up to look at her face, then saw the lone tear running toward the pillow, where it merged into the already stained fibers.

In that moment, the passion left him, and shame settled in its place. Love didn't ask for another's abasement and he did love her. If he hadn't known it before, if he had only thought that it was her beauty and flesh that called out to him, he knew now that he could never harm her soul. Not like last time, when he had forced her, to both their surprise. He hadn't planned to hurt her then, but realized that it was her pain he had planned for now. Realized now that he could truly not force her body, nor her heart.

He rose from the bed, his emotions dead in the cold glare of self-examination.

"Get dressed," he said quietly.

Her eyes registered confusion, until she realized he meant what he said. Then they held relief, a fact that stabbed his already wounded heart.

She sat up on the bed, her bare feet barely touching the floor. "So, you'll let me go then? And not require . . ."

"You can go," he said abruptly, already donning his own

clothes with a somberness reserved for someone in preparation for a funeral.

"But why?"

He damned her curiosity. Couldn't she just get dressed without questioning him? Without forcing him to admit to her as he had to himself that he had sunk so low that he didn't think he could ever recover his own esteem? That he would forever know that he was no better than a rapist lurking in the dark waiting for his prey?

"It doesn't matter," he said. "Just know that this will be the last time I ever ask anything of you and that I truly regret all that has happened between us."

"Everything then?" she asked. There was a touch of hurt in the question.

"Woman, what do you want from me?" *Will you please choose one road or another! You don't want any part of me, yet you want me to want you! Well, I'll not be the fool in this game anymore! Just get dressed, and I'll get you a cab.*"

He turned from her, trying not to listen to the rustling of clothing as she silently dressed.

He stood now fully dressed with his back to her, allowing her the dignity he had stolen earlier.

"You can turn around now," she said, and he turned to find her standing quietly, beautifully regal in a green velvet and tulle dress. She'd been wearing green when he first saw her eons ago. Around her neck was a gold locket in the shape of a heart. She'd worn it that night also. She had told him that it was an anniversary present from her late husband. The color of the dress set off the glow of her skin, the luster of her reddish hair. Lust and desperation had blinded him earlier. He realized at this moment that this would be the last time he would see her.

"Let's go." He held out an arm, and for a second she seemed hesitant to touch him. He wondered that a man already dead could still feel pain.

He escorted her down the steep stairs. The state of the hostel was shameless, but indicative of the owner's near poverty.

As bad as this home was, it still was heads above the stifling, windowless apartments nearby that at times sheltered nearly twenty people.

They reached the door, opened it. He let her precede him. He had just descended the three stairs when he heard a familiar voice.

Chapter 36

Joseph thought he heard a woman's voice, strangely familiar, floating to him on the wind. "What else happened, David?" But the words drifted away, quickly replaced by someone else's.

"You left too soon, rich man. You no give me the chance to win some a tha money in your pockets. Now, dat's no like a real gentleman, such is yo'self."

Joseph stared in comprehending fear at the barely lit figure of his poker partner, Roberto Salvatori. Something gleamed in his left hand. Staring harder, Joseph made out the silhouette of a switchblade.

"You no walk too fast, rich man. Not very smart. Easy for someone to follow, tho it cost me much to hire a cab afta your own. And the cold, she hits the bones real hard when waitin', but I find waitin' worth the while." The glimmer of teeth was barely perceptible in the darkness. Joseph peered around. There were still folks about, but none the likes who would come to someone's rescue. They would more likely join in on the fun. But the only one he was worried about was the woman on his arm, who was clenching him in a way that would have earlier made his heart beat faster. Now, it just reminded him that he had something more valuable to protect.

"Roberto, you never were one to take your losses like a good sport. But I'm not going to argue with you over funds.

Here . . . all right, I'm just going to reach into my pocket to get my wallet, nothing else."

Still, he could feel the Italian's nervousness. He had to disengage Rachel's nervous hand to reach for the wallet that might save them both. Damnably, he had left his own knife at home, so he was at a disadvantage.

Another figure neared them, and he held out hope that maybe there was a Samaritan among the denizen of thieves. But that hope was quickly dashed as he soon realized that his disadvantage was doubled as the man stopped next to Roberto.

"I got the ride. Hadda kill the driva though," the man said, his accent a fading brogue, indicating how long he had been in America. But different species were known to band together after a common prey. Joseph knew that his luck had just run dry, but inopportunely when the dearest thing he had ever possessed was with him. Unfortunately, Roberto also noticed.

"Not mucha man, are you? Lovely whore like dis would keep a real man busy for hours. At least, dat's 'mount of time wha I thought I was gonna have to wait. 'Magine my surprise when I seen you two comin' out the door. Told myself, rich man no know how to pleasure a woman. Good thang Roberto knows how."

"Wait, you damn cur . . ."

"Ah, ah, now," Roberto waved the knife like a censoring finger. "Don't make dis an unpleasant experience. We just gonna take a ride."

"Here!" Joseph threw the wallet at Roberto. His partner quickly grabbed it up from the ground. "There's over a thousand in there, enough to keep your sorry ass for a month of days! Given my reputation, I'm hardly one to call in the police. So, just let me and the lady go, and we'll call us even for tonight."

A bitter laugh ensued. "Rich man think we even. Lemme tell you, rich man, we ain't never gonna be even. You always gonna have ev'ythang you want, while a bum like me havta kill himself on the docks just to keep a measly wormy bread on my plate. Even yo nigger whore is bedda than soma the Irish shanties that put out fo a whole week's pay. But see, rich man, I gonna get me a taste of the good life, if just for dis night. I gonna know the fun life, like a rich man knows."

Roberto waved the knife, indicating they should begin walking to a vehicle parked across the street. Joseph recognized the insignia on the calash; it was the same he had hired to pick up Rachel. His guilt was hardly piqued as he realized that his actions tonight had already cost a life. His whole focus was to get Rachel, if not him, out of danger. The danger he had put her in.

Roberto forced them into the calash, Joseph first, then Rachel. Then he squeezed in next to her, his knife pressed at her breast. "Just so you no get any hero ideas. You move, dis knife go in, unnerstan?"

Joseph nodded. The other man took the driver's seat and hit the lash across the horses' backs, causing them to whinny in protest.

"No so rough you Irish stupido! More easy, so dey do wha you say!" Roberto yelled at his cohort. Soon, the calash headed down the street. Joseph could only pray that they survived their destination.

Chicago, 2006

Tyne didn't understand. Why did Joseph believe he killed Rachel? From what he had just told her, they had both been victimized by criminals.

But he had put Rachel in a situation that obviously led to her death. That would make anybody feel responsible, as though he had killed her himself.

"Joseph, don't you see, you weren't the one who killed Rachel," she said softly.

"But I did kill her," David said quietly. "I didn't mean for it to happen. God forgive me."

Tyne closed the space between them even farther, felt safe enough to stroke his hair, to comfort him.

"No, you didn't kill Rachel, Joseph."

When he looked at her, the hardness of his eyes caused her heart to skip a beat. "I know what happened to her, you don't! You couldn't possibly know!" His eyes clouded over, and he began again.

New York—November 14, 1879

Joseph knew they were in more trouble than he had anticipated when the calash stopped in front of an old warehouse at the south end of the long pier that ran along the East River. It was late into the evening, past the time when even the straggler dock men worked. Besides, it was Friday night, when hardworking men were eager to lighten their pockets of the change they had been paid. Given the solitude of the place, Joseph figured there was only one reason the men had brought them here—to dispose of their bodies. It might have been their plan for him all along, but they were more than willing to accommodate Rachel, as well.

A chill wind came from the river, as well as the smell of discarded garbage that had been cast into its waters.

Roberto got down first, his knife still aloft in the air, should either of them get any ideas. Joseph's only plan at this time was to let himself be sacrificed to save Rachel, if that was even a remote possibility. He just had to find the perfect time; if he couldn't kill them, he would occupy their attention totally, and hope that Rachel could get away.

She had been quiet throughout the ride, even when the fiend took opportunities to feel along her breast, probably hoping to rile Joseph into action. Joseph had reined in his anger, though, knowing that it would better serve him later.

Like the true lady she was, Rachel had maintained a dignified silence, never letting the ruffian see her fear. Even though she knew she could die this night, she would not die cowering. Joseph felt an ill-timed pride in the woman who would have his love always—and an unbearable guilt that he had brought her to this.

"Step down, and don't cha try nothin'," Roberto warned, more to Joseph than Rachel, whose arm the man latched onto, his knife again at her breast. The other man descended from the driver's seat. He looked avidly at Rachel and said, "Now for some real fun, huh, Roberto?"

Roberto said nothing, but smiled, an evil expression obvious even in the dingy lights that scarcely lit the dock. He pulled at Rachel, his anticipation obvious, steering her toward the decrepit building. The door gave way easily with one swift kick of Roberto's boot, and in a matter of seconds, all four of them were inside.

Joseph's heart fell even more as he made out two more figures in the lit interior. The warehouse was nearly empty, except for a few shipping boxes lining either wall. A rickety ladder rested against the floor of a second landing, which held more boxes. The air was cold and stale.

The first man, Joseph did not recognize, not that it mattered. But the other, he knew all too well. Charlie Rhodes. Obviously, he and Roberto had hatched the scheme together, more out of a mutual resentment than mere robbery itself. Charlie had never had any love loss for Joseph, especially since he was more likely than not to lose to the latter's usually expert skills. Tonight had been a rare fluke. But Joseph's loss tonight had obviously not persuaded Charlie from his nefarious intent to see his gambling nemesis dead.

Charlie stared at Rachel. "What the hell is this? It was just supposed to be him." He nodded a head at Joseph. "Whatcha go and bring this nigga bitch here for?"

"What else we gonna do wit' her?" Roberto blasted back at his partner. "She wit' him, she die wit' him. 'Sides," he leered at her figure, "she a fine lookin' whore, worth the trouble, 'ey?"

Charlie and the fourth man seemed to think it over for a second, sizing up Rachel, whose cloak had been discarded in the calash at Roberto's insistence. The men's features slowly began to mimic Roberto's ugly leer.

Joseph cast a sidelong glance at Rachel. For the first time, he saw fear in her profile. She had expected death, maybe had even hoped for escape from despoilment from the first two men. Now that there were four, she had obviously given up hope of any escape.

Charlie stepped to her, pinched her nipple, causing her to gasp. "That hurt, missie? Gonna be more of it, just you wait. Gonna make your fancy man watch us have fun wit' ya. Then gonna watch as we make him show us wha he do to you in the dark."

"Please, if any of you are Christian men. . . ." she began to plead.

"Aah, I don't think Christ gives a care for the likes of you, no how," the fourth man piped up. Dark haired with blotchy skin, an ugly scar ran across his brow, marring what might have been a handsome face a long time ago. But age, drink, drugs, and the way of the street had sapped him of all virtue a long time ago.

Roberto handed his second partner, their driver, the knife, so that he could commence with unbuckling his pants. Rachel stepped back, which gave Joseph the chance he had been waiting for. He quickly shoved Rachel aside and lunged for the man holding the knife. He hadn't been as careful as his partner, and Joseph easily wrenched the knife away from the startled man.

In a split second, he grabbed Rachel's arm, the knife waving in the air toward three men, including Roberto and Charlie. He desperately pulled her toward the door and felt hope again the nearer he backed away from his captors. But where was the fourth man? The answer came in the unmistakable impression of the neck of a gun in his back.

The fourth man had anticipated Joseph's move. "Now, we're not gonna leave before the party's started, are we? You gotta watch us have at your whore, now don't you? That'll be the last thing you see on this earth."

The other men were closing in. Roberto had kicked off his pants, his stained long johns tattered in various places. He groped at the obscene bulge between his legs as he advanced toward Rachel. "All dis for you," he taunted her. Joseph's hand was still around Rachel's arm. He felt the shudder go through her. He couldn't imagine her horror. In his other hand, he still held the blade.

"Now, drop the knife slowly," the man behind him directed. "Otherwise, I'll blow a hole in your back big enuf to dock a steamer."

Joseph knew that he was dead, whether he obeyed the man or not. There was no reasoning with these animals. And Rachel was dead, too. They would use her, then kill her. The only thing he could do was give her a clean, quick death so that she would not have to be despoiled by these men.

His hand acted almost before his brain had stemmed over the decision. With a quick, easy move he brought the knife against the pliable skin of her neck. It gave way easily, a cascade of blood squirting her would-be attackers. The fourth man, reacting to Joseph's sudden action, cocked the hammer of the gun. But when he sought to shoot, there was only a click indicating a jammed chamber. In that moment, Joseph dropped Rachel's dying body to the wooden floor.

"What the . . ." the man started at the gun, and in that flat second, Joseph lodged the knife into the man's gut. Grief and vengeance moved him in his quest that none survive this night. Without a knife or another weapon, Roberto was already backing away, then he turned to run in the opposite direction. At that moment, his driver tried to make a pass around Joseph, seeking escape through the door. But Joseph reached out and rammed the knife into the back of the fleeing man's neck. Blood spilled from the wound when Joseph pulled the weapon away.

By now Roberto had reached the ladder that led up to the second story. Joseph ran the span of feet that separated him from his quarry. Roberto was nearly halfway up when Joseph kicked the ladder from beneath him. The already ponderous man fell heftily to the floor with an "Ooommph," landing on his back. His ugly face was uglier with fear. He began crawling away.

"Please, no do it! I was no gonna kill you! It was Charlie what planned it all! You see, it was his cousin you killed that time! He figured tonight would be good since you already drunk on the drugs and all! It was Charlie! Charlie!" This last was almost a scream.

But Charlie wasn't here, having escaped in the melee.

The man sought to continue his plea, but Joseph pulled him up with one arm as though his weight was nothing. Then he slammed Roberto against the nearest wall, his hatred focused on this pathetic fool who was probably nothing but a pawn, but who had been too willing to hurt Rachel and to kill them both. There wasn't an ounce of human left inside Joseph. Just predator instinct. His humanity lay dead on the floor where Rachel rested.

Without a word, for the man didn't deserve even that courtesy, Joseph plunged the knife into his neck, forever freezing Roberto's pop-eyed horror on his face. Then he brutally pulled the weapon from the still warm flesh and slammed the blade into the man's heart. The blood shot at Joseph, got into his mouth. The body half twisted as it fell to the floor, spraying the filthy walls red. The man's blood was already soaking into the wooden floor.

Joseph stood for what seemed like an eternity, staring down at the dead man, trying to steel himself for what he must do. He had survived, when he had not planned to. She had not, as he had so desperately wished. There was nothing he could do to save her. He turned slowly.

She lay a few feet away. He walked slowly toward her, already knowing what he would do with her body. Already feeling the eternity of grief and shame he would feel for his lifetime. For several lifetimes.

Chapter 37

Chicago, 2006

Carmen Carvelli ran her finger down the names listed alongside the mailboxes. This had to be the building, it had to be. Her vision couldn't have been wrong. She had wasted enough time driving around, at one point taking a wrong turn that had cost her precious minutes. Now standing in front of the brownstone, she found the name she'd been searching for. T. Jensen. Tyne Jensen, the name of the woman David had told her about. Carmen rang the bell once, twice in quick succession, then a third time. She shivered in the cold, closed her eyes in a quick prayer as she waited for a response. And saw David brandishing a knife. The same vision she'd had twice now.

"Please, c'mon, c'mon," she pleaded to the wind.

But was only met with silence.

He bent solemnly over Rachel's lifeless body. Her beautiful vacant eyes stared up at him.

He heard a motion and looked up. And there she was standing in front of him. It was all confusion. Rachel was dead . . . and alive.

From somewhere, the sound of bells chimed. Their cheery sound mystified him. They were so incongruous to the moment.

He saw the other Rachel walk toward the door and push a button. He heard a distant voice that seemed familiar yet he couldn't figure from where.

"Please, my name is Carmen Carvelli. My son, David, is he there with you?"

Rachel said something he couldn't make out, pushed a button in the wall. A waspish buzz sounded and she opened the door, waiting for someone.

He stood from the lifeless Rachel, moved toward the unfamiliar Rachel who was still so beautiful, yet so different. The hair was not long, nor reddish, but dark. The lips, fuller. The eyes were still those of a doe and they sparkled as he remembered. She turned as he reached out to her and her eyes widened with fear. Fear of him.

He took another step closer, thinking to comfort her, to tell her everything would be all right. That he would never let anything happen to her again.

But she backed away, her eyes staring at his outstretched hand. "Where did that come from?"

He stopped and looked down. In his hand was the knife that had taken Rachel's life. The same knife he'd used to avenge her death. Not his own, but the one he took from one of the bastards who sought to rape her. Strange. It was no longer bloodstained.

Another gasp. Another voice. "Oh my God, David!"

He looked up to see an older woman just in the doorway. Again, the voice and face were familiar, but he just couldn't grasp why he knew her. She had called him David. Just as Rachel . . . no, not really Rachel . . . had done earlier. Why did they insist on calling him this name?

"David, please," the other one, the beautiful one, pleaded. There were tears in her eyes. He felt the need to kiss those tears away. He took a few more steps, and the other woman pulled something from the reticule she clutched in her hand.

"David, please, I'm begging you!" The older woman had tears in her voice. He saw the gun in her hand. Saw that her hand was shaking. He had to get the gun away from her before she hurt herself. Before she hurt Rachel. He couldn't stand the thought of losing Rachel again.

He approached the woman, reaching out. Then there was a loud explosion.

He felt himself falling back, felt the impact of his body hitting the floor. He shifted his head and saw Rachel lying next to him, her eyes still vacant. She was so near he could reach out to touch her. As he felt her cold flesh, he thought that this was as it should be. He should have died with her that first time.

He closed his eyes and waited for death to take him.

Chapter 38

Carmen Carvelli stood listening to the bleeps that tracked David's tenuous hold on life. Every pause on the monitor caused her own heart to miss a beat. She clutched the cold bed railing as she looked down at her son, still unconscious after six hours. He was too pale, as though the transfused blood refused to flow through his veins. She placed a trembling hand to his forehead, tracing a finger along his flesh. He no longer felt clammy, but he was several degrees cooler than normal. The doctor—she couldn't remember his name—had told her that David was expected to pull through, but that the next few hours were critical. She wanted to believe everything would be OK. But there were many things that could still go wrong. She could still lose him.

And it would be her fault. She had only meant to aim at his hand to make him drop the knife. But the gun had jerked in her nervous clutch, and the bullet nicked an artery in his right forearm instead. David nearly bled to death before the paramedics got to the apartment minutes later. The doctor told her that eight pints of blood had to be pumped into him to keep his heart going during surgery.

She barely remembered all that had happened between that first horrible moment and now. She looked at the clock; it was just a little past three A.M. With the harsh fluorescent lights and the closed blinds, Carmen didn't notice the passing of time. The room was a vacuum removed from reality. Occasionally, she heard the steps of someone passing by, otherwise the corridor was a tomb. The only reason the attending doctor had allowed her in this late (or early) was because of the circumstances. David could still die, and she needed to be by his side in case he took his last breath.

The horrible nightmare of the previous hours intermittently flashed through her mind. David, being wheeled away. The police station, dirty and cold. Tyne in a haze of shock. Yet the young woman had been alert enough to speak to the first officers at the apartment. To give Carmen an alibi she hadn't asked for. The story offered was that Carmen and David had been visiting Tyne. At some point Carmen had reached into her purse for something, and had pulled out the gun she kept for personal safety. Somehow the gun had accidentally gone off.

A simple lie. The two officers had looked at both women skeptically and then loaded them into waiting squad cars to take them to the station. They hadn't had time to get the story straight, so Carmen just restated the lie with a little detail when she was questioned alone. She told the officer (who reminded her a little of David) that she'd been reaching for her cigarettes, had pulled the gun out because it blocked her search. That somehow the safety had shifted and the gun had gone off.

The police held her for a couple of hours, during which she pleaded to see her son. Without any evidence, they couldn't do anything but let her go . . . for now.

Everybody was waiting for David to regain consciousness to tell his side of the story. If he lived to tell it.

The only thing was, even if he came out of the coma, he probably wouldn't remember anything.

Carmen hoped desperately that was the case.

She would rather go to jail than have David tormented with the realization of his past life, the deeds he could not undo, in this lifetime or any other. He was no longer that shadowy stranger that she'd seen standing in the middle of the apartment, his hand clutching a long knife. He was her David, her son.

She touched him again. This time he stirred. And she held her breath.

"So, what exactly did happen?" Tanya pressed, her eyes unwavering. Tyne was finding it hard to meet those eyes.

Tyne sighed, looked at both Tanya and April, who, despite her protests, had come over to the apartment anyway. They were sitting side by side on the sofa, their faces hard with a no-nonsense threat to them. She had had to field so many questions last night, first from the police, then the media who had brought vans around early in the A.M. And later that morning, she'd put in calls to her family and to Sherry to fend off another round of queries before the story hit the air, hoping to avoid this very confrontation.

Her mother and Sherry, even Tyrone, had accepted her explanation, all of them concerned but thankful that no one had died. At least not yet. But her sisters were another matter. They wanted the full details of what happened last night. And they weren't buying her story. But what could she tell them? It was like she had been through some bad drug trip, with fantastic illusions playing her senses. Except the illusions had been real. David, no longer Joseph, lying on the floor, bleeding. Tyne shuddered as she remembered the paramedics loading a very still David onto a gurney, wheeling his nearly lifeless body from the apartment. She kept her eyes averted from the bloodstained carpet. Yes, last night had been all too real.

Her sisters sat together on the couch, April occasionally taking a peek at the carpet, then looking back at Tyne. Tanya refused to break her stare. Through some damned sixth sense, they knew she was lying. And she didn't know what to tell them. She definitely couldn't tell them the truth.

"I told you exactly what happened, Tanya. I'm not going to keep explaining. It was an accident."

Tanya shook her head. "What was he doing here anyway? I thought this thing was over between you two. And what in the goddess' name was his *mother* doing here? Tyne, it makes no sense."

April nodded her agreement. "And his mother just happens to have a gun that just happens to go off? I'm not buying any of this, Tyne. He brought the gun over, didn't he? He came over to hurt you."

"No, no, he didn't! He wasn't trying to hurt me. He just wanted to talk. His mother . . . I don't know, she just dropped by . . ."

"After midnight?" April countered.

"Look, I don't know why she dropped by, she just did. And it was her gun, not David's. She was trying to get something from her purse and the gun came out, went off . . ."

"And you told this to the police?" This time from Tanya.

"Yes, yes, just like I'm telling you. What do you want me to say, Tanya? That David came over here to kill me? It wasn't like that. He didn't lay a hand on me. The shooting was an accident, that's all. And I don't feel like discussing this any further. I haven't had but a few minutes sleep since last night and I don't feel like being questioned by the damn Gestapo! You're both worse than the police."

Her sisters glanced at each other, some unspoken communication passing between them. Then they stood. Tyne rose from her chair, waiting.

"We're going, for now," Tanya warned. "But this conversation isn't over, Tyne. And whenever you think you feel up to telling us the truth, we'll be ready to listen."

Tanya walked to the door. April started to follow, but then the younger woman grabbed Tyne, planted a kiss on her sister's cheek. "I love you Tyne, and I'll be damned if I'm going to let you go through the mess I had to go through. I'll do everything in my power to make sure that doesn't happen, OK? Even if it means you have to hate on me for a while."

Tyne felt tears brimming. She looked into April's eyes, so open and full of concern. If both of her sisters were pains, it was because they loved her. And April had reasons to be hesitant about Tyne's story; she, too, had once been on the other end of her sisters' questioning. Had once been the one to offer excuses that just didn't sound right.

Tyne hugged April, looked over at Tanya standing near the open door. Tanya also had tears in her eyes.

"One day, I'll tell both of you everything," she promised softly. "Just not today. I need time. OK?"

Tanya nodded slightly, opened the door, then turned back. "You're not going to see him again, are you?" The question came out more like a plea.

When Tyne didn't answer, both sisters sighed, shook their heads. They both seemed to be appendages of a single mind. But they said nothing more as April shut the door behind them.

Tyne stood there, looking at the door, wishing she could call them back, wanting to ease this burden off her heart. She needed desperately to talk with someone, someone who could understand. But she barely understood it herself.

In the last hours, she'd gone over not only last night, but all of those other nights in these past few months, the dreams, the inexplicable feelings about David, her fears, even before she knew what to be afraid of . . .

She had thought she was just playing along when she pretended to be Rachel.

But sometime during everything that happened last night, the truth had hit her and she could no longer run from it.

It frightened her more than anything that had occurred. Because she didn't know if she could reconcile her life with that of a woman she didn't know, a woman so entrapped by her circumstances and bad choices that it had cost her life. She found it hard to feel a connection, and yet there was. A connection that had nearly destroyed David and might still destroy him.

She needed to know more. About Joseph, about Rachel. And from what little she had learned in a short conversation with Mrs. Carvelli, she knew the woman might have the answers she needed. But she would have to wait.

For David.

She said a silent prayer.

Minutes later, the phone rang.

Chapter 39

Tyne listened half-heartedly to the excited murmurings on the other end of the phone as she sat at her desk. Regina Stewart was talking so rapidly she ran out of breath at intervals, had to stop then start again. Throughout the deluge, Tyne nodded as though the other woman could see her. She did feel gratified that the story had led the city to investigate Webber Tires and that the investigators had already found several environmental violations near the surrounding areas of the plant, violations that might force the plant to close. Regina continued to thank Tyne profusely.

"I'm so glad, Regina. Really I am." She *was* glad, but her heart just wasn't feeling the woman's joy. In the last few weeks, her heart had been elsewhere.

When she hung up, she closed her strained eyes. Already, her desk was strewn with the clutter from two projects Sherry had given her in the last week. Photos had to be sifted through, people had to be called, interviews arranged. Weeks ago, this phase would have excited her. Now, she only felt exhaustion.

Tyne looked up from her notes at the knock on the door and blinks in surprise. It was open and David stood in the entrance, looking like he wasn't sure he could enter. Or that she would want him to. Almost a month in the hospital had nearly washed his skin of any healthy color. And he was thinner than ever before. Still, when he smiled, the brilliance of it masked the obvious ravages of pain and illness.

She stood up, walked to the door, her steps slow but sturdy.

"David, it's so good to see you." She gave him a peck on the cheek to answer any unvoiced concern about his welcome. He held her eyes for only a few seconds before looking away, as though he was afraid of what he might see there.

She led him to one of the chairs fronting her desk. Instead of returning to the other side, she took the seat next to his. She peered at his face, searching for a vestige of the man who had possessed him, who had stood in her living room that night. But he was just David now, no signs of Joseph anywhere in his features. Although there were new lines visible around his eyes and his mouth. But these would probably disappear once he was fully mended. She was glad to see life in those green, sometimes hazel, eyes. He was on the way back. And hopefully, Joseph was gone forever.

"I just wanted to come by to . . ." he paused, searched for a word. ". . . to thank you."

"There's nothing to thank me for, David. I was glad to help, especially with you being wounded."

"No, not that, although I do owe you for that, too. But I wanted to thank you for the other . . ."

She leaned forward, reached out to touch his hand. Could he know?

"I remember everything." He looked down, unable to meet her gaze. "Everything. About you—about her." He didn't need to say her name. They both knew whom he meant.

"David, don't force yourself to think about it."

"But I have to think about it. I tried not to believe for so long, that this thing was coming over me, that something was taking control. It wasn't until that night that everything became so clear. And so horrible. I was that man, a man who killed the woman he supposedly loved, a woman who had to die because of his lust, his selfishness."

Tyne didn't know what to say to assuage his guilt. She had hoped he wouldn't remember anything about that night. Still, maybe it was good that he did. Maybe, they could talk openly about it now.

She rose, walked behind her desk and retrieved the microfilm printout from the middle drawer. She'd had it for nearly a week now, ever since she'd met with Mrs. Carvelli at a small café downtown. Initially, when Tyne had called Mrs. Carvelli with questions, she'd resisted the woman's suggestion that they meet face to face again, but Mrs. Carvelli had been insistent that there were things Tyne needed to know. Things that were best said in person and not over a phone. They had met for coffee, quietly going over that horrible evening and everything that had occurred before the shooting. Even verbalizing what she had seen and heard had not made it truly real to Tyne. The whole evening had begun to take on the dimensions of an illusion that would fade away with time. But then Mrs. Carvelli had handed Tyne the newspaper printout she'd found in the library archives. And a parcel of faded letters. And suddenly the whole thing became very real.

Tyne sat next to David again and handed him the printout and the letters. He opened up the article that had run in the January 10, 1880 edition of the *New York Times*. His ashen skin seemed to pale even more as he looked at the picture of the man next to the headline.

Joseph Luce, Sole Heir of Luce Fortune, Dead at 29.

The photo was grainy after so many years, but the impression was indelible—handsome in the smug way that men used to wealth seemed to emanate without effort. Dark hair, dark eyes that reflected a brilliant smile. A congeniality that masked a dark soul. The face of the man David had once been.

Tyne had memorized nearly every word of the article, knew every angle of that face. The story would have been a scandal in its day. Son of an elite New York family killed in a

common alley fight. The other man had been named Charles
Rhodes, 42, a stevedore, residence unknown.

Still holding the printout, David unfolded one of the age-
weathered letters, began reading Rachel's words. His hand
was trembling.

"Your mother gave me those. She got them from a college
student who'd been researching about Rachel. There were so
many things I needed to know and the letters helped me understand a little about Rachel . . . about who I'd once been."

David's head shook slowly as he continued reading. "I still
don't understand how or why—and, the knife . . ."

"I don't know. Even your mother couldn't explain that.
Maybe Joseph's guilt was strong enough to bring the past
into the present. To make things as they were. Which could
explain your physical change, and the knife."

He looked up at her, his eyes brimming with tears. "Tyne,
I would never have hurt you . . . at least I don't think I would
have."

He sounded so uncertain, her heart quavered.

"My dreams were always leading me to you," he said quietly.

Tyne thought about her own dreams, their strangeness and
yet how real they had been. Especially the knife that had terrified her. Yes, the dreams had been leading both of them,
warning them.

He stopped reading as though he couldn't bear it anymore.
Closed his eyes. He leaned back his head and it seemed that
the last of his strength left him at that moment.

He still needed something from her. Something only she
could give.

"David, your mother told me that you . . . that Joseph . . .
was probably seeking absolution from Rachel that night.
Well, it may be too late for Joseph, but it's not too late for
you. If I were still Rachel, and you were still Joseph, this is
what I would say: I forgive you. And I understand. That
night, you were about to do the right thing and release me,

except everything went wrong after that. In the end, you did what you thought was best for her—for me. Joseph saved Rachel from something horrible and he avenged her death. So, from my point of view, there's nothing more to feel guilty about. You need to live David's life and let go of Joseph's. He's long dead. And so is Rachel. Because I'm no longer her. I'm Tyne. A flesh and blood woman who cares deeply about the man sitting next to her, and who has no qualms about giving her heart."

She reached over, kissed him softly, carefully. His lips were salty with tears freely flowing down his face. She touched his cheek, then pulled away, and let him weep.

After a few minutes, the sobs waned. She caressed his hair, dark and curly. There were a few strands of gray that hadn't been there before.

He drew a deep breath, smiled. He seemed stronger some-how, as though the tears had expunged the last of his former life, the vestige of Joseph's remorse.

"So how should we do this?" he asked. "Let's say we start over."

Tyne smiled. "Sounds good to me."

He reached out a hand. She gave him hers and he enclosed it in a warm grip.

"Guess introductions are in order, then. My name's David Carvelli."

Her smile broadened as she shook his hand. "And mine is Tyne, Tyne Jensen."

As they held hands, Tyne said a silent prayer in her heart for Rachel and Joseph, and hoped that finally they were going to have a happy ending.

Only time would tell.

Here's a scintillating look at
Alison Kent's
DEEP BREATH.
Available now from Brava!

been ordered not to move by her stylist, she might nev
stopped laughing.

When Harry told her he'd arranged not only this appc
ment but another with the hotel boutique's personal shop
for jewelry, shoes and a dress, she'd asked him if he thougl
she was made of money.

He'd pulled out his wallet, handed her a five to pay back
the tip, then reminded her she was the one donating to
General Duggin's Scholarship Foundation tonight.

Making sure she arrived looking the part of a wealthy col-
lector rather than pack rat was the least he could contribute
to the cause—a cause he'd then started to dig into, asking her
questions about her family and the importance of the docu-
ments Charlie had sent her to find.

Since she'd been stuck on the pack rat comment, frowning
as she ransacked her duffel for the sandals she knew that
were there, thinking how she really had let herself go since
being consumed by this quest, she'd almost answered, had
barely caught herself in time.

The story of her father's wrongful incarceration and her
determination to prove his innocence had been on the tip of
her tongue before she had bit down. If Harry knew the truth
of why she wanted the dossier, he would quickly figure out
she had no intention of delivering it to Charlie Castro.

Then, no doubt, they'd get into an argument about the
value of her brother's life versus that of her father's name,
and he'd want to know why the hell were they going through
all of this if not to save her brother.

She really didn't want to go there with Harry. She was having too much trouble going there with herself. Finn would
understand; she knew he would. As long as he was alive to
do so when this was over . . .

At that thought, she groaned, the sound eliciting the stylist's concern. "What's wrong, sweetie? Too much color? Not
enough? The highlights are temporary, remember? Three
washings max, you'll be back to being a brunette."

"Oh, no. I was thinking of something else," Georgia as-

While Georgia had holed away in the suite's monstrous bathroom to shower, shave, shampoo, and pull on a clean pair of undies, her T-shirt and jeans, Harry had been busy. Busy doing more than getting dressed and ratcheting up the who-is-this-man-and-where-did-he-come- from stakes.

He wore serious grown-up clothes as beautifully as he wore casual, and as well as Michelangelo's David wore his marble skin.

She'd walked out of the steamy bathroom and only just stopped herself from demanding what the hell he was doing breaking into her room before she realized her mistake. He was that amazing. And her heart was still dealing with the unexpected lust.

The man was the most beautiful thing she'd seen in forever. Her first impression made from Finn's truck when looking down from her window had been right on the mark. But he was so much more than a girl's guide to getting off.

His smile—those lips and dimples, the dark shadow of his beard—was enough to melt even the most titanic ice queen. Not that she was one, or anything . . .

Sitting as she was now in the hotel's salon, having her hair and makeup done, she kept sneaking looks over to where he sat waiting and reading a back issue of Cosmo. Every once in awhile he'd frown, shake his head, turn the page. If she hadn't sured the other woman, meeting her reflected gaze. "I hadn't even looked . . . "

But now she did. And she swore the reflection in the mirror couldn't possibly be hers. "Wow," was the only thing she could think to say, and so she said it again. "Wow."

"Yeah. I thought so, too." The stylist beamed at her handi-work—and rightly so. Georgia had never in her life looked like this. The highlights in her hair gave off a coppery sheen. Her layers, too long and grown out—she had been desperate for a new cut, had been trimmed, colored, and swept up into an intricate rooster tail of untamed strands.

And then her face . . . was that really her face? The salon's makeup expert had used a similar color scheme, spreading sheer terra-cotta on her cheeks, a blend of copper and bronze on her eyelids, finishing off with a gorgeous cinnamon-colored glaze on her lips.

And all of it matching the beautiful ginger-hued polish on the nails of all twenty fingers and toes. She could go for this girly girl stuff. Really.

Especially when she lifted her gaze to meet Harry's in the mirror. He stood behind the stylist, his shoulders wide in his designer suit coat, his hands jammed to his lean waist, his smile showing just a hint of teeth.

She had no idea when he'd moved from where he'd been sitting to her chair, but the look in his eyes, the fire in his eyes, and the low sweep of his lashes was enough to make her swoon.

It had been so long since a man had shown that kind of interest in her that she didn't know what to do, how to react, to respond. Except the truth was that it wasn't the men. It was her.

She had refused to let any man close enough to do more than notice her skill for ferreting out valuable antiques for years now, longer than she could remember.

But now, here came Harry into the middle of her personal catastrophe, a veritable stranger who had the body of a god and a killer smile and eyes that were telling her dangerously sexy things about wanting to get her naked. He was helping her in ways that went above and beyond.

And she still had the night to spend in his room. "Can we charge the makeup to the room? I'll pay you back."

"Sure." His eyes sparkled. His smile grew wicked. "And it's my treat."

The stylist swept the cape from around Georgia's shoulders and Harry offered his hand to help her from the chair. It was a Cinderella moment that she had no business enjoying, but she couldn't help it.

She hadn't done a single thing for herself in so long that it was impossible to brush aside this feeling of discovering someone she'd thought lost.

She was well aware of why she and Harry were together, the full extent of what was at stake. But it had been years, literally years, since she'd considered herself attractive—not to mention since she'd felt confident that someone of the opposite sex found her so.

Harry did. She didn't doubt it for a minute. Even if it did up the nerve-wracking factor of the long evening ahead in his company.

While Harry tipped the stylist and settled the bill, she took the bag of cosmetics from the cashier, absently noticing how the attention of every woman in the salon, whether overtly or subtly, was directed toward the checkout station and the fit of Harry's clothes.

She wanted to laugh; here she was, panicking over sleeping near him when he could crook a finger and have any woman here in his bed.

And then she didn't want to laugh at all.

She wanted to grab him by the arm and drag him out of there, leaving a battlefield of bloody cat scratches in her wake. Like he belonged to her or something, and how ridiculous was that? He was nothing but a man who happened to be in the wrong place at the wrong time, who was going out of his way to get her out of a jam.

Finn would have done the same for a woman in need. Her

ex, hardly. They'd been married, and he wouldn't have done it for her. Unless there was something in it for him . . . hmm. Too bad she hadn't snapped to that before.

Harry scrawled his signature across the bottom of the ticket then handed the pen to the cashier. Georgia cocked her head and considered what he could possibly hope to gain from helping her out. He was going to a lot of expense . . . and sex was the first thing, the only thing, that came to mind.